Death in a locked room

Maggie said, "Sarah and I will go have a peek in the window while you try the door."

Donna followed Olivia to the den door and pounded on it. "Dale? Open the door!"

They knocked and shouted. After a moment Maggie came flying down the hall. "Move over!" she shouted. "Let's get that damn door open!"

She was carrying a crowbar. Olivia pulled Donna aside and watched, astonished, while Maggie rammed the bar between door and jamb. She braced a foot against the door frame and then levered the bar violently back and forth until the door sprang open with a piercing, agonized creak.

Donna gasped.

Dale Colby lay prone, splayed on the plaid carpet, his half-turned face resting in a dark stain.

Olivia's mind refused to consider what that stain might be. . . .

Bantam Crime Line Books offer the finest in classic and
modern American mysteries.
Ask your bookseller for the books you have missed.

Rex Stout

Too Many Clients
The Black Mountain
Death of a Dude
Death Times Three
Fer-de-Lance
Plot It Yourself
Some Buried Caesar
Three for the Chair
Too Many Cooks
And Be a Villain
Death of a Doxy
Three Witnesses

Max Allan Collins

The Dark City
Bullet Proof
Butcher's Dozen

Loren Estleman

Peeper
Whiskey River

Dick Lupoff

The Comic Book Killer

Meg O'Brien

The Daphne Decisions
Salmon in the Soup

Virginia Anderson

Blood Lies
King of the Roses

William Murray

When the Fat Man Sings
The King of the Nightcap
The Getaway Blues

Eugene Izzi

King of the Hustlers
The Prime Roll
Invasions

Gloria Dank

Friends Till the End
Going Out in Style

Jeffery Deaver

Manhattan Is My Beat
Death of a Blue Movie Star

Robert Goldsborough

Murder in E Minor
Death on Deadline
The Bloodied Ivy
The Last Coincidence
Fade to Black

Sue Grafton

"A" Is for Alibi
"B" Is for Burglar
"C" Is for Corpse
"D" Is for Deadbeat
"E" Is for Evidence
"F" Is for Fugitive

David Lindsey

In the Lake of the Moon
coming soon: Mercy

Carolyn G. Hart

Design for Murder
Death on Demand
Something Wicked
Honeymoon With Murder
A Little Class on Murder
coming soon: Deadly Valentine

Annette Meyers

The Big Killing
Tender Death

Rob Kantner

Dirty Work
The Back-Door Man
Hell's Only Half Full
Made in Detroit

Robert Crais

The Monkey's Raincoat
Stalking the Angel

Keith Peterson

The Trapdoor
There Fell a Shadow
The Rain
Rough Justice
The Scarred Man

David Handler

The Man Who Died Laughing
The Man Who Lived by Night
The Man Who Would Be
F. Scott Fitzgerald

Jerry Oster

Club Dead
Internal Affairs
Final Cut

M. K. Lorens

Sweet Narcissus
Ropedancer's Fall
Deception Island

Benjamin M. Schutz

A Tax in Blood
Embrace the Wolf
The Things We Do for Love

Monroe Thompson

The Blue Room

Diane Shah

As Crime Goes By

Paul Levine

To Speak for the Dead

Randall Wallace

Blood of the Lamb

Stephen Greenleaf

Impact

Margaret Maron

Corpus Christmas
The Right Jack

Jane Haddam

Not a Creature Was Stirring
coming soon: Precious Blood

Denny Martin Flinn

San Francisco Kills

P. M. Carlson

Murder Unrenovated
Murder in the Dog Days

Max Byrd

Fuse Time

Bob Reid

Cupid

MURDER IN THE DOG DAYS

(Maggie Ryan 1975)

P.M. CARLSON

BANTAM BOOKS
New York · Toronto ·
London · Sydney ·
Auckland

MURDER IN THE DOG DAYS

A BANTAM BOOK / JANUARY 1991

Grateful acknowledgment is made for permission to use the following excerpts: "Blowin' in the Wind" by Bob Dylan. Copyright © 1962 WARNER BROS. INC. All rights reserved. Used by permission. "I Feel Like I'm Fixin' To Die Rag." Copyright © 1965 ALKATRAZ CORNER MUSIC CO. Words and music by Joe McDonald. All rights reserved. Used by permission. "The Scout Toward Aldie" by Herman Melville is available in The Poems of Herman Melville, Douglas Robillard, editor, New College and University Press, Schenectady, 1989. "Mental Cases" by Wilfred Owen is available in The Poems of Wilfred Owen, Chatto & Windus, London, 1963.

Map by Jackie Aher.

ISBN 0-553-27778-2

Published simultaneously in the United States and Canada

PRINTED IN THE UNITED STATES OF AMERICA

RAD   0 9 8 7 6 5 4 3 2 1

To all the heroes
wasted in an unheroic cause
and to all the survivors
who courageously bear witness
to a truth the rest of us don't want to believe

Fear no more the heat o' the sun,
  Nor the furious winter's rages;
Thou thy worldly task hast done,
  Home art gone, and ta'en thy wages:
Golden lads and girls all must,
As chimney-sweepers, come to dust.

—CYMBELINE, *act IV, scene ii*

Sunlight seems a blood-smear; night comes blood-black;
Dawn breaks open like a wound that bleeds afresh.

—WILFRED OWEN, "MENTAL CASES"

Author's Note

For sharing their wisdom, my warmest thanks go to Robert Knightly, Patricia King, Kay Williams, Joanna Wolper, Bill and Elizabeth McElroy, Carolyn Wheat, Malvin Vitriol of the Milton Helpern Library and healer and truth-teller Elizabeth Ann Scarborough; but most of all to the extraordinary Kate Miciak, whose vote of confidence rescued this book from formless limbo.

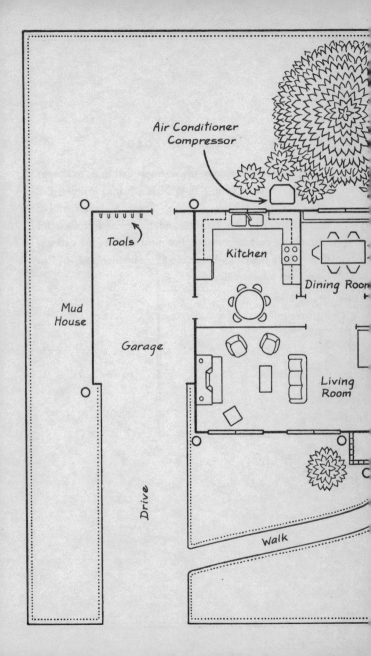

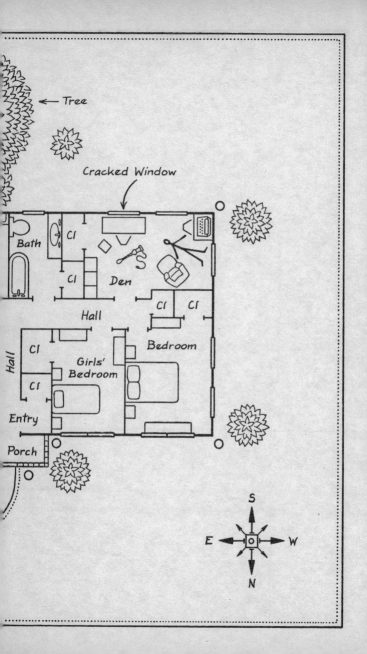

Mosby,
Virginia

MONDAY

AUGUST 4TH
1975

Chapter 1

The big graying air conditioner in the window of the so-called city room of the Mosby *Sun-Dispatch* groaned piteously. Olivia Kerr scribbled a last correction into a pre-release story about the filming of *All the President's Men*, leaned back in her chair, and stared at the machine suspiciously. For ten days it had been laboring, with only partial success, to convert the polluted ninety-eight degree Virginia haze outdoors into livable air. "When that thing goes on strike," Olivia declared, pointing at it accusingly with a freckled finger, "I do too."

Rumpled Nate Rosen switched off his tape recorder, peered around the edge of his cubicle and nodded. His thin, mournful face looked longer every day as his hair receded a bit further. "I'll be right on your heels," he agreed, with a worried glance at the suffering air conditioner.

"This heat wave is a killer."

"Not a metaphor," he informed her, tapping the page he was working on. "Guy up in New York got shot in a fight over a fire hydrant. And he's the third this weekend. Dog days."

"Yeah. I wish I could say I can't understand people fighting over trivial stuff like that. But right now I can," said Olivia. "I'm glad I'm off to the beach."

Nate raised his eyebrows. "Aren't you afraid you'll get freckled?"

"Hey, one more crack like that and I'll ask you if you aren't worried about getting bald."

"Don't rub it in, O cruel maid," grumbled Nate, turning back to his keyboard.

Olivia pulled the barrette from her humidity-frizzed hair. In romantic moods Jerry called it chestnut-colored. Of course he'd also been known to point out that it matched the stain in the sink. The lout. The only possible response had been to whack him with a pillow. Olivia grinned to herself. The resulting pillow fight had quickly turned bawdy. Very bawdy. With Jerry, romantic moods came in a lot of different flavors.

She twisted her hair up away from the nape of her neck and clipped the barrette across it. Then she stood, tossed the strap of her bag over her shoulder, and went to look out the window. Jerry wasn't down there yet. Today only a few people had ventured out, shuffling sweaty and exhausted along the sidewalk through the unmoving pool of sultry, half-toxic air.

The door of the managing editor's office opened and a round woman arrayed in black came out, smiling and nodding behind her. She hadn't been smiling when she went in. Edgerton had smoothed some more feathers. Well, that's one of the things editors did. Olivia looked out the window for Jerry again.

"Hey, Liv!"

Damn. "Yeah?" she answered, turning reluctantly from the window.

Edgerton was pudgy, moist-lipped, imperious. "Wire service just sent in some more on the Joanne Little trial. Work it into the story." A yellow page from a legal pad dangled from his plump outstretched hand.

Olivia's conscience told her she'd better not bolt for the door. Damn conscience. Doing the rewrites on the Little story and writing the associated features was her chance to break out of the women's pages. True, Edgerton had given her the assignment with the assumption that it was a feminist issue. But it had already grown beyond that. She crossed the room to take the paper. "What is this?" she asked, trying to decipher Edgerton's uninhibited scrawl.

"Kunstler just got out of jail. Had a few choice words about Judge Hobgood." Edgerton puffed the information at her close-range, blanketing her with coffee breath.

Olivia stepped back, wondering how he'd got the woman in black to look so happy. Maybe she had an olfactory problem. "I'll bet he did." Why couldn't they keep Kunstler locked up until she'd left for the day? She hurried back to her cubicle and grabbed her copy of the story. What a circus this case had turned into!

Joanne Little admitted stabbing her jailer with an ice pick; the trial was meant to determine whether or not she had done it in self-defense when he tried to rape her. But the spicy ingredients of race, sex, and Southern justice had turned it into a national extravaganza. Joanne Little's defense team played to the visiting reporters with relish. This morning they had attempted to add the famed New York lawyer William Kunstler to the team, but Kunstler had promptly insulted the judge and been jailed instead.

"You should have made a run for it," said Nate when Edgerton was safely back in his office.

"Nah. This is the best story he's ever let me handle." She cranked paper into her typewriter. "Biggest thing he ever gave me before was Ann Landers' divorce."

"What about Patty Hearst?"

"Dale Colby had that while it was hot. He didn't assign it to me until it was dead. But if they ever find her I'll be set."

"So what? Good stories don't pay any better, and the hours are worse. Don't know why you bother."

"You want to know why?" Olivia squinted at Edgerton's scrawled notes. "Because when they make the movie, I want Robert Redford to play me." She ignored Nate's snort and settled down to type.

In fact, she decided grudgingly, Edgerton was right. This new quote made the story better. Kunstler, upon being released, had said about the judge, "I think the man is determined to see this woman convicted by any means necessary, in violation of his oath as well as the Constitution, and that constitutes in my mind a criminal act." Nice. Manipulative, of course; Kunstler knew what news hounds wanted. So all over America, people like Olivia were putting it into the papers and TV news, maybe publicizing the very real difficulties of black women in the South, maybe just publicizing Kunstler. Every now and then Olivia wondered uneasily if it was Joanne Little or North Carolina that was really on trial. But what the hell, North Carolina had never even ratified the constitutional amendment giving women the vote. Olivia typed in the quote. Take that, North Carolina.

Beyond the wheezing of the air conditioner, she became aware of music somewhere outside. Sixties music, guitar and the sweet blended harmonies of Peter, Paul and Mary singing "Puff the Magic Dragon." Then her attention was distracted by the opening door. A thickset man with a pink complexion, curly brown hair and loosened necktie shoved in. He held the limp jacket of his light summer suit tossed back over his shoulder. "Hey, Edgerton!" he yelled.

Edgerton stuck his head out of his door. "Hi, Leon. What can I do for you?"

"Get that bastard reporter off my back! That asshole Colby!" the chunky newcomer demanded.

"Colby again? Okay, okay, simmer down. Too hot today to get steamed up. Come on in and tell me the problem." Edgerton, with a scowl at the music drifting in the window, gestured the thickset man into his office and closed the door.

Olivia picked up her revised story and tossed it onto the big central table. Nate was standing at the window now, hands in pockets, gazing out with amused eyes. "Who's that?" Olivia whispered to him, jerking her thumb at the closed door.

"Edgy's visitor? That's Leon Moffatt. Colby should tread lightly. The widow Resler didn't look too happy either."

"The plane crash story?"

"That's the one. Moffatt's father went down in it." Nate pulled his hands from his pockets, retrieved a note that fluttered to the floor, and pushed the current issue of the *Sun-Dispatch* toward her. Dale Colby's report was on the bottom of the front page, reporting the latest information about a small chartered plane leased to Congressman Knox last January. Olivia skimmed it. She could see why Moffatt and Mrs. Resler were upset. Without actual libel, Dale implied that the survivors of the five victims were better off now than before the crash. Including the congressman's office. Thin ice there, Dale. But knowing him, she was sure he had plenty to back up his statements. A very careful reporter.

Nate added, "Listen, you're going to the beach with the Colbys today, right? You might just breathe a word in his ear."

"Okay." She picked up her shoulder bag.

"And tell me, Liv, isn't that the love of your life down there now?"

Olivia joined him at the window. "Oh, Jesus Christ."

It was Jerry Ryan all right. Even from the second floor there was no mistaking that lanky build, those black curls. He was standing between his sister Maggie, also lanky and curly-haired, and her brawny, balding husband Nick. With amazing energy for such an oppressive day they were belting out the song about the magic dragon. Olivia giggled. "God, can't turn my back a minute!"

"Pretty good imitation," Nate observed. It was true; Nick was accompanying them expertly with his guitar, and all three were warbling away with gusto. Before them, unaffected by the exhausting sultriness, a tiny girl not yet three was dancing. The heat-wearied passersby forgot their discomfort for a moment to smile at her and at the singers.

Olivia sprinted for the door. "Listen, Nate, when Edgy comes out tell him the story's there on the table. See you tomorrow!" She escaped and ran downstairs.

The heat hit her like a wall when she opened the front door. Dog days. She was dripping by the time she reached them. They had started on "Blowin' in the Wind." She caught Jerry's eye but he only winked and held up a cautioning hand. "How many times must the cannonballs fly?" he sang. Her little niece, still dancing, was trying to sing too. "Answer blowin' inna wind!" she chirped. Olivia had to smile. She hadn't heard little kids singing those songs for years. It was a whole different age now. No Peter, Paul and Mary hits. No Woodstock. No peace marches. All gone. Except maybe for Maggie. Pregnant again, Jerry's sister was recycling an old red maternity T-shirt emblazoned with a peace sign. And recycling the old songs too. Nostalgia time.

The handful of listeners applauded heartily when they finished. Jerry took a sweeping bow and loped over to Olivia. "Hiya, Livid. Aren't we great?"

She tried to contain her smile. "You're a bigger ham than Nick is! And you don't even have the excuse of being an actor."

"Listen, the instant the MD business starts to drag I'll be off like a shot! I mean, this is *fun*! Besides, the Maggot was wearing her peace shirt. How could I resist?"

"Yeah, it's all my fault." Maggie, leading her little daughter, rejoined her brother with a grin. Her eyes were the same laughing jay-blue of Jerry's. "Kid sisters are always to blame. Are you a kid sister, Liv?"

"No, thank God."

"Some people have all the luck. Hey, how's Joanne Little doing?"

"She'll win hands down if her lawyers don't clown around once too often. And speaking of clowning around, are you guys finished? Ready to go pick up the Colbys?"

"Hey, look!" Maggie's husband called gleefully. Nick O'Connor was a big, bald, pleasantly homely man who periodically appeared in TV commercials selling beer or paper towels. Olivia was sorry she hadn't been able to see him in any plays, but they'd all been in New York. Right now he was picking coins from the open case where he was about to stow the guitar. He jingled them jubilantly in his hand. "We made seven bucks!"

"Wowee!" Jerry scooped up small Sarah, grabbed Maggie's hand, and capered over to inspect the haul. "We should have left the guitar case right next to the sidewalk!"

Olivia shook her head, got out her keys, and climbed into the driver's seat of the Ford passenger van parked a few steps further up the street. She turned on the air conditioner and tapped the horn. Within seconds the others piled in, still jabbering excitedly about the commercial future of their little quartet.

Dale Colby lived in the Sandford subdivision, a set of nearly identical one-story ranch houses grouped around a small park. A century ago it had been woods and farms traversed by Union soldiers in search of the Confederate Army. What they'd found was Mosby's irregular cavalry band, who struck and then melted back into their home woods in the best guerrilla tradition. Today the area had a reputation for low prices and good schools, no trace of its bloody past.

Olivia pulled into the driveway behind the Pinto. Donna Colby, a neat, worried-looking blonde, opened the front door for them. "Oh—please come in. Sit down a minute," she said. "Dale's on the phone. He's—well, he's not feeling too well today." She waved them into the immaculate living room with a flutter of her hand.

Olivia said, "Donna, do you remember Jerry? And this is his sister Maggie Ryan. Her husband Nick O'Connor. And this is Sarah."

Donna smiled brightly at their greetings. "Glad to meet you. This is Tina, with the Barbie dolls. Say hello, Tina."

A girl about nine was sitting on the hearth. She looked up and said, "Hi!" She exchanged a solemn glance with Sarah, who trotted over to inspect the dolls. At another nervous wave from Donna, the two men sat in the wing chairs.

Donna continued, "And Josie, with the book. Josie, put your feet down!"

A twelve-year-old girl on the pink-flowered sofa sullenly removed her sandaled feet from the cushions.

Maggie glanced at the book and murmured to the girl, "My favorite character is Gollum. Who's yours, my preciousss?"

Surprised hazel eyes flicked up. The touch of interest before defiance returned. "The Nazgûl," Josie declared.

"Right! The Ringwraiths!" exclaimed Maggie approvingly, perching on the arm of the sofa. "I always wanted to be able to fly too. I still want to be an astronaut."

"Really?"

"Sure. As long as I can still have a hobbit-hole. Maybe on the moon."

The girl rewarded her with a tiny cautious grin. "I know where there's a hobbit-hole."

Olivia left them to discuss Tolkien and turned back to Donna. "Shall we go rouse Dale?"

"Well—" Donna looked nervously at the hallway that led back to the den. Dale, theoretically on vacation, had been working at home for the last three weeks, doctor's orders, while he adapted to a new medication. But Edgerton, not the easiest of managing editors, continued to send him assignments. Not that Dale would want a real vacation.

"I'll go," Olivia told Donna. "I have something to say to him anyway." She marched through the hall to the last room, a den outfitted with file cabinets and an IBM typewriter that put the old machines in the *Sun-Dispatch* office to shame. Dale was a neat worker, his notes in careful stacks. Even the brass lamp perched at the edge of his desk was polished.

Dale was on the phone. "Of course I'll be discreet, Mrs. Resler. Thanks so much."

"Lying to sources again, Dale?" teased Olivia, when he'd replaced the receiver.

He turned in his desk chair, not amused. He was a handsome man with shrewd hazel eyes and sandy hair, but small teeth made his smile seem miserly. "Hello, Olivia."

"How are you?"

"Rotten. As usual."

"It'll gradually improve, Jerry says."

"Yeah. Everyone who isn't going through it says that." He stood up, moving easily, Olivia saw, not the little hesitations and hurries that had characterized his last weeks in the *Sun-Dispatch* office. He'd be back to full-time soon.

Behind Olivia, Tina ran past into her own room across the hall. Little Sarah was right behind her. Dale winced.

"I've got a message for you from Nate," Olivia said.

"Oh?"

"Yeah. Leon Moffatt stopped by to complain to Edgerton about something you were doing."

"Moffatt?" Dale's eyebrows crept up in pleased inquiry.

"Yeah. Mrs. Resler came to complain too. But Moffatt really seemed furious. Edgy whisked him into the office out of earshot. But Nate thought you'd want to know."

"Moffatt! All right!" Dale hurried back to his chair. "Listen, Olivia, I won't be able to—"

"Sunshine on my shoulders," bellowed John Denver's recorded voice from across the hall.

"Goddamn it, Tina, turn that off!" roared Dale, charging to the door so vehemently that Olivia stepped back. In the sudden silence that followed he spotted his wife at the end of the hall. "Donna! Bring me one of those sandwiches you made!"

"A sandwich? But the picnic—"

"I can't go to the beach now! I haven't been able to have my nap yet. Besides, this story is getting interesting."

Olivia regarded Dale with amusement. A true reporter. Dale at work was a perfectionist, even rigid, with files that were actually orderly and a strict self-imposed schedule. She could never run her life that way. But she shared the insanity that relegated all things, even sickness and trips to the beach, to a lower order than the demands of a story. Still, she said, "Nate suggested that you go easy."

"Aw, come on, Olivia, you know better than that."

"Yeah. I do."

Donna came hurrying down the hall with a plate containing a wrapped sandwich, a little bag of potato chips, and a mug of coffee. "Dale, the children wanted to go to—"

"Right! Exactly!" He took the plate and plunked it onto the table. "Take them away!"

"You mean go without you?"

"Right."

"But honey, I was hoping you'd get some rest."

"Donna, honey." Dale took her by the shoulders. "I'll take my nap first, I promise. And if you take my daughters away a few hours, I may even get some work done." He released Donna and rolled his eyes at Olivia. "Never, ever try to work in the same house with kids!"

"Yeah. My niece has already taught me that," Olivia agreed. "Come on, Donna, I guess he's serious."

Donna Colby was not only an immaculate housekeeper but a good organizer. The picnic basket she'd raided for Dale's lunch was packed, towels and toys ready. Nick and Jerry carried them out to the van and lifted Tina into the back seat. Olivia held open the door that led from kitchen to garage while Sarah jumped from the step with Maggie's help. Josie came running back in through the garage, coltish and stiff-legged, and bounded awkwardly past them and across the kitchen.

"What's the rush, honey?" asked Donna, who was picking up the last bag from the kitchen table.

"Tina forgot Ken and Barbie." Josie disappeared into the dining room and the hall beyond. Olivia heard her sandals slapping unevenly on the hardwood floor.

Dale's roar could be heard all the way to the garage. "Damn it, Josie, aren't you gone yet? I'm trying to make a call!" A whoosh, a slam, a click of bolts closing.

Josie, looking small and white, beelined from the bedroom to the garage, Ken and Barbie clutched in her fists. Donna looked after her despairingly, then stepped into the dining room. "We're leaving, honey. Bye."

There was no response. Donna waited a moment, steadying herself with a hand on the wall, then turned and came back into the kitchen with a tremulous smile. "He's really not feeling very well. And he's so involved with this story."

Olivia tried to think of something charitable to say. "It's tough to dig up stories even when you're healthy."

"Yes, and there's other pressure. He got a letter this morning from his first wife. I don't know what it said, but—" Donna shrugged. "It's hard for him these days."

"Hard on the kids too," Maggie observed. She and Sarah had negotiated the step and were watching Donna too.

"Yes. I wish the doctor had waited until they were in school before he started this new drug." Donna, her face drawn, followed them through the hot garage to the van. "They were in camp this summer, but it only lasted through July."

"Well, let's take them to the beach," Maggie said pragmatically, opening the van door. Jerry had turned on the air conditioner. They climbed into the coolness gratefully and headed for distant Bethany Beach.

Thunderheads came boiling down from the northwest as they finished the picnic dinner. A cool gust of wind hit Olivia's damp back and sent goose bumps running along her skin. "God, that's great!" she exclaimed. "I haven't felt cold for months!" She joined Nick and Maggie, who had started to pick up toys and sandals from the water's edge. "Guess it's time to get back."

"Right," said Nick. "I think Donna will be just as glad."

It was true; they had hardly arrived before Donna had sought out a phone to call Dale, though the line was busy so she soon gave up. She had been pleasant, had sat out the swim but had joined in the wild volleyball game that pitted the women—

including little Sarah—against Nick and Jerry, who made up for their reduced numbers by shouting sexist comments such as "Here you go, doll babies," or "Hurry up, dainty Maggot!" It had been impossible to keep score, especially since the men insisted that points scored by women were more delicate and therefore smaller than their own robust variety. Donna had smiled about it too. Afterwards, though, she had seemed restless, as though uncomfortable outside the well-ordered home she ran.

The wind grew stronger. The younger children, excited by the looming black clouds, shrieked and ran around. Maggie didn't help by suggesting to Josie that it looked like the arrival of the evil Lord of the Nazgûl on his unholy winged steed. Josie had been quiet all day, haughtily rebuffing her mother's sympathetic questions, refusing to put on her swimsuit and collecting shells and pebbles instead. But she enjoyed Maggie's suggestion and began to instruct Tina and Sarah about ways to save Barbie and Ken from doom. Sidestepping the darting children, the adults threw toys and towels into the van helter-skelter, no trace remaining of Donna's careful packing. Even so the first drops were falling as they finally rounded up Sarah, wriggly and sandy in her little red swimsuit, and closed the van door. The return trip, through heavy rain, was slow. At last they drove through the last of the storm into an oddly cool, cloudy twilight. The world seemed stunned by its sudden scrubbing.

The children were inspired all over again by the wet unfamiliarity of the yard. Tina ran to the side of the garage. "The little house is gone!" she squealed, pointing at the muddy remnants of some earthen creation. Josie renewed the doomsday chronicle of the beach, which required much running about and flapping of arms. Nick and Jerry joined in, chanting "When shall we three meet again, in thunder, lightning, or in rain?" to the delighted screams of the girls. Olivia had to grin at them. It was true, the relative coolness was invigorating.

She helped Maggie carry some of the towels as far as the kitchen door. Donna, visible through the dining-room door, was calling timidly, "Dale?" There was no answer. She turned back, hand trailing along the wall, and returned to the kitchen with a shrug. "Probably on the phone," she said with a quick apologetic smile.

"No danger he won't know we're back," observed Olivia as they sauntered back to the van. The excited squeals continued, punctuated by Nick's and Jerry's hilarious versions of doom-laden Nazgûl squawks.

Maggie pulled another towel from the van and shook sand from it into a puddle. "Is anyone else hungry?" she asked.

"We just had a huge basket of sandwiches," Olivia objected. She grabbed a towel and hurled it at Jerry as he ran flapping by. He caught it and came over to help.

"Yeah, I'm hungry," he said, fishing a pink plastic swim ring from the van. "Pizza, right, Maggot?"

"With anchovies and extra cheese!" she agreed enthusiastically.

Tina galloped past her mother and there was a crash.

"Oh, dear!" Donna, her hand at her mouth, looked down at the picnic basket she'd just dropped onto the wet driveway.

Nick was already kneeling to pick up the scattered contents. "Nothing broken except the jar of pickles," he said, handing her a packet of paper plates. "But the napkins got wet."

They cleaned up, repacked the basket, and tucked all the toys and towels inside the kitchen door. Then Nick and Jerry took Tina with them to the shopping center to get pizza. The others wiped their shoes and went inside. It seemed stuffy after the rain-washed air outdoors.

"Dale!" Donna called. There was no response. She put a kettle on the range and pulled out a pitcher and some tea bags, her face troubled.

Olivia frowned. Damn it, Dale was acting like a total asshole today. No story could keep him *that* busy. "I'll go get him," she said.

The office door was closed. She banged on it. "Hey, Dale!"

No answer. She listened, but if he was on the phone the other person was doing a hundred percent of the talking. A paper napkin drifted across the polished floor of the hall in the soft air-conditioned breeze. Olivia stuck it in her pocket and hammered on the door again.

Still nothing.

The knob turned but she couldn't budge the door itself.

She went back to the kitchen. "No answer," she said. "I heard him say he was going to take a nap."

"Not many people could sleep through this homecoming," Maggie observed with a doubtful glance toward the bedroom hall. She was squatting on the vinyl floor, belly bulging, to help Sarah get into her little blue shirt and shorts again. "You tried the door?"

"I couldn't get it open. Will you come try, Donna?"

"Sometimes he bolts it." But Donna looked increasingly uneasy.

Maggie straightened. "Sarah and I will go have a peek in the window while you try the door."

Donna followed Olivia to the den door and pounded on it. "Dale? Open the door!"

They knocked and shouted. Josie, her hazel eyes curious, sidled along the wall behind them to watch.

After a moment Maggie came flying down the hall. "Move over!" she shouted. "Let's get that damn door open!"

She was carrying a crowbar. Olivia pulled Donna aside and watched, astonished, while Maggie rammed the bar between door and jamb. She braced a foot against the door frame and then levered the bar violently back and forth until the door sprang open with a piercing, agonized creak.

Donna gasped.

Dale Colby lay prone, splayed on the plaid carpet, his half-turned face resting in a dark stain.

Olivia's mind refused to consider what that stain might be.

Chapter 2

Holly Schreiner strode up the puddled cement walk, walking point in plainclothes, mechanically registering what details she could see in the dusk. The Sandford subdivision: smallish fifties ranch houses, decent middle-class homes decked with petunias and tricycles, the summer-toasted lawns soggy but unrevived by the brief rain, the azalea bushes droopy too. Stormwater still dripped from their branches and she pulled her twill skirt aside to avoid them. This house faced north, had kids' bikes in the garage next to a Pinto. A Ford passenger van, this year's model, sat in the driveway. Beyond the garage, a patrolman watched them approach. In the yard next door a woman and a teenaged boy observed them all. Holly stepped up onto the cement platform that was trying to pass for a porch. Gabe Mercer stepped up beside her. Gabe wasn't a bad partner to work with. He'd come on to her once, of course, but that was practically a job requirement. Take good notes, always carry your gun, and proposition female partners. Luckily she was senior enough to put that down quick. She wouldn't date cops anyway. To them there were only three varieties of woman cop: nympho, dyke, or frigid. They called Holly Ice Maiden. She was content.

Gabe was younger than Holly, already too pudgy. Not that she should point fingers, she was no Twiggy herself. He punched the button.

She heard the bell chime inside, heard the plop-plop of water from a drainpipe at the corner of the garage, heard the squeals of children down the block. Heard the chopper. The throbbing rotor crescendoed suddenly overhead, pounding the humid air, hammering the spike of memory into her gut. A wave of nausea. Her stomach began the crawl toward her throat, lifting ahead of it a spreading fan of image and odor: steamy air weighty with the stench of charred red flesh, red mud oozing through the cracks in the wall, reds everywhere in a fantastic palette from maroon and brick-red through scarlet to petal pink. . . .

Steady, Schreiner. The door was opening. The chopper had passed. She swallowed acid and planted her crepe-soled sandals a little further apart, bracing herself, her ID held out before her. A uniformed town cop peered out at them, graying, big-bellied, suspicious. She drew herself up to her full five five, fixed him with the stolid, unblinking cop stare she practiced in front of the mirror at home, and said crisply, "Holly Schreiner and Gabe Mercer. County Homicide."

Reassured by the shield and by a glance at Gabe's round face, the cop nodded. "I'm Higgins."

"What have we got?"

"DOA in the back room."

They followed him into the house. From somewhere in the rear came a child's shrill chatter. Comfortably machinelike again, Holly checked off the details. An arch from the entry hall into a living room with gold wall-to-wall carpeting, flowered sofa, wing chairs. Sibilant sound of central air-conditioning. Newspapers stacked neatly on a shelf, big-screen Sony TV in the corner, expensive stereo components on the bookshelves, Barbie and Ken dolls dressed for a rock concert and then abandoned by the brick fireplace. The bookshelves were filled, except for a gap near the stereo. Across the room, another arch led into the dining room. From a door in its wall, kitchen probably, two people craned their necks to catch a glimpse of the newcomers. One was a tall, dark-haired woman, the other a girl, twelve maybe, who chewed solemnly on the knuckle of her forefinger. "Family?" asked Gabe.

"Yeah," Higgins confirmed. "And friends. Found the body. I told them to wait in the kitchen. It's out of the way, other end of the house."

"Fine." Holly and Gabe followed him around the corner and down a short hall. First door on the left was a bath. Two bedrooms were on the right, one sporting white-painted bunk beds, probably advertised as French provincial. A yellow plastic tape recorder sat on the pink rug, a John Denver poster looked out from the wall. Barbie and Ken's resplendent two-story colonial house stood atop a white dresser. Holly had missed Barbie, had already been in high school when the curvy dolls had first swept the nation. Born too soon. She asked Higgins' sweat-rumpled back, "Ambulance been here?"

Higgins nodded, scrabbling in his pocket for a card where he'd jotted down names and numbers. "Couple of seconds after we got here. Pronounced him DOA and left him for us."

He waved vaguely at the last door on the left. A den. Gray metal file cabinets, battered Naugahyde recliner with the footrest up, big oak desk, gray metal typing table bearing an IBM electric typewriter. Big windows to the south and west gave a twilight view of the backyard and side fence. From the vent, air brushed softly past her face. As she stepped into the room, Holly saw that the doorjamb was splintered.

The body sprawled on its back between the typing table and the recliner. The neck and shoulders were twisted, scalp and face gashed, dark blood soaking the plaid carpet. A few feet away lay a metal lamp base, shade mashed, bulb shattered. Holly squinted at it. Blood on the base. She said, "Fill me in, Higgins."

He pulled another card from his shirt pocket. "Guy's Dale Colby. Reporter for the *Sun-Dispatch*. Wife and two daughters, in the kitchen now. Friends too. They were away swimming, got back about nine, yelled for him. Didn't answer so they tried the door." He frowned doubtfully at Holly. "What they say is, it was bolted from the inside. They broke it down."

"Wonderful." Frowning too, Holly turned to examine the door. It held a standard brass barrel bolt installed about a foot above the doorknob. The bolt was in its locked position, barrel jutting past the end of the door, the strike that should be on the doorjamb now dangling from the end of the bolt. The screws of the strike had taken a chunk of wood with them. It would fit the splintered scar in the jamb. "Okay. Crime Scene will check it out." She looked at the windows, three of them, gauze-curtained, all clamped closed. One looked cracked. "Higgins, you secured the yard outside these windows, right?"

"Yeah, my partner's there."

"Good. You better get back to the family. I'll talk to them one at a time."

Cautiously, she squatted by Colby's body, grateful for the few moments before the forensic technicians arrived with their bustle and black jokes. Colby was wearing a crisp short-sleeved blue shirt, blue jeans, heavy leather belt, sandals. He'd soiled himself in death, that was common enough, but otherwise his clothes were uncommonly neat. He lay on his back, his head and neck twisted oddly aside. The gash in his skull and forehead over his right eye did not seem deep but had bled profusely. The blood was drying now, thick, caked black in the sparse brown hair. Something was odd about it, about the angle of the face. She decided it was the way the blood had spread toward his temple and right ear; most of it should have run down across his forehead the other way, toward the left. Didn't quite match up with the stain on the carpet either. And there were purplish hints of lividity on the up side of his neck. "Wonderful," muttered Holly in disgust. "Paramedics or somebody rolled this body around."

"Yeah?" Gabe glanced over his shoulder.

"Well, could be God temporarily repealed the law of gravity." She touched the taut neck gently; it was rigid. But when she lifted his forearm a couple of inches, the hand dangled limply. Rigor just starting. Well, she already knew it hadn't happened in the last half hour. Wait for the ME to give her the official guess.

Gabe was peering at the oak desk. "Looks like some violence here." He pointed at the edge of the table, where a gash showed in the wood. "Hard to date it, though."

"Yeah. Still—" Holly's eyes traveled to the recliner. "Damage on the arm of the chair there too. Stuffing looks clean. Let's keep it in mind."

Gabe leaned across the desk, his paunch dented by the edge, and peered at a plate with interest. "Looks like he ate lunch here. Tuna sandwich, potato chips, I'd guess."

"You can't think of anything but food, Gabe. Only one person?"

"Only one coffee mug. Mm, lemon drops."

"Don't eat the evidence, Boy Wonder."

"I won't. Yet," he promised. "Guy's got a tape recorder here. Some messages by the phone. Priscilla Lewis. Mitch Mitchell. Mrs. Resler. Leon Moffatt."

"Good." Holly was checking Colby's pockets and making notes. Not much there; some loose change, house keys, penknife neatly folded. No handkerchief, no billfold, no cards. Maybe in the back pockets; she'd leave it for the technicians.

Gabe, peering into the top desk drawer, whistled. Holly straightened and joined him.

"Looks like he expected trouble," said Gabe.

A pair of Colt .38's gleamed in the drawer, extra cartridges next to them. Holly shook her head. "Kids in the house, and the drawer doesn't lock." She looked back at the door, wondering if the weapons were the reason for that bolt.

"S'pose this is important?" asked Gabe.

He indicated a newspaper. Today's *Sun-Dispatch*. His stubby finger pointed at a byline: Dale Colby. Holly skimmed the story, an update about that plane crash back in January. Congressman Knox. The story made it sound as though most of the families were better off now. Names: Moffatt, Resler, Lewis, some others. "Yeah. Let's start with these names," said Holly.

She pulled a pad of graph paper from her shoulder bag and sketched the room quickly, the position of the windows, the furniture, the body. Someone else would do a measured map, there would be countless photographs, and if she was lucky she'd never have to try to explain her crude sketch in a courtroom. But she needed it to help organize her own mind. God help her, it needed organizing. Okay, lamp there, outlets there and there, air-conditioning vent there, bulletin board there. She gave a last look around the room but saw nothing that she should add. "Gabe, launch the Crime Scene boys when they come moseying in. I'm going to go tackle the witnesses."

From the den end of the hall, she walked along the polished floor to the dining room, gold-carpeted like the living room. A pair of big windows gave a dusky view of the only tree in the backyard. Pineapple-patterned wallpaper, a top-of-the-line thermostat near the door to the kitchen, Audubon bird prints lined up on the walls. She paused at the kitchen door.

The kitchen was large, with maple cabinets and yellow countertops. Towels, pails, and a pink swim ring were heaped next to the door to the garage. Holly thought of her own swim ring, a patched inner tube. On the counter, pizza boxes and a pitcher of copper-colored liquid sat next to an incongruous crowbar by the sink.

Her eyes skimmed the group clustered around the maple breakfast table. There were three women, one red-haired, one blonde, and that tall one with black curls she'd glimpsed earlier. Two men, one a rangy fellow, also with black curly hair, the other burly, and balding. There were also three little girls. The smallest was bouncing vigorously on the knee of the big bald man, singing an enthusiastic off-key version of "Puff the Magic Dragon." Wonderful. Holly's hand clenched on her notebook. "I'm Detective Schreiner. Which of you is Mrs. Colby?"

"I—I am." The speaker was the woman with blonde hair pulled back, gentle mouth, a kicked-puppy look in her brown eyes. Holly knew that look: shock, bewilderment, disbelief. The older child, the one she'd glimpsed earlier at the kitchen door, had the look too. She was still chewing on her knuckle. Holly's heart went out to her. Her suffering had already begun. But the middle-sized girl was sneaking an amused glance at the youngest, who hadn't paused in her high-pitched song.

"I'd like to talk to you a moment, Mrs. Colby. I'll see the rest of you too in a few minutes. Are the children okay?"

"We'll manage." The woman with black curly hair answered. She was lean but roundly pregnant, a red maternity T-shirt over navy shorts showing off long rawboned arms and legs. There was a peace sign printed on the shirt. "Go on now, Donna," she added gently, touching Mrs. Colby on the elbow. Still stunned, the blonde woman lurched to her feet. She was dressed in a flowered yellow shirt and blue shorts. Holly led her to the living room sofa.

"Sorry we have to bother you now, Mrs. Colby," she began. "I know this is a terrible shock for you. Just a few questions. For the record, your name is Donna Colby, is that right?"

"Yes." The word was murmured. She wasn't looking at Holly. Her head was turned toward the back of the sofa where a printed rose seemed to engross her.

"Your husband's name?" Holly started gently, with the straightforward questions, easing Donna Colby into the interrogation.

"Dale. Dale Colby."

"And you have three children?" She was thinking of the little girls in the kitchen.

"No, two. Josie and Tina. Mark is Felicia's son."

Holly paused. "Mark?"

Donna Colby's soft bruised eyes returned to Holly's face, puzzled. "Yes. Felicia's son. Oh, I'm sorry. Felicia was Dale's first wife."

"I see. Dale had three children. Your two girls, and before that Mark? Back when he was married to Felicia?"

"Yes."

Holly noted it down. Time enough to place the third child later. Probably belonged to that fertile peacenik. She asked, "Where do Mark and Felicia live?"

"They live in Pennsylvania. Harrisburg. That's where Dale came from." Donna Colby herself came from around here, Holly decided. Her educated voice had a soft Virginia blur.

"Okay. Do you work, Mrs. Colby?"

"Yes, I'm a teacher at Honey Creek."

"And your husband?"

"A reporter. For the *Sun-Dispatch*."

"What kind of reporter?"

"City news."

"Had he worked there long?"

"Yes. He was working there when I met him. He came here when he divorced Felicia, and I think he started with the *Sun* right away." The puzzlement returned for a moment, the gentle mouth twitching. "I don't understand. Somebody beat him. He was all bloody. But how? Somebody went in there and beat him!"

"We'll try to find out, Mrs. Colby." Holly's attention was caught by the door chime. Gabe hurried past the arch to admit a crew of men with valises. "Excuse me a second." Holly walked over to them. Howie Winks was there too, paunchy and grizzled, an old-style detective marking time till retirement. He was big enough to be nicknamed Wee Willie Winkie, and resentful that Holly was likely to make detective sergeant soon while he never would.

"Well, if it ain't the Frost Queen," he said, beaming. "How ya doing, sweetheart?"

Holly ignored him. "Gabe Mercer here will get you started," she said to the others. "Two general things. Figure out how the perp got out of the room. Also, the body's not in the original position."

Winks snapped a quick salute. "Yes ma'am, Ice Maiden!"

What a boring old hairbag Winks was. She gave him a big bared-teeth smile. "That's the right attitude, Wee Weenie!"

Winks turned an interesting shade of purple while the others tried not to smirk. Holly said, "See you in a few minutes," and went back to her witness.

Donna Colby looked at her blankly. The shock of what had happened still blockaded her senses. Soon hideous reality would come crashing into her world. But at the moment blessed numbness dammed the pain, and Holly must make what use of it she could. She flipped over a page of her notebook. "All right, Mrs. Colby, tell me what happened when you came home."

"Well—" She paused, examined her hands, tried to gather her thoughts. She spoke in a monotone. "We were away all afternoon. At the beach. Then the storm came, and we drove back. I called to Dale that we were back, then went out to help the children get their things out of the van. The men went to the shopping center to get pizzas and the rest of us came inside to fix some iced tea. I called to him again." Her voice broke suddenly. "Oh, God! I can't—I always thought I would die first! I thought—"

"Yes, Mrs. Colby," said Holly soothingly. "What happened after you called to him again?"

"I'm sorry." Donna Colby pressed her hands to her temples and took a deep breath. "Olivia—she's a reporter too, she knows

Dale from work—she knocked on the door but he didn't answer. Then I went too, and we knocked and called. And we were getting worried. So I tried the door but it was bolted."

"I see."

"I don't understand!" Donna Colby cried out. Her self-control cracked. She reached toward Holly in appeal, tears starting. "It was bolted! How could anyone—even if Dale let them in, they couldn't bolt it again after they—"

"Yes, Mrs. Colby." Holly broke in, firm and reassuring, to deflect the outburst. "We'll check into it. You can depend on it."

"Thank you," said Donna with a little choking sound.

"Now, what did you do when you realized the door was bolted?"

"Well, he usually takes a nap. I thought maybe he was asleep." Donna Colby was trying to revert to her numbed monotone again, but a tremor underlay her words. "Then Maggie went to look in the window and came running back in and said hurry up, we had to get the door open. So she did, and—" She stopped. The next part was the unspeakable, Holly knew. Donna Colby turned her face back to the pink flower on the back of the sofa, tracing the outline with a forefinger. "All that blood," she murmured. "I just don't . . . Why?"

"I know, Mrs. Colby." Holly tried to keep her voice soothing in the face of the incomprehensible. A husband and father lay twisted in the den. Why? *Tell me why.* And the others, so many others. A flash of reds at the back of her eyes. A blue-green stench. A tiny whispered beat, *ten, eleven. Twelve.* No more. Hey, cut the bullshit, Schreiner. Just get the details. Ain't no time to wonder why, whoopee we're all gonna die. Holly flipped to a new page, keeping her voice colorless. "What did you do when you got the door open?"

"We all ran in—I don't remember, it was so—I couldn't—the blood. Maggie went to him. Sent Olivia to call an ambulance. Told me to keep the kids out, take them to the kitchen."

Holly noted it down. This Maggie sounded like a real take-charge type. "Okay. And then what?"

"I don't remember much. She made me leave, take care of the kids."

"What was she doing?"

"I don't know. There was so much . . ." The word escaped Donna and she stared at Holly in mute terror before finding it again, with an almost pitiful triumph. "Confusion. The men came back. Maggie will tell you," she added hopefully, trying to be helpful. All her life, probably, being nice had kept her out of trouble. But now she'd hit the big trouble, and Holly knew that no weapons, even niceness, could help now.

"I'll ask her," Holly said. "Was your husband lying on his back?"

"No—yes—I don't remember. It's so confusing. Maybe . . ."

"I'll ask the others." Holly skimmed over her notes and clarified a few so she would remember later exactly what Donna Colby had told her. Not that it was much. Still, she tried to be patient. Civilians were rotten witnesses, by and large. The sight of blood knocked their brains out of commission. Often their stomachs too.

Maybe Donna Colby would be more useful on background. Holly scribbled a new heading as she asked, "Mrs. Colby, did your husband have any enemies?"

"Enemies?"

"People he disagreed with? Maybe from work, from somewhere else?"

"No, not that I—well, he was always saying that someone was going to be mad about something or other he wrote. But except for a few letters no one ever did anything."

"Do you know of anyone recently who might be mad?"

"I don't remember." Her voice was almost a whisper.

Holly looked at her closely and waited. Donna Colby had twined her fingers together in her lap and was frowning at them, as though they held some association that could not break through her numbness. But no words came. Finally Holly prompted, "He was working on a story about a plane crash."

"Yes, he thought he'd found something about that explosion." Almost gratefully, Donna looked up at Holly again. "He was talking to the families. But I don't know what he'd found, he didn't tell me about things very much."

"Was he working on other stories too?"

"Yes, he usually was. But I think that was his main one this past week."

"Did he seem nervous or excited recently? Any unusual behavior?"

"No, not really." Donna's voice was steadier now that she didn't have to focus on the horror of the scene in the den. "Except he was in a terrible mood because of the new drug making him so queasy. Didn't talk about much else the last three weeks."

"What new drug?"

"L-dopa. It still made him sick. So—"

Parkinson's, then. "Was his disease advanced?"

"No, no. Very mild. It's been under control with other drugs, it's just that the doctor wanted to phase in this new one. But it's hard to get the dosage right and Dale felt really sick sometimes."

"Nausea is the main side effect, though. The drug isn't dangerous," said Holly thoughtfully.

"I know. People with Parkinson's live a long time, the doctor said."

Well, Doc, somebody with a brass lamp just wiped out that theory. Holly asked, "Can you think of anyone who might have done this? Who maybe had a grudge against him?"

"No, not really. I mean, the blood—who would break in and do something like that? But they didn't break in, did they? The door was bolted! I just don't understand!" An edge of hysteria was creeping into Donna Colby's voice again.

"We'll try to find out, Mrs. Colby," Holly soothed. She shifted to a calmer subject. "Right now let's just go over the time. You said you were away at the beach. When did you leave?"

"Right after lunch."

"Twelve? One?"

Donna Colby nodded. "Yes. A little after twelve, I guess. We were going over to Bethany Beach so we had to drive a ways."

"Right. Who went with you?"

"Everybody. Except Dale, of course."

"Everybody in the kitchen now?"

"That's right."

"Anyone else?" Holly pursued patiently.

"No."

"Okay. You were all there all afternoon?"

"Yes. We took a picnic."

"What time did you come back?"

"Well, the storm hit after we ate and we started back then. We got here about nine o'clock."

The call had come at nine thirty-eight. Sounded about right; they hadn't found him immediately. Holly closed her notebook. "Thank you, Mrs. Colby. I'll talk to you again later, but this has been very helpful for now." She stood, and Donna Colby stumbled to her feet too. "Let's go on back to the kitchen."

"Detective Schreiner?" Donna Colby's hand on her arm was hesitant, pleading.

"Yes?"

"Do you think the children are safe? I mean, from whoever broke in?"

"Try not to worry, Mrs. Colby. We'll be keeping an eye on things." The mighty arm of the law, safeguarding the trusting public. Except for occasional fuck-ups, of course: a murder here, a rape there, muggings, assaults, terrorist attacks. So hey, what do you expect, Schreiner, perfection? You like it any better when the mighty arm of the law doesn't count at all?

Holly led Donna Colby back to the kitchen. The two younger girls, and Higgins, were listening raptly to a story the bald man was telling them. From the crime scene at the far end of the hall came the murmur of voices, suddenly punctuated by a burst of laughter. The older girl jerked upright, pulling away from the comforting arm of the pregnant woman in the peace shirt. They should have moved them out of here.

The pregnant woman anticipated her. "Do you suppose we could take the kids to a neighbor's, until those guys are finished?"

"I was just going to suggest that." Holly kept the annoyance from her voice. "Do you have a friend near here who could help, Mrs. Colby?"

Donna Colby's brow contracted in confusion. "A friend?"

"Maybe the woman next door?" prompted the pregnant woman.

"Next door. Oh, Mrs. Morgan. Betty. Yes, maybe."

"Okay. You can go with Officer Higgins." Holly glanced at the freckled, russet-haired woman, then back to the pregnant one. "Are you Maggie?"

The pregnant woman bounced to her feet. "Right. Am I on next?" Intensely curious blue eyes, a gawky boniness made ludicrous by the distended belly under the peace sign. "I want to tell you something about—" Her eyes slid to the twelve-year-old, then back to Holly. "About the room in there."

Yes, this was the take-charge hotshot. Holly hoped she was observant as well as bossy. She nodded. "Yeah. You're on next. Let's go."

Chapter 3

"We'll sit in the living room," said Holly.

"Okay." The pregnant woman kissed the smallest girl and squeezed the bald man's hand before turning toward the door. The curly-haired man put a hand on her shoulder as he too stood to go next door with Higgins and the others. "See you soon, Maggot," he said seriously. Holly's fist tightened on her pen.

"Thanks, Jerry." A small smile. They resembled each other: hair, eyes, rangy build. Family, Holly decided. The whole pack of them had probably spent the sixties jamming helpless daffodils into National Guard rifles. Well, doesn't matter now, Schreiner. Your job is to find out why Dale Colby got wasted this afternoon. So get on with it.

"Your name is Maggie?" Holly asked as the woman joined her.

"Yeah, not Maggot. That's just big-brother talk. Hasn't called me anything else since he first heard the word in second grade," she explained. She moved smoothly, athletically, in contrast to her angular, lanky appearance. With a curious glance at Holly, she asked, "Do you like being a detective?"

"I've had worse jobs."

"I'd like the puzzle side of it. And the sense of helping people, putting things right. But there sure are a lot of forms to fill out. A lot of rules. Don't you get tired of those?"

Wonderful. A witness who was trying to interrogate her. But it was interesting that she had apparently encountered police red tape sometime or other. Well, plenty of demonstrators had rap sheets. Holly made a mental note to check. For now, she said neutrally, "A necessary evil. Would—"

"Right. Chain of evidence, they tell me. When did you decide to join the police?"

Holly felt her jaw tightening. Steady, Schreiner, she warned herself. So okay, your chief witness turns out to be a pushy, inquisitive, demonstrator type, and irritates the hell out of you for various reasons. But your job is to find a murderer. Holly pulled her eyes from the red T-shirt with the peace sign, reassembled her professional shell of neutrality, and waved at the sofa politely. "Please sit down."

"Okay." Those blue eyes, disconcertingly alert, were appraising her. "Unless you want me to show you first how the body was lying when we arrived."

Holly halted beside the sofa. "What do you mean?"

"As soon as I broke in I rolled him over. I thought you knew if a body was moved."

"We knew," said Holly shortly. So this was the culprit, not the paramedics. Idiot civilian. Well, find out what happened. Keeping her voice flat, she repeated, "You're saying you broke into the room, and you moved him?"

Maggie nodded. "Yeah. To see if I could help him. Want me to show you?"

Holly snapped open her notebook to underline who was in charge. "First let me get your full name."

"Oh, right." She combed back her feathery black curls with bony fingers. "Margaret Mary Ryan, R-Y-A-N."

"Address?"

"Two-sixty-eight Garfield Place, Brooklyn. I'm here visiting my brother."

"His name?"

"Jerry Ryan. Four-oh-seven-three Markleman Road."

A posh area compared to this one, a pocket of big prewar houses, young professionals. Holly asked, "Is he a lawyer? Doctor?"

"Doctor." The glint in Maggie's eyes revealed appreciation of this deduction. "Have you lived here long?"

"Nine years. Mrs. Ryan, shall we—"

"Yeah, I thought you didn't sound like Virginia. Started out in Ohio, myself. Where were you before?"

"Let's go talk to the ME." Brusquely, Holly marched past her to lead the way to the back hall and den. She stopped at the door. Several men were working in the room, and plump Doc Craine, the medical examiner, was squatting next to the body. The position was already chalked onto the carpet. "Dr. Craine," said Holly, "we've got a witness here says she saw the original position of the body."

He looked up at them, little shrewd eyes with puffy lids. "Hello, Schreiner. Yeah, let's hear it." Maggie Ryan started to step in past Holly, but Holly grabbed her arm and Doc said, "Hey, no, don't come in. Just tell us about it."

"Okay. He was on his stomach." She stood in the door squinting at the scene, cool, detached, but Holly could see that her hands were clenched together behind her. Not so unruffled, after all. Holly remembered, eons ago, her own first encounters with death, her younger self struggling to stay calm, objective. It was the only way to get the job done. She repressed an unwelcome stirring of empathy with the witness and readied her notebook as Maggie continued, "The jaw and neck were already stiff so their position hasn't changed any. The blood was pretty well dried on his face, the head lying on that stain on the carpet. Left arm bent, upper arm maybe forty-five degrees from the body, elbow bent at seventy degrees." Other Crime Unit men were peering at the carpet too, trying to visualize what she was describing. "Right arm extended beyond his head, fingers near the lamp base. Legs—I'm not real clear on the legs. My impression is that they weren't totally straight, but they weren't curled up either."

Doc Craine peered at the body closely again, probably checking lividity stains, and nodded curt approval. Holly fished out her graph paper and sketched in a second little stick man next to the first on her floor plan. "Is there anything else different about the scene now from what you saw?"

Maggie surveyed the room. "No, except the drawers were all closed. God, are those guns? Wonder why he didn't try to grab one? Defend himself?"

"And what about the door?" Holly insisted, keeping her on track.

"Closed, bolted."

"You said you were the one who broke in."

"Yes. Donna and Olivia knocked at the door and yelled and couldn't rouse him. So I went out to peek in the window, saw he was in trouble. I ran back in. Had to pass through the garage and there was a crowbar on the wall so I grabbed it. Pried the door open." She glanced at the splintered wood beside her. "Looks like I really messed up the jamb."

"Yeah, it's a strong bolt," agreed Holly. "Where's the crowbar?"

"Crowbar. Oh, yes, I took it to the kitchen with me when Officer Higgins sent me out of this room."

"Anything else you remember that's different now?"

"No." A slow shake of the black curls. A vision nudged at Holly: dark curls bunched above a tight bandage, reddened with seeping blood. She turned away. God, she was tired tonight.

"Let's go back and sit down," she said.

Maggie lingered a moment, frowning at the room. "Sure don't see how anyone got in. Or out again." Then she fell into step beside Holly, glancing sideways at her. "Have you worked in Homicide long?"

"Two years," said Holly wearily. "And yes, I've seen plenty of dead bodies, and no, I don't like to see them. Let's get on with this, okay?"

"Hey, I'm sorry, I don't like to see them either. I'm just nosy by nature." Maggie touched Holly's forearm apologetically but Holly jerked away and walked to the other end of the sofa. Maggie shrugged and perched on the edge of the near sofa cushion, long legs stretched out past the coffee table, eyes brightly studying Holly again. "And I'm interested when I meet women with unusual jobs. I'm a statistician, myself. Homicide work must be pretty exhausting. Psychologically too, right?"

Holly, tight-lipped, smoothed the flowered cushion unnecessarily and sat down. Psychologically exhausting, yeah, you could say that. But why did this damn curly-haired peacenik care? Why did she keep worming past Holly's defenses? Maggot, her brother called her. Pesky. But what the hell, in the last few years Holly had dealt calmly with witnesses of all types—surly, drunk, antagonistic, hysterical, violent, even amorous. Nothing so difficult about this one, right? So quit acting like an asshole, Schreiner, and get on with the job. Ignoring those inquiring eyes, Holly took a deep breath, balanced her notebook on her knee again, wrote "statistician," and said in a colorless voice, "Mrs. Ryan, you mentioned that the jaw and neck were stiffening, and the blood already dried when you first reached the body. So why did you roll it over?"

"He was lying there, obviously hurt. So I turned him over to start CPR." Maggie's hands were clenched together again, the knuckles white. "As soon as I tried to move his jaw to open his airway I noticed the rigor."

A disgustingly admirable course of action for a mere civilian.

Holly asked, too sharply, "You couldn't tell he was dead?" Steady, Schreiner.

But Maggie had picked up on Holly's skeptical tone. Her blue gaze was chilly as an ice storm. "No, I couldn't tell! Not that first minute. I touched his back, okay? It didn't register that he was cold, only that he wasn't breathing. Sorry I disturbed the scene of the crime, but my first impulse was to try to save his life!"

"Yes, of course, you did right," Holly admitted. For a moment the blue eyes held hers, angry but puzzled too, Holly thought. Then the bony shoulders in the red shirt shrugged and Maggie seemed to accept the truce. Holly asked, "Now, did you notice anything else that might help us?"

"Stuff I'm sure you noticed too. Cracked windowpane. Gouges in the edge of the desk. Story about the crash of Representative Knox's plane last January. Lunch eaten. Lamp bashed and bloody. Some notes by the phone, and a tape recorder on the desk. And a bunch of tapes missing by the stereo there."

Holly looked at the gap on the shelves indicated by the pointing finger. "You say missing. You saw tapes there earlier?"

"Yes. I sat on the arm of the sofa here while we got organized to go to the beach, talking to one of Colby's daughters about a book. I remember noticing how neat Donna kept everything, books, magazines, tapes. Even newspapers. At home we drown in newspapers."

"I see." Holly made a note about the missing tapes. "What were the tapes?"

"I couldn't read the labels from here."

"We'll ask. Did you notice anything else?"

"Not that I can remember now." She leaned forward eagerly. "But the big problem is how it was done. I mean, that door was really bolted. From the inside."

"We'll get to that. Right now let's go over what you did from the time you arrived." Sometimes that jogged memories, and Holly had to admit that this annoying witness seemed to be more observant and a hell of a lot less dazed than poor Donna Colby had been.

Maggie leaned back and flopped a rangy arm along the back of the sofa. "Okay. We arrived sometime around nine. The kids had been cooped up during the drive, and it was cool. So they all wanted to play, and ran around. We encouraged them, I'm afraid. You'll find lots of little footprints all over the yard. And Nick and Jerry ran around too. But I don't remember them going in the backyard."

"The children were in the backyard?"

"From time to time."

"By the den windows?"

"I wasn't there. I know they ran all the way around the house sometimes, but I didn't see the exact route."

"And the rest of you?"

"Let's see. Donna went in as far as the dining-room door for a second, called to Dale that we were back. Then she came back out and helped us unload the van. She left the kitchen door open and we just stuck things inside the door. It took a while because we hadn't really packed carefully to leave the beach. The storm was coming and we just tossed things in the van, so we needed a lot of trips unloading. Oh, and Donna dropped the picnic basket on the driveway and we had to clean up all that too."

"About how long did this take?"

"Twenty minutes, maybe. We also had to discuss getting pizza and who was going to go get it. You know."

"No one wondered why Mr. Colby didn't come out?"

"Yeah, sure, it crossed my mind, but not enough to worry about at first. No one said anything about it, if that's what you mean."

"Okay." Holly wrote that down. "Then what?"

"Nick and Jerry and Tina were elected pizza committee, and they took the van to Cedar Lane Center for it. The rest of us went into the kitchen. Donna called Dale again and started fixing iced tea. I was looking for my daughter's clothes in the heap. She was still in her swimsuit. Olivia finally went down to knock on the den door."

"Right."

"And the rest I've told you. Donna got worried and went to help Olivia, and I popped outside to look in the window." She straightened her leg and waggled a sandal toward Holly. "You'll find my footprints out back too. I stood right outside the window."

"I see." Holly noted it down.

"Do you have any idea whether he was killed before or after the rainstorm?"

"The ME will tell us. Any special reason you ask?"

"Just curious. If it was before the storm, any traces of a person out there might have been wiped out by the rain, right? Not by us?"

"Maybe," said Holly noncommittally. "Now, you all used the kitchen door when you came in?"

"Kitchen door. Every one of us."

"Every time? There was a lot of running in and out, wasn't there?"

"Not as much as you'd think. We came through the garage as far as the kitchen door and tossed things in from out there. But when we did finally go in, there were a lot of us."

"No one used the front door, then?"

"*We* didn't." A ghost of a smile.

Holly took the point and nodded resignedly. She and all the other cops had trooped in that way. Colby might as well have got himself killed in the middle of a busy intersection. However the perp had entered, the traces were mostly covered over. Well, let the Crime Scene boys sweat that problem. Holly said, "Okay, let's go back to the discovery of the body. You turned him over to try to help, and found out he was dead. What happened next?"

"Well, while I was turning him over I was yelling for Olivia to call an ambulance and the police. After I'd figured out I couldn't help him I looked back at the door. Little Josie was there, and Donna, gaping. Donna was trembling. I was afraid she'd get hysterical or faint or something. So I told her to get Josie the hell out of there, to take her to the kitchen. And I asked her to check on my daughter because I'd just dumped her in the kitchen on my way in with the crowbar. That sort of brought Donna to her senses. She rallied around pretty well. I stayed in the room with the body. By the door."

"Did you move anything?" Holly demanded. She caught the glimmer of incipient anger and added hastily, "I have to ask. There are a lot of questions I have to ask."

"Yeah, okay, I know." Maggie sprawled back into the corner of the sofa and pushed her fingers through her curls. "I keep thinking we're on the same team, but you can't assume that yet, can you?"

"I try not to assume much." Holly made herself meet Maggie's eyes. Appraising eyes, skeptical yet friendly.

Still sprawled, Maggie dropped her hands to rest on her round belly and shifted her gaze to the big blank TV. "Okay, I'll play your rules. The answer is no. I didn't move anything or touch anything except poor Dale. I didn't step anywhere except on the carpet between Dale and the door. The only reason I stayed in that room at all was to keep other people from running in and touching things. Kids especially."

"So you were the only person in the room after the door was pried open?"

"Well, no. Jerry came in."

"Your brother." Wonderful. Whole platoons of Ryans tramping across the crime scene.

"Right. He and Nick and Tina arrived with the pizzas. I hollered down the hall for him to come."

"Why did—" Steady, Schreiner. No need to squawk at her.

But Maggie was already defending herself, straightening up, gesturing with those lean, graceful hands. "Look, I wanted to be absolutely sure! He's a doctor, damn it! We stupid laymen aren't all that confident about our medical judgments. A guy is lying there, bloody, he's been attacked—but we don't want to believe he's dead. We cling to hope too long. Can you understand that?"

"Yes, of course, Mrs. Ryan. I just—"

The front door opened. Holly turned to look at it, almost grateful for the interruption.

It was Higgins' partner that she'd seen outside. Patterson, said the nameplate under his shield. He was escorting a blonde woman, trim, a carefully made up forty. Red flare-leg slacks, a sleeveless white blouse, wavy hair sprayed stiff. She was gesturing indignantly at the policeman.

"Look, what is this? What's going on?" she demanded. She spotted Maggie and Holly, and appealed to them. "Can you tell me what's happening? I just want to talk to Dale. Is this some new trick of his?"

"You want to talk to Dale?" Holly asked, standing up. "About what?"

"He knows about what! I've been phoning him about it for days!" She paused to eye Holly's unpowdered face and plain twill skirt belligerently. "Listen, who are you? Why should I talk to you?"

Holly held up her ID. "Detective Schreiner," she said. "Who are you?"

"Jesus, what next?" The blonde rolled her eyes at the ceiling in exasperation. "I come to talk to Dale and he sics the cops on me! He's the one you should be after! Don't you know that? Look, I've got papers!" She fumbled in her big white handbag, pulled out a red chiffon scarf, a Holiday Inn motel key, a romance paperback, finally an official-looking document that she waved under Patterson's nose. "See? Right there! Judge says he's supposed to pay Mark's tuition! Well, he hasn't! Won't answer my letters, won't even pick up the phone any more! And then I come and the cops won't even let me see him!"

"You're Felicia Colby, then," said Holly.

"Damn right! That's my name right on the paper here!" She jabbed at the document with a shiny red nail.

"Okay, we'd better discuss it." She was surprised at the depth of her own relief. Tomorrow, she told herself, she wouldn't feel so raw, she could cope with Maggie Ryan better. Maybe she'd be tired enough to sleep tonight. Glancing down at her notes, she was astonished to see that pages of information had resulted from this tense, half-bungled interview. Meanwhile Felicia Colby's story might be very interesting. Without looking up she said, "Patterson, take Mrs. Ryan here next door, all right? We'll get an official statement tomorrow."

Maggie had been observing the angry Felicia Colby with frank curiosity. Now she looked sharply at Holly. "God, you're exhausted!" she said sympathetically. "Bummer of a job some days, isn't it?"

Her unquenchable friendliness tugged at Holly, challenging her to confidence, connection, friendship. Damn Maggot. Holly's hand clenched defensively on her notebook. "See you tomorrow," she said tightly.

"Okay. We ought to talk about how it was done." Maggie's glance lingered a moment as she stood, heron-like with her rounded torso poised over those long legs. Then she turned to the blonde. "Felicia, sorry we met this way. I'm Maggie. See you later." She waved at them both and started for the door. Patterson quirked a dubious eyebrow at Holly and followed her out.

"What was all that about?" demanded Felicia Colby. "And where's Dale?"

Holly was scribbling in her notebook. The peacenik was right, of course; how Colby was killed was the first problem, and she'd better check soon to see what Crime Scene was finding.

But for now she turned with relief to the angry and bewildered Felicia Colby. "Mrs. Colby, please sit down," she said gently, gesturing to the sofa. "I've afraid you can't talk to Dale Colby. You see, a little earlier today he was killed."

"Killed? Dale?" Felicia sank suddenly into the sofa cushions, her eyes darting wildly about the room and finally settling on Holly. "And you're a cop—"

"Yes, Mrs. Colby. And I have a few questions for you."

But Felicia Colby's bright red lips had clamped shut. Another tough interview coming up. Yet Holly knew that this one would be easier, because this time she'd be contending only with the witness. Not with that black drowned part of herself.

Chapter 4

For the sixteenth time, Olivia twitched back the mist-green satin drape of Betty Morgan's front window to peer toward the Colby house next door. The night was black now, but the glow from a streetlight reached as far as the Colby walk and light from the living room windows splashed onto the still-glistening lawn. Two policemen stood in the driveway, shadows against the light, talking. Their rumpled regulation summer shirts together with nightsticks, holsters, and notebooks made their silhouettes look lumpy, barnacled. Two more men, in plainclothes, were moving around the periphery of the house, studying the shrubbery with flashlights.

"Hey, Maggie's coming!" Olivia exclaimed as the Colby front door opened at last. Instantly Nick and Jerry were at her side, peering out too. Nick held a drowsy Sarah against his beefy shoulder, and the little girl whimpered resentfully at her father's sudden movement. He patted her back and murmured, "Let's not be tetchy and wayward, now."

"Look at Maggie," said Jerry. "Quizzing the police."

"Wish I could!" Olivia muttered to him, enviously watching Maggie's conversation with the officer escorting her toward them. This was the height of frustration. Her friend and coworker had been killed, and Olivia was simultaneously horrified and eager to discover anything she could to help. And more than that: she was the first reporter on the scene, she had inside information, she knew the victim, the witnesses, the first doctor to examine the body. But here she was, cooped up in the house next door, and every time she'd try to compare notes with Jerry or asked the dazed Donna a question, a discouraging word from the cop Higgins in the corner shut her up again. She hadn't even had a chance to call the paper yet. She'd tried to get information from Higgins, but he'd brushed off most of her questions, explaining that a statement for the media would be issued in good time. Off the pigs. Though Olivia had to admit that she was also inhibited by Donna's shock; she couldn't ask Jerry anything too graphic in front of her even if Higgins would let her."

"I feel bottled up," she grumbled quietly to her husband.

"Yeah, I can tell." His fingers touched the nape of her neck lightly, a strangely comforting sensation. "The minute they uncork you, you'll be fizzing all over the place with questions."

"You make me sound like Alka-Seltzer."

"No, no. Champagne," Jerry corrected her gallantly. But he was distracted too, glancing from window to front hall.

Maggie and the other officer appeared in the archway. Maggie's eyes and smile first sought out Nick, who nodded at her across the blue cotton of their slumbering daughter's back. Then she turned to Donna and her children, a flicker of concern crossing her face. The three were huddled together on the sofa, a picture book sitting unopened on Donna's lap. Maggie crossed to her. "How's it going, Donna?"

Slowly, Donna's brown eyes focused on her. " Fine," she said without inflection.

"Josie? Tina? You okay?"

Josie was staring stonily at her own toes, but Tina wriggled impatiently on the sofa next to her mother and whined, "I want to go home."

"We can't just yet," Maggie said gently. "Do you want to take a nap? Like Sarah?"

Tina twisted her head around to look at the small girl. "Sarah's a baby," she pouted.

"Well, I know how to pretend to be a baby," Maggie declared. She lay down on the shag carpet on her back and bicycled at the ceiling. God, thought Olivia, what kind of family have I got myself into? But Tina was distracted from her complaint. She laid her head back in her mother's lap and imitated Maggie from the sofa before an enormous yawn slowed her circling legs again, testimony that Maggie's reading of her problem was correct.

Plump Betty Morgan, making the best of her enforced role as hostess, bustled in from the kitchen laden with a tray of cups of hot chocolate. "Oh, goodness!" she exclaimed, halting in surprise.

Maggie looked up sheepishly from the floor. "Oh, hi. You must be Mrs. Morgan." She stood up, surprisingly nimble, and explained, "Tina and I were just pretending. I'm Maggie Ryan. Thanks for helping us out."

Olivia could bear it no longer. "Maggie, what's going on?"

"Police investigation. Tedious but necessary."

"Who was the woman in the red Vega? Blond, red pants?"

"Felicia Colby." Maggie was looking at Donna as she answered.

Donna blinked. "Felicia's here?"

"She said something about Mark."

"Her son," said Donna. "She's been after Dale for—"

From his straight chair next to the arch, the cop Higgins cleared his throat. "It's better if you don't discuss it."

Jeez. Olivia steamed ahead with a different question. "What were you and the other policeman talking about on the way over?"

Maggie glanced at Higgins. "Not about the case! About the county detective in charge of this investigation. Detective Schreiner."

"What about her?"

"He says she's good. Started undercover in Narcotics, got promoted fast when they let women in the regular force. One of the first women to make detective. She's earned a fistful of commendations. Do you agree, Officer Higgins?"

"That's the word," said Higgins, looking at her suspiciously from under gray brows.

"You've worked with her before?"

"No. She's new. Anyway we don't get a lot of homicides around here." He shifted in his chair, as though startled by his own loquaciousness.

"But what did *you* think?" Olivia asked Maggie.

"Me? Oh, I agree. She's good. Totally professional. Oh, thanks, Mrs. Morgan!" She accepted a cup of cocoa with a smile. "You know, nothing's as comforting as chocolate."

Betty Morgan beamed. "I think so too! And the weather has cooled off enough, don't you think? Here, Josie, won't you change your mind?"

The girl looked sideways at her sister, who was now leaning against Donna's arm, sipping sleepily at her cup. "Okay," she consented. Betty Morgan distributed the rest of the cups, even coaxing Higgins into accepting one. He took it with a suspicious look, propping it on one uniformed knee. Well, with that paunch he was probably right to view it as the enemy.

A car door slammed and Olivia whirled to look through the

curtain again. The old red Vega's lights went on, and she saw the blonde at the wheel as the car pulled out past the streetlight. Was there a second person in the car too? Then the other cop appeared in the archway. "Who's the reporter?" he asked Higgins.

Higgins nodded toward Olivia. "Redhead."

"Okay, ma'am. You're next."

At last! Olivia thrust her chocolate into Jerry's hand and raced across the room. As she passed Maggie, she heard, "Don't ask her anything personal."

"Oh?" Olivia slowed.

"But you might ask her if the Colbys should be arranging for a place to spend the night. I doubt if they'll be finished over there any time soon."

Olivia glanced at Donna. "Good point. See you soon." She went through the door Patterson was holding for her and into the fresh damp night.

Detective Holly Schreiner was in the hall talking to the pudgy male detective when Olivia and Patterson arrived. Olivia had a moment to study her: sturdy, muscular rather than fat, with mid-length khaki-colored hair. She was dressed in conservative tailored summer skirt and blouse, comfortable sandals. Only the holstered gun not quite hidden by her loose blouse betrayed her occupation. Olivia was fascinated: cops had been the other side for so long, college demonstrations against the war, feminist marches, and now that she was a reporter they too often served as tight-lipped obstacles to getting a story. But this cop was a woman. An ally? She'd soon know.

"Let's phone them right away, Gabe," Schreiner was saying to the pudgy detective.

"Sure," said Gabe. "But Harrisburg may take a while. It's almost eleven already."

"Yeah, well, get it in the works. And I want to know about Ryan too. Margaret Mary. Check New York City on her."

Wow, so her sister-in-law was being checked! Olivia wondered if she would be too. It came home to her suddenly, viscerally, that this was real, not just a newsworthy event, not happening to someone else. Dale was really dead, and that fact had entangled her, her relatives and friends. She remembered writing about colleagues and relations of Joanne Little's murdered jailer, laughing at some of their claims about the victim's flawless character. Would her own claims be any less biased?

Well, she'd try. Stay objective, collect facts, use her skills to help figure out what the hell had happened here. Don't ask anything personal, Maggie had warned. But the questions of the official interrogation itself would be revealing. She might be able to read between the lines, find out what the police were thinking.

She focused again on the detectives. The one called Gabe was heading down the hall for the den again. Detective Schreiner's serious dark eyes, underlined with weariness, turned to Olivia. She said, "You're Mrs. Kerr?"

"Ms. Yes," said Olivia.

"Right." There was no flicker of sisterly approval, but no hostility either. "You worked with Dale Colby?"

"Yes, since I started at the S-D a year and a half ago."

"Let's sit down." Schreiner gestured with her notepad toward the sofa in the living room. Olivia followed directions and settled into the cushions, feeling strangely self-conscious to be taking part in this formal rite of truth-searching. Solomon, Pilate, Oliver Wendell Holmes: the law's lineage was ancient and solemn compared to her own profession's checkered history. Embraced by the creaky scaffolding of rules of evidence and due process, she and Detective Schreiner would play their appointed roles in the attempt to pick out the currents of truth in the muddy-bordered runniness of reality. Olivia's role was to be witness, source of information. How many times had she bantered about sources? And now that was her own sole function. But Detective Schreiner was more than curious reporter. Her role was weightier: priest of logic, justice, retribution. She studied Olivia with those grave eyes and began the ritual questions: full name, address, date of birth, ID.

"You said you've been working at the *Sun-Dispatch* a year and a half?" Her voice was courteous but colorless.

"That's right," said Olivia. "Mostly features, some news rewrites."

"Did you know Mr. Colby well?"

Olivia shrugged. "Not well enough to know what's going on now. Socially, he and Donna came to our Christmas party last year. That was about it, until this picnic. Mostly we talked at the office, joked around."

"Can you tell me anything about his current work?"

"Only a little." Olivia saw that her hand was squeezing the arm of the sofa and relaxed her fingers consciously. "You see, he was working at home temporarily while he got used to his new medication. The way I understand it, Edgerton considered him half-time this month, and Dale sent stuff in from home."

"Edgerton?"

"Kent Edgerton, our managing editor. He kept him pretty busy. Dale was calling in a couple of times a day or sending a messenger. Once or twice he asked me to stop by here to pick things up on my way in. Dale was definitely doing a lot of reporting. He's such a workaholic anyway, I don't think half-time made any difference to either of them. Except he was doing all his interviews by phone."

Detective Schreiner's head was bent over her notepad, the ash-tan hair drooping over her face. "Was he due to go back to the office soon?"

"Week after next, I think. But that's just a manner of speaking. Normally he'd be away from the office a lot, getting interviews and so forth."

"I see. Well, what can you tell me about his current stories?" The detective lifted her eyes to Olivia. She didn't smile much.

Olivia leaned forward on the sofa, forearms on her knees, hands clasped as she thought. "Today he was working on a follow-up on that Representative Knox plane crash back in January. He'd been doing stuff on the progress of the new subway lines into Virginia too. The I-66 controversy."

"Can you explain about the plane crash? If it was in January, why was he still writing about it?"

"They're still investigating it, you see. Representative Knox wasn't happy with some of the original work. He said it was too hasty. He got them to repeat some of the tests."

"Why would they be too hasty?"

"Well, it was a small plane. Five deaths. Not like a big commercial plane crashing. But Representative Knox was scheduled to be on the flight originally, so naturally he wanted a thorough investigation."

A quick nod as Detective Schreiner wrote it down. This interested her, Olivia thought, trying to remember what else she knew about that crash. She'd have to check the files tomorrow. And Nate Rosen—he'd done some of the early reports on that story. Though mostly it had been Dale, out in the January weather, shuffling back into the office with snowflakes melting on his coat, grousing about the congressman's press aide.

The detective asked, "What had the new investigation found?"

Olivia leaned back in the sofa and crinkled up her face in the effort to remember. "Let me think. A couple weeks ago they reported the pilot's last words. I know that they concluded he hadn't seen trouble coming. But there was going to be another report. It wasn't out yet, that's why I can't tell you much. But soon, I think."

"Had Dale said anything about it recently?"

"Not much. He said he'd started talking to relatives of the people who died in the crash, updating their ideas. But I don't know what he found out."

"Who were the relatives?" The detective's voice was still neutral, but her posture had altered slightly, her back straighter, her eyes more alert. Olivia felt an uncomfortable little shiver of complicity with the power structure. She felt like a snitch. But, hell, this wasn't a political struggle, was it? They all wanted to find Dale's killer. Anyway, it wasn't confidential.

"Moffatt," she said. "There was someone named Moffatt, a rich businessman, who died in the crash. His son Leon came to the office today. And, well, he was complaining about Dale."

"I see." The information went briskly onto the notepad. Official now. Part of a different order of reality. "What was his complaint?"

"Very general. He called Dale an asshole reporter."

"Mm. Did he say why?"

Olivia shrugged. "Probably he did, but not in my hearing. Edgerton took him into his private office. You'd better ask him." And I'd better too, she thought eagerly. This was important. She and Nate and Edgy should get their heads together as soon as possible.

"Had Moffatt been to your office often?"

"No. At least, not while I was there."

"Okay. Now, do you know who else he was talking to about this crash?"

"Representative Knox's office, obviously. But I really wasn't keeping track of that story." Dumb, she thought to herself; she should have asked Dale more questions. A national politician involved in this almost-local story. The airfield was in this county, the hills where it had crashed not far away. But even Dale hadn't seemed too excited about it. Except— She said slowly, "I saw Dale for a minute before we left for the beach. I told him Moffatt was upset at him, and he seemed pleased. Like he was finally getting somewhere."

There was a little amused twitch at the corner of Schreiner's mouth, as though she recognized that situation. Olivia blurted, "Your job is a little like a reporter's, isn't it?"

"A little."

"Wish I could get search warrants and things," Olivia observed enviously.

"Wish I didn't have so many forms to fill out." Schreiner's tired eyes looked at Olivia almost kindly. "Now, Ms. Kerr, I'm going to read you some names. Tell me if you recognize any of them. First is John Lewis, also known as Corky."

"Corky Lewis. No, don't recognize that name."

"How about Priscilla Lewis?"

"No."

"Moffatt we've done. How about Ann Kauffmann?"

"Guess I'm striking out. No."

"Frank or Doris Resler?"

"Hey!" Olivia bounced upright on the sofa. "I've heard—listen, Mrs. Resler was in the *S-D* office today too, talking to the editor! Not upset like Moffatt. But there's something else. Dale was on the phone to Mrs. Resler when I stopped in right before we left! Doris, you said?"

"Doris and Frank. Can you tell me anything about them?"

"Resler. Resler." Olivia pressed the heel of her hand against her forehead. "Frank Resler. A lawyer, maybe."

"Yeah. Criminal lawyer."

"Hey, if you know already, why—oh, hell, same reason I do the same thing. Fresh angle." Olivia looked eagerly at the detective as a stratagem occurred to her. "Maybe if you told me a little about the others I'd remember more."

"Okay. First tell me about the phone call. How do you know he was talking to Mrs. Resler?"

"I just heard the end of the conversation. He was saying sure, Mrs. Resler, I'll be discreet."

"Discreet about what?"

"I wish I knew. But he hung up then."

"I see. Can you tell me anything else about the Reslers?"

"Not yet. But I'll sure look them up."

"No doubt," she said drily. "Do you recognize the name Peter Church?"

"Peter Church. Yes, actually," said Olivia, surprised. "I remember now, when I saw the list of crash victims in January, he was the only one I'd even heard of. He was one of Representative Knox's aides."

"And where had you met him?"

"I didn't meet him, just talked to him on the phone about press releases last year."

"Ann Kauffmann was another aide in Knox's office," offered Schreiner.

Olivia filed away the information. "I'd heard there was a second aide. But I don't know anything about her. How about those first people you mentioned? The Lewises?"

"Corky Lewis was the pilot. Priscilla Lewis is his sister."

"I see." Olivia decided to find out about Corky, maybe at the little airstrip where the plane had taken off. "I'm sorry, I don't know anything about them."

"Anything else you can tell us? About Church, about any of the other names?"

"No. But we've got stuff in the files at the office. Dale probably has good files here at home too, knowing him. And of course Representative Knox's office will have a lot of information."

"I see." Schreiner paused to read through her notes again. A thorough woman, obviously tired but still alert, double-checking everything. Strange to be in law enforcement, Olivia thought, a traditional man's job even more than the newspaper business, where it was tough enough to get yourself taken seriously. And yet Olivia could imagine the appeal. Not just curiosity, or desire to be allied with the power of the law, or a yen for excitement, though all that was real enough. But to see life at the raw edges, to be part of the forces that knit it back into order after it had been ripped apart—

Come off it, Olivia scolded herself, or next thing you know you'll be signing up at the Police Academy yourself. You, who tried to get yourself arrested for peace at least twice. But plenty of women really had signed up. From traffic cops to detectives. And jailers, she thought suddenly. If Joanne Little's jailer had been a woman, the tragedy would not have occurred. And what was it like to be a jailer? She could sell Edgerton on this, she realized. Tie it in to the Joanne Little story, a whole series on women in law enforcement.

Detective Schreiner had finished skimming through the pages. "Okay, Ms. Kerr," she said, and pointed with her chin at the bookcases. "Do you remember any more tapes on the shelves earlier today?"

Olivia stared at the empty space. "I think—look, I can't swear to it, but I think so. And if they were stolen it might be important."

"In what way?"

"Well, a lot of us use tape recorders for some of our interviews. If Dale had been asking someone the wrong questions—"

"I see."

"But it doesn't really narrow things down unless we find the tapes."

"Right." Schreiner wrote it down and asked, "Is there anything else you can tell me about Mr. Colby's work situation? Did he get along with the others at work?"

"Yeah." Again Olivia felt that sinking sense of being personally entangled when she'd much rather be an observer. "The usual relationships at an office. Nothing deep. We'd talk about stories, or just joke around, or grouse. Probably the same as police do."

"No enemies at work?"

"No. Not that I know of, anyway."

"You mentioned grousing. What did Mr. Colby grouse about?"

"His medicine, or people who wouldn't be interviewed, or the weather—all the usual stuff."

"You think he was unhappy with his work?"

"No! Look, you asked about grousing, right? That doesn't mean he always did it! He worked hard, kept things organized tightly. If anything, he groused less than the rest of us because he didn't gossip as much. I really don't think it was one of us!"

The serious eyes studied her a moment, and Olivia felt furious at herself, realizing that getting emotional hurt more than it helped. But Schreiner just said mildly, "Fine. I'll stop by your office tomorrow to follow up some of these things with the others. Now, could you tell me how you came to schedule this picnic with him?"

"Oh, it was pretty casual, really. A couple of days ago he called and asked me to stop by to take some of his stuff to the office. I came to the door and we both complained about this heat wave. I told him we were planning a picnic with Jerry's sister on Monday, and I saw his little girls behind him in the hall and just impulsively asked if they'd all like to come to the beach with us." Olivia smiled faintly. "The kids both gave him this bated-breath look, and he said sure, it would be good to get out of the house. The little one clapped her hands. He told her to settle down and she did, but it was clear that we were all committed."

"But in fact he didn't go," the detective pointed out.

"No, damn it. He didn't." A wave of loss surged up through Olivia, surprising her. Dale hadn't been a close friend; recently she hadn't even seen him that often. But he was a presence in her life all the same, grinding out solid, tightly researched stories that they all respected. A hardworking man with an odd little smile she'd never see again. She clasped her hands on her knees and blinked at them.

"When did he decide not to go, Ms. Kerr?" Detective Schreiner's cool professional voice pulled her back.

"It was—" She found she had to clear her throat. "It was when I was talking to him, I think. He seemed a little edgy with everyone. Then I told him about Moffatt's visit, and he called for Donna to bring him a sandwich and to take the kids away so he could take his nap and do some work."

Schreiner's pen was scribbling rapidly across the page. "Do you know what he planned to do next?"

"No! I would have told you first thing!"

"Yes, of course." The grave eyes appraised Olivia. "Now, could we go over the order that things happened? What was he doing when you arrived?"

"I came to the den door and he was on the phone with Mrs. Resler." She went through it all again. After that she explained about coming back from the beach, the games and banter that had culminated at that hideous frozen moment when Maggie broke into the den.

At last Detective Schreiner closed her notebook. "Thank you, Ms. Kerr. I'll probably have follow-up questions later but that's all for tonight."

"Okay." They stood and Olivia said diffidently, "You know, Detective Schreiner, I'm planning a feature on women in law enforcement. Right now I'm doing the Joanne Little trial, and it seems to me women would have handled it a lot better, don't you think?"

"Not for me to say." Schreiner's attention was distracted as she maneuvered her notebook into the patch pocket of her skirt.

"Yes, but—anyway, I wondered if I could interview you sometime about it. Just on what the job is like for a woman."

Detective Schreiner's gaze was direct but opaque, impenetrable. "That wouldn't be appropriate. Especially while this case is open."

"Yeah, I understand that right now we've got this official relationship too. But I wouldn't be asking anything about this case. It would be a lot more general. And I could conceal your identity, that's no problem."

"Even so—look, Ms. Kerr, you've been following the Little trial. You've seen how the lawyers scrutinize every move those officers made."

"Yeah, but those guys were dolts! Made one blunder after another!"

There was that twitch of amusement again at the corner of Schreiner's mouth. "Well, I'm not a dolt, Ms. Kerr. I want this investigation to be as blunder-free as possible. Look, why don't you call the D. C. Public Information office? Out of this jurisdiction would be best. Maybe they could set up something for you. A ride in a patrol car."

Olivia looked at her: an ordinary, pleasant-faced, sad-eyed woman, totally unreachable behind the fortifications of her official authority. Well, we'll just see about that, Ms. Blunder-free Detective Schreiner. You want to be a pig, I'll write about pigs. To hell with your D. C. patrol cars. Aloud Olivia said politely, "Right, that's a good idea. Oh, and one other thing. Should the Colbys be making arrangements to stay somewhere tonight? Your people won't be finished here for a while, will they?"

"No, not for a while. Tell her to make the arrangements, and as soon as I've talked to the last two of you, everybody can go."

"Fine." Outwardly docile, Olivia went back to Betty Morgan's.

But Donna seemed incapable of thinking of anyone to stay with. "Don't you have a friend? Another teacher, maybe?" Maggie asked. She was lounging in Betty Morgan's leather recliner, the sleeping Sarah curled into the bit of her lap that hadn't been usurped by her belly.

Donna nodded. "Roberta. But she spends August in Maine."

"Your sister? Jill?" Betty Morgan suggested. She stood twisting her hands in the arch of the dining room. Two lanky teenage boys, probably her sons, had appeared and now sat drinking Cokes at the table behind her.

"No. Jill moved to California," Donna said.

"Other relatives?" asked Nick from the rug next to Maggie's chair. Last in line to be interviewed, he was waiting for Jerry to return from next door, his hand resting lightly on Maggie's ankle.

Donna shook her head mutely.

"What about Dale's family?" he continued gently.

Donna looked stricken. "Oh, we'll have to tell Grandpa Colby. Oh, dear."

"He's mean," muttered Josie.

Olivia glanced at Betty Morgan, who turned pink. "Yes, well, I'd love to help, Donna, you know that. We could manage. Of course Randy and Bo's rooms are always a mess." She smiled, half proud and half apologetic, at the teenagers. "But, let's see, you could take our room, and we'll put the sleeping bags in for the girls. And we can open the sofa here and—"

"Don't be silly," said Olivia. "It's sweet of you, but we've got four bedrooms and only two of them in use. Donna, you can come with us."

"No, I don't want to be a bother. Maybe a motel."

"No, no, it's all settled. We'll stick together."

"But—"

"I *want* you to come!"

So it was settled. Donna continued to protest feebly, thinking Olivia was just being polite. But Olivia caught Maggie looking at her ironically, and knew that at least one person realized that she had spoken the truth and was pleased as punch.

Chapter 5

"So you first realized there was a problem when you got back from buying the pizza?" Holly asked.

Jerry Ryan was leaning back into the corner of the sofa, one bony elbow on the armrest, the other arm extended along the sofa back. He had his sister's deep blue eyes and curly black hair, but in him the family lankiness looked craggy, mature. Being female lightened Maggie just enough to give her that teenage-boy appearance that Holly found so unsettling. Besides, Jerry showed less of Maggie's inquiring friendliness. This Ryan didn't make the same outrageous demands on Holly that his sister did.

He was nodding. "Olivia met us in the driveway, in fact. Heard the van arrive and came out to meet us. And I'm glad she did. Nick and I were roistering about, singing 'Rocky Mountain High' for young Tina. But I took one look at Liv's face and knew there was trouble. She explained as we went hurrying in. Maggie yelled down the hall at us to keep everyone in the kitchen, and then asked me to come look."

"Because you're a doctor."

"Right." He pressed his hands together and examined his knuckles. "But there was nothing I could do."

"He was clearly dead?"

"For hours."

"Why do you say that?"

His head came up alertly and he frowned at her. "Am I wrong? Well, you've got the experts in there. I'll admit that my experience is limited. Even when I worked in ER we managed to save most of our patients. My guess was based on memories of the olden days in med school. Hell, I'm not a bad doctor. You've probably seen more dead bodies than I have."

"Probably. Even so, I'd appreciate your top-of-the-head reactions, Dr. Ryan. It could help."

Jerry Ryan shrugged. "Okay, as long as it's unofficial. I mean, you do have the experts. I didn't do any tests. Just checked for respiration, pulse, stiffness."

"Rigor?"

"Right. Rigor was clearly present in the small muscles, face and neck. But not in the larger muscles, at that point. Lividity was well advanced."

Holly nodded. That agreed with her own observations.

Jerry concluded, "So, unofficially, I'd guess he'd been dead four, maybe six hours."

"Why not more?" Holly was writing it all down.

"He wasn't cool to touch yet so I figured it was closer to four hours than ten. But hell, your guys have thermometers. They should come pretty close."

"Right." She looked up from her notebook. "I'm asking because your sister didn't realize he was dead until she turned him over."

"Yeah. Well, of course lying on his back with his neck askew, it seemed obvious to me at first glance. But front-down, the way she saw him? He'd look more natural. I might have done the same thing. Tried to get him into position for CPR even while checking for signs of life." He met Holly's gaze. "My sister's no dummy."

True. So get off her case, Schreiner. "I wasn't suggesting that she was, Dr. Ryan," Holly said levelly. "Just trying to get an idea of how things were. What would you say about the cause of death?"

"Not much without an autopsy."

"Unofficially, Dr. Ryan," she said patiently.

Jerry shrugged. "Someone clobbered him on the head with a brass lamp."

"Subdural hematoma?"

Interest quickened in the blue eyes. "Yeah, I'd tell them to look for that. They teach medical jargon to detectives now?"

"I used to be a nurse." Until they'd told her she got too involved with her critical patients, exhausted herself, became a safety hazard to them.

"Aha. And you left for better pay?"

"Partly." She gave her stock answer. "Mostly I got bored with the parade of hemorrhoids."

Jerry Ryan's appreciative laugh was infectious. "You're absolutely right! Medicine is supposed to be so exciting, but after a while only the life-and-death stuff really satisfies." Holly had to agree; she'd only lasted a few months in nursing once they'd moved her away from the critical patients. He sprawled back into the sofa corner again. "So. You recommend detecting for jaded medics?"

"It's okay." Amazing how all these people wanted to spend their time discussing her job. Get him back on track, Schreiner. She picked up two evidence bags from the sofa beside her. "These seem to be prescriptions for Mr. Colby."

Jerry glanced at the labeled bottles inside. "Yeah. Anti-Parkinson's drugs."

"I recognize one. Artane," said Holly. "Anticholinergic, right?" In Parkinson's patients, she knew, the critical balance between two brain chemicals, dopamine and acetylcholine, was upset because their brains didn't produce enough dopamine. Tremor and other symptoms resulted. The usual treatment was based on suppressing acetylcholine with anticholinergic drugs like Artane, so that the two brain chemicals would be in balance again.

Jerry nodded. "Yeah. Dale told me at our party he'd been taking it for years. Up to a high dose by then so his physician was going to add a low dose of L-dopa." He indicated the second bottle.

Holly had read newspaper stories about L-dopa a few years ago. It was a real breakthrough, achieving the critical chemical balance in the brain by increasing dopamine instead of suppressing acetylcholine like the older drugs. Starting L-dopa slowly was sound medical practice. Nothing weird there. She asked, "Dr. Ryan, do you have any ideas about how someone might get out of that room?"

"You mean, if I'm so sure somebody bashed him, how did the somebody get out." His forehead wrinkled. "I don't know. I'd look pretty carefully at the windows. Or maybe the door was already splintered and something else was holding it closed somehow when they were trying to get in. But why ask me? You've got other experts to tell you about that."

"Yeah. We'll check it out." Holly debated taking Jerry in to talk to Doc Craine. But Doc would have found all the same things, and he got prickly at second-guessing. More than once she'd been snapped at herself for offering a medical observation. So wind this up, Schreiner. There's still a lot to do tonight. She asked, "Can you think of anything else, Dr. Ryan? Anything odd or even obvious that might have affected this death?"

"Only that locked door. Aside from that—well, my wife's a reporter." He gave a little shrug, suddenly seeming very vulnerable. "So I can't help wondering what the hell he did to get someone that angry."

"Yeah." Holly nodded and closed her book. "We'll find out. Thanks, Dr. Ryan. We'll want you to sign a statement tomorrow, but that's it for now. As soon as I talk to Mr. O'Connor we'll be done."

"Good."

Nick O'Connor was a broad, burly man, with expressive eyes that could move from dark sorrow to twinkles to lively curiosity in an instant. His head was nearly bald but his khaki shorts and unbuttoned polo shirt revealed plenty of curly hair on legs and chest and arms. He was a comfortable man, easy to talk to. Holly took him quickly through the departure and return from the beach. He confirmed the other accounts and apologized for not being able to add anything. "As things worked out, I never even saw Dale Colby, before or after the trip to the beach. Maggie and Olivia can help you more."

Holly nodded and decided to risk another topic. "Mr. O'Connor, your wife seemed very familiar with police procedures."

"Oh, yes. She's been called as a witness in homicides before."

Homicides! Whoopee, Schreiner, you're on track now. Holly tried to hide her excitement. She said flatly, "I see."

But Nick O'Connor must have sensed a problem. He explained, "Yeah, she'll do everything she can. She's helped convict two or three already."

"Really?" She felt an unprofessional pang of disappointment.

"The only one still open is a kidnapping from a couple of years ago. Maggie still gets calls every few months from the New York detective on that case. Lugano."

"I see." Holly wrote "Lugano" in her notebook. Check to see if Dale Colby could be connected to that case somehow.

"You seemed surprised when I said homicides," Nick observed mildly.

"It's unusual." Holly was guarded.

"Yeah, but you must have been interested in something when you mentioned that she seemed familiar with police procedures."

His guileless brown eyes were concerned, eager to help. What the hell, she might fish out another fact. She shrugged and admitted, "I just noticed her shirt. Lots of people got arrested in the sixties for demonstrating."

He grinned. "Sure did. Almost got arrested myself, and I'm a vet."

Too old for Vietnam. "Korea?" asked Holly dubiously.

"No, a few years later. I knew a little German, so they sent me to Berlin. The Wall."

"Then you weren't in combat."

"No."

"And you were a protester?" She couldn't keep the skepticism from her voice. Plenty of Viet vets protested their war. But someone older, someone stationed in Germany?

"Yes, I was." Elbows on knees, he was leaning forward thoughtfully, looking past her toward something far away and sad. "There was this kid one night at the Wall. Just a teenager. Came scrambling toward us from the other side. They machine-gunned him. He lay there in the searchlights and bled to death. And we weren't allowed to help. We just—watched. It was so pointless. And he wasn't the only one. So damn pointless!" He leaned back, passed a chunky hand over his face, and murmured, "Did heaven look on, and would not take their part? It changes your thinking, you know. That kid's never left me. I try not to think about him, but he's there. So when people started marching to stop some other pointless shooting, I marched too." He glanced at her, found her studying him intently, and shrugged. "Sorry. You don't need all that. The short answer is no, I've never been arrested for demonstrating and neither has Maggie."

"Okay." She looked down at her notepad but found that the letters were blurry. *Did heaven look on, and would not take their part?* She riffled back through the pages blindly and remembered something. Gratefully, she changed the subject. "Oh. I didn't ask you what you do."

"I'm an actor."

Oh, wonderful. All this case needed was an actor. Quoting stuff. Had he been putting her on after all? And asshole Schreiner practically blubbering over it. Holly was suddenly deeply weary. She wrote down "actor" and underlined it twice, slashing at the paper.

"You might have seen me in one of those AT & T commercials recently," he said, then added uncertainly, "If you ever have time for TV."

"Not often," said Holly. "But I'll watch for it."

He shook his head. "Hardly worth watching for. But it helps pay the bills."

"Yeah. Now, can you think of anything else that might help us, Mr. O'Connor?"

"Nothing more at the moment. But I'll keep trying."

"Thanks." Holly looked at his friendly, homely face. Oh, hell, it was possible he'd really felt all that. Didn't make any difference anyway, did it? She closed her notebook. "Let's go next door."

The night was fresh, not cold but far from the hot dark blanket of humid air she'd grown used to over the past ten days. As she and Nick O'Connor walked across the damp grass toward the lit windows of the Morgan house, Holly tried to get her thoughts into formation, reviewing the story these people had given her. Dale Colby, hardworking reporter, temporarily housebound, disturbing some people as he inquired into that plane crash. The lawyer's widow, Mrs. Resler, asking him to be discreet. Wealthy Moffatt's son charging into the newspaper office swearing at Colby. Two congressional aides. The congressman himself, certainly the most visible target, deciding at the last moment not to go. The pilot, Corky Lewis: not much on him from these folks, but Colby had been interviewing his sister Priscilla, quoting her in his story. Holly would check the newspaper tomorrow, talk to the editor. Edgerton, his name was. Also the other reporter that Olivia Kerr had mentioned, the one who had worked on early stages of the story Colby was following up.

And then there was the domestic front. A stunned widow, two unbelieving little girls. She hurt for those little girls. She'd seen too many children who'd lost parents, too many kids mangled and grieving. She hoped she wouldn't have to talk to the kids long. But she'd have to talk to neat blonde stunned Donna Colby again, get a few more details about Colby's life and last days. And get her view of the ex, for what it was worth. Felicia Colby had appeared opportunely, claiming she and her son had just driven down from Harrisburg, furious at Dale's neglect of his son and then shocked into silence when she heard of his death. Maybe true. Holly had arranged to talk to her and the boy first thing tomorrow.

And the others, this batch of Dale's friends that he hadn't gone to the beach with after all. His colleague the reporter, a red-haired Brenda Starr parody, bubbling over with solemn eagerness to help, yet always with an eye out for a story. Her husband the doctor, lanky, observant, but claiming not to know the Colbys well. His sister, the take-charge Maggie, able to bear children, break down doors, flip over dead bodies, interrogate police detectives, and stop wars in a single bound. Pah. Holly faced another unpleasant follow-up interview there. And Maggie's husband, the husky gentle vet beside her now. An actor. Jesus, wouldn't you know it. Fact and fiction, the true and the counterfeit, slithering like mud through her grasping fingers.

So cool it, Schreiner. Why should it be any different this time?

At the Morgan house her little crowd of witnesses looked up at her as she entered. Maggie, sprawled in a recliner with her daughter asleep in her lap, regarded Holly and Nick with lively interest. Jerry sat in a ruffled side chair that was too small for his gangly frame. His wife, perched on the arm of the sofa, was in the midst of pinning up her red hair but paused to look at Holly eagerly. Donna Colby sat on the sofa between her daughters, the younger drowsing with her head in Donna's lap, the older watching Holly with exhausted anxious eyes. Across the room through the dining-room arch, a plump woman with a friendly nervous smile sat at the table with two teenage boys. Holly crossed to her first. "Mrs. Morgan?"

The plump woman stood, wiping her hands on her skirt. "Yes?"

"I'm Detective Schreiner. Thanks for letting us use your house."

"Oh, it's no trouble, really. I want to help."

Mrs. Morgan had told Higgins she and the boys had been out this afternoon, so they didn't have to be interviewed right away. Holly turned to the others. "I'd like to thank all of you for your help tonight. As soon as you can, tomorrow if possible, please stop by the station and we'll get a statement typed up for you to sign. I'll be talking to several of you again too, so I'll need to know where you'll be tomorrow."

"That's easy," said Olivia. "Our house."

"The Colbys too?"

"Well, until you're finished with their place."

Holly was not pleased. Nick explained, "Donna's other friends are out of town, and Jerry and Liv have more space than Betty here."

"Of course, I'd be glad—" Betty Morgan faltered. "I mean, if you'd rather—"

Holly looked at the Colbys: Donna exhausted, bruised by events; the girls so young to be facing this. She'd seen kids face worse. But it seemed cruel to make them stay here next door while their familiar home was made ghastly by police barriers, lights, chatter. She sighed. These witnesses would talk among themselves anyway. People always did. "It's all right," she said. "We'll try to be finished with the house as soon as possible. If any of you will be at work tomorrow, please give Officer Higgins your phone numbers so we can reach you if necessary. You can go on now."

She watched them get up. Maggie gathered up her sleeping daughter tenderly as she stood. Nick murmured something to Donna Colby, then picked up Tina carefully. Olivia handed a business card to Higgins, then hurried to Donna's side and helped her solicitously to her feet. Jerry too went to speak to Higgins, probably giving an office phone number. Maggie, cradling her daughter in her arms, said something encouraging to Josie, who was clinging to her mother's side. They all shuffled out toward the front door.

Maggie paused in the arch and looked back. "Detective Schreiner?"

"Yes?"

"You'll probably want to talk to Bo Morgan."

Who the hell—oh, must be one of Betty Morgan's sons. Holly looked back at the boys at the dining room table. One of them was studying her guardedly. He was maybe fourteen, stringy blond hair, gangly arms and legs, bad skin, an Incredible Hulk T-shirt. "You're Bo Morgan?"

"Yeah." He glanced at his mother and added, "I mean yessum."

"And you have something to tell us?"

"Oh, it's no big deal." Bo wriggled uncomfortably in his chair. "It's just, like I was listening to tapes in my room this afternoon."

His mother bleated, "His door was closed! I thought he'd gone out with Randy and his friends! That's why I told the other policeman no one was here! I just found out that—"

"It's all right, Mrs. Morgan," Holly soothed her. "Let's hear what Bo has to say."

The center of attention again, Bo writhed unhappily. "It's just, well, like I looked out the window and saw this guy over at the Colby's."

"What kind of guy?"

"Oh—sort of average. Old guy."

"Old as Officer Higgins? Older? Younger?"

"About the same. Thinner."

Most of humanity was thinner than Higgins. She asked, "What time was this?"

"I wasn't like watching a clock."

"Well, maybe you can work it out by what you were hearing on the tape," Maggie suggested.

She was still in the archway. Holly glared at her. "Ms. Ryan, isn't it time you took your daughter home?"

But pleasure was dawning on Bo's face. "Hey, yeah! I was listening to 'Born to Run' so that would make it—well, like three-thirty, about."

Maggie flashed a wide smile at Holly. She shifted her sleeping child to one arm as she reached for the doorknob. "Goodnight. See you tomorrow, Detective Schreiner." The door slammed behind her.

Holly unclenched her teeth and turned back to Bo. She found a new page in her notebook and asked, "About three-thirty, you said?"

"Yeah."

"And what did the man do?"

"Just stood at the front door a minute. Then I guess someone answered cause he went in."

"Did you see him come out?"

"Yeah. Maybe after—let's see." He screwed up his face, calculating song times, no doubt. "Twenty minutes later, about."

"What did he do?"

"Just walked to his car. Blue Ford, '73."

"Good. He didn't seem agitated?"

"Nah. Just regular." Bo rocked back in the dining chair. He was beginning to enjoy this.

"So there was nothing different about him when he left?"

"Nothing I could see. Except he had a package."

"He didn't have it when he arrived?"

"Maybe, maybe not. I didn't notice him till he was already at the door, and those bushes might of like hid it."

"What did the package look like?"

"Brown paper. Maybe a grocery bag folded over. Shoebox size."

"Good." Holly was pleased. This might be something. "Bo, could I look out the window where you saw all this?"

Suddenly he looked uneasy. Had he been lying? Making up these helpful details? He muttered, "Hey, I don't like people in my room."

His mother giggled. "He won't let me clean it, even. And it's such a mess!"

Bo's brother was hiding a smirk. Bo said sullenly, "She always gets my mags all mixed up."

Holly realized what the problem was. She explained carefully, "I just want a look through the window, Bo. I'm not going to check your housekeeping. And it'll be a lot more trouble for everybody if I have to get a search warrant."

"Oh, of course you can look without a search warrant!" exclaimed Betty Morgan. But Holly waited for Bo to work things out in his head and give her a quick miserable nod before she followed Betty down the hall.

His room was in the front of the house, the corner nearest the Colby's. She walked around to the far side of the bed and looked out the window. The view was as he'd described it. Even lying on the bed he could see across the Colby driveway to their front porch. This kid's testimony might someday be important.

She turned and surveyed the room quickly. A chaos of posters, rock albums and tapes, electronic equipment, huge stacks of Marvel comics, candy-bar wrappers, soft-drink cans. But the bed was made. She lifted the nearest corner of the bedspread with her toe. There was his stash: papers, a bag of grass, plus a couple of bright pills. An easy reach from his pillow. Mom looking the other way, consciously or unconsciously. Well, Holly wasn't into illegal searches tonight.

When she looked up again, Bo was standing in the doorway watching her, eyes terrified.

Holly joined him and closed the door behind her. "It all checks out, Bo," she said. "You have a good view of their door. Let's get down all the facts. This could be a real important statement."

The boy nodded mutely and followed her back to the dining room.

Chapter 6

At the upstairs den door, Olivia gripped the knob and pulled the door partway closed. "Okay, everybody, if you need anything, just let us know, okay?"

"Okay." Donna, still puffy-faced but no longer weeping, was sitting stiffly on the edge of the open sofa bed. Tina was already lying on the other half, her eyes wide open, her lower lip trembling. Her mother was smoothing back her hair from her forehead in little mechanical strokes that couldn't have been very comforting. Josie huddled alone on the extra cot, legs pulled up, her face hidden against her knees.

It was nearly midnight. Olivia had finally phoned her sleepy editor, who'd told her to stick with Donna now and check in early tomorrow. Maggie had urged Donna to call her relatives and friends and, obediently, she had: her sister Jill, the nursing home where her mother lived, her cousin Ann, a teacher at Honey Creek School named Linda who promised to notify the principal for her, and finally Dale's parents in Roanoke. Donna had gotten through all but the last with numb determination, but halfway through the last call, she began shaking her head at the telephone, stammering, "No—no! You can't—please—no!" Her hand was trembling as she hung up.

"What's wrong, Donna?" Maggie asked her gently.

"He says—he says he'll take them!" Donna murmured.

"The girls? Of course not! He doesn't have the right!" Maggie exclaimed vehemently.

Tears were trickling down Donna's cheeks. "He doesn't?"

"I wish it was that easy! But for years Parkinson's had to be treated by suppressing acetylcholine with anticholinergic drugs, so the two brain chemicals would be in balance."

"Is that what Dale took?"

"Yes. But about five years ago they discovered that L-dopa could increase dopamine in the brain. So now they can restore the balance two ways."

"Can you get too much L-dopa?"

"Possible. But it's not likely that was Dale's problem. He was on a very light beginning dose of L-dopa, and even that was still causing some nausea. He wouldn't likely take too much."

"Not on purpose," Nick said.

"Also, he was still taking the anticholinergic," Jerry continued. "The same drug that he'd been taking for years. He was at the highest dosage of that—probably that's why his doctor wanted him to add the newer drug at this point. I suspect he was suffering some mild side effects from the anticholinergic. Reduced secretions—dry mouth and so forth."

"Suppose he took too much of his old drug?" Maggie asked.

"Restlessness, floppiness. Plus forgetfulness. And maybe hallucinations. Psychedelic effects, little people having parties, writhing designs on the rug."

"Wow." Maggie was sitting cross-legged on the floor now, listening avidly. "Sounds like fun. Would he maybe take too much on purpose?"

"No," Olivia said firmly. They didn't know Dale.

"Not the type?" asked Nick dubiously.

"Well, now that you mention it, he's not. Wrong generation. Too uptight to play games with his medicine. The whole time I've worked with him I've never seen him restless or twitchy. Slow, yes. A couple of times he sort of froze, couldn't move his feet."

"Yeah, that's typical of Parkinson's," Jerry confirmed.

"But the real reason Dale wouldn't overdose is that he was working on a story. He was a good reporter, damn it! And he wouldn't risk forgetfulness or hallucinations if a story was breaking."

"In any case," said Jerry, "tripping wouldn't have the charms for him that it does for some people. To patients with this sort of chemical imbalance, being normal is the amazing and glorious thing."

"So an overdose is unlikely," Nick summed up. "He'd been taking one drug for years with few problems even at high dosages. The other was prescribed in low—"

He was interrupted by a sharp rap on the door. Olivia hurried to answer it.

A couple stood there, erect in dark raincoats, the woman with steely gray hair, the man angular and balding. He said, "We've come for our grandchildren."

"What?"

"Josie and Tina. Our grandchildren." The man emphasized his point with an impatient tap of his furled but dripping umbrella.

Maggie was at Olivia's shoulder now. She scanned the grim pair and asked, "Are you Dale Colby's parents?"

"Yes!"

"Well, I'll go fetch Josie and Tina's parent," said Maggie sweetly, and breezed up the stairs.

Olivia decided not to ask these people in. Well, not unless Donna wanted them. It was raining again but the porch was a broad comfortable turn-of-the-century model where they could all talk easily enough. So when the man motioned to go in, she didn't budge, just smiled and said, "They should be down soon." All the same she was glad to note Nick and Jerry behind her in the arch to the living room.

Donna, wrapped in Jerry's navy terrycloth robe, looked frail and uncertain as she descended the stairs. Olivia gave her an encouraging smile and said, "Would you rather talk on the porch?"

Donna's frightened eyes checked the pair outside, then Olivia, then the comforting bulk of Nick and Jerry. She seemed to take heart. "Yes," she said.

Mr. Colby's lips tightened but he moved aside to let the phalanx of women out. Nick and Jerry remained inside, shadowy linebackers. Olivia waved at the wicker chairs. "Have a seat," she offered.

"No need for that." Mr. Colby refused conciliation and glared at Donna. "We came for Josie and Tina."

Donna stared at her feet.

Maggie said, "You're saying that you want to help Josie and Tina?"

"Yes, that's it." Mrs. Colby spoke for the first time, with a furtive glance at her husband.

"That's natural, at a time like this," said Maggie agreeably. "I'm sure there will be a lot of ways to help them."

"We want them with us," said Mr. Colby.

"You mean Donna too, of course?" inquired Maggie. Donna was observing her now, brown eyes amazed, occasionally flicking a nervous glance at Mr. Colby.

Mr. Colby said impatiently, "No, not enough room, and she's a bad influence."

"Oh? In what way?" Olivia asked indignantly.

"Well, look what she did to our son!" exclaimed Mr. Colby. "Broke up his marriage. Let him catch that disease. And now let him get murdered!"

Mrs. Colby sobbed. So did Donna. But they both stood rigidly apart from one another.

Mr. Colby added angrily, "She's a bad mother. Just the way she was a bad wife!"

"Well," said Maggie in that sweet voice, "the fact remains that Donna is the person who has the right to decide. What do you say, Donna? Do you want Josie and Tina to go with their grandparents?"

Donna's lip trembled. She shook her head.

"Not even for a few days?" Maggie continued.

Donna looked at her feet again. Olivia was exasperated with her. Okay, so right now she was devastated, that was understandable. Hard to be liberated in the midst of tragedy. But if she'd stood up to these people long ago they'd be more reasonable now. Wouldn't they?

And Mr. Colby was blustering again. "We're not talking about a few days, young lady! We're talking about my grandchildren's future!"

"So are we!" exclaimed Olivia hotly, unable to keep silent any longer. "What makes you think—" She broke off. Maggie's hand, a powerful gymnast's hand, was squeezing her wrist painfully.

"It's Donna's decision," Maggie repeated gently. "Donna, I know it's hard right now. But you have to take control of your life. You have to decide what's best for your girls."

Donna looked at Maggie and drew a deep breath. Then, blonde hair alight in the glow from the porch lamp, she squared her shoulders in Jerry's robe and said, "It would be best for the girls to stay with me."

Olivia cheered silently. Mr. Colby shouted, "You'll regret this! We'll—we'll—"

Olivia said, "If you cause them any trouble, Donna can get a court order to keep you away."

There was a spark of astonishment in the old man's eyes. He waved a fist at Donna. "You do that and I'll disown them! You, them, everyone!" He grabbed his wife's elbow and steered her from the porch. "I'll disown them!" he repeated, as though relishing the sound of it. "You hear that? I'll disown them!" They disappeared down the front walk.

Donna stood there dazed until Maggie put her arm around her and drew her inside.

"Whew!" said Olivia as they rejoined the men. "I hate to insult your family, Donna, but they really are unreasonable."

"Can I really get a court order?" Donna asked in wonder.

"If you want one," said Maggie. "You have lots of rights, you know."

"But Dale's father is so . . ."

Maggie gave her hand a squeeze. "Yes. But I have a feeling that he's mostly bluster. Stand up to him the way you did tonight and your girls will be fine."

"I'm not very good at standing up to people."

"You did fine."

"I wish he would disown us," said Donna with feeling. She glanced at the staircase.

"Fine. Then there's no problem. Do you want to get back to your girls, now?" She squeezed her hand again encouragingly and released her to go back upstairs, then Maggie joined the others drifting back into the living room.

Jerry said, "Boy. I hope that man's the murderer. I'd love to lock him up."

"Just what I was thinking," said Olivia indignantly. "Should have asked him for an alibi."

"Well, I'm sure Schreiner will ask," said Nick. "Now, where were we?"

"Drug overdoses," said Maggie. "I suppose the cops will know to test for overdoses of those medications?"

"Yeah," said Jerry. "Schreiner said she used to be a nurse."

"Really?" Olivia was fascinated. "But she's such a cold fish!"

"I don't think she's a cold fish." Maggie was thoughtful. "I think she hurts."

"Well, the effect is the same," snorted Olivia unsympathetically.

"All cops act like cold fish," said Nick. His lively eyes suddenly grew stony, watchful; his usually mobile face became neutral, impenetrable; his pleasant voice shifted to a flat contralto. It was an amazing transformation. "What time did you return from the beach?"

Jerry clapped his hands. "God, that's Schreiner!"

"Why do they do that?" Olivia wondered.

Nick shrugged. "They never know if they're talking to the

damsel in distress or to the perp. It's a grim job and they can't afford mistakes."

Maggie pulled them back to the problem at hand. "Okay, so Dale's medication is not likely the problem, and—"

"Wait a minute," said Olivia. She glanced apprehensively at the stairs and lowered her voice. "Could Donna maybe slip extra medicine into his sandwich? Or his coffee? I mean, she wouldn't, but—"

"She didn't," Maggie said. "Or we might all be hallucinating right now. I know because Sarah went running into the kitchen about the time Dale asked Donna for his lunch. I followed Sarah. And I saw Donna pour his coffee from the same Thermos all the rest of us drank from. She poured it into a mug that she took from the dishwasher."

"And the sandwich?"

"I was by the table and she asked me to hand her one. I just randomly grabbed one from the basket and put it on the plate she was fixing for him."

"And the potato chips were in a sealed packet," Olivia remembered. "Another theory shot. Thank God."

"Well, the medication was involved in one important way," Maggie pointed out. "It kept Dale close to home. So the murderer must have known his house."

"Doesn't help a lot," Olivia said morosely. "He got out occasionally, though not a lot during this heat wave. And he got some of us to come to his house. Even did some interviews there if he could talk people into stopping by."

"But from the murderer's point of view there was a real advantage to knowing where he'd be. He wasn't out running around unpredictably the way you usually are, Liv."

"That's true. But still, how did the killer get out of the locked room?"

"How about the air-conditioning?" asked Nick. "No one would have to get in or out if maybe some kind of gas could be fed into the system."

"Not carbon monoxide," said Maggie. "He wasn't pink. Right, Jerry?"

"Right. But we're really in never-never land here. Cyanide, mustard gas—these things leave signs too. I didn't see any signs. But of course there's always a chance the police will find something."

Back to the damn police, to Ms. Ride-in-a-patrol-car Schreiner. Olivia leaned back, exasperated, stretched out her toes to kick angrily at the coffee table, and jammed her fists into her pockets. "Damn, I wish we didn't have to leave it all to them!"

"Schreiner's got access to labs," Maggie pointed out reasonably. "She's got lots of trained people. No need for us to meddle."

"Well, maybe not. Not about *how* he died, anyway," Olivia admitted as another thought occurred to her. "I mean, you're right, all the theories we've come up with so far require some kind of evidence. Blood tests or door wedges or whatever. But we're already ahead of the cops when it comes to Dale's life, right? I can talk to Nate and Edgy tomorrow and find out about the stories he's worked on. Donna can probably help us a lot once she's had some rest, and—"

"Donna's energy should go toward helping the police," Maggie said.

"Yeah, I know, of course. But if we talk to her we can help her think of things to tell the police." Olivia pulled her hands from her pockets and gestured upstairs. "I mean, Donna's mind isn't working all that well right now. We can help."

"Well, it's true that things make more sense when you know more background," Maggie admitted.

Olivia didn't answer. She was staring at her hand, at what she'd just pulled from her pocket. A paper napkin. The napkin that she'd picked up from the hall floor outside Dale's locked door, before the horrible discovery had wiped it from her mind.

Jerry nudged her in the ribs. "What've you got, Liv?"

"Oh." She dragged her eyes from the folded square, met his blue ones. "It's, um, maybe a clue!"

"Donovan's Bar?" he asked suspiciously, taking the napkin. The green logo, complete with shamrock, filled the corner.

"You found it at the Colbys'?" Maggie guessed.

"Yes. On the floor outside the den door when I first went to knock on it. I'm sure it wasn't there earlier, before we went to the beach."

"Yeah. You would have noticed. Donna's a good housekeeper." Maggie was on her feet, hurrying to the phone in the hall. She brought back the directory.

"Yeah, that's why I picked it up," Olivia said. "It seemed almost sacrilegious on that polished floor. So where's Donovan's?"

Maggie's tracking finger paused on the page. "What do you mean, Donovan's? I'm looking for the county police number."

"Hey, wait a minute!" Olivia snatched the book away and turned to the D's. "Schreiner won't be at headquarters anyway," she added lamely.

"You're not saying you're keeping this from her!"

"No, no," Olivia said soothingly. "I just mean, she's got more than enough to do tonight."

"That's not what you mean, Ms. Woodward-hyphen-Bernstein," said Jerry darkly.

Nick returned to the point. "It might help the cops if they know about it right away."

Cornered, Olivia protested, "Do you really trust Schreiner that much? She wears all that more-official-than-thou armor. But if she wants to learn things—well, hell, she just wasn't very open with me."

"Not her job to be open with us," Nick said. "Besides, she did tell you a little about the plane crash victims."

"Yeah, but I know what Liv means," Maggie said slowly. "Schreiner's got her own agenda. I think she wants to solve the crime, basically. But that armor you talk about has some odd cracks in it."

Nick nodded thoughtfully. "Yeah. She didn't talk to me long. But there was a moment—I was talking about Berlin, and for a minute there we connected. Then suddenly the defenses went up again."

"Right. That kept happening to me too. Swings back and forth."

"So how can we trust her?" repeated Olivia, sensing an ally.

But Maggie betrayed her. "I trust her more than I trust us," she said vehemently. Olivia was surprised at the dark emotion in her eyes. "Last time I meddled in police business somebody died. I don't want to mess things up again."

"Well, nobody's asking you to." Olivia put down the phone book and stood up briskly. "But just in case you hadn't noticed, it *is* a reporter's business to ask about things. So I'm going to go ask." She grabbed her shoulder bag from the table.

"Hey, Liv, can't it wait till tomorrow?" Jerry protested.

"This is a bar. Now's the time." She hesitated, thinking of one A.M. at some bars she knew. "Though I wouldn't say no to some company."

"Hey, I have to make hospital rounds five hours from now!" Jerry complained. "And I was hoping to have a couple more minutes to talk to Maggot while she's here. We were so busy yesterday seeing the Mosby Museum and the battlefield, and this morning she was tooling around Maryland while Nick and I took Sarah to the Smithsonian. And then the beach. So can't you do this tomorrow, Liv? I don't even know what my own sister's current projects are!" He glanced at Maggie. "Well, except for the obstetrically obvious."

The hell with it, she could take care of herself. Olivia put her hand on the doorknob. "I'll be back in an hour or two."

"Hey, Liv, please!" Jerry said.

Nick lumbered to his feet. "I'll play backup for you, Liv," he said.

"I can manage." But she was pleased.

"No, let's let these Ryans chatter away. Leave them to their remembrances of days foregone. I tune out anyway when the talk turns to life in grade school."

"Great! Well, let's go!"

"Listen, be careful, Olivia." Maggie was rummaging through a straw handbag. Olivia realized suddenly it was Donna's. "Here," said Maggie, and handed her a photo from the wallet.

"Oh. Right." Olivia took the snapshot. In it Dale smiled his miserly smile, his arms around his two girls. "This could speed things up."

"Take care," Maggie warned them both.

Olivia waved, flung open the door, and dug out her keys as she ran through the rain to the van.

"Thanks for coming along," she said to Nick as she flipped on the windshield wipers and pulled out of the driveway. "But it wasn't really necessary."

"I know. But in some bars, being alone would say something that you'd have to waste a lot of time explaining away."

"Sexists," grumbled Olivia.

"The millenium has not yet arrived."

"Yeah, tell me about it."

He grinned. "So where is this Donovan's Bar?"

"Other side of the S-D offices. Fringy area."

It was a working-class bar. Lots of jeans and plaid shirts, few women, a TV with sallow color propped on a high shelf in the corner. It was tuned to a wrestling match.

Olivia hauled herself onto a bar stool. Nick sat next to her and told the bartender, "Coupla Millers."

Olivia didn't want a Miller. But her flash of indignation was followed by grudging admiration. Maybe she wouldn't have to use her press card yet. Nick sounded local. He sounded like her plumber. And her plumber would probably order a Miller for her.

The bartender was middle-aged, a surprisingly handsome man with smoky gray curls and only a hint of belly. His shirt was green plaid. "There you go," he said genially, pushing two foaming glasses across the worn bar toward them.

"Rain feels good after all that heat," said Nick.

"Yeah, you said it! It was like living in a goddamn fry pan," he said. He glanced up at the TV.

"Right. Goddamn fry pan." Nick guzzled half his beer. A burst of laughter came from a group watching the wrestlers. Someone swore good-naturedly. Nick said, "Nice place you got here. Congenial, y'know?"

"Yeah, well, Dale said it was okay." Olivia hoped she didn't sound too prissy. She took a swig of beer and eyed the bartender. "You know Dale?"

No guilty starts, just a bored shrug. "Can't say as I do."

"I bet you do. Here, look." She dug into her bag and pulled out the snapshot. "That's him. See?"

The bartender took the photo and squinted at it in the combined light of the lamp and the TV. He shook his head. "No. He's not one of our regulars."

"Maybe he just came a couple of times." Disappointed, Olivia took back the photo. "You sure you don't remember him? Newspaperman. Wrote about that plane crash over on Blue Hill back in January."

"Nope." He shook his gray curls again. "Don't know the guy." His eyes strayed to the TV again, then back to Olivia's doubtless crestfallen face. She wished she had Nick's control. The bartender took pity and threw her a sop. "I remember that plane going down, though."

"You do?" Damn, she sounded too eager.

"Yeah. Old Ernie got all excited, said he knew the pilot."

"Ernie?"

"Guy who comes in here sometimes. Said he'd heard of the guy in Nam."

Bull's-eye. Olivia found herself squeezing her beer glass with both hands in her excitement. She stared blindly at the TV, thinking how to follow up. But the bartender caught a signal from one of the tables and bustled away to take the order.

Nick had been studying his beer with sleepy plumber's eyes. Now he looked up, as though recognition had at last penetrated his weariness. "Ernie!" he said. "Hey, wasn't that the guy brought Dale here?"

"Maybe so," said Olivia cautiously.

"Carpenter," Nick said. "Wasn't that it? Ernie Carpenter?

Hey!" He waved the bartender over again. "Is this guy we're talking about Ernie Carpenter?"

"Doesn't sound right to me," Olivia said dubiously, and thought she caught a glint of approval in Nick's eye.

"No, not Carpenter. Hey, Mike!" The bartender hailed a sunburned man at one of the tables. "What's Ernie's last name? You know, the guy with a beard? Dog in his truck?"

"Ernie," said the sunburned man. "Grant, ain't it? Something like that."

"Grant? You sure? The Ernie I'm thinking of lives on—what street did Dale say?" Nick turned to Olivia.

"Vienna Road." Olivia named the area where her plumber lived.

"Nah. Must be a different guy," the sunburned man said. "Ernie Grant talks about his farm. Appleyard Road. Off Vale."

"Yeah. Different guy. You're right." Nick slumped over his beer.

Olivia wanted to find out more about this Ernie Grant, but she couldn't think of how to ask without getting the bartender suspicious of her motives. In a moment Nick nudged her. "Ready to go?"

She realized that the noisiest table of drinkers had just paid and were filing out. Only a few people were left in the bar. She didn't want to look conspicuous. "Sure," she said. "Let's go. I'll follow up tomorrow."

Chapter 7

One A.M.

Holly plopped onto the Colby sofa and kicked off her sandals. She was tired to her bones. She'd just seen Colby's parents, a cold bristly old couple from Roanoke who seemed convinced that poor Donna had caused their son's illness if not death. She'd sent them packing. About time to wind things up for the night. Crime Scene had just finished this room—inspecting the windows, the book-shelves where the tapes were missing, even checking out the Barbie and Ken dolls lying on the hearth. Winks had been full of crude comments about Barbie's spectacular shape and how well she'd sell in a life-size version. Holly had ignored him, and they'd all moved on after a while to the back of the house. She could hear their voices now back in the kitchen.

Dale Colby's body had been removed an hour ago. Doc Craine was long gone, and the local uniforms, Higgins and Patterson, had been relieved by the night shift. Colby's den had been searched and sealed, and they were nearing the end of the methodical search of house and yard. The Latents man had been full of sarcastic comments about blundering flatfoots when Holly had told him that a witness had seen someone enter the front door that afternoon. But he'd dutifully dusted the doorknob with its mass of overlapping cop fingerprints. He was much happier with the interior. Donna apparently kept most of the surfaces in the house cleaned and polished regularly, and he'd picked up satisfyingly clean prints. Whether they belonged to anyone besides the Colbys and their visitors remained to be seen.

God, she was exhausted.

Outside, they had done what they could in the sporadic rain, under artificial lights. She'd return tomorrow in the daylight to see if anything had been missed. But for now, as soon as Gabe decided they were done in the kitchen and garage, it was time to take a break.

She laid her notebook down beside her, scooted forward on the cushion a little, stretched out her legs, and slumped back to rest her head on the top of the sofa back. She let her eyes close. Not that she was sleepy. Her body was exhausted, her mind jumpy. Same as last night. Christ, what a fiasco. And he'd seemed, for a few minutes, so understanding. Genuine.

But hell, so had that goddamn actor tonight. The whole goddamn world was a con. A shitheap.

She'd even conned herself for a while. Imagined herself a healer. Worked her butt off helping hundreds of critical patients, thousands, in country and later in post-op at St. Mary's. And then she'd lost two in a row, though she'd worked her butt off, and she got the shakes so bad with the next one that they transferred her. You're working too hard, they said, you're a safety hazard to your patients. They'd sent her to work with outpatients and it hadn't taken much of that kind of boredom to show her she was no longer a healer. So she'd followed in Pop's footsteps and joined the cops. It suited her. She got to use her brain, her adrenaline, her reflexes. But she didn't have to put on a cheery face. Didn't have to pretend she was a healer.

Not that cops didn't con each other, con their superiors, con the public. No different from doctors and nurses, that way. Or reporters. Or federal employees. Or goddamn statisticians, flashing their little tables of numbers, counting the nonexistent, glibly proving the untrue. But as a cop you didn't have to believe the cons. Sure, you filled out the stacks of forms, took the jokes and needling of your so-called brother officers, listened to the bullshit the public handed out. But sometimes, every now and then, you could touch reality. Dig through the shit and come up finally with a fact. Because one thing at least wasn't false. Death at least was genuine.

She had pills at home. Darvons. Enough, counted into a brown bottle that sat on the middle shelf of her kitchen cabinet. Last night, weary after a hot day of typing useless reports, the emptiness an ache inside her, she'd opened the cabinet to get out a can of fish for her cat. Behind her a curtain stirred and the hot cruel sunlight flashed from the brown glass. God, it would be so easy. Hesitantly, she'd touched the bottle with her fingertip.

Behind her, Country Joe had mewed plaintively.

"Sorry, Joey." Holly had pulled herself together, taken out the cat food. Country Joe had studied her with his amber eyes as she opened the can, scraped it into his dish, and set it on the floor. Then he stepped over to it in his gentlemanly way, not what you'd expect from a scuffed-up battle-scarred tom, and began to nibble at it.

Holly had moved restlessly to the window and looked out at the heat-wilted foliage of her building's courtyard. She'd chickened out again. A commercial ended and a woman on the radio began to sing "I think I'm losing my mind." Billie Ann's letter, carried unanswered for months in Holly's wallet, said the same thing. Angrily, Holly had switched off the radio. Time to get out, Schreiner. Maybe try the Banana Tree. Okay, so it hadn't worked out before, but maybe someday. At least they mixed a good drink.

She'd showered, made up her eyes carefully to hide the hollowness, put on her jade-green dress and strappy high-heeled sandals, and gone out into the muggy evening.

At that time of night you could get to D.C. in under an hour. The sun had set but the brief walk from the car to the Banana Tree set her sweating again. Dog days. She hoped her mascara wouldn't run. Inside she'd ordered a gin and tonic and was feeling better by the time someone edged up to the bar next to her and said, "Hey, you're looking gorgeous tonight, baby."

Not Mr. Goodbar, not that one. The conversation hadn't gone anywhere, had fizzled on both sides inside ten minutes. But the next guy was a little different. Well, she'd thought so at the time. Alec, he'd introduced himself. "Like the English movie actor."

"I'm Holly," she said. "Like 'Deck the halls with boughs of.'"

He smiled. A nice, shy smile. "Pretty name. But I bet kids teased you when you were little."

"Yeah. Holly-ween, my brother called me." She had a sudden image of Chuck at twelve, sitting on the other end of the porch steps on a hot night like this one, both of them drinking Kool-Aid and thinking of clever ways to mutilate each other's names. "Or he'd call me Hollow, and tap his head."

"Yeah. Know what you mean. I was usually saddled with Smart Aleck. Or sometimes Alas and Alec, even though the rhythm's all wrong." He slid onto the seat next to hers, a fair-haired man, skin reddened from the summer sun, crinkles around his eyes. "I work at OSHA," he said. "Engineering stuff. What do you do?"

"I'm a nurse." Only once had she been asshole enough to admit she was a cop. Exit Romeo, running.

"Did you always want to be a nurse?"

"When I was little I thought I'd be a glamorous singing star and marry Elvis Presley. But it turned out there were more applicants than openings."

He laughed. "Yeah. After I outgrew my fireman period, I decided my real calling was to be a millionaire. But I couldn't figure out what the entry-level job was."

"Not nursing," Holly informed him.

They'd talked for a pleasant hour before he'd said, looking nervously at his glass, "It's getting pretty noisy in here."

They all said that. Holly flashed on the interchangeable apartments: shag rugs, Naugahyde sofas, grocery-store wine, towels that never saw bleach. But she'd said, "Yeah. I'm getting tired of shouting too."

"Let's go to my place, okay? It's not far."

Schreiner the slut. But she shook off her misgivings. Better than home. And maybe Alec really was different. He was lonely, she knew, and sensitive. And maybe he'd hold her. She was so hungry for someone to hold her.

The shag rug and the sofa were regulation issue. But he'd surprised her by bringing out a cold bottle of real French champagne and a pair of crystal champagne glasses. "Hey, I'm impressed. Is it your birthday or something?" she'd asked.

"No. But I think I've just met a very special person."

Somehow even then it didn't sound like a cliché, because he said it with a little sheepish grin. She drank the champagne, and he stroked her cheek with timid fingers, and pretty soon they were in the dim soft lamplight of the bedroom, clothes heaped on a chair beside the king-size bed.

And she'd been right. He had held her. Even afterward, cradling her in gentle arms, murmuring drowsily to her that she was the most perfect woman he'd ever met. She'd clung to him, trying to believe, almost succeeding, almost happy.

But then, gazing dreamily past his shoulder in the dim light, she'd noticed the door. A closet, she'd thought as she passed it on her way in.

Skip it, Schreiner, she warned herself.

Alec shifted in her arms, rolled away, settled into deeper sleep with a sigh.

There was a moan.

Dread filled Holly. But she knew what she had to do. She sat

up slowly, pushed back the hair from her eyes, and tiptoed to the
door. It was ajar, just an inch or two. Dusky light from an unseen
source cast long shadows across the room within.

The moaning was louder.

She pressed the door open gently and stepped in.

It was a long room, crammed with close-spaced ranks of cots.
Bodies lay on the cots. All dead. The moan hummed in her head.
She tiptoed closer, looking at each. A young man with skin roasted
black. Another swathed in blood-soaked bandages, a symphony of
reds, only the black curls visible. The next with guts spilling
sausage-like onto the sheets. Another lay on his stomach, the open
wound in his side writhing with maggots chewing the dead flesh.

But there was something she had to find.

She crept on. Limbs torn off. Jaws missing. Then a young one
in a white starched student cap, head turned away from her.
Gently she reached for the chin, gently turned the face toward
her.

She screamed.

It was herself.

A rough hand shook Holly's shoulder. A male voice demanded,
"Hey, what's wrong?"

She whirled, lighting-quick as she'd been trained, found the
vulnerable hollow of the throat, dug her fingers in hard. He
yowled and jerked away. "Hey, what the fuck? What are you
doing?"

Holly dove for the floor, snatched her .38 from the purse she'd
nudged under the bed. The cold metal sent a shiver up her arm.

With a shock she realized there was a champagne glass on the
night table before her.

And next to her, the king-size bed.

The dream was disintegrating around her like a rotting curtain,
black shreds dripping into nothingness.

She looked back over her shoulder. Alec, naked and terrified,
was backing toward the door. Holly dropped the gun back into the
bag and turned toward him, still on her knees, palms held out.

"Sorry, Alec," she faltered. "Just a bad dream."

"Fuck your dream!"

"Yeah." She was shaking, drenched in adrenaline sweat. She
pulled herself up to sit forlornly on the edge of the bed and
dragged a sheet around her shoulders.

"Yeah, okay." A little bravado was returning to his tone. He'd
had a hit of adrenaline too, now stood shivering at the foot of the

bed, arms wrapped across his chest. Hugging himself, not her. "But look, maybe you better go, okay?"

"Okay."

"I mean, you're some crazy broad, attacking me like that!"

"Yeah. Sorry." She'd crept to the chair, pulled on her jade-green dress again and her fancy sandals, stumbled out to her car, and—

"Ahem."

Someone cleared his throat, cutting through the memory, jolting her back to the present, to the Colby sofa. Holly's eyes flared open. Pollard stood there, the patrolman who had relieved Higgins. There was a suspicious look in his eye. The look cops got when they figured they had proof she was just a dumb broad after all, because she was doing something they all did themselves. Holly sat up and said, "Yeah? What do you want, Pollard?"

"Lady here wants to see you. Name of Ryan."

Wonderful. One-thirty in the A.M. and she still wasn't rid of that one. Holly lurched to her feet and said, "Thanks, Pollard," in dismissal. She pushed her hair back from her face, noticed unhappily that her feet were still bare, and finally raised her eyes to meet Maggie's. "Yeah? What is it, Ms. Ryan?"

Maggie's expression was compassionate. "I know you're beat. I'm sorry to come butting in again, but—"

"Yeah, I know, you thought of something important," Holly broke in, cutting off the friendly voice. She reached back down to the sofa to retrieve her notebook, struggling to raise her defences again. She pulled out her pencil, stared at the peace sign woodenly, and said, "What is it?"

Maggie read the signals correctly and became more business-like. "Well, it's only important to little Tina. She really misses her Barbie dolls. If you don't need them here, it would be a comfort to her if you'd let me take them to her."

Poor kid. The irony of it hit Holly hard. "Having trouble sleeping, is she?" She was still too shaky to hide her bitterness. She'd known kids who couldn't sleep, nor eat, nor walk. She muttered, "Well, kid, join the club."

Maggie's blue eyes flamed with anger. "Jesus, what is this? I come here to ask you to help out a little grieving girl, and that's the answer I get? Look, I'm sorry you don't like me. But don't take it out on the kids!"

Civilians didn't understand. Holly tossed her notebook despairingly onto the sofa. Don't cry, Schreiner. Be strong.

Maggie pushed her fingers back through her curls. "Look, I'm sorry," she said in a softer voice. "But I just don't understand the problem. Is it something I said? Or—maybe you don't like kids at all. I'm pregnant, is that it?"

"Of course not! Why don't—"

Maggie glanced down at her T-shirt. "My politics, then. You were pro-war?"

Holly jerked her traitorous gaze away from the peace sign. "Don't talk bullshit!" she said roughly.

But Maggie realized she was on the right track. The compassion was back in her voice now but the questions continued relentlessly. "I'm sorry, I know no one was in favor of it, exactly. But you had a connection, didn't you?"

Holly's fists were clenched, wanting to smack her into silence.

"A brother, maybe? Wounded?" Maggie's soft voice was insistent. "Or a boyfriend killed?"

Holly's control snapped at last. "Yeah, smartass, you think you're so clever! But you're as dumb as everyone else in this goddamn counterfeit country! You think every Vietnam vet is male!"

For a fierce triumphant instant, Holly saw shock and disbelief reeling in the blue eyes. Then, comprehension dawning, Maggie murmured, "Jesus! Jesus, of course, an Army nurse! No wonder— look, I'm sorry, I didn't think!" She reached out sympathetically to touch Holly on the arm. "What was it—"

"What was it like? It sucked." Don't cry, Schreiner, if you start you'll never stop. She snatched up Barbie and Ken from the hearth and jabbed them into Maggie's hands. "Here, I hope the kid will be okay. And now if you goddamn peaceniks can restrain yourselves from spitting on me, I've got a murder to solve!"

Mosby,
Virginia

TUESDAY
MORNING

AUGUST 5TH
1975

Chapter 8

"Oh, Christ," moaned Olivia.

She had just closed her eyes, and someone was already nudging her awake.

"Liv, I thought you might want to go see Felicia."

Olivia pried her eyes open. The world was blurry, full of loathsome gray early light. A small figure swam into view. Little Sarah, industriously sorting through the drawers in Olivia's dresser. Another figure next to the bed. It was Maggie, dressed today in a sky-blue sundress. Olivia turned her head away and scowled bleary-eyed at the empty pillow beside her.

"Jerry just left for his hospital rounds," Maggie informed her cheerfully.

Hospital. So it was six o'clock. Hateful early-bird Ryans. Olivia peeled her tongue from the roof of her mouth and mumbled thickly, "Who's Felicia?"

"Felicia Colby. Dale's first wife."

Dale. Oh God. With a crash, reality broke over Olivia, swamping her with regrets and questions. She jerked upright, rubbing her eyes, her mind churning with images. Dale sprawled in his den. His family, Donna and the kids. The story about Representative Knox's plane. And the bar last night, hearing about Ernie Grant, the pilot's friend. And there was Leon Moffatt. And Mrs. Resler. And Felicia Colby, yes.

"Yes," said Olivia. "I want to see her. But why so goddamn early?"

"I don't know where she'll be later."

"You do know now?"

"Yes. Maybe."

Olivia clambered from the bed, grabbed her fresh undies out of Sarah's small hands, and whisked into the bathroom. "Be with you in a sec," she called over her shoulder.

A splash of cold water on the face, a quick rinse of the teeth, a grimace at the straggly-haired creature in the mirror. Looked like she'd only had two hours' sleep. Not far from the truth, really. Last night when she'd returned from the bar with Nick, Jerry had still been wide awake, demanding a blow by blow account. And even when they got to bed they were both still alert, as though Dale's fate underlined their own pulsing life, their own warm tingling senses. Maybe they should have lain sober and depressed in his honor. But sex framed by death seemed somehow doubly precious, a tiny affirmation that despite the waiting void, at that moment life was still triumphant.

At *this* moment, though, she didn't feel triumphant at all. Olivia picked up her hairbrush and returned to the bedroom, brushing. "How do you know where she is?"

"She pulled out her Holiday Inn key when she first arrived at Dale's yesterday. I happened to notice the room number."

"So this isn't a sure thing."

"No appointment, no." Maggie was helping Sarah count Jerry's socks. "How many of your leads are sure things?"

"Yeah, okay." Olivia finished pinning up her hair and pulled a yellow blouse and flowered skirt from her closet. "It's just that at six A.M. after a late night, sure things are a lot more attractive than maybes. Is anyone else up?"

"The Colbys are still sleeping. Donna had sedatives in her purse, I noticed."

"You're sure a noticing kind of person," grumped Olivia. "How about Nick?"

"He's downstairs reading. Said he'd mind the store in case Donna wasn't quite coping."

"Good. Do I have time for a cup of coffee?"

"Why don't you have one with Felicia?"

"Eleven!" caroled Sarah triumphantly, holding up a sock.

Olivia gave her little niece a sour look. "Rotten number for socks." She looked out the window. Her van was blocking Maggie's Camaro in the driveway so she might as well drive. She found her car keys and slouched down the stairs.

Sarah elected to come with them and Olivia drove through damp streets and highways gloomy in the clouded dawn. Rumbles of thunder threatened from beyond the hills. They passed the old farmhouse, now the John Singleton Mosby Museum, as they turned onto the highway.

"They hid in the woods," Sarah announced.

"Right," Maggie agreed.

"You see them hiding, Aunt Liv?"

"Huh?" Olivia was concentrating on keeping her eyes unshut.

"No, Sarah," Maggie smiled. "It was Mr. Taynton's grandpa, and the police chief's grandpa. They were hiding in the woods a long time ago. Before Aunt Liv was here."

"Who are you babbling about?" Olivia asked peevishly.

"Mosby's guerrilla fighters. Nice old fellow at the museum showed Sarah the paintings and uniforms and explained how they ambushed Union soldiers."

Sarah bounced up and down in the backseat. "They jumped out, and blam! blam! blam!"

"God, I'm raising a hawk," lamented Maggie.

At the Holiday Inn, Olivia followed directions and pulled into a parking slot. Maggie walked confidently up to Room 84, peeked brazenly through a crack in the curtain, then banged on the door.

A shirtless young man in jeans, with unkempt brown hair, opened it. Oh God, wrong room. Olivia stepped back.

But Maggie was more awake. "Mark Colby?" she asked.

"Yeah?" The young man raised his eyebrows in inquiry. Olivia's heart contracted. It was one of Dale's expressions.

"I'm Maggie and this is Olivia. Friends of your dad's."

His mouth twitched. He said, "Yeah?"

Olivia said, "We wondered if we could talk to you and your mother a minute before you go back to Harrisburg."

"Who is it?" Felicia Colby's blonde head appeared next to her son's. She was dressed in a pink ruffled robe. She stared at Maggie a second, then said accusingly, "You were at Dale's yesterday!"

"Right. So was Olivia here. I thought maybe you'd be interested in comparing notes, while the police aren't around."

Felicia chewed at her lower lip a moment. She was already carefully made up, Olivia saw. Full fifties war paint.

Sarah tugged at Maggie's hand. "Wanna pee!"

"Oh, dear." Maggie looked apologetically at Felicia, who was smirking down at the little girl. "I'm sorry. Mrs. Colby, could Sarah use your rest room?"

"Yeah, go ahead." Felicia stepped back from the door. "God, I remember Mark once at that age, screaming in the middle of the supermarket."

Mark stalked to the window, whisked back the curtain, and stared out at the unlovely parking lot. Olivia, sliding into the room in Maggie's wake, said to Felicia, "Listen, we don't want to bother you now if it'll be more convenient later. We just wanted to make sure to catch you before you left."

"Well, I'm leaving as soon as I can," Felicia said. She was lighting a cigarette. "I've got to stop by the police station this morning. Thought I'd go right after breakfast. Are you a friend of Dale and Donna's?"

"Not a close friend, if that's what you mean. I worked with Dale at the *Sun-Dispatch*. I'm a reporter too. I hardly ever see Donna."

"What about what's-her-name in there? Maggie?"

"She met him for the first time yesterday."

"How'd you both get mixed up in this?"

Olivia leaned against the wall. She needed coffee. "Chance, really," she explained. "I impulsively asked Dale and his family to go to the beach with us, since it was so hot. But when we picked them up, Dale was working on a story and decided to stay home. We got back eight or nine hours later and he was dead."

At the window, Mark's back was rigid. Felicia bowed her head, the heel of her hand against her forehead, smoke pluming from the cigarette between her fingers. "God, I still can't believe it. I just talked with him last week!" She raised her eyes with a bitter smile. "No, that's wrong. Talked *at* him. He was in one of his snits."

"Mother," said Mark, glancing at her from his position at the window.

"Hey, look, don't get uptight," Felicia told her son. "Nobody expects the ex to feel chummy toward a documented deadbeat. I've got proof," she explained, turning to Olivia. "Court papers telling him to pay up."

Maggie emerged from the bathroom with Sarah. "Why don't we all go have breakfast? Give ourselves a few minutes to talk things over."

"Yeah. Get your shirt on, Mark." Felicia stubbed out her cigarette and disappeared into the bathroom to change.

A few minutes later they were settled into a corner booth in the motel restaurant, the four adults on the semicircular banquette upholstered in antique-silk patterned plastic, Sarah queening it over them all from a high chair on the open side of the table. They ordered and to Olivia's relief the coffee came immediately. As soon as the waiter left, Maggie handed Sarah a picture book from her bag, then looked across the table at Felicia and said, "Okay. What do we all want to know?"

"I didn't say I wanted to know anything." Today Felicia's blouse was a vibrant turquoise. She fumbled in her bag and drew out a fresh cigarette.

"No. But you came along instead of throwing us out. And you're in an odd position, just like us. We found the body, so the cops are interested in us. You turn up, same day, mad at Dale. So the cops will at least be interested in your alibi."

"I wasn't even here! I was on the road three hours."

"And in Harrisburg before that?" asked Olivia.

"Yeah, where else?" Felicia looked at them narrowly. "It happened earlier? Is that it?"

Maggie shrugged. "It's possible. I'm no expert, though. So you were in Harrisburg until six or seven?"

"Yeah. I left after work."

"And people saw you up until five or so?"

Felicia blew out a cloud of smoke. "God, you're as bad as that policewoman last night! No, yesterday afternoon I had to check inventory. Guy that usually does it for me was on vacation. So after lunch I was mostly alone in the supply room. Nan saw me in the ladies' once, and that's it."

"Okay. And the detective probably also asked you why you drove down yesterday. Why not call or write? You often did, right?"

"No more often than I had to." Felicia tipped her head back, smoke streaming from her nose.

Olivia leaned forward. "Well, why did you come then?"

Mark broke in. "It's just that I have to mail in deposits for college. It's not so amazing to get worried about college fees in August!"

"No, it's sensible," Maggie agreed soothingly. "But it's a bad coincidence that you turned up here on that particular day. The detectives are probably looking askance at you."

"Askance," said Felicia. "Good word. That's what that police-woman does, all right. Looks askance."

"At us too," agreed Olivia. "We know it happened while we were gone. But she has to be suspicious of all of us."

"How did he die, anyway?" Felicia tapped her cigarette into the thick glass ashtray.

Olivia hesitated and said, "They don't seem to know." It was all very well to learn things from Felicia and her son, but Olivia's instinct was to protect information not yet published.

Maggie seemed to have no such qualms. "Best guess is that he got hit with a brass lamp base," she said. Her eyes were on Mark and she ignored Olivia's warning kick under the table.

"Who would do that? Why?" Mark asked urgently. He had that intense, quizzical Dale look again. But the waiter arrived with eggs and pancakes, and there was a flurry of sorting out juice and toast, and getting Sarah's French toast properly syruped.

When things settled down Olivia said, "There are a whole lot of questions. The police have to do tests, fingerprints and so forth, and find out if it really was the brass lamp. Nobody seems to know why it happened either. I'm wondering—well, he was working on a story about an unsolved crime. Maybe he got too close to an answer."

"Oh, he always said that!" Felicia exclaimed. "He always said, 'They're really going to be gunning for me now!' Every time he had a story more exciting than a zoning meeting." She snorted. "Sometimes even then."

"Yeah, we all feel like that," Olivia admitted, wondering uneasily if Kunstler would sue about anything in her Joanne Little story.

"But it never happens, does it?" Felicia demanded.

"Hardly ever. But there was this reporter in—"

Maggie broke in. "Well, who did *you* think did it?"

"That woman!" said Felicia. Mark shot her an exasperated glance.

Maggie nodded. "Donna. Well, it's true a lot of murders are domestic."

"Yeah, it's not so unusual, is it? Wife wants his money but not him. Especially if—" Felicia stopped, poked at her egg with a fork. "But of course, maybe it really was a story. Anything's possible. What was he working on?"

"Plane crash story," said Maggie. "Olivia's going to check into it, find out about what Dale might have discovered. Did he mention it to you?"

"Are you kidding? I was lucky to get anything more than hello-goodbye. That man's cold shoulder was a full-fledged iceberg."

"Mm. Maybe he felt guilty about owing you money."

"Guilty? Not him. He was just irresponsible!" Felicia's turquoise-lidded eyes sparked with indignation. "And spiteful. He couldn't believe I'd really divorce him. Went into his usual stony silence, trying to control things. When it finally sank in that I'd left for good, he skipped town himself. No forwarding address. It took me a year to get the divorce final."

Maggie was looking thoughtfully at the boy. "He ran out on Mark too?"

"No!" said Mark hotly. "He was avoiding Mother. You know it's true," he said, turning to Felicia. "He sent me cards. Christmas, birthday. I was just a little kid but he sent money too."

"Who told you that?" his mother demanded.

"Nan Evans. She said he sent money back then."

"Yeah, instead of the child support he owed, he'd send five bucks for your birthday," snapped Felicia. "But he did send cards. That's how I tracked him down finally. The postmarks on Mark's cards were all different. I figured he had to be working somewhere in the middle of the postmarked towns. So I got a map and looked at all the newspapers from places in the area. And sure enough, there he was, writing for the *Sun-Dispatch*. I knew he'd never give up his byline."

"God, you know reporters, all right!" Olivia had to respect this bit of investigation.

Maggie nodded approvingly at Felicia. "Must have been especially tough, with a little kid to take care of."

"Oh, I learned how to cope, all right," said Felicia proudly. "Raising a kid alone, you have to be a juggler. Breadwinner, nurse, PTA, and still find time to buy an ice cream cone. But Dale didn't have to pay me a thing. I mean, he was supposed to send child support but he hardly ever did. I went back to work as a secretary and pretty soon noticed that the big employers were using computers. Back to night school, data entry and even programming. I'm in the state finance department now. I supervise a hundred and fifty people."

Maggie beamed at her.

"But college is expensive," Olivia pointed out.

"You said it! And damn it, he's shortchanged Mark all his life. I mean, maybe I could have gone after him earlier, but you pay a lot of legal fees and they get one month's payment and say case closed. But for college—" She poked at her egg again.

"Who took care of Mark?" Maggie asked. "He was pretty small back then, right?"

Felicia nodded. "Yeah. My mom watched him a couple of years. Pretty soon he was in school, but she kept on helping out while I went to night school. Wasn't easy, but we made it, Mark and I." She smiled proudly at her son.

"Did you ever see your father, Mark?" Maggie asked.

"Yeah. Not at first. But he did send those cards. And later he'd send me copies of articles he'd written. About five years ago he took me to the World Series. Mostly to explain about his disease, I think." Mark cleared his throat. "To tell me it wasn't hereditary."

Olivia was touched. Maybe Dale had run out on his financial responsibilities, but it showed some thoughtfulness to try to head off worries in a son he barely knew. But Felicia, lighting a cigarette, muttered, "Too bad he didn't send us the ticket money instead. Mark doesn't even like baseball."

"So how was he supposed to know?" Mark flared at her. "Last thing he'd heard, I was in Little League. He was trying, Mother!"

"Well, he never tried hard enough."

"Shit." Mark leaned back in the booth, arms crossed, a frown on his young face.

Maggie said gently. "It's tough to lose your dad twice." Mark's sullen face crumpled and he looked away.

"Hey, come on," said Felicia angrily. "We're not here to fish for sympathy!"

Maggie nodded. "I know. I can see you managed very well without him. But he owed you both, and there's a lot of questions now that may never get answered. Mark's right to feel bad about that." She leaned forward toward Felicia, bony elbows on the plastic tabletop. "But we're back to the first question, aren't we? Why are you here? What do you want to know from us?"

Felicia ground out her cigarette and asked without looking at them, "Do you know if Mark inherits anything?"

"Rabbit book!" exclaimed Sarah imperiously.

Mark sputtered with choked laughter. Maggie and Olivia joined in, and even Felicia managed a halfhearted smile at the little girl. Sarah beamed, pleased at the effect of her comment. "Rabbit book," she repeated proudly.

"Yeah, okay, *chouchoute*, just a minute." Maggie removed Sarah's sticky plate from in front of her. The original stack of French toast had disappeared. "Do you know anything about his will, Olivia?" she asked, dipping a napkin into a water glass.

"Not offhand. But we could check with Donna. Though she didn't have any idea about insurance so I don't know if she'll know about the will."

Felicia snorted. "That one's never had to manage for herself."

Maggie had swabbed off Sarah's face and hands, and now handed her the book again. "We'll find out for you," Maggie promised. "The police will probably let Donna back in the house today, and she can check her papers then. If it's not there it may take longer to find out."

"Yeah. It's just that they want tuition," Felicia explained. "And I'm afraid if I ask the police, that detective will look askance."

Maggie grinned. "She probably will. Now, do you mind telling me about—well, about how you happened to marry Dale?"

Felicia looked at her sharply but answered with nonchalance. "What's to tell? I was nineteen. No crystal ball around to tell me it wouldn't work. I thought a reporter was real glamorous. Admired his brains. He was smart."

"Yes," Olivia agreed.

"And ambitious. And he had everything organized, under control. There was a fire in my building, where I was a secretary. And he came to cover it. And everyone was running around tearing their hair, but Dale was so cool, taking notes. Really impressed me. My golden lad." She shook her blonde head, bemused by her remembered younger self. "That's why finally I couldn't take it. He had to be in control, everything had to be just so. I could never come up to his standards."

"What were the grounds for divorce?"

Felicia looked at Maggie levelly. "Abandonment," she said after a moment. "Because he ran off to Virginia. It was easiest, my lawyer said." She leaned back against the antique-textured plastic. "My turn, okay? Tell me about the brass lamp."

Maggie complied. "He was in his den, working on the story. The lamp was in his den too. Apparently someone came in and struck him. Liv, I've been meaning to ask you. Where was that lamp sitting when you saw him?"

Olivia cringed to hear her dropping facts into Felicia's lap. But they did owe her something for telling about her soured marriage. At least Maggie had said nothing about the room being locked. Olivia said, "It was at the right end of the desk, near the edge."

"So it would have been easy for someone to grab."

"And you found him when you got back from this trip to the beach?" Felicia asked.

"Yes. He talked to Olivia before we left, and was dead by the time we got back."

"So that woman probably didn't do it. Well, what the hell. Dale never made things easy. I just hope it doesn't mess up the settlement of the will. Not that we really expect anything," she added grimly.

"We'll find out what we can for you. Um, one other question. Mark didn't come in last night when you came to Dale's."

"No. He waited in the car. I was going to show Dale the papers alone. Then depending on how he reacted, Mark would see him or not."

"Mark?" Maggie asked. "Did you want to see him?"

"I didn't want to beg," the boy said stiffly.

"God, how many times do I have to tell you, it's not begging! He owes you!"

"Not any more, Mother," said Mark bitingly. "Maybe his estate owes me. But he's out of our control now. For good."

"Yeah." For the first time Felicia looked regretful. "Poor old Dale. Maybe he's happy at last."

They paid the bill and said their farewells.

On the way out Olivia called Detective Schreiner to tell her about Donovan's Bar. But Schreiner couldn't come to the phone. Olivia left a message that she'd be at the newspaper and hurried to the car through gusts of rain-laden wind.

"Felicia did pretty well, raising Mark alone," Olivia observed as she switched on the windshield wipers and lights.

"Yeah. Though it wasn't exactly alone." Maggie was arced over the seat back, buckling Sarah into the backseat.

"What do you mean?"

"Well, Dale stuck around for a couple of years. And for a few more years her mom did a lot of baby-sitting. Twelve hours a day at times, by my calculation. With that kind of free help you're not raising a kid alone. Still, I think Felicia made the right choices. Got herself and Mark out of the situation as fast as anyone could in those circumstances."

"That's what I meant. She's got a right to feel bitter, too." The rain intensified as they drove out of the parking lot. "Do you suppose Felicia and Mark could have come down early and then pretended they'd just arrived?"

"It's possible. But if one of them killed him, I'd think they'd want to get back to Harrisburg and pretend they'd never left. Still, they may have reasoned that if they were seen they should have an excuse for being here." Maggie frowned at the sheets of rain chopping at the road. "And someone did go into the Colby's around three-thirty, when Bo was looking out the window."

"Not Felicia, though. Bo said it was a man, right? Not a blonde woman."

An impressive boom of thunder delayed Maggie's reply. "Felicia's fairly tall and broad-shouldered. And when Sarah and I were in her bathroom, we saw a wig form."

"A wig?" Olivia banged a fist against the steering wheel. "You mean that pile of blonde hair is a wig?"

"That's what I mean."

"Jesus Christ. I thought it was the blue-ribbon winner in the Clairol County Fair."

Maggie grinned. "Maybe that too."

"What's a wig?" demanded Sarah.

Maggie looked over her shoulder at the little girl, her hands shaping a phantom wig around her head. "It's like a hat that you can put on or take off, but it looks like hair."

"Like my hair?"

"Your hair isn't a wig. But a wig might look like your kind of hair. Or it might be blonde, or brown, or red like Aunt Liv's."

"A wig," said Olivia. "So Felicia could take it off, and maybe put on Mark's clothes—or Mark could have done it himself, of course."

"Unless they really were in Harrisburg."

"Yeah."

"And there's a second car. Bo saw a blue Ford, not a red Vega."

Olivia thought about it a minute. "I'll check the motel desk. Find out what time they checked in, what license number they gave. Because she already had her motel key when she arrived at Dale's, right?"

"Yes," Maggie agreed.

"Of course that'll only help if they did check in much earlier than they said. If they waited to check in until after they'd done it—"

"Still, it's worth a try. Ouch! Sarah, don't grab my hair! It's *not* a wig!" Maggie untangled small fingers from her curls. "And you're supposed to keep that seat belt on!" She twisted back again to resettle the lively child.

Olivia glanced sidelong at her sister-in-law. With caffeine coursing through her veins, she had finally located the source of her puzzlement at this foray into the dawn. "I've got a question for you," said Olivia.

"What?" asked Maggie.

Olivia looked back at the sluicing rain. "Last night you said leave it to the police. You said you didn't want to snoop. You said I shouldn't snoop. So why did you wake me at dawn to go snoop?"

"Oh, that," said Maggie guiltily. "It's just—well, I told you I had to go back to fetch Tina's dolls last night."

"Yeah."

"Well, I talked to Detective Schreiner when I was there. Just for a moment. And Liv, she's shattered. She's a very competent woman but she's living right on the edge of a breakdown."

"Shattered?" Olivia asked.

"Emotionally, yeah. Behind that cold facade. And Josie and Tina need gentleness now. Not coldness." She gazed out at the Mosby business strip, cafés and hardware stores, florists and frame shops. "Wish I could keep Schreiner from interviewing those kids— Anyway, the quicker this thing is cleared up the better. So I decided maybe this time snooping was the least of the possible evils."

"I see."

"For starts, there's a friend of my mother's who works in Representative Knox's office."

"Hurray!" Olivia grinned at her. "Welcome to Snoopers Inc!"

Chapter 9

"Well, my freckled friend, what are you doing here so early?" Nate Rosen swung into the *Sun-Dispatch* city room, hooking his umbrella onto the rack and casting a glance at the clock. Seven-thirty, she saw. He turned back, beaming the smile that never quite brightened his mournful eyes. "And why are you playing in our illustrious colleague's file cabinet?"

Olivia looked at him bleakly. "He's dead, Nate. Dale's dead."

"Dead?" Nate stopped in midstride to stare at her. Implications chased each other across his face. "Dead?" His smile wavered. "You're kidding!"

Olivia closed her eyes and shook her head. "No. Didn't Edgy call you? I told him last night."

"How the hell can he be dead? The Parkinson's? But they said it wasn't fatal!"

"No, no. Worse than that." Olivia pushed back from the files and collapsed into Dale's chair. "He was murdered."

"You're kidding!" Nate said again. He dropped his rain-beaded briefcase onto his own desk and came around the big central table to stare at her accusingly. "At the beach?"

"No, no. I've got to ask you—well, first let me tell you what happened."

"Please!" He propped himself half-sitting against the shorter of the file cabinets. His yellow shirt was already rumpled.

"Okay. We went over to pick them up. They were all ready except that Dale was on the phone."

"Yeah."

"I went back to his den to tell him what you said about going easy with Moffatt. And he seemed glad that Moffatt was upset. He decided instantly to stay and work on the story. Said it was getting interesting. Called for his wife to leave him some lunch and sent us on our way."

"Wait a minute. You're saying that after all that planning he didn't go with you?"

"Right. Just sent his wife and kids with us, said he could work better alone. But when we got back about nine, he was dead."

Nate shook his head in disbelief.

"And it's weird, Nate. He'd been hit on the head with his own brass lamp. But the door was bolted from the inside."

"Liv, you're putting me on!" He straightened with an impatient flip of his hand.

"No, Nate. I know it's crazy, but it's true."

He studied her suspiciously. "God, Liv, if you're lying . . ."

Olivia felt her mouth trembling and willed it still. "About something like this? I only wish I were, Nate."

"Shit." He licked his lips. "You say he was working on the plane crash story?"

"Yeah. You were on it too for a while, right?"

"Yeah. I was first on the scene, in fact. Picked up some talk on my CB and zipped over to Blue Hill. Edgy put Dale on it too because there was so much those first days, with Representative Knox's office making pronouncements and the air investigation so complex."

"So what's your feeling? If Dale got too close to the truth about that crash, do you think Moffatt or someone would kill him?"

Nate shook his head again. "Christ, Liv, I can't quite absorb this."

"Yeah, I know! Neither can I! But it happened. I saw him lying there. His wife and kids spent the night at our house because there were detectives all over theirs. It really happened. And I want to know about Dale's work."

He was beginning to believe her. He shoved his hands in his pockets and went to stare out the window. He'd worked with Dale for ten years, Olivia remembered. Maybe twelve. Much longer than she had. They weren't buddies, but they weren't enemies either. Not like Nate and Corey on sports, who seemed to grate on each other and did their best to avoid each other. Ten years, though—that was a long time. Ten years ago she herself had been starting college. God, how much she'd changed! Getting into the peace movement, the women's movement. *How many times must the cannonballs fly?* Woodstock, Kent State. *And it's one, two, three what are we fighting for?* Editing her college paper, landing a mini-job on a suburban weekly and soon, miraculously, this one on the *Sun-Dispatch,* complete with salary. Well, in a manner of speaking. Meeting smart, loony Jerry, who understood her hunger to uncover truth and tell the world. A busy ten years. And all that time Nate and Dale had been slogging away together, cranking out the stories side by side.

Nate still faced the window. "How do you think it happened?" His voice sounded thick. He cleared his throat.

"I don't know what to think, Nate. Maybe it'll all come clear when the police find out what kind of Houdini got out of that locked room. But since I can't figure out that part at all, it makes more sense to start looking for motives."

"So that's how the plane crash story fits in."

"Well, I know that's what he planned to work on that afternoon."

"Moffatt was mad as hell, all right," Nate said, turning back toward her.

"I know! What's with him, Nate? Why is he so made at Dale?"

"Dale was keeping things stirred up. He and a *Post* reporter were nagging at Knox's office all the time."

"But wouldn't Moffatt be glad of that? Wouldn't he want to find out how his father died?"

Nate pulled his hands from his pockets, frowned absently at the scrap of paper he'd pulled out, and walked across to his own chair. Olivia pursued him and sat on the center table facing his cubicle. Nate said, "I don't know the answer to that. Moffatt the younger is a contractor. I talked to him a few times that first weeks. He was stunned, angry—well, that's not unusual." Nate still wore his thoughtful frown.

"No. It would be more suspicious if he wasn't. But I still don't know why he'd be mad at Dale."

"Yeah. Mrs. Resler, now, she's into appearances. Reputation. Almost from the first day she was full of anxiety about how her husband would want things to look. Really yelled at me when I suggested in one story that he was on suspiciously good terms with some of the scum he defended."

"Was he?"

Nate looked hurt, his mournful face twice as piteous as usual. "Would I lie, Liv?"

She gave him a little smirk. "Not in print. Not if they could catch you."

"No trust left in this evil world," he grumbled. "Even the young and fair are cynical. But in fact, I know that one Bob Bates came back to Resler after he was released, and Resler got him a job at the water treatment plant."

"Hope he wasn't a poisoner!" Olivia swung her legs from the edge of the table.

"No. He'd conned his way into a bank job, then blew up their armored truck. Resler got him off most of the counts but Bates had to go inside for a couple of years. Most of the money was never recovered."

"And then Resler got him a job. No wonder you were suspicious! So how did Mrs. Resler dare object to your story?"

"Well, her version is that her husband was humane, all milk of human kindness. He tried to help offenders because it was the moral thing to do. My story, she said, made him sound like a criminal himself."

"And did it?"

Nate shrugged. "*I* thought it was neutral."

Olivia gripped the edge of the table and leaned forward eagerly. "But Edgy listened to her. Right? That's why he transferred the story to Dale?"

Nate held up his arms as though to ward off blows. "God, girl, you go for the jugular, don't you? Yeah, La Resler is the reason he switched." His look was half exasperated, half admiring. "Look, you damn reporter, you want to know about the plane crash or about my brilliant career?"

"Nate, it's weird, I know." Olivia looked down at her toes in her damp sandals and decided not to complain yet that he'd called her 'girl.' She shared his sense of being off-balance. "I've felt schizophrenic ever since it happened. We're reporters, yes. But we're also friends of Dale's, so we're involved too. Almost like sources for each other."

"Yeah."

"And when the cops come, you'll see that we're suspects also."

"Suspects?" His startled eyes jerked up to stare at her, the full impact of the situation registering at last. "God, Liv, this is a mess!"

She smiled sympathetically. "I promise not to write it up to make you sound like a criminal."

"Back to that, are we?" Nate snorted. "Okay, I'll take you to meet that ex-con Bates and see what you think. It was a big favor Resler did him. And his widow is keeping up family tradition."

"And you can't help but wonder why."

"Right."

"What does Bates look like?"

"Fangs, warts, a squint . . ."

"Nate, come on!"

"Oh, he looks average enough. Even respectable. But shifty, somehow. Never know what's going on in that brain."

"And Mrs. Resler approved of helping him?"

"Not only approved, but announced her intention of setting up the Frank E. Resler Memorial Trust to aid poor fallen felons like him."

"Wow. Okay. Because remember I said Dale was on the phone when we got there to take them to the beach? He was talking to Mrs. Resler. He told her he'd be discreet."

"Really!" Nate's eyebrows climbed.

Edgy bustled into the room, tossing everything but his take-out coffee onto the table. Olivia had phoned him late last night with the first details. "What's new on Dale?" he asked.

Olivia jumped off the table and tried to look more dignified. "Not a lot."

Edgy glanced at Nate. "I tried to call you last night."

Nate nodded. "I, you know, met somebody. Got back late."

"Real late," said Edgy.

Olivia broke in, "I was about to tell Nate, I interviewed Dale's ex-wife this morning."

Nate whistled. Edgy pried off the lid of the take-out cup and asked, "The golden-tressed Felicia? Is she around?"

God, these guys knew Dale so much better than she did. Why the hell hadn't *they* taken him to the beach? She said, "Yeah, very interesting. She and her son drove down from Harrisburg last night and arrived a few minutes after the police."

"My, my," said Nate. He seemed pleased rather than jealous that she'd brought in this tidbit. Not ambitious, was the newsroom scuttlebutt about Nate. Not hungry enough. But it made him easier to work with. He asked, "Did she say why she came after all this time?"

"She said Dale was supposed to pay Mark's tuition and he hadn't."

"I see. Money. Her usual topic."

"Any truth to her story?" Olivia demanded.

Nate shrugged. "I don't know the legal situation. Dale was pretty burned up at her, yeah. Complaining how there was no getting away, she was always trying to boss him around. She sent the divorce papers right to this office, way back when."

"Before my time," said Edgy.

"Yeah, Mueller was still editor. He thought it was a hoot. But Dale was furious. Muttering about castrating females. Said he'd never give her a penny."

Olivia, hackles rising, said, "I don't think she wanted it herself so much. She just thought Mark deserved support."

Nate shrugged. "Same difference."

"Nate, you know it's not! Mark was his son too! Why should the woman be stuck putting in all the time to raise him, and all the money too?"

"Who says life is fair? Anyway, I just meant—"

"The whole Judeo-Christian tradition says we should try to make it fair!"

"Okay, okay," Edgy put in. "Now we all understand Felicia's said of it. Are the police checking her alibi?"

"They're checking all our alibis," said Olivia. "Yours and mine too."

Startled realization flitted across Edgy's face. Like Nate, like her too, he came a little late to understand the peculiar dual role they played in this murder. He turned to the coffee urn, verified that no one had started it yet this morning, and said in an annoyed tone, "Cops'll be here too, won't they?"

"I'm sure," said Olivia. "The detective in charge seems very thorough."

"Does he know yet how the killer got out of that room?" Edgy asked.

"If so, she's not talking," said Olivia, enjoying the momentary confusion the pronoun caused. "So it seems to me we should look for motives. We know as much about Dale as anyone. I know he stayed home to work on the plane crash story. So maybe we should compare notes."

"Right." Two more early arrivals came through the door, scattering raindrops onto the floor. Edgy turned, picked up his stuff from the table, and beckoned Nate and Olivia with a jerk of his head. "My office," he said.

Sitting on the worn pads of the visitors' chairs in his office, Olivia and Nate told him about Mrs. Resler's call and Felicia Colby's visit. In the big room outside the venetian blinds of the door, people filed in, wet and grouchy, to begin work. Olivia concluded the account and said, "That's what we know about those two. We were wondering about Leon Moffatt too."

"Moffatt?" asked Edgy.

"He wasn't very happy with Dale yesterday," Nate reminded him.

"No, he wasn't."

"Did he tell you why?" Olivia asked.

Edgerton tented his fingertips and frowned at the acoustic tiles in the ceiling. "Basically he wants this investigation to go away. His father's estate is on the verge of being settled but, he says, every time there's a new story the estate's lawyers hedge again. I told him they'd hedge anyway."

"They think *Moffatt* might have blown up the plane?" exclaimed Olivia. If he had—

"Right. They'd look like fools if they turned over the bucks to him and then found out he'd arranged the accident himself."

"What kind of guy is he?"

Edgy shrugged. "I was a senior at Maryland when he was a freshman. Came on a football scholarship, but he flunked out his second year. Ended up working on road crews. Finally his dad took pity and helped him get started in this construction firm."

Tarnished son of a successful father, then. Skilled at sports but not able to fulfill the dream of college. She asked, "How is he as a businessman?"

"Haven't heard any complaints," said Edgy.

"He was mad at Dale, though. Like Nate said."

"Yeah, he wants it all over with. Who wouldn't?"

"Does he have an alibi for the plane crash?"

"No one does," said Nate. "The explosive was put on board before the plane was fueled for the flight, but no one knows when. Could have been almost any time on the three days before the crash, at a poorly guarded little airfield. Can you prove you weren't there?"

"I see what you mean," said Olivia, glad for being alibied by so many others yesterday at the beach. Still, she preferred Moffatt to Felicia Colby as Dale's killer. Knee-jerk feminist, she scolded herself. If women are equal they can kill too. But there were objective things that made Moffatt seem more likely. She said, "The kid next door to Colby's saw a man arrive around three-thirty yesterday."

"Really?" Edgy and Nate spoke almost together. "Is that when it happened?" Edgy added.

"They don't know yet. But I bet it works out that way."

"Well, we can't ignore other possibilities until it's official," Nate chided her.

"Okay, I know. But I think we should find out where Leon Moffatt was yesterday afternoon. I'll talk to him."

"Hold it!" Edgerton held up his damp beefy palm. "Nate talked to Moffatt before. He's the logical one to interview him now."

Nate, who had been frowning at his shoes, looked up and nodded.

Olivia swallowed her fury. Didn't want Edgy to think she was an emotional female. "I found the body," she reminded him coolly. "I'm the logical one to do this story."

Edgy gave her a tight smile. "Never said you weren't. There'll be a lot of people to interview. You're both on it. For starts, Liv, you draft something on the discovery of the body. Nate, do a sidebar about his career. You do the obit too. Don't mention the stories he was working on yet, but get out and do those interviews. I want Nate on Moffatt, Liv on Mrs. Resler. You two divvy up the rest." He glanced at his watch. "I'll talk to you again about two, okay?" They both nodded, and he added, "If you're quick enough right now you'll be out of here before the police catch you."

"Good point," Olivia said. Schreiner could hold them up for hours. She followed Nate back into the main room. "So what do you say?" she asked him. "Any problems with Edgy's plan?"

"No, it's a good idea for you to take the widow Resler. She'll remember my alleged unfairness. But I'd like to see Bates. How about we write this stuff, then I'll catch Moffatt, you catch Resler, and we'll meet Edgy back here after lunch? Maybe hit the congressman's office this afternoon."

"Fine." If she was quick enough at Resler's, she might also be able to squeeze in the pilot's friend that she'd heard about last night at the bar. Nate would be finding stuff too, he knew so much about Dale. She started for her cubicle, then paused and looked up at Nate's sad eyes. "I didn't mean to be prickly in there. I'm glad we're both on it, Nate."

"Don't sweat it." He punched her shoulder lightly with his fist. "A little determination never hurt a reporter, kid."

"Damn right, old man."

They popped into their respective cubbyholes to bang out the first reports of Dale Colby's murder.

Chapter 10

At first light Holly revisited the Colby house. Couldn't sleep, might as well detect. The day was rainy and gusty and there wasn't much chance of finding anything outside. Still, she wanted a daylight view. She waved at a red-eyed Officer Pollard on the slab porch and started around the house, trying to keep her mind open to possibilities. Last night also the garage door had been open, the Pinto in the drive. At the back of the garage was the door to the backyard, a pegboard hung with tools next to it. Bikes, other typical suburban garage stuff, but neater than most. She moved on to the side yard, a narrow strip of grass between the Colby garage and the Morgan house. Bo's bedroom windows at the front corner, blinds down now. Probably still asleep. Farther along, a disturbance in the mud next to the garage wall. She squatted. Looked like a floor plan. A little foundation for a mud house, now melting in the rain. She used to build houses like that. Clay dirt, that was the best, stuck together for nice solid walls. Her brother helped, sometimes. Other times buzzed it on his scooter, pretending to be a bomber, destroying it just as thoroughly. Holly's wails didn't stop him. Important lesson there: wailing was not a good weapon. The next time around, she'd built her mud house behind anti-scooter fortifications of brick and rock.

She straightened and moved on, around the back corner of the garage. Downspout at the corner, rainwater dribbling out now. Yard mostly grass, a few bushes near the foundation, one tree. Here was the door next to the tool pegboard, a little slab of bare cement probably billed as a patio. High windows over the kitchen sink inside. The compressor for the air conditioner next, painted buff to match the house. The maple tree in the yard shaded the big dining-room windows. More foundation bushes along the house wall. The small bathroom window next. And then the windows of Dale's den. The second of the three on this side was the cracked one. Under it, bushes and muddy earth. It had been photographed last night under floodlights but she still was careful where she put her foot when she stepped closer to peer in. Yes, Maggie Ryan's story checked out; she could have seen the body in enough detail to know there was a problem. Then run back to the garage door, grab the crowbar from the pegboard, run through the kitchen and hall to break in. Holly looked carefully at the windowpanes and frame. Putty smooth, frames unmarred. No way to open them from outside. Everything solid, sealed, neat.

At the corner, another downspout oozing water. She squinted at the guttering along the roofline. No holes there either. Crime Scene had checked the roof last night, the attic crawl space too, but she made a note to be sure they'd remembered the gutters. But everything looked airtight from here. Same thing around the corner on the west side of the room. Here, instead of evergreen bushes, a narrow gravel strip divided wall from lawn under the den windows. But there was no way into that room.

At the front corner of the house, windows to Dale and Donna's bedroom, curtains drawn. Another downspout. More evergreen plantings. Next, the girls' bedroom window. And then back to the front door, the slab porch.

A fruitless survey.

She sighed, waved good-bye to Pollard, and headed for the station house. Felicia Colby would be arriving in half an hour to make her statement.

"Thank you very much, Mrs. Colby." Holly took the typed statement that Felicia Colby had just signed and smiled officially at her. "I'm sure you want to be on your way. We appreciate your stopping by."

"Sure." Felicia Colby stubbed out her cigarette and gathered her handbag and clear plastic scarf into her lap. "This is so unbelievable. You'll keep me posted about what's happening, won't you?"

"We'll be back in touch," said Holly. Gabe had already tried to contact Nan Evans, the woman that Felicia said she'd spoken to yesterday afternoon. But Mrs. Evans was apparently en route to work, since no one was answering either at home or at her office.

"You see, it's just that we're so far away," Felicia explained, tying on the plastic rain scarf. "It's hard to keep up. And it's pretty important to us."

"Yes. Well, of course we can't give separate news bulletins to all the interested parties. Perhaps you could arrange something with the newspaper. I'm sure they'll have full coverage."

"Oh. Maybe Olivia. That redhead."

"You know Olivia Kerr? Did your ex-husband introduce you?"

"No, I just met her this—" Felicia stopped, eyes narrowing. "Hey, I'm not getting her in trouble, am I? Or me?"

Wonderful. This witness primed by the news hounds already. Holly asked, "She found you and talked to you already?"

"Yeah. Reporters do that, you know." Felicia clutched her bag defensively. "They asked me the same things you did, pretty much."

"They?"

"You know that woman with the black curly hair? Maggie. The one you were talking to yesterday?"

"Yeah. I know." Holly closed her eyes a second.

"Well, she was there too."

"No doubt." Holly had a sudden surge of nostalgia for the Kelly case last month, decent hardworking witnesses who spoke their piece, shut up, and stayed out of the way. But hell, you had to take them as they came. Dale Colby had been a reporter. Naturally he'd know other reporters. And naturally they'd be curious.

No excuse for Maggie, though.

"Well, if it's okay I'll get in touch with her," Felicia said.

"Sure." Holly stood up and Felicia did too. "We'll let you know if there are any developments that concern you. And of course as the investigation proceeds we may have further questions you can help us with."

"Okay."

Holly walked her to the waiting area where Mark was sitting. The boy looked haggard, as though he'd been walking point on a night patrol. He stumbled to his feet as they approached. "Thank you both for your help," Holly said.

"Sure. We just want to get this settled," Felicia repeated.

"We all do." Holly watched them out the door, then returned to her desk. Moffatt next, she thought. And the pilot's sister, Priscilla Lewis. And the newspaper. Check with Crime Scene, see if the Colbys could return to their house. And at some point, she'd better face up to the rest of the interview with Maggie, who had wanted to talk about how the murderer had gotten out. With a little luck, Crime Scene would have found the forced window or whatever it was that had been used. But if they hadn't, she might as well find out what Maggie had to say. The first on the scene. She was observant, bright, persistent, in addition to being a shit.

How had it slipped out? Holly hadn't told anyone about Nam for years. It was so much simpler to leave it behind her, leave it alone. And if you didn't watch the news, if you threw yourself into your job, it would leave you alone too.

Usually.

Right after she'd DEROSed at the end of 1967, she'd seen her parents for a few days on leave before reporting to Walter Reed to finish out her enlistment. She'd brought out her photos, eagerly tried to tell her mother something about that astounding year of challenge and horror, achievement and disillusion. She showed her a photo of herself and Billie Ann dressed in fatigues, grinning at a Montagnard child. Then a shot of the 18th's original tent hospital in Pleiku. Twelve-hour shifts minimum, she'd told her, often seven days a week. "Yes, you wrote how busy you were," said her mother.

"More when there was a Mas-Cal."

"A what?"

"Mass casualty. The choppers would come in from the combat zones, run the guys in and we'd triage. Then—"

"What's that?" asked her mother politely.

"Three priorities. Like if a guy had maybe run into a grenade and had a lot of frag wounds but nothing serious, he'd have to wait till we weren't busy. If he was hurt bad but we could save him, he was an Immediate and we'd take him straight to the OR. Operating room. The others, well, we'd send them to Expectants, give them a shot of morphine, and—"

"Expectants?"

Still staring at the photo, Holly explained gently, "Means the poor fuckers were going to die."

"Oh, honey!" exclaimed her mother. "You mustn't say that!"

Holly had glanced at her, thinking for an instant that her mother meant they should not have given up, should have tried to save everyone. Then she'd realized what the problem was. The chasm between them that she'd been struggling to bridge suddenly yawned into a gigantic gulf. Hopeless. She'd gathered up the photos and stood up.

"Honey, don't be angry. You know I just want what's best for you. You've been in a very crude place, I know, but you mustn't use such language. You're home now. You must put it behind you."

None of her friends wanted to hear about it either. "Tell us a funny story," they'd plead. "Like M*A*S*H."

So she'd put it behind her.

Ignored the news. The body counts. The demonstrations.

Torn up the letter to Billie Ann she'd started to write.

Gotten out of nursing because the emergency wards stirred up the adrenaline and the nightmares, and the other wards bored her to distraction.

She'd worked hard. Drunk hard. Put it behind her.

Until this year. In January, the mad scramble as the last Americans scurried onto helicopters. Peace with honor. Whoopee. In March, overhearing a snippet of a news program that stopped her in her tracks. The South Vietnamese had pulled out of Pleiku. No fight. Just plain pulled out. All her boys had fought to keep Pleiku for the south. They'd lost legs, faces, brains, lives. All wasted. Why? Why?

Did heaven look on, and would not take their part?

Don't ask me I don't give a damn.

She still struggled against it but since then she'd hardly had an undisturbed night's sleep. Her defenses were eggshell-thin. Work usually still helped, but last night, a swollen belly and a peace sign had snapped her like kindling.

"Holly."

She realized it was the second time Gabe had called her. "Sorry," she said. "Just thinking deep thoughts. What's up?"

"You're looking a little raw this morning."

"I'm okay. What've you got?"

"Two things. One local, one national."

"Wonderful."

"Yeah. The local—well, here he is."

Holly looked around to see a frail old man of erect military posture, wearing a light gray summer suit, his long face elegantly lined with wrinkles, his pale eyes troubled. He seemed vaguely familiar.

Gabe said, "Mr. Taynton, this is Detective Schreiner. Mr. Taynton is the curator at the John Singleton Mosby Museum."

Holly remembered him now. Every historic affair that Mosby held included a speech by this man, a walking encyclopedia of the Civil War guerrilla battlefield in the area. One of his grandfathers had fought with Mosby. Against the prevailing winds of the glorification of the Union cause, Taynton and his friends took their stand, staunchly championing the valor and nobility of the losers.

Holly wondered if anyone would ever do the same for her boys.

She shook his hand and asked, "How can we help you, Mr. Taynton?"

"Our museum has been robbed," he said shakily.

Gabe put in, "He's given the details to us already, but he wanted to talk to you."

"I'm sorry to hear Chief Posey is on vacation," said Taynton fretfully. "Good friend of mine."

"We'll help you, Mr. Taynton," said Holy in resignation. Looked like bouncing it back down to the local uniformed cops was not an option. "What was taken?"

"Our wonderful painting of Colonel Mosby's forces. Cut out of its frame—it's terrible!"

"Any leads?" Holly asked Gabe.

"Yeah. Mr. Taynton says a tour bus arrived from D.C. at opening time. He gave them the tour and they were back in the bus heading for Manassas already when he noticed the missing painting."

"Nothing like this has ever happened!" Mr. Taynton was clearly very upset despite his rigidly dignified bearing. Holly could understand; to him this was violation of a shrine, of a sacred trust. "We've had some vandalism outdoors, of course—but when I walked into that room and saw the bare wall—"

"I thought you said it had been cut out of the frame. Was the frame there?"

"It was broken into pieces, on the front steps. Strips of the canvas still tacked on the stretcher on the back but the painting cut out. And the tools were there—razor, crowbar, glass-cutter."

"Looks professional, then. Not just someone grabbing it on impulse," Gabe pointed out.

"Okay, Gabe, get Winks on this. Tell him to contact Manassas right away." She turned to Taynton. "We'll do our best."

"It's so distressing!"

True. With the chief and three senior detectives on vacation, they were already stretched thin. But Mr. Taynton had clout around here, so they'd have to make room for his problem.

Gabe returned from escorting Taynton to Winks. Holly sighed. "Shit. I needed him to follow up the Colby thing."

"Well, here's more on Colby," Gabe told her. "Remember I said there was local news and national news?"

"Congressman Knox?"

"Got it in one. D.C. called. A Sergeant Thornton. Says they're up to their ears now what with guys on vacation—"

"Yeah, tell me about it."

"So he can't put anyone on it there, but he's set things up so we can visit the congressman at ten. He said there'd be two of us."

Holly glanced at her watch. "Shit. I'd wanted to hit Moffat and the pilot's sister first."

"Yeah. But you know how much more important a congressman's time is than a cop's."

"Yeah, I know." Rear echelon motherfucker. She looked over her desk. Nothing but a note to call Olivia Kerr, who probably just wanted the latest for her story. She'd catch her later at the newspaper. Holly said, "Okay, Boy Wonder, let's go. Can't disappoint the bigwigs."

Knox's office was pretty much what she'd imagined: thick carpet, dark masculine furniture, personable young brunette in a linen suit at the reception desk, the Ohio state shield flanked by well-lit photos of the congressman smiling with Johnson, with Ford, with some schoolchildren, with a hog. A less well-lit photo of him smiling with Nixon. The brunette took them to an inner office where the real-life Knox, also smiling, put down a sheaf of papers, stood up to show off expensive tailoring on a trim athletic frame, and said, "Glad to meet you. Please sit down," with a practiced handshake. Then he assumed a more sober face. "But is my understanding correct? This terrible business of the plane crash has brought on another tragedy?"

"We don't know yet, sir." Holly studied him: longish face with photogenic smile creases, intense eyes, hair cut carefully to disguise a receding hairline.

He raised his eyebrows. "Oh?"

"A reporter was murdered. One of the stories he was investigating was the January crash. But as yet we don't know that it was related to his death."

"I see. Colby? That's the one the district police said, right, Dot?"

"That's right." The brunette nodded.

"Dale Colby, of the Mosby, Virginia *Sun-Dispatch*," Gabe confirmed.

"Just spoke to him the other day." Knox shook his head. "Unbelievable!"

"What was the subject of your conversation?" Holly had her notebook out.

"Well, in fact, I just said hello on my way into this office. Carol took care of him."

"Carol?"

"Carol Carson. Runs the office here, right, Dot?"

"That's right," agreed the brunette.

"Can you tell me anything about Mr. Colby's interest in the crash, sir?" Holly asked.

"Not really, except that he's been one of the most persistent in asking for updates. Generally he just took the releases, came to the scheduled news conferences, that kind of thing. I didn't have any reason to give him a special interview."

"I see." Washington papers or Ohio papers would get the interviews. Yet Dale had kept chipping away. She asked, "Did you have any sense of whether he was interested in some particular angle of the investigation recently?"

Knox shook his head regretfully. "I'm sorry. Just didn't talk to him enough."

"What is your own idea about the cause of the crash?"

"Terrorists," he said confidently.

"Terrorists?"

"I'm one of the sponsors of an anti-terrorism bill. And I was planning on being on the plane until an important vote came up at the last minute."

"So you think you were the target?"

"Makes sense. Kennedy, King . . ."

And Knox, yeah, sure. Holly asked, "Have there been any attempts since?"

"Not that we know of. Maybe the publicity about the crash made them realize we'd be on the alert."

"What about the other sponsors of the anti-terrorism bill? Any attempts to harm them?"

A testy frown flitted across the photogenic face. "Not that I know of. But Carol Carson could probably help you."

"Yes, we'd like to talk to her too."

"Fine. Dot, why don't you take them over there?" Knox picked up his sheaf of papers again.

Chapter 11

Carol Carson's office, behind the reception area, was less grand than Knox's swagged and paneled room, but just as masculine. Carson herself was stocky, gray-haired, and dynamic. Nothing grandmotherly about her except her age. This was Rosie the Riveter thirty years further along. She was leaning back in her chair, talking to someone in the corner, when Dot opened the door to announce Holly and Gabe. Carol Carson stood up behind her massive teak desk and extended her hand.

"Glad to meet you!"

"Same here." Holly entered to shake hands and glanced at the person getting to her feet in the corner.

Wonderful.

"You've met Maggie Ryan, I understand?" asked Carol Carson.

"Yes. And today I seem to be following in her footsteps." Watch it, Schreiner, don't sound cranky.

Maggie shrugged airily. Today there was no peace sign, just a sky-blue summer dress that drifted gently across her breasts and belly. She said, "I told you I was curious."

"Well, Ms. Ryan, sorry to interrupt, but—"

"Hey, it's okay! I'll just grab a Coke for Sarah and see you later, Mrs. Carson."

"Fine. Don't go far. I'll dig out that photo you wanted to see."

"Great! Bye for now."

"Bye!" piped Sarah. Gabe wagged his fingers at her and she giggled. He beamed and shut the door behind them.

"Please sit down," said Carol Carson. "Interesting young woman, isn't she? From Ohio."

"She wanted to see a photo?" Holly asked.

Carol smiled. "Yes. Her mother is mayor of a town near Cincinnati, and I have a photo of her at a conference we both attended once."

"I see." Holly noted it down.

"She was asking about the plane crash investigation too. That's why you're here?"

"Yes. The congressman said you could fill us in on that."

Carol Carson handed over a folder of papers. "Here's the press packet. Exactly what Dale Colby received. Everything we know about it."

Holly glanced through the papers. CAB reports, interviews, Xeroxes of newspaper articles, brief bios of the victims. She passed it on to Gabe. "Mrs. Carson, could you tell us something about the people who died?"

"Whatever I can."

"Mr. Moffatt. What was his connection with the congressman?"

"He was an Ohio man. Made his money here in Washington but kept an interest in Ohio politics. Like Mr. Resler. They were going back to Ohio for a fund-raising conference. Always supported us, served on committees."

"I see. Do you know Moffatt's son Leon?"

"Not well. I've met him, of course. He was something of a disappointment to his father for a while. But they'd reconciled recently."

"The son was upset about the stories being written."

"Really?" Carol Carson shrugged. "Maybe it's just that he wants things settled. Mrs. Resler feels the same way."

"Did Leon Moffatt talk to you about your investigation?"

"Yes. Said basically he wanted it over with. He asked about our findings, just like the reporters. But this was back in June, and we had only the preliminary results to pass on."

"I see. Have other people expressed an ongoing interest in this investigation?"

Carol Carson smiled, pulled open a file drawer, and handed Holly a list of names. "These are the people we mail to on this topic. The asterisks indicate relatives of the victims. I thought you might ask so I made you a copy."

The list was dauntingly long. But the relatives, except for the few with Ohio addresses, were already on her own list. "Thank you, Mrs. Carson. Can you tell me if any of these people are—well, unusually interested in some way? Persistent, or angry, or with odd questions?"

"Not really." Carol Carson's brow wrinkled. "Moffatt's son has been in, as I said. Mrs. Resler has checked in frequently but not antagonistically. She's also asking us for advice on the foundation she's establishing in her husband's memory. Priscilla Lewis was upset because her brother—he was the pilot—had some medals that disappeared, and she wanted us to check with the Air Force to see if it would be possible to get replacements. Ann Kauff-mann's father was extremely distraught—it's natural, she was still in college, she was—she only worked with us a few weeks, from about Thanksgiving, I think—and of course, her father was, um, upset—" Carol Carson stared down at her own well-groomed hands, both spread tensely on the blotter of her desk, as though pressing away an unwelcome image.

Holly played it gently. "He'd lost his daughter. He might have said something he didn't really mean."

Tears hard as diamonds stood in Carol Carson's eyes. "He said Chappaquiddick. He said she had died in shame. It's not true! There was nothing shameful, only tragic!"

Gabe's glance flicked toward Holly, silent congratulations at pulling out this bit. Hanky-panky involving the virile Knox? Holly moved smoothly on. "Did he know it wasn't true? Or was he upset enough to believe it?"

"Oh—I don't know. I think it was just the first rush of grief."

"Did he feel the press was reflecting badly on his daughter?"

Carson pulled herself away from her thoughts, frowned, and then said, "Oh, I see. You want to know if he might have had a grudge against Colby. I'm afraid you'll have to ask at the newspaper. We corresponded with him only in Ohio, so I don't know if he even knew Colby's work."

"I see." Holly turned the page. "Tell me something about Peter Church."

"My predecessor," said Carol Carson soberly. "A talented man. He'd been with the congressman about ten years."

"What does the job involve?"

Carol Carson smiled. "Just about everything! Meeting constit-uents, making up schedules, meeting the press, running the office here and in Ohio—you name it."

"Advising on votes?"

"Sure. There are lots of other advisors too. His legal advisor, other experts. But I'm the one in touch with the grass roots, to tell him what'll fly politically."

"So yours is a position where you could make enemies."

"I do my best not to. Peter did too, of course. But there are always idealists who think it has to be all or nothing. They don't understand that there are people just as idealistic on the other side, and the best we can do is compromise."

"So it's possible someone might have thought Peter Church had sold out?"

"Yes. I've thought about that, obviously. Since I'm in the hot spot now," Carol Carson admitted. "Ours is a rural district, has its share of good ole boys who admire frontier justice. But blowing up a plane doesn't seem quite their style. A rifle out the window of a moving pickup truck would be more likely."

"Yeah." Holly had to agree with her; the good ole boys were not as promising as some other leads.

"My own feeling is that it's likely a terrorist organization upset about the bill."

"Yes, the congressman mentioned that. But no one has claimed responsibility for the bombing."

"No. But maybe they don't want publicity, they want to try again." Obviously Carol Carson had thought this out too. She leaned forward, emphasizing her point with a stubby, neat index finger jabbing at the desk. "So if Dale Colby had found out something incriminating, they'd definitely want him out of the way."

"You think the congressman is in danger, then?"

"We're taking precautions, yes."

"Are there any particular terrorist groups you suspect?"

"Not really." Carol Carson handed over another paper. "Here's a list. You probably know most of them. A few are apparently limited to Ohio."

Holly skimmed the list. Free Kolumbus. Symbionese Liberation Army. Now there was a thought. Patty Hearst had disappeared, reappeared as Tania, disappeared again, and was still at large despite the efforts of parents, cops, the FBI. Maybe the SLA had perfected getting in and out of locked rooms. She handed the list to Gabe and said, "Thanks, Mrs. Carson. Do you know if any of the co-sponsors of the bill have had threats?"

"Not that I know of. That's why we're paying special attention to the Ohio groups on our list."

"I see. Can you think of anything else that might help us now?"

"Not really. But—well, I did get a call from Colby yesterday afternoon."

"Yesterday afternoon? What time?"

"About two-thirty. But it was strange. Gibberish, almost. Identified himself, and I asked what I could do for him. He said something, sounded like Moffatt. Then something I couldn't understand and he hung up. I thought maybe he'd dialed the wrong number and really wanted someone else."

"I see."

"I wonder if Dale Colby might have somehow been a step ahead of us in his investigation. Maybe that's why this tragedy occurred."

"That's possible."

"So if you discover anything that might help the congressman, please let us know right away so we can protect him."

"Of course, Mrs. Carson." Holly stood with a surreptitious glance at her watch. Almost eleven. She'd better make her calls now, because by the time they got back to Virginia everyone would be at lunch. She asked, "May I use a phone?"

"Of course. Use Line five, from Dot's desk." She walked around the desk and opened the door for them. "Oh, good, Maggie. You want to come back in? I'll get your mom's picture out."

Holly nodded curtly at Maggie and headed for the receptionist's phone to make her calls to Latents and the ME. Gabe occupied himself with Dot.

They started for the elevator. "God, that prissy suit of hers is hiding some real bazooms," Gabe said with relish.

"Yeah, and did you notice the congressman?" Holly faked enthusiasm. "Hung like a stallion."

Gabe reddened. Amazing how shocked men were to discover that women had eyes too. She let him think it over a moment because they had other things to discuss. Finally he said, "Uh, so what has Latents got?"

"Confusion," Holly reported glumly. "Two unidentified prints, both in the living room."

"Well, they may work out."

"Probably the kids' friends. Not much progress on the locked room, either. So far all they've done is confirm that the crowbar Ryan said she used really was the one used. They haven't found anything on the windows."

"Shit. I was betting on them. What about the ME?"

Holly stabbed the elevator button. "Doc said he wasn't finished."

"Wouldn't even give you a guess?"

"Oh, yeah. I pressed him and he got huffy. Said if he had to go to court this afternoon, he'd have to testify that the guy died of a heart attack."

"You're kidding!"

"He said it wasn't a simple concussion. Doc has to do some more work. And the toxicology results aren't all in but what they've got is all negative."

"Shit. What about time of death?"

"Sometime between noon and nine P.M."

"We know that already! He won't pin it down?"

"He was edgy, Gabe. Says there's been a fuck-up somewhere. Body temperature, rigor and lividity all pointing different directions. So he won't even guess until he double-checks everything."

"Shit."

"Yeah. It means no shortcuts for now. Us, we better keep all our options open."

The elevator doors slid open and they entered the cubicle. As Holly turned around to face the front she saw that someone had boarded behind them. "Hi," said Maggie soberly, hoisting Sarah and balancing her on her hip. "Turning into a tough case, isn't it?"

Holly rolled her eyes toward heaven.

Holly left Gabe to write up the reports on the Knox and Carson interviews and headed through a fresh thunderstorm for Leon Moffatt's office. It was not far from the Dulles access interchange, on the less fashionable side of a collection of low office buildings. A shiny maroon-on-buff sign that read Moffatt and Pulaski was stuck onto a gray-painted cinder-block wall next to double glass doors. Inside, the small reception area featured brown carpeting and a dramatically made-up young woman attempting to look like Raquel Welch. She was poking carefully at a typewriter keyboard, trying to keep long fingernails intact.

"I'd like to see Mr. Moffatt, please," said Holly.

"Oh, okay. What's it about?" Grateful to be released from her nail-threatening chore, the secretary stood up. Her slinky red blouse was slit most of the way to her belt.

"Police business." Holly held out her ID. "I'm Detective Schreiner."

"Oh, my God. The Blankenship thing?"

Blankenship? Holly hadn't heard anything about Blankenship. But experience had taught her that the best reaction to unexpected information was often silence. She inclined her head but didn't answer. The young woman knocked on the door at the back of the room and then pushed it open. "Mr. Moffatt, sir. Lady here says she's police." She turned back and nodded to Holly, her thick-lashed eyes wide with interest. "He says go right in."

"Thank you, Miss—um—"

"Rosalie York." She watched curiously as Holly entered Moffatt's office.

Leon Moffatt was big, thick-lipped, pink as a boiled ham. He smiled quickly and offered Holly a damp hand. "Well, the police are prettier every day! How are you?"

"I'm Detective Schreiner, Mr. Moffatt. I'd like to ask you a few questions."

He looked out into the reception area, puzzled. "You here alone, Miss Shiner?"

"Yes. I'm in charge of the investigation."

"Yeah. August, everyone on vacation, right?" He closed the door when Holly said nothing. She'd decided it would be a waste of time to tell him she was competent. Occasionally being viewed as a dumb broad had its advantages, lulling witnesses into saying more than they might to a man. But she drew the line at acting like Raquel Welch. He smiled at Holly again. "A lady detective!"

"I have a few questions for you. About Dale Colby."

"Yes, poor guy. I'll be glad to help you if I can." He motioned for Holly to take the big leather chair near the desk. She sat and found herself sliding back into its depths. It had been sized for football players like Moffatt, not for women. She put her notebook on her knees and looked coldly at Moffatt until he finished examining the fit of her trousers and sat down too. She wondered what he'd think if he knew there was a .38 strapped to her ankle under the flare legs.

Interesting, wasn't it, that he already knew that Colby was dead. Of course, by now Olivia Kerr and her buddies at the newspaper had probably phoned everyone that Dale Colby had spoken to the whole last six months.

She opened her notebook. "Now, my understanding is that Mr. Colby was interested in the plane crash last January."

"Yeah, that's true enough." He leaned back in his big chair.

"Had he been asking you about it recently?"

"God, honey, what didn't he ask about? He kept coming back with questions all the time. Don't know why he did, I could never tell him anything. I mean, I could tell him a little about Dad's business, but that was it, right? All this other stuff—" His hands gestured argumentatively. "I mean, how was I supposed to know anything about that crash? I wasn't there!"

"What do you think caused the crash?"

"Well, like I told Colby, the experts are saying terrorism. I'm no expert but I think that makes sense. I couldn't figure out why Colby was asking me."

"Maybe he thought you'd know if someone had a grudge against your father." Holly thought about scooting forward in the big chair but it was steeply slanted as well as slippery. She settled for a steady gaze.

"Who knows?" Mofatt, despite filling his chair better, didn't seem very much at ease either. "I don't know all that much about my father's business, honey. I didn't work with him."

"Did you think the investigation was progressing well?"

"God!" Moffatt snorted. "I don't know why they haven't quit by now! You know that congressman hasn't found a damn thing that wasn't in the first report. But it just goes on and on!"

"Don't you want them to find out why your father died?"

"Oh, yeah, yeah, of course," Moffatt conceded. "Except they should know when to quit, honey. Doesn't do any good to keep going over the same old stuff. Beating dead horses. The facts don't change, right? No matter how often you go over them?"

Wrong, Moffatt. A fact that made no sense the first time through might combine with another later on in a way that made the whole configuration shift. But aloud she said only, "It must be a problem for you that the investigation is still open."

He shrugged. "No big deal. Of course I want to settle the estate, honey, who wouldn't? But the lawyers say we gotta wait. So we wait."

"They're sitting on a lot of money that's rightfully yours?"

He didn't blink, he'd seen it coming. Probably Colby had asked him too. Or Olivia or the ever-present Maggie. He said smoothly, "I don't know how much. Doesn't matter anyway. The important thing is that they get it settled eventually. Damn slow lawyers! It's not just me, but all the others—you know, prolonging the agony. We just want to get it behind us, not have all these questions all the time." He smiled quickly. "Present beautiful company excepted!"

"What was your relationship with your father?"

A grimace of disgust. "It was fine! Someone's been trotting out that old stuff about college for you. Don't listen to them, honey."

"I'd like to hear your side."

"Look, it's no big deal. I'm not the only guy who wanted to break away on his own at that age. Dad was a successful man and had a lot of strong opinions. So I get to Maryland, football scholarship, coeds falling at my feet, fraternities lined up wanting me to pledge . . ." He had forgotten her legs, was blinking out the window now at the rain drenching the brick commercial row across the street. Holly wondered if he had ever again reached the ego-gratifying pinnacle of those heady days.

"Your dad must have been pleased," she prompted.

He slammed a heavy fist onto the table. "Never satisfied! He wanted me to go the executive route. Didn't like the courses I chose, didn't like my grades . . ." He looked at his fist, still clenched on the table, and pulled himself together. "Well, fathers are like that. They think they know what's best. I don't hold it against him."

Yeah, tell me another one. Holly turned the page. "He made you leave Maryland?"

"In a way. I got to drinking—you know, at that age, you want to try everything, and the parties were fun. It's easy to get carried away. And I was under all this pressure from him."

Pressure. Sure, Moffatt. Were your buddies maimed and dying all around you? Or were you maybe working twenty-hour shifts in the operating room? Holly damped the licking flames of contempt and asked levelly, "How did he find out you were drinking too much?"

"Well, my grades were shot sophomore year." Moffatt was not looking at her any more. His elbows were on his desk, his fleshy fists against his eyes. "I coulda got that under control, you know, it was just I was young yet. And one night I hit a tree and this girl I was with got hurt. Goddamn cunt sued." He cleared his throat. "Pardon my French. Anyway, Dad had to pay a whole lot even out of court. That was the end for me."

"What happened to her?" Holly inquired mildly.

"She said her face and arm got hurt. I mean, big deal, you face that stuff in a game all the time!"

Holly noted it down without asking if the goddamn cunt had been supplied with helmet and protective pads. If the elder Moffatt had paid up, the young woman must have had a damn good case against young Leon. Enough smashed bones and stitches to convince Moffatt's high-priced lawyers they couldn't win. Holly decided to look up the case later. She said, "So you had to leave college."

"Yeah. And Dad said he was finished with me, to get out on my own. Join the Army or something." He uncovered his eyes. "Well, that seemed dumb. I had a good lottery number. So I signed onto a construction crew."

"I see. Did your father stay mad?"

"For a while. But I got my act together, married Judy. He liked her. Came to the wedding and everything. Then I got a chance to buy into this outfit with Horse Pulaski. Dad came round then. It's a good business, too."

"Your dad invested in it, then?"

"Yeah, sure. Like I say, it's a good business."

So the official line was wild oats followed by mature reconciliation. Ho hum. But possibly true. Holly asked, "When Dale Colby talked to you, did he have any particular line of questioning?"

He smiled. "He asked pretty much the same questions as lady detectives ask." When she didn't smile back he coaxed, "C'mon, honey, loosen up! You could be real pretty if you'd smile!"

Holly turned crisply to a new page. "Now, just a routine question. Can you tell me where you were yesterday afternoon?"

"Sheesh." He looked at her a moment, frowning, then shrugged and answered with exaggerated businesslike coolness. "Windover Country Club. Had lunch there with a client about one o'clock, went to golf with another at two-thirty. Finished about five."

"And after that?"

"Drinks, home to the wife. Normal day."

Holly looked at him directly. "On a normal day are you angry enough at Colby to visit the *Sun-Dispatch* office and complain?"

A spasm of pain crossed his face. "God. I've never had good timing."

"Could you explain what made you so angry yesterday morning?"

A look of cunning that didn't suit his jowly face flickered through his eyes and was gone. "He just asked so many questions. He was asking about Tracy again."

"Tracy?"

"The girl who sued. I was fed up. But, listen, I bet when you ask other people, they'll be fed up with his questions too. Maybe he was just doing his job but it gets on a guy's nerves after a while."

"Yeah. Who else do you think was fed up?"

He became vague. "Oh, you know. Maybe somebody connected with that congressman Dad liked so much."

"Okay. Can you tell me anything else about Dale Colby?"

"Not really. I didn't know the guy."

"Anything else about your dad? Did he have enemies?"

He rolled his eyes up. "Everybody asks the same thing! Look, I really didn't know the details of his business. Ask his partners, his employees." He looked at the watch that dented his pudgy wrist. "Now, Miss Shiner, I do have an important lunch appointment soon."

Holly sat still. "Yes, I understand that you're very busy, Mr. Moffatt. Just a couple more questions. Can you tell me about Blankenship?"

For an instant Moffatt looked as though she'd walloped him with a two-by-four. Then he shrugged again, very casually. "That's all settled. Last fall it was settled."

"And how did the settlement affect you?"

"We could manage!" he said vehemently. "Obviously we weren't that happy about it because we weren't to blame. But it's a good business, like I say. We can swing it." He stood up. "I really do have to get ready for a meeting."

"Did Colby ask you about Blankenship?"

"No more than he asked about anything else! Now—"

She cut him off by grabbing the arms of her chair and shoving herself erect. "Thank you, Mr. Moffatt. I'll get back to you as the case develops."

"Yes." He smiled his thick-lipped smile and got up to open the door for her. "Good-bye, Miss Shiner."

"Detective Schreiner, Mr. Moffatt. Good-bye."

The reception area was empty. No people lined up for important lunch meetings, not even a receptionist at the moment. Holly started down the hall, spotted the ladies', and went in.

Moffatt's secretary was at the mirror, carefully arranging an elaborate Raquel Welch hairstyle. "Oh, hi," she said.

"Hi, Rosalie." Holly dropped her bag on the sink counter next to Rosalie and pulled out her own brush. "Your hair's gorgeous," she said in an admiring tone.

"Thanks. Takes time, though. You ever think about dying yours?" Rosalie asked, in the instant comradeship of two women sharing a mirror.

Holly looked at her own dull sandy-brown mop. "I've thought about blonde," she admitted.

"Oh, you'd look great! Course you'd have to use a little more mascara so you wouldn't look too washed out." Rosalie replaced her hairbrush and began to hunt through her big bag.

"Yeah, that's the problem," Holly told her confidingly. "This is a crazy job I've got. I got maced once at a demonstration. Cried for ten minutes, and my face looked like a zebra's. I never wore mascara to work again."

"God, I never thought of that! Me, I get caught in the rain like today and it takes two hours to recover." Rosalie produced a lip brush and began lining her mouth carefully.

Holly edged toward the topic she wanted. "You like working for Moffatt?"

"Sure. See, I'm not that fast at typing. Probably have to do grocery checkout except dear old Porky likes my style." She gave a quick hip-wriggle and grinned at Holly in the mirror, then sobered. "What were you asking him about?"

Holly pulled out her own light lipstick. She looked faded next to the younger woman. Eyes hollow, face permanently taut in a way that Rosalie's lipliners and purple eye shadow could never help. "We talked about a lot of stuff," she answered. "Like Blankenship."

"God, what a mess!" The heavily made-up eyes fluttered at Holly's image anxiously. "Is it going to be all right? I mean, I want to know because after the ruling Leon said he might have to let me go."

Holly colored her upper lip in two strokes before she said, "I don't think it will come to that. You're an important employee, right? The firm needs you."

"Yeah, sure. But if the firm is bankrupt?"

"Well—" Things were slipping into place. Holly asked, "But isn't Moffatt getting an inheritance?"

"Yeah, but I don't think that's coming through soon. The lawyers are sitting on that money."

"Still, they should be able to hang on for a while." Holly finished her mouth and dropped the lipstick into her purse.

"Maybe." Rosalie looked glum. "But it's been a year since Leon lost the suit, and he's just about run out of excuses."

"Lawyers can usually think of new ones."

"Yeah. Hey, thanks, that cheers me up." Rosalie tossed her makeup back into her bag and carefully tucked her shiny blouse into her belt to give maximum emphasis to her cleavage. She knew what Leon liked about her, all right. She picked up her bag, said, "Well, see you," and teetered toward the door in her high heels.

Holly watched the door close before pulling out her notebook to write herself a memo. So Leon Moffatt's "good business" was maybe on the edge of bankruptcy. As of last fall. And his dad had probably had his fill of bailing out his clumsy son. How convenient for Leon that his stubborn father had checked out just in time for him to inherit what the old man wouldn't give. And how annoying if a nosy reporter like Dale Colby noticed how convenient it had been.

Check the country club to see if Leon's alibi held up.

Look up the Blankenship case.

And look up Leon's rap sheet. He probably had a string of DWI's besides the crack-up with poor Tracy.

But right now Holly was only four blocks from the insurance firm where the pilot's sister worked. Priscilla Lewis. Talk to her next.

Chapter 12

Priscilla Lewis turned out to be a few years older than Holly, with dark wavy hair and smile lines flavoring her eyes. When Holly identified herself she glanced at the big clock high on the wall of the open-plan, beige and buff office. "I was about to go to lunch," she explained in a pleasant voice.

"If you're not meeting anyone, we could go together," Holly suggested. "I could use a bite myself. I just have a few questions about a reporter named Dale Colby, and about your brother."

Priscilla Lewis studied Holly for a moment, then picked up her phone and cancelled her appointment with someone named Ben. She gathered her things and smiled at Holly. "Okay. Let's go. Is the Rosebud Café all right?"

"Sure."

Over tuna salad Holly told Priscilla Lewis about Dale Colby's death. Priscilla expressed shock and confirmed that Colby had called her several times since the plane crash. "I don't think I helped him that much, though I wanted to," she said. "They don't seem to be making much headway. But it's probably something political having to do with Knox, don't you think? I don't see how it could have been directed at Corky."

"A lot of people are angry at Vietnam vets."

Priscilla's eyes were sorrowful. "Some were. I think now most people just want to forget about it."

Leave it behind you, right. Holly said, "Your brother had no enemies?"

"Not that I knew of. Or that he knew of, except maybe himself."

"Himself?"

"He was such a sweet kid." She glanced apologetically at Holly. "Okay, he was a man, but I'm the older sister. I still remember Corky as a snaggletoothed kid who was fascinated by flying. Only reason he joined the Army was to learn to fly a helicopter. He already had a private pilot's license but a chopper was a new challenge. He was just nuts about flying."

"When did he join the Army?" Holly's notebook lay on the table beside her iced tea. She picked up her fork left-handed so she could take notes with her right.

"Let's see. In 1970, I think. He'd had officer training. He was sent to Vietnam in 1970 as a captain, and he extended his tour. Finally got back late in 1972." She shook her head sadly at her salad. "He wasn't the same guy."

"Yeah. What did he do then?"

"Applied to be a civilian pilot, TWA, I think. But he got a look at the regulations and decided he couldn't take another big organization. He'd been in charge of missions in Vietnam."

"I know." Holly remembered the frustration of nursing after she'd returned. They'd actually told her to get instruction in IV's—she, who had started hundreds of them, who had even done surgery during pushes. "So he wanted to make his own decisions?"

"That's it. Corky signed on with this charter company because there's a variety of assignments and only a couple of bosses. He was doing okay. As far as the job goes, I mean. But his private life—well, he left his wife and little son. Got a divorce. His wife said he'd been drinking a lot. Seemed depressed all the time. It was true, I could see it. He wasn't the happy-go-lucky kid I remembered." Priscilla looked out the window. Cars whirred past a few blocks away on the Dulles access road. "Sometimes we'd be kidding, you know how brothers and sisters are. And he'd just sort of drift away. He got into fights at bars, too. Things he'd never done before."

"But he didn't have enemies?"

"Not that I know of."

"I'm sorry, but I have to ask this too. Was he upset enough that he might have been negligent? Or booby-trapped the plane himself, even?"

Priscilla smiled patiently. "Don't apologize, everyone asks that. The investigators, the reporters. I'm sure he didn't contribute in any way. See, most of the trouble was a couple of years ago. He was doing better by this year."

"Better?"

"Yes. First of all, it never affected his work. I met the guy who runs the charter company, oh, two years ago, maybe. We talked about Corky. He said Corky was moody but he was the best pilot they had. Really praised him. And that was right when Corky was having his roughest patch, right after the divorce and everything."

"Okay."

"But he got better after that. It's funny, I just figured out why a couple of weeks ago."

"Why?"

"About a year and a half ago he met another vet who'd been in Vietnam. Guy named Mitchell. Mitch, everyone calls him. He was one of the guys who threw their medals away. Do you remember? Back in 1971?"

Holly nodded mutely. The scene had shaken her: the angry veterans hurling their bronze and silver stars like grenades at the government that was still sending boys to Nam. The foul odor of the war had filled her nostrils again. She'd flipped off the TV and gulped a double Scotch to send that image too into the set of memories she would ignore.

"Well," Priscilla continued in her soft voice, "Mitch belonged to a group when he was in New York. You know, Viet Vets Against the War?"

"Yeah, I've heard of them."

"And they had these rap groups up there. Well, after Mitch moved down here he started a group. They meet over on Ewell Street near the feed store."

"And your brother joined them?"

"Not exactly joined. It's pretty informal. But he stopped in often, talked to them. And—I don't know how to explain it. For a while he got worse, it seemed. Angry, disgusted. That's why I didn't think it was helping him. But a couple of weeks ago I remembered that he'd said he was finally facing it. Letting it out. And it was such a relief to him to find other guys who were hurting too." Priscilla's eyes were damp. "He'd never told me anything about it. I asked him why and he said he didn't want to drag me into it too."

"I see." Holly's mouth was dry.

"He said I couldn't understand. Maybe—well, I know some things I probably couldn't understand. I remember one night a new guy had dropped into the rap group. Corky phoned me, very late at night. He was shaky about it. Crying. But he said he had to face it. I don't know who the guy was. Someone Corky had met in Vietnam soon after he arrived."

"What was it about?"

"I don't know. I just know Corky was upset. But ready to face it, you know? Not depressed."

"When was this meeting?"

"Maybe around Thanksgiving. At Christmas I asked him if he'd seen the guy again but the other vet never came back." Priscilla stirred her iced tea and spoke as though reading her thoughts in the ice cubes. "Corky was so hard to talk to after the war. So hard. Maybe he was right, maybe I couldn't understand him any more."

Yep, that happened. Unexpected grief welled up in Holly's throat at this tiny tragedy of a brother transformed, wrenched from his sister. She swallowed the last of her tuna as soon as she could get her throat to work, sipped some tea, and changed the subject. "What were the terms of your brother's will?"

Priscilla shook her head with a sad little smile. "Everything he had was supposed to go to his son. Skipping his ex-wife, you know? But it turned out that after his debts were paid there was only about three hundred bucks."

"Can you think of any reason someone would want to kill him?"

"No. Colby kept asking that too. And of course I wasn't really communicating with Corky so well. But what could it be? Not money. Not any problem at work. No girlfriends. And he didn't seem worried." She shook her head fretfully. "No, that's wrong. He was always depressed, angry. But it really seemed to be getting better those last months. Like I told Colby, I guess that rap group was—helping."

At the little catch in her voice, Holly looked up from her notes. Tears were sliding down Priscilla Lewis's cheeks. Holly pulled a paper napkin from the container and handed it to her. "Here," she said gently.

"Thank you." Priscilla mopped her face. "I do miss him."

"Yeah."

Corky Lewis did not seem a likely target for terrorists or any other bombers. It was really more because Priscilla had told Colby about the rap group that Holly decided to take a look at Mitch Mitchell before going to the *Sun* office. She turned into Ewell Street, in the commercial area around a former railroad spur. There were a few offices, some boarded up, some serving the businesses there. Cement, agricultural supplies, plumbing. One window had two signs: a big white-on-orange Office for Rent and underneath, a hand-scrawled card that said Viet Vets Survival Counseling.

She was a cop now. It was all behind her, further every day. Besides, Mitch probably wouldn't be in anyway.

Holly knocked.

"Come on in!"

A small room crusted with cream-colored paint, chipped to reveal former days of turquoise or forest green. Gray-green marbled linoleum worn to its black backing along the path from the door. Scarred desk shoved against a wall, covered with leaflets. An oscillating fan. A telephone. A Bob Dylan poster, curled ragged at the edges. With a red marking pen someone had printed "How many times must the cannonballs fly?" across it. A battered brown sofa, several mismatched chairs. A brown metal wastebasket full of cigarette butts sat proudly in the center of the room.

Two men in jeans and T-shirts lounged on the sofa, both smoking. One was lanky, weak-chinned, with a prominent Adam's apple. The other was shorter, muscular, with shaggy black hair and a mustache. The thin drawn skin of a burn scar replaced half his left eyebrow and fanned back across his forehead until it disappeared under the long hair. In the back of her mind the blue-green slime oozed, the stench turned her stomach. She blinked it down and forced herself to face him: a man who was healed, healthy, alive. "Hi, babe," he said cheerfully. "What can we do for you?"

"Priscilla Lewis said you knew her brother Corky."

"God, yes." Abruptly serious, the scarred man leaned forward, elbows on knees, stubby cigarette dangling from his fingers. "What a waste," he said bitterly. "It never ends, you know? Good man, Corky."

"Did a reporter named Colby call to ask about him recently?"

"Last week, yeah." He stretched his arm toward the wastebasket and began to grind out his cigarette against the side. "You from that paper too? Like I said to him, I can only tell you general stuff about how we work here. Everything in the rap group is confidential unless a guy decides to tell someone else himself."

"But Corky Lewis is dead now."

He looked up at her, right hand still holding the butt against the wastebasket. There was fierceness in his eyes but his voice was mild. "Lady, I don't betray the dead."

She was startled, ashamed and yet strangely joyful. This man was on the same side of the chasm. She said, "I'm not asking you to."

"Good." He leaned back again in the sofa and waved his hand toward the chairs. "Hey, sit down if you want. I'm Mitch and this is Bill."

Holly sat on a worn oak desk chair. "I'm Holly Schreiner."

"And you're from that paper?"

"No. The reporter you talked to—Dale Colby—was killed yesterday. I'm a detective."

Very slowly, Mitch crossed his arms. The left one was taut-skinned and hairless like his brow. "Shit. A detective. A cop." His voice had gone cold.

"Yes. Colby was murdered."

"So naturally you look for the nearest Viet vet to pin it on. We're all killers, right?" He popped his hands suddenly to his head and rayed out wiggling fingers. "And all wacko besides!"

Bill laughed uneasily.

"Look, I'm not here to spit on you," Holly protested. The words brought echoes of last night: nosy Maggie, and herself as prickly as Mitch was now. And Alec calling her a crazy broad. She explained earnestly, "I'm looking for whoever murdered Colby. It's my job. That's all."

Mitch dropped his hands and studied her a minute. "God, you're serious, aren't you? But I still can't help."

Bill stood up nervously and flicked his cigarette into the wastebasket. "Gotta get back to work."

"Okay. See you later, hombre."

They both watched him leave.

Holly said, "Priscilla told me Corky was getting a lot from your group. But he was upset by another vet who came once."

Mitch shrugged, his expression unreadable.

"Look," Holly said, "another man has been killed. If you know anything that'll help make sense of his death, please tell me."

Uneasiness flickered in Mitch's eyes. "Can't," he said.

"Well, can you tell me what you told Colby?"

"Sure. Doubt if it'll help, it was pretty general. No names. Just Intro to Viet Vets Lecture One."

Holly fished out her notebook. "I'd like to know what you told him."

Mitch stretched across the sofa arm to pull open a desk drawer. Inside was a pack of cigarettes and a lighter. "Smoke?" he asked.

"Thanks."

He lit both cigarettes, handed her one, then propped a foot on the wastebasket, crossed the other over it, and lounged back on the sofa again. "Okay. About the rap group. It's just a bunch of guys who went over to Nam because they were about seventeen and they believed in John Wayne, right? Freedom, democracy, truth, helping the underdog, ask not what your country can do for you, you know?"

"Yeah." She knew.

"Okay, about two days after you arrive you find out it's all a fraud. Freedom and democracy are just not top priorities. Shit, it was our side that cancelled the elections, right? Fraid they'd lose to Ho. The army we're helping doesn't want to fight and it's half Cong anyway. You airlift them to some battle and some of them turn around and fire at our fucking helicopter!"

"Right," Holly muttered. She knew that. Why tell anyone? Why couldn't he forget?

He went on, "If you take a hill you have to turn it over to ARVN and they lose it. You learn real fast that whatever it is the gooks want, it ain't us. So okay, forget freedom and democracy and helping the underdog. Now at least you know the truth. But you've got to survive to tell it. And help your buddies survive."

Should she tell him she was there, stop this gush of painful stories? But she wanted to know what he'd told Dale Colby. She nodded and tapped ash into the wastebasket with a shaky hand.

"But your buddies get killed," Mitch continued. "Not for democracy, not for freedom, not even for a piece of territory. But really dead. You're terrified. You're full of hate and grief. You want revenge. Kill the enemy, says the brass. Up the body count. They send you into some ville. No Cong. So you start raping and shooting out of pure frustration." Mitch paused and eyed Holly suspiciously, a little frown contracting his good brow. "Hey, about now women usually start whimpering, no, no, that's terrible, no decent person would do that."

Holly shook her head. "No," she said hoarsely. "You're right."

"You bet your sweet ass I'm right. In that situation just about anybody would do it. John Wayne himself would do it. I mean, part of you knows it's wrong but part of you is really enjoying the revenge. Except it's a phony revenge. You mow down maybe twenty people. And you find no weapons. But you count twenty Cong and no civilians. If they're dead they're Cong, right? Keep the brass happy. All dead gooks are Cong." He leaned forward intently, mismatched arms on his knees, and said softly, "And that's when you find in your heart that you've lost the war.

Because you don't even stand for truth any more. You've joined the goddamn fraud."

Holly nodded mutely. Why, why, why? Don't ask me I don't give a damn. She didn't want to hear. How many times must the cannonballs fly? She wanted to forget.

Mitch said, "You okay?"

"Yes." Get it together, Schreiner, stay cool. She took a long pull on her cigarette.

He said, "See, I've got to explain where the rap group comes from."

"Yeah. Go ahead."

He tapped ash into the wastebasket and leaned back again. "Okay. One thing stays real, and that's dying. So you lock your guilt and pain away in the back rooms of your mind, and concentrate on surviving. You slog on through the swamps, the rats. The jungle rot. The leeches. The terror. You get sick, you get wounded, but you survive. A fantastic achievement. And finally the good old Braniff freedom bird takes you away, back to the land of youth and innocence and John Wayne."

"Disney World," said Holly.

Mitch laughed, a short bitter burst of appreciation. "You got it, sister. And back in Disney World, well, you don't expect parades, you know you didn't liberate France or take Iwo Jima. But you did your best, you survived in a damn tough job. So what happens? You get back and half the country thinks you're scum because you went. The other half thinks you're scum because you lost."

Holly bowed her head. Mitch's words hurt, ripping open wounds she'd thought were safely scabbed over. Why wouldn't he shut up? Nothing to be done about it now. She cleared her throat and asked, "Why not forget it, then? Leave it behind you?"

"Oh, sure, you try that first. Try to forget. Numb out. But you fail. Of course you fail. How can a human being let his buddies go unremembered? That's where the rap group comes in. Guys come in here, claim they don't remember. But they're having nightmares, or violent outbursts, or flashbacks. Or they've built walls to keep away life." His words pounded at her. "That's phony forgetting, just as phony as the war. So the rap group is a place to confront reality. It hurts, sure. But we help each other through the pain. Then a guy can move on. Reorder his world. Renew his life."

"You can do that?"

"We can help a guy do it for himself."

"Doesn't it hurt you to hear it?"

"Sure. I'm no machine. I'm human, so it hurts." His eyes were fierce again. "But avoiding it is phony. And I've had it with phoniness, sister. I've seen Death's face and Death's backside, and I survived. And I'm going to make my survival mean something. This group is my way of wrestling one little bit of Disney World into something worthy of my dead. Something authentic."

Something authentic.

She'd written it in her book. She blacked it out with careful strokes of her pen.

"Anyway," Mitch added more gently, "while a guy is figuring himself out he's damn fragile. No way am I going to expose him to the cops until he thinks he's ready."

The cops. That's you, Schreiner. Get the information. She asked, "No matter what he's done?"

A bitter grin. He jerked a thumb at his own chest. "I've done worse, sister. I personally have done worse. And Disney World tried to give me medals for it."

That TV image of the hurled medals bubbled to the top of Holly's mind. "Yeah. I understand." She cleared her throat again. "But what if he can help us find why some other guy died? Make sense of it for his family?"

Mitch looked uneasy. "I hear you," he said. "About making sense. But I can't break a confidence."

"Yeah."

They both ground out their cigarettes.

"Look, I'll tell you what I can do," Mitch suggested. "I'll give the guy your phone number. But it's totally up to him and I'll tell him that too."

"Yeah. Okay." She was touched by his protectiveness. She scribbled her name and phone number on a page, tore it out for him, and asked timidly, "Are there women in the rap group?"

Mitch laughed. "God, no! What would a woman know about it?"

She swallowed and said, "Well, I was a nurse. I saw a lot of deaths."

He looked interested but shook his head as though trying to be kind. "Ain't the same, sister. I mean, nurses prevent deaths. Our guys were pulling the trigger. Even if we did it to survive, even if our fucking country told us to, we've got to deal with guilt. Depression. Rage."

"Yeah. I understand."

"No! I'm saying you *can't* understand!"

Holly blinked down at her notes. Even Mitch thought she

shouldn't feel the way she did. She must be crazy. Schreiner the crazy broad. The scum of the scum.

She put on her impassive cop look, closed her notebook, stood up. "Thanks for passing on the message, Mitch. I'll wait for his call."

"If he calls—you'll remember what I said?"

Holly paused at the door, bleakly. "Oh, yeah. I'll remember." She went out into the rain.

Chapter 13

Olivia sat stiffly in a living room in Westwood Heights, amidst carved teak, an immensely thick blue-on-ivory Chinese rug, a photo of Frank Resler gazing from a carved wood frame, raw-silk walls. The dumpy woman across from her was in silk too, black mourning silk that should have minimized her stoutness but instead sliced across her body at the wrong places so that her thick neck and thick legs glowed in pale contrast. She should have been wearing a comfy housedress, but clearly she felt an obligation to blend into her elegant surroundings.

Her handkerchief, at least, was a plain white cotton workaday model, slightly damp.

"My husband was devoted to his clients," Doris Resler told Olivia. "I know Mr. Colby and that other reporter thought someone might have been dissatisfied but I don't see how that could be! Why, Frank worked so hard for each and every one of them. And Mr. Edgerton agreed with me."

No wonder she'd looked so satisfied as she left Edgy's office yesterday. Olivia put down her coffee cup on the ceramic Chinese table. The air-conditioning here was set a notch higher than most and the hot drink had brought a film of moisture to her face. "What kind of clients did he have?"

"Why, all kinds," said Doris Resler. "They were accused of muggings, robberies, murders, negligence, pollution—"

Pollution? "Some of his clients were corporations?" Olivia asked. Made sense. It would take a lot of fees from muggers to buy that rug.

"Well, some, yes. Took up a dreadful amount of Frank's time. Frank always said he preferred to work with ordinary people. Help them out, help them remake their lives. Like Bob Bates." Doris wiggled forward to the edge of her chair. "Have you met Bob Bates?"

"No, not yet." He'd blown up an armored truck, Nate had said.

"Oh, well, let me call him. I think you'll understand why I want my husband's work to go on." Doris Resler hopped up and scurried to the French doors, fat calves and small feet twitching along below the black silk. To Olivia's surprise, she opened the door and called out, "Bob? Bob, come in and meet someone!" She returned to her chair with a satisfied smile at Olivia. "He's coming. I've given him the spare room over the garage, so he can help out. You know, I think if I could have introduced Bob to Mr. Colby he would have understood better. But Mr. Colby wouldn't come. He was getting to be like that first reporter, that Jewish fellow, so sure that someone might have had a grudge against Frank." She looked back at the man who was entering through the French window.

Bob Bates was middle-aged and middle-sized, lean and tanned. He carried himself humbly, though the quick eyes under handsome brows seemed shrewd enough. His brown hair was silvering at the temples, which added a touch of distinction. In fact, if it hadn't been for a purple snake tattooed on his forearm, he might have been mistaken for a banker. Or a lawyer, like Resler? Olivia stole a peek at the photograph framed in ornate carved wood that sat centered on a Chinese chest like a little shrine. No real resemblance, but the same air, the same type. Except that Frank Resler, in the photo, looked definitely haughty rather than humble.

Doris Resler was saying, "Bob, I was just telling Olivia about you. She works at the same paper as poor Mr. Colby who was killed."

"Killed?" The handsome eyebrows climbed Bates' forehead. "You mean hit by a car or what?"

"No," Olivia explained. "He was murdered at his home. We know he was working on the story about the plane crash last January, so we thought we'd ask you if you remembered his general line of questioning recently."

"I see," said Bob Bates slowly. His voice was educated enough. With a pinstripe suit he could probably walk up to any bank in the country. Could even get some employee to lead him to their armored truck. As long as that snake was hidden. Bob asked, "So you're thinking that something he was investigating may have caused the trouble?"

"Well, I've got to look into the possibility. The reason for the plane crash is still unknown." At Olivia's words, Doris Resler gave a sniffle and brandished her big cotton handkerchief. Olivia went on, "I mean, if Dale had learned something about who caused the tragedy, the guilty party wouldn't want it published, right?"

"Are there other possible reasons for Colby's death?" Bob wanted to know.

"Sure. But this story is a definite possibility too," said Olivia tartly.

Bob Bates smiled. Good teeth too. What on earth had possessed him to get that tattoo? He said, "Well, I'll be glad to tell you whatever I can to help. Though I'm afraid it won't be much."

"Can you tell me where you were yesterday afternoon?" Olivia asked boldly.

"I was right here, working in the garden," said Bates glibly. "The garden suffered terribly in the heat wave."

"Oh, yes, it did," agreed Doris Resler.

"And what time did you get back, Mrs. Resler?"

"Back?" The widow looked puzzled.

"You were at the *Sun-Dispatch* office around noon."

"She arrived here before one," said Bates. "And we worked on foundation business all afternoon."

"Now, Bob, let me tell you why I asked you to come in," Doris Resler said pettishly, as though she didn't understand the relevance of Olivia's question or Bob Bates's answer. "You see, Miss Kerr was just asking about Mr. Colby's idea that one of Frank's clients might have been angry at him. I just wanted you to explain how good Frank was."

"He was a hell of a guy," Bob Bates confirmed. "I'm the first to admit I had a serious drinking problem. Blacked out for days sometimes. Couldn't keep a job. I ended up resorting to some very unscrupulous things." He was clenching and unclenching his hands in tension or distress at the recollection. The play of muscles in his forearm made the purple snake writhe in an oddly voluptuous way. Bob's eyes flicked up, catching Olivia staring at it. She could have sworn there was an edge of mockery in his voice as he concluded, "I was arrested."

"I see," said Olivia heartily, hoping that her warm cheeks just meant the room was hot.

"Luckily I was working for a firm that was concerned about its own possible liability, and they went to the top. To Frank Resler."

He bowed his head toward Doris, who smiled a tearful proud smile. "And Frank not only got me a lighter sentence than I deserved, he turned around my life."

"How?" asked Olivia.

"Advice plus concrete help," Bob Bates explained. "He encouraged me to join AA. And when I got out of prison, he helped me financially while I took a couple of business courses. Really showed he had faith in me."

"And now you have a job?"

Doris started to say something but Bates said quickly, "Yes. I'm working for a hardware wholesaler. Mosby Hardware."

"And the firm you were working for before?"

The snake rippled on his arm. Why hadn't Nate mentioned it? Of course Nate had spoken to him back in January, and had been pulled off the story soon afterward. Bates said wryly, "Well, of course they didn't want me back. I'd blown up their truck, after all."

"No. I meant, were they held liable?"

"No. Frank got them off scot-free."

Hah. Olivia had been sure that the picture Doris Resler had presented, of a lawyer devoted to kind treatment of reformed criminals and only grudgingly spending time working for corporations, was oversimplified. Bob Bates's story made it clear that he, at least, would not have enjoyed Resler's services if he'd had to depend on his own resources. And he'd served time while the corporation he worked for hadn't even paid a fine.

Bates was watching her closely. "I was guilty, you see." That hint of mockery was in his voice again. "They'd put me in a position of trust but Frank proved I was the one who'd tricked them. No, I've faced up to it now. I was guilty. Now I must move beyond that."

"You've paid your debt to society, you mean," Olivia said ironically.

But his eyes moved to Doris Resler and he responded seriously. "No. Time in jail is punishment, all right. But it doesn't help society, or help the victims."

Doris had been quiet as long as she could stand it. "That's what Frank always said! And he tried to instill in his clients the desire to do better, to improve the world."

"Was he successful with many clients?"

"Quite a few, yes," Doris replied. "I know you reporters are very cynical people. But Bob here, and Mrs. London, and William Schultz—oh, there are quite a few. And Frank used to tell me he wished he could set up an organization to aid offenders, help them find their talents."

"Aren't there other groups that do that already?" Olivia had personally written a feature on one of them.

"You mean the literacy programs and church counselors?" Bob Bates managed to sound contemptuous even while maintaining his air of humble courtesy. "Yes, those people mean well, and of course they help some. But they don't really get a man back into society."

"Yes, Frank's idea was much more ambitious," Doris explained. "It would work like AA partly, but it would have funding for necessary support mechanisms."

"Support mechanisms?"

Doris Resler looked as uncertain about the term as Olivia was. "To, well, support the people after they've served their time. And so that's what I'm doing, as a memorial to Frank. It's my duty and joy to carry on his work!"

"I see." Olivia looked from plump triumphant Doris to smooth, humble, tattooed Bob. She was afraid she understood. "You said like AA," she ventured cautiously. "So there's a role for people like Mr. Bates?"

"I'll do what I can," said Bob Bates.

"He's an enormous help!" Doris explained. "Of course that nice woman in Representative Knox's office helps some, and Frank's law partners with the legal stuff. But Bob is the one who's crucial. Because he really knows." She beamed at her husband's protégé.

Olivia tried one last time. "But there must still be a few clients who served time and didn't understand that your husband did his best. Because they still went to jail, or something."

"Ungrateful, you mean." Bob Bates shrugged.

"Yes. Or opponents, maybe, who might think Mr. Resler freed someone who deserved punishment."

"If so, they didn't bother Mr. Resler. They'd be more likely to go after the person they thought was guilty. That was certainly who I was mad at."

"You never heard him talk about ungrateful clients, Mrs. Resler?" Olivia asked.

"No. He was a very positive person, you see. He was more interested in success. Well, every now and then he would complain that someone wouldn't help him defend themselves. But they all thanked him in the end. They knew he did his best."

"He explained things to us," Bob Bates added. "We knew what was possible."

"I see," said Olivia.

Bob Bates said humbly, "It's important to have a memorial to such a fine lawyer and human being."

"Frank Resler will never die!" declared Doris through her damp handkerchief.

Enough, Olivia decided. She stood up abruptly. "I'm glad I met you, Mr. Bates. And thank you very much for your help, Mrs. Resler. I'll be back if I hear of any developments."

"Yes, thank you." Doris Resler was on her feet now, smiling anxiously. "You do understand now, don't you? Now that you've talked to Bob?"

"Oh, yes." Olivia let them walk her to the door. "I understand."

Her last view of them as she turned from the walk into the driveway was of Doris Resler closing her expensive paneled door while Bob Bates stood protectively beside her, murmuring comfort into her ear.

Olivia looked at her watch. She still had an hour and a half before she had to meet Nate and Edgy. She decided to stop by her own house.

Nick and Maggie were in the living room finishing a plate of sandwiches. The three children were in the dining room, Josie staring out the bay window at the yard, Tina and little Sarah inventing an adventure for the Barbie dolls. Olivia couldn't hear them because John Denver was singing on the stereo. "Hi," she said to Nick and Maggie, grabbing a sandwich. Tuna. "Where's Donna?"

"At the funeral director's," said Nick. "One of the teachers at her school came by. The one called Linda that she called last night. She wanted to know what she could do to help. So I said I'd watch the kids if she'd take Donna to arrange the funeral. I thought maybe a few minutes away from the kids and us strangers might be good for her."

"Good idea. Poor Donna." Olivia shed her shoulder bag onto a chair and dropped into another near them to eat her sandwich. "She's such a traditional woman, isn't she? Mother, wife, schoolteacher. Perfect house, perfect kids."

"Coping with Parkinson's isn't my idea of perfection," Maggie mumbled around a mouthful of tuna sandwich.

"God, I didn't mean it was a picnic!" Olivia exclaimed. "I know it's damn tough. Hell, coping with a reporter is tough even without Parkinson's. Just ask Jerry."

"Right." Maggie grinned.

"But that's really another example of what I meant," Olivia

explained, munching a pickle. "Perfect nurse. All those traditional roles she did so well. And now this happens. It must be especially hard for someone whose life revolves totally around someone else. I mean, she wouldn't have the resources she'd have with more of a life of her own."

Nick was shaking his head sadly. "The resources you think you have don't save you," he said gently.

Belatedly, Olivia remembered that his first wife had died. He'd experienced Donna's tragedy firsthand.

Maggie said, "It's tempting to turn our backs, to say Donna's different and we'd never get hurt like that, because we've arranged our lives better. But Nick's right. We're all vulnerable."

"Yeah," Olivia admitted awkwardly. Then, in a burst of honesty, "God, I hate thinking I could be devastated like that! It's almost easier to think of dying myself."

Maggie reached for her hand and squeezed it. "Yeah." After a moment she asked gently, "So what's the news, newswoman?"

Olivia returned to the puzzle. "Just saw Mrs. Resler. Weird situation there."

"Weird? How?"

"Okay. Rich widow, right? As soon as they finish investigating the plane crash, she'll be even richer. Apparently her husband was interested in helping his clients after they got out of prison. So she's setting up a foundation to help such people. Self-help groups plus money and education, I gather. Frank Resler's name will never die."

"Well, that sounds a normal enough goal," said Nick.

"Yeah, but what worries me is the self-help expert. Ex-con named Bob Bates. Near as I can see, he's the guiding force behind the foundation. I wouldn't be surprised if he arranges things so he can skip with the Resler Foundation money one of these days."

"Why did he go to jail?"

"Apparently he got a bank to hire him. He's smooth. Well-bred yet humble. A con job of some type because the bank was worried about its own liability when he blew up their armored truck."

Maggie was interested. "Blew up?"

"His own words."

"So besides being a con man, he knows explosives."

"As in making a plane crash. Right. Plus, he knew Resler's situation, and obviously the widow turned to him immediately when her husband died."

"Why was she asking Dale Colby to be discreet?"

"She was upset at his suspicion that some of Resler's clients might be ungrateful enough to blow up his plane. But meanwhile there's dear Bob Bates patting her hand consolingly and getting her to set up the foundation."

"And what were they doing yesterday afternoon?"

"He lives on the premises now. They say they were working on foundation business all afternoon. The call to Dale was just one example."

"Very interesting," said Maggie. "A couple to keep in mind. How about Moffatt?"

"Nate's going to tackle him."

"Because someone in the construction business would know explosives too."

"Right. Now, what did you find out from your friend in Congressman Knox's office?"

"I found out she's half in love with Knox. And maybe because of that, she's most nervous about the accusations of Ann Kauffmann's father. Ann was a college student, temporary aide to Knox's office."

"Hanky-panky with a sweet young thing?" That always made good copy. Olivia thought of Wilbur Mills and Fanne Fox.

"Yes. Mr. Kauffmann claims his daughter was done in as in Chappaquiddick."

"Wow." Olivia took the last sandwich so she could think better. "But Dale didn't say anything about that."

"It's probably not true. Carol Carson denies it vehemently."

"Dale was always super-careful with his stories, too," said Olivia. "Wanted to be in total control of the facts. That was his real strength as a reporter. Triple-checking."

"There's another problem," Maggie pointed out. "Let's say for some reason Knox wanted to get rid of the girl. He could find someone to blow up the plane, I'm sure. But he wouldn't blow up another aide and two major donors at the same time, would he?"

"You're right. Still, it's worth nosing around. What are you doing next?" She stood up to inspect herself in the mirror over the mantel and brushed a crumb from her mouth.

Nick said, "The police called just after Donna left to say the Colbys could go back home, except the one room should stay sealed. So we can help get them settled."

"Is Donna in any shape to talk to?" Olivia asked hopefully.

"Still pretty zombie-like."

"You think she'll let down her hair with her friend?"

"Probably," said Nick. "May or may not help you."

"I'm worried about Josie too," said Maggie soberly, with a tiny jerk of her head toward the immobile girl in the dining room. "She just sits there like a stone."

"Poor kid."

"Anyway, Nick and I can get the Colbys settled in again. Then I'll check on Ann Kauffmann's story."

"Fine." Olivia retrieved her bag.

"I also want to call the woman in Harrisburg that Felicia mentioned. Nan Evans," Maggie said.

"Felicia's alibi. Right," Olivia said. "That's great. I've got to meet Nate and my editor at two, and I'll follow up on the pilot. We could meet back here late this afternoon."

"It's a deal."

Olivia looked at her watch as she puddle-hopped back to the van. Still plenty of time before she was due at the *Sun-Dispatch* meeting. With sudden decision, she pulled out the address she'd looked up in the phone book after she and Nick got back from the bar last night. She'd get the interview with the pilot's friend out of the way now. Ernie Grant, she'd written. Appleyard Road off Vale.

The hills northwest of Mosby were cut-velvet green, as though some titanic seamstress had dropped the rumpled fabric across Virginia, clipped areas yielding suddenly to the deeper pile of forest and underbrush in a gigantic pattern that couldn't be read from Olivia's lowly vantage point. It was like this investigation, Olivia thought. She was too close to see the logic of it. Fragments of pattern would attract her attention—Bob Bates' influence on the widow Resler, Felicia Colby's fierce battles for her son, Leon Moffatt's fury at Dale in the office yesterday. But what was design, what was background?

She drove past a great gash in the earth, a construction project, green stripped away by giant Tonka toys that grunted across the muddy landscape, carving it into a different shape. At one end of the gash a couple of houses with matchstick skeletons were rising from the bared earth, substanceless until a skin of clapboards would make them suddenly real and solid. Above her, ranks of clouds nosed their way balefully over the crests of the hills like a pack of furry dark beasts grazing the sky.

Appleyard Road was the next right. Olivia almost overshot it, but managed to pull the van around by veering into the wrong lane briefly. The road, narrower than Vale, twined upwards, tucked into the folds of the hills. On her right, on the other side of the hill from the construction project, the land was divided into fields by a wire fence, but they were overgrown meadows rather than tilled crop fields. On ahead were woods, posted against trespassers. Old woods. Ghostly in their dampness. Union soldiers in these parts had lived in dread of Colonel Mosby's raiders, who materialized from these very woods to strike and melt away, back into genial civilian farmers once again. She remembered a fragment of Melville's poem about Union cavalry troops returning to camp after one such bloody encounter: "Each eye dim as a sickroom lamp, All faces stamped with Mosby's stamp."

The mailbox peeped suddenly from the massed Queen Anne's lace beside the road. Grant, it said. Good Union name. Beyond it, half-hidden by the high grasses, a wide crushed-stone driveway led back toward a cluster of buildings. Red barns, solid but peeling in places. A sturdy square white house with a full-width porch sitting in an acre or so of ragged lawn. From the corner of her eye she glimpsed a shadow moving in the patchy hedge beside the drive. She drew up behind a Chevy pickup truck, as close to the house as she could get, and peered out suspiciously at the hedge. No one. Mosby's ghost, maybe.

Olivia squinted at the house. The windows facing the porch were cracked open, the curtains within stirring in the breeze. And the truck was here. So maybe someone was home, though in the country you never knew. Could be out riding a tractor or feeding the hogs. She picked up her tape recorder and notebook, gave the silent hedge one more careful look, and opened the van door.

An explosion of noise sharp as guncracks, a flash of fang and brown fur. Olivia shrieked and slammed the door again in the face of the raging dog. German shepherd, part of her mind catalogued, while her heart kicked in her chest like a rabbit in a sack. Goddamn German shepherd.

"Sarge!" A male voice broke authoritatively through the hoarse bombardment of barking. "Off!"

Sudden silence. The big animal, tan with smoky black saddle and mask, trotted wagging past the front of the van toward Olivia's savior. "Lie down," the man said conversationally, and when the dog dropped, "Good dog. Hey, lady, you can get out now!"

"Are you sure?" Olivia's mouth was dry. Her heart was still thudding.

"Sure I'm sure. Old Sergeant Rock, he won't do a thing unless I tell him to."

What would Woodward or Bernstein do? Or Gloria Steinem? They'd get out and get the story, Olivia decided unhappily. She pushed down the door handle, eyeing the dog unwaveringly. Nothing. She pushed the door open a crack. He didn't budge. She took a deep breath, sternly instructed her knees not to collapse, and climbed out.

Sergeant Rock lay calmly on the porch.

"You're a brave lady," said the man.

"Thanks, I guess." If this was what brave felt like, she'd hate to try fear. She flicked her gaze to the man for a brief instant. A short dark beard, nice smile with dimples, but dull brooding eyes. *Dim as a sickroom lamp.* He wore jeans, a maroon plaid shirt with the sleeves rolled up, a Day-Glo orange vest and billed hunter's cap. Upright against his shoulder, pointed casually at the porch ceiling, was a rifle. Fancy telescopic sight, the whole gleaming with the sheen of loving care.

Sergeant Rock blinked sleepily at her.

"He's a very obedient dog," Olivia said, as much to convince herself as to the man.

"Oh, yeah. He's been to school. Attack dogs like this, they get heavy-duty training. Total control."

"Well, that's good." Olivia licked her dry lips. "Um, I'm looking for Ernie Grant."

"That's me."

"I'm Olivia Kerr."

"Hi, Olivia Kerr." He grinned again, the smile lines disappearing into his beard. "And Sergeant Rock you've already met."

"Yes, I sure have. Um, I was wondering if you'd talked to a guy named Dale Colby recently." She was poised to leap back into the van if the dog or the rifle moved. Drops of rain were beginning to fall again, but she sure as hell wasn't going onto that porch.

But Ernie Grant merely shook his head. "Dale Colby. No, I don't know him."

"Middle-aged guy, sandy hair—can I show you a picture?" She glanced fearfully at the dog.

"Just a minute." He swung open the front door. "Sarge, inside!"

The dog ambled in politely. Ernie Grant shut the door on him and smiled at Olivia. "He wouldn't do anything, but you still seem nervous," he explained.

"Yeah. Thanks. He's quite a dog." Olivia pulled out the photo of Dale and walked up the porch steps. Ernie leaned the rifle next to the door behind him and studied the picture.

"No," he said, shaking his head again. "Never met him. How come you ask?"

"Well, he was a reporter."

"A reporter?" Wariness flared in Grant's dark eyes. Olivia decided to go step by step.

"Yes. He was working on a story about a plane crash. Do you remember? Back in January. Representative Knox's plane?"

She had his attention now. The skin around his eyes had tensed as he studied her face. "What about it?"

"Well, I was told you knew one of the guys in that plane. The pilot. Corky Lewis."

He stared at her, unmoving. She wasn't sure he'd heard.

She said nervously, "Well, did you?"

"Did I what?" His gaze was on her but his thoughts could have been on the moon.

"Were you a friend of Corky Lewis?"

"A friend." The dimpled smile returned suddenly. "A friend of ole Cap'n Corky. You want to know if I was his friend."

"So you did know him!" She had begun to wonder if the bartender had somehow misremembered. "Well, I was wondering if you could tell me a little about him."

"What's it to you, lady?" He was wary again. "What are you really after?"

There was a story here, all right. There was also Sergeant Rock and that rifle. Olivia wished she'd brought Nate along. Or Nick. She held out her palm in a gesture of appeasement. "Sorry! Let me explain how I got involved."

"Yeah. Do that." He hooked his thumbs in his belt loops, the immemorial no-nonsense position. Olivia decided to avoid nonsense.

She said, "Dale Colby was a friend of mine. He got killed while he was working on a story about the plane that crashed. He was talking to a lot of people. The congressman, and that developer Moffatt, and the lawyer's widow. So I thought maybe he'd talked to you. And—"

"He didn't. Why would he talk to me?"

Olivia smiled nervously. The Donovan's Bar napkin glowed in her memory. This man, not Moffatt or Bates, had been at Dale's despite his claims not to know him. And she realized uneasily that the nearest humans were those guys in the bulldozers back around the hill at the turnoff. Working in that clamor of mechanical noise they'd never hear a scream or even Sergeant Rock's barking from over here. Olivia said soothingly, "Well, Dale talked to a lot of people. But if he didn't talk to you, well, that's all I wanted to know." She moved down the steps toward the van. "Sorry to bother you."

"Wait."

Olivia turned, still backing toward the van. "Yeah?" she said in what she hoped was a friendly confident voice.

He came down the steps toward her. "This Dale you keep talking about. What paper is he with?"

"Mosby *Sun-Dispatch*. And so am I."

"You're a *Sun-Dispatch* reporter too?" He looked incredulous.

"Yeah. But if Dale didn't talk to you, that's okay, never mind." She swiped raindrops from her forehead, took another step back.

"Hey, I think you ought to come inside a minute."

"No, it's okay," Olivia soothed. "Sorry I bothered you." Her fingers finally found the handle of the van door.

"I don't want to hurt you. I just want to make a call." He jerked a thumb toward the farmhouse door. "C'mon."

"Well, make your call and I'll check back with you a little later, okay?" Olivia wrenched open the van and jabbed her keys into the ignition as she slammed the door behind her. She spun the wheel and started backing up. She had to make a K-turn to clear the pickup truck and switch directions without going into the ditch. But the driveway was plenty wide.

Ernie Grant was running up the steps back toward the farmhouse door. She was free. Or was he going to release the dog? But Sergeant Rock couldn't get into the van anyway. Olivia completed her turn and began to roll down the driveway. She'd be back, of course. Bring Nate, maybe even tip off the cops. Because there was one hell of a story here. She could taste it.

Then the world lurched.

Green unkempt hills zipped upward to the left, thick tangled weeds of the ditch careened toward her in a blur, clarifying at last into the rain-sparkled cheeriness of Queen Anne's lace and black-eyed Susans nodding welcome a few inches from her eyes. Her forehead rested somehow on the steering wheel.

Ernie Grant was opening her door, slinging the rifle back over his shoulder, grabbing her wrist to help her out. "I'm not going to hurt you," he said gently. "Just hang around until I make my call, okay? I'll help you change your tire in a few minutes."

Her tire. Olivia gaped at the van, which tilted drunkenly into the ditch, rain sliding down its roof, front tire flat as an old toothpaste tube. Mystified, she rubbed her forehead with her free hand.

"Did you hurt yourself?"

"Bumped my head."

He peered at it solicitously without releasing her wrist. "It'll be okay. C'mon, let's go in."

There was no choice now.

Help would come eventually.

He said he wouldn't hurt her.

Her job until then was straightforward if not simple.

Survive.

But one tiny unregenerate corner of her mind was dancing, thinking, what a story!

Mosby,
Virginia

TUESDAY
AFTERNOON

AUGUST 5TH
1975

Chapter 14

Kent Edgerton was five eleven, maybe a hundred eighty-five, brown hair, brown eyes. The managing editor was wearing a short-sleeved button-down oxford shirt with khaki trousers, no tie. Holly had refused his offer of coffee. She was wired enough already, after that talk with Mitch. But she had herself back in grip now. Focus on Dale Colby, Schreiner. On details that might add up to answers. No need for coffee. Besides, the *Sun-Dispatch*'s scuffed urn looked like the twin brother of the sludge producer back in the station house.

But Edgerton had taken a foam cup of the stuff himself before leading her to his office, which was built at the end of a big room where people typed in cubicles, answered phones, and moved in and out in response to purposes she couldn't guess. The office had interior windows so Edgerton could watch the activity in the large room. He took his coffee to a big battered desk already strewn with empty cups as well as stacks of papers.

"How long did Mr. Colby work here?" Holly asked him after the preliminaries.

"Must be fifteen, sixteen years," he replied. "I've only been here eleven years myself. He told me he'd worked in Harrisburg before."

"Did you know him well?"

"As a newspaperman, yes. Socially, not much. We each had our own circle of friends."

"Who was in his circle of friends?"

"Don't really know." He sipped at the coffee, small eyes surveying her as she was surveying him.

"Neighbors? Drinking buddies? Poker players?"

"God, I never thought about it. I knew him only as a newspaperman. Seemed to be a workaholic."

"Tell me about him as a newspaperman."

"Reliable," said Edgerton promptly. "Compulsive checker of facts. Really solid stories. Kept the best files of any of us."

Holly nodded. It fit the picture of Colby that was forming in her mind. Workaholic, yes. A neat person, clothes unrumpled even in squalid death, married to a woman who kept a neat, unrumpled house. Tidy, no loose ends. In his job as in Holly's it was difficult to tie off all the loose ends, but apparently he did his best. She glanced out the interior window at the big room. Most reporters' cubbyholes had surfaces stacked with paper, used coffee cups like Edgerton's, notes taped crazily to walls and file cabinets. Dale's home office had been much better organized. The desk surface had been orderly: phone book squarely next to the phone, the oval dish of lemon drops lined up with the axis of the desk, even the dirty lunch dishes stacked neatly in a corner to be taken away. The latest equipment all through the house: IBM Selectric, labeled files, Sony TV, thermostat, even coffee maker. No sludge for Dale Colby. His bedroom closet neat, shoes lined up. Tools on the garage pegboard hung carefully, each on its own silhouette. Only that lamp out of place.

"What was Colby's reaction when he found something that didn't fit?" Holly asked.

"Like a hound dog on a scent," Edgerton said. He'd finished his coffee already. "Most of us have that basic instinct. But he was especially likely to keep working at a story until every *i* was dotted. Dale took inconsistencies almost as personal insults. His greatest strength was his tendency to keep after stories until he understood every nuance."

"And his greatest weakness?"

"Same thing, really." He poked at the used foam coffee cups on his desk, arranging them in a military row as though in unconscious homage to Dale Colby. "He'd hold on too long. Fairfax scooped us several times because Dale was checking something in his last paragraph and didn't get the story in. Most of us prefer to get it out fast even if we have to cut the last paragraph."

"Did he usually tell you what he was checking?"

"If it was hot stuff. Or if I asked why the hell he hadn't filed the story yet."

"Do you know what he was checking yesterday?"

"No, damn it." He picked up one of the foam cups and began to pinch off the rim in tiny fragments. "He was working on the plane crash story. We'd printed his update yesterday and I had the feeling he was using that piece in part to rattle cages. Certainly Moffatt and Mrs. Resler called in about it."

"You think one of them might be upset enough to be involved with his death?"

"Hell, I don't know." The foam cup had been destroyed. Edgerton began to pick up the pieces and drop them into another of the cups. "I keep asking myself who would benefit. He had a first wife, you know, a tough blonde—"

"Yes, Felicia Colby. Do you know her?"

"Just acquainted. She came here once years ago, claimed he owed money."

"Do you know what she was doing yesterday?"

"No. Oh, hell." Edgerton gave Holly a grim smile. "I apologize. In this business we're all a little paranoid, you know. All sure that someone will become furious about the story we just wrote and pop by with a sawed-off shotgun. It really doesn't happen often. But something like this raises our own fears. I'd love to have it turn out to be a domestic squabble."

"I understand." It was one of the small hurdles of detective work: witnesses who were eager to prove that the victim had shown bad judgment in a way that they never would, so that they could continue to feel invulnerable to crime and death. Whoopee we're all gonna die: a deep truth much avoided here in Disney World. Well, give Edgerton credit, Schreiner, he has a little insight. At least he realized he was harping on the unknown Felicia Colby because the alternative was admitting that newspaper work, his own work, might be dangerous.

Holly said gently, "But in case it's not domestic, maybe you could just fill me in on his work situation."

"Well, that's the other thing," Edgerton said. He began to stack the surviving foam cups, nesting them inside one another. "He was doing so much work at home these days. Oh, he'd stop by the office occasionally, or he'd go out for a really important interview, but he really was feeling lousy so he cut down on the activity."

"Didn't that interfere with his work?"

"God, I really admired him. Yes, of course it interfered, but he drove himself hard and kept producing the stories. He's never liked our Virginia summers, and on top of that he had all the nausea from the drug—well, I don't know how he did it. But the stories were good."

"You're the one who assigns the stories, is that correct?"

"Yes. And I did what I could." He added the ninth and final cup to the tower he'd built, then dropped the entire construction into his wastebasket. "He had his long-term assignments like the plane crash and the extension of the Metro into Virginia. I tried to give him stories without a lot of legwork—follow-ups, rewrites. But things where you had to get out and talk to a lot of locals I'd give to Nate or one of the others. Like preparations for the Bicentennial or the effects of the heat wave." He glanced out the interior window, eyes roving over the scene in the big room. "But all that might have changed soon."

"What do you mean?"

"Well, he was having the attacks of nausea, of course. But this new drug was really miraculous. This spring he was slow and shuffly at times. Sometimes not fit for face-to-face interviews, and on the phone he often sounded, well, stupid. The publisher and I had actually talked about giving him medical leave, but we knew it would break his heart. Then came the L-dopa. It improved his walking and his speech. Wonderful to see him so much better. As soon as his stomach adapted, he'd be ready for anything again."

So Colby should have been feeling optimistic overall, despite the temporary unpleasantness of adapting to the medication. Holly tried another tack. "Did he have any conflicts with his co-workers?"

"No. I mean, what can I say? He wasn't the most popular, he wasn't the least popular. Last spring a few people avoided him, they couldn't cope with the funny speech and wooden expression. But it wasn't anger or hate, just discomfort. Besides, he was very work-oriented. Didn't stand around gabbing a lot. I don't think he had time to make enemies."

"He'd been here quite a few years. He was senior reporter?"

"Yeah. He and Nate Rosen were the two old-timers in the newsroom. Earned as much as some of the editors."

"What would his next career step be?"

Edgerton reached for the foam cups, discovered he'd thrown them all away, and picked up a stray paper clip instead. Staring at it instead of Holly, he said, "Managing editor."

Aha. Check this out, Schreiner. "Your job," she said neutrally.

"Yeah."

"Who chooses the managing editor?"

"The publisher. Schanfield."

"What was Schanfield's opinion of Colby?"

Edgerton propped his fingertips against each other, pursed his lips at them, and said, "Oh, hell, there's no reason to make a big secret of it. Seven years ago the old managing editor left. Mueller."

"Okay."

"Colby was appointed the new managing editor."

"Colby was? Not you?"

"Right. Nate, Dale, me, and a couple of outside guys were in the running. Schanfield liked the solidity of Dale's work. We didn't know about the Parkinson's yet, it hadn't advanced much. Anyway, Colby was chosen."

"And?"

"Turned out Dale was a lousy manager. He was just as compulsive as ever and wanted everyone to write stories exactly the way he would. Freaked out if someone followed up a lead he hadn't known about first. So after two months of rages and people threatening to resign Schanfield demoted him again."

"And promoted you."

He gave a small shrug.

"Wasn't Colby unhappy about it?"

"Maybe. Half relieved, though. He couldn't have thought he was doing well. We made up a face-saving story, said he was the only one with the background to cover a government scandal at the time. I gave him the two biggest stories that came up next. He was civil, turned in the stuff. We worked together okay. He was a damn good reporter."

A suspiciously harmonious changeover. If Dale Colby had inspired resignation threats seven years ago he might still have enemies despite Edgerton's protests. And Colby couldn't have felt kindly toward the man who'd replaced him, whatever Edgerton claimed. Dig into that a little with the other reporters. Holly turned the page. "Do you know if he'd received any threats recently? About something he was working on?"

"Only story he was working on with that potential would be the plane crash. Just a second." He stepped around his desk to the door and yelled, "Hey, Nate! Come here a minute!"

A man who was listening to tapes in one of the cubicles glanced at Edgerton and punched the machine off. He removed his earphones, stuck the entire apparatus into a drawer, and walked toward them: five ten, thinning dark hair, dark eyes, slim build. His eyes had a sad cast, like a basset hound's. Holly shook his hand as Edgerton introduced them.

"Glad to meet you, Mr. Rosen."

"Call me Nate. Terrible thing about poor Dale."

"Yes. We hope you can help us."

Edgerton explained. "She was just asking about that damn plane crash story. Wondering if he'd had any threats. I don't know of any but I thought maybe you'd heard something."

Nate shook his head slowly. "Moffatt yesterday was the closest to a threat, and you know more than I do about that."

"He was peeved," Edgerton told Holly. "Thought Dale's story was delaying the settlement of his father's estate."

"But it doesn't make a lot of sense," Nate said. "Because Dale was getting most of his stuff from the congressman's investigation, right? He wasn't out sifting clues himself much. So why would anybody think Dale was the only one who knew something?"

"That's true," said Edgerton. "And even suppose he was the only one. If it was important he'd file a story so quick the world would know about it the next day."

"You're saying that if he knew something incriminating, he'd learned it very recently because he hadn't reported to you yet?" Holly asked.

"Right," Edgerton confirmed.

"And I'm saying that even if he did know something, it's not likely that he was the only investigator to know whatever it was, with all the people the congressman had working on it," Nate explained.

"We'll check on it," said Holly. "I'd like to know exactly what Mr. Moffatt said."

Edgerton shrugged. "I didn't take it that seriously. But yeah, he said 'I'm gonna kill you guys. I'm gonna sue you for every penny you've got.' I talked to him a few minutes and he simmered down and left, asking me to tell Colby to ease off."

"I see."

"So I figured it was just talk. Maybe I was wrong."

"Right. We're checking his alibi. Now, one of the victims was a young woman named Ann Kauffmann."

"Yeah." Nate Rosen nodded.

"I understand her father was very upset, said her reputation had been ruined."

Edgerton looked inquiringly at Nate, who shrugged. "Dale mentioned it once. But he never published anything because he couldn't verify it. He said the guy was broken up and lashing out at Knox. Dale said he could understand, if it was his daughter he might go crazy too."

"Yeah. So he hadn't published anything detrimental to Miss Kauffmann's reputation?" asked Holly.

"Nothing."

"But if he had received some sort of verification yesterday—"

Nate nodded in mournful confirmation. "Anything's possible."

"There's Mrs. Resler. I understand she was concerned about the latest story too."

"Concerned about her husband's reputation," Nate explained. "She's setting up a foundation to help ex-cons. Jumpy about it being misinterpreted."

"Olivia Kerr's just been talking to her," Edgerton said. "She'd have the latest."

"Yes, I want to see her," Holly agreed. "I have a note that she called earlier today. Asked me to get in touch with her here. Is she around now?"

Edgerton glanced at his watch. "She was due back twenty minutes ago to talk to me, so she should be around somewhere." He leaned out the door again and bellowed, "Liv! Hey, has anyone seen Kerr?"

A general shaking of heads. Edgerton shrugged as he turned back to her. "Probably got delayed. You know how the investigation business goes."

"Yeah. Okay, something else I have to ask. Where were you yesterday afternoon?"

"God," said Edgerton. "Well, I was here until two, then went to talk to Schanfield at the Montmartre Restaurant. Back here at four."

"I was out interviewing for the heat-wave story." Nate tapped the newspaper on Edgerton's desk. Front page weather story. "Got back at four-thirty to write this up."

Holly noted it down. "Thanks. Well, if you have nothing to add now, maybe I could go through Colby's files here."

"Sure thing. Liv'll be here in a minute, I'm sure. Nate, why don't you show her where Colby's stuff is? Of course most of the current stuff is at his home."

"Yes. Thanks."

As Nate led her toward one of the cubicles, Holly said, "Colby was managing editor for a short time, I understand."

"Yeah. Few years ago."

"What happened?"

"Drove us all crazy. He'd assign a story and then we'd find out he was calling up behind our backs to find out if the person really said what we reported. Don't know when the guy slept, he was trying to do the whole damn thing single-handed."

"Lots of bad feelings?"

Nate looked at her mournfully. "Sure, back then. But if nobody clobbered him during that two months, there's no reason to do it now."

They had reached one of the cubicles and Nate stopped. Holly asked, "Did Dale get along with Mr. Edgerton?"

"They weren't buddies. But they worked together well enough."

"It just seems that Edgerton replacing him might have bothered Colby," Holly pursued.

Nate shrugged. "If so he kept it to himself. But then, what else could he do? Sorry I can't help on that."

Holly studied him a moment. If there was any friction between Edgerton and Colby, she wouldn't hear about it from this man. She said, "Okay. Thanks."

Nate gestured at the desk. "This is where Dale worked when he was in."

"Yeah. Thanks, I'll just look through it."

Colby's files were not enlightening. Well-organized, yes, but most of the material related to months-old stories. The recent material had been in the house files she'd seen already. After twenty minutes Holly closed the drawers and leaned back in the desk chair. Colby had posted lists of phone numbers and schedules neatly in front of his desk. They seemed to be the same lists she'd seen next to the phone at his home. The sloppy stacks of papers on top of this desk, Nate had said, were not Colby's. "Overflow from the rest of us," he'd admitted shamefacedly. "Any of us go on vacation, we find everybody's extra crud on top of our desk if we're dumb enough to clear it before we leave."

So, Schreiner, you've found what there is to find here. On to the next task. She'd put off Donna Colby long enough. Donna should be back at her home now, maybe in better shape to talk about her husband's last few days. Maybe Holly could talk to the children too, though she doubted that they'd know any more than Donna.

She stopped by Nate Rosen's desk. He was on the phone but when he saw Holly he said into the receiver, "Look, let me get back to you, okay?" and turned promptly to Holly as he hung up. "What can I do for you?" he asked.

"Has Olivia Kerr come in?"

"Haven't seen her yet." His mournful eyes skimmed the room,

searching, then he glanced at his watch. "Strange. She said she was going to talk to Mrs. Resler. Shouldn't take her this long."

"Well, I'll have to see her later. Tell her to leave a message at the station house about where I can reach her."

"Okay. You got any statements for the press?"

"You've got the thing about the man in the blue Ford we want to talk to?" In the neighborhood canvass that morning, Gabe reported, a lot of people had been away at work, but a retired man at the end of the block had confirmed Bo Morgan's story that a man in a blue Ford had left the Colby house around four o'clock.

Nate rolled his pencil in his fingers. "Yeah, we've got that. Also that you're following up a number of leads."

"That sums it up, then," Holly said.

"Can't you say who looks most likely?"

She let a grin twitch at her mouth. "Sure. You can say that we're especially interested in the movements of Dale Colby's colleagues at the *Sun-Dispatch*."

"Touché." Nate smiled back weakly.

She started for the door. "I'll talk to you later."

She checked back with Gabe at the station house. A couple of things had come in, he said. Most notably, a detective named Lugano in New York wanted her to call. She dialed the number at Gabe's phone, half-sitting on the edge of his desk.

"What've you got on this Ryan woman?" Lugano demanded.

"Nothing," Holly admitted. "We've got a homicide, she was first on the scene. She's also got four witnesses putting her miles away at the time it probably happened. What've you got?"

"The same. Nothing," Lugano said. "She was a witness in a kidnapping here. Kid got back safely but the ransom disappeared. What can I say? We've been watching the Ryan woman and her husband because I have a gut feeling they know more than they're telling. But they sure as hell don't act like they got any cash out of it. Had high hopes once, she bought a Camaro. But it turned out to be used, and she'd got a big government contract at her business. So I'm left with a gut feeling."

"Yeah, same here. Well, if anything shows up, I'll let you know."

"Ditto."

Holly hung up and turned back to Gabe. "Damn. Nothing there. Any word from Doc Craine on time of death?"

Gabe rolled eloquent eyes toward the ceiling. "He's getting mulish. 'No one, including me, will ever know if you keep pestering me every ten minutes.'" His imitation of the irascible doctor was clumsy but recognizable.

"Yeah, I know that mood," Holly said glumly. "Well, let's concentrate on the guy Bo Morgan saw. Have the photos come in?"

"We've got Bates already, standard mug shot. I sent Driscoll to Maryland to pick up Moffatt's. He should be back soon."

"Fine. Moffatt's is from quite a few years ago, he was only in college. But maybe it'll do. Listen, I'm going over to Colby's now to talk to Donna. Maybe I'll pick up Bo Morgan and bring him back afterwards to look at the photos. You dig out a few others for a lineup, okay?"

"Okay."

"Anything else?"

"Not on Colby. On the painting—you remember that stolen painting? Colonel Mosby on the battlefield?"

"Yeah."

"Well, Winks and a couple of Manassas detectives searched the whole tour bus. Nothing. And then old Taynton called back. Said it wasn't the picture he'd reported missing after all. They found that one, fallen behind the chest where it's hung."

"So we can quit looking?" asked Holly hopefully.

"Not at all. There really was a broken frame on the steps, and those tools. So Taynton says he'll call back to describe the painting that's really missing, soon as he figures out which one it is. And we're to stay on the job, he says. To honor our noble soldiers in gray."

"Yeah."

"Otherwise he'll serve our heads on platters to the chief when he gets back."

"He's got the clout to do it, too. Damn. It must have been handed off to someone here in Mosby. Well, keep Winks on it. Find out if anyone else was around the museum this morning."

"Right-o."

In the unmarked car again, Holly paused for a moment to look over her notes. She'd learned a lot since last speaking to Donna Colby, and had plenty of new questions now: about the people Dale Colby was currently writing about, about his feelings toward his demotion and replacement as managing editor by Edgerton, about his son Mark and ex-wife Felicia. Donna, though doubtless still dazed by the sudden collapse of the life she knew, might be able to focus on specific questions about Colby's last weeks.

But when she arrived the Colby yard was a scene of confusion.

Donna, screaming, came darting up the driveway, past the Colby Pinto and a black Camaro. Nick O'Connor was chasing Donna. Back by the front door Maggie held a weeping Tina in her arms while little Sarah clung to her mother's sky-blue hem. As Holly pulled up to the curb, Nick reached Donna and seized her by both wrists.

"Donna, it'll be okay," he said soothingly.

"Josie!" she shrieked, looking around wildly.

"Donna, it'll be okay! I'll find her!" Maggie called.

Holly had pulled on the brake. Okay, Schreiner, cool and quick. Her damn revolver was in an ankle holster today, under the flare legs of her slacks. She snatched it out and leaped from the car. Without raising the gun she said to Nick, "Let her go."

"Oh, Christ, here comes Annie Oakley." Maggie's exclamation dripped contempt.

Donna was still sobbing, "Josie," over and over. Nick looked apologetically at Holly. "She's kind of hysterical," he explained.

"Let her go."

He shrugged and released Donna's wrists. Donna raced to the middle of the street and looked up and down. "Mrs. Colby?" Holly called.

"Josie!" Donna sobbed as though the others didn't exist. She turned and ran back past Holly to the garage to peer inside.

Nick was standing quietly, watching the distraught woman. So okay, Schreiner, cool it, he's no threat. She planted her foot on her car bumper, reholstered her gun and asked him, "What's going on? Where's Josie?"

His sad eyes turned from Donna to Holly. "She's disappeared."

Chapter 15

At the porch steps Olivia balked. "I could wait here, couldn't I?" she suggested. "Without the van I . . ."

"C'mon."

She pretended to stumble on the steps but even though her arm was slicked with rain, the sudden jerk didn't loosen Ernie's grip. Loosened her shoulder, though. Ouch. Hand-to-hand combat with this guy was clearly out even if she could somehow eliminate the rifle and dog. He bent his head and asked, "You okay?"

"Uh—yeah, sure. A little woozy from, you know, the van." She thought she heard voices. With a wrench of hope or fear or a combined thrill of both she realized there were people talking inside. Allies? Or assistant captors? She babbled on, "And the steps are wet."

"Okay, we'll go slow." He helped her carefully up the steps and across the porch. Olivia's rabbity heart began bouncing when she saw Sergeant Rock behind the screen door, tail waving, tongue lolling from the enormous jaws in a doggie grin. "Look," she said, "he makes me so nervous. Couldn't we—"

"Yeah," said Ernie, unsurprised. "He's an attack dog."

"Well, I mean, couldn't I wait out here?"

He opened the door, shoved her in, and said mildly, "Just let me make this call."

Clearly there was no choice, so she said, "Okay." He obeys Ernie, she told herself. Keep Ernie happy and everything will be

A-OK. Right now you better notice every detail in case you need it to get away.

With that task in mind she managed to ignore the big shepherd except for one fearful glance. She looked at the two doors. The screen had a hook, but Olivia saw that there was no lock. The inner wooden door, standing open now, boasted a dead bolt but had a twist knob inside. So with brief fumbling she could let herself out, if the opportunity ever came. Ernie hooked the screen, and shoved the door closed with his foot. Sergeant Rock sniffed at her civilly enough while Olivia resolutely looked past him at her surroundings.

She was in the front corner of a living room. It didn't seem to match Ernie's outdoorsman personality. A pinky-beige carpet carved in a vaguely floral design stretched wall-to-wall and on into the dining room through an arch. The windows, one next to the front door looking out on the porch and one across the room at right angles giving onto the driveway extension, sported inexpensive mauve drapes that moved in the gusts of wind. Under the driveway window sat a sofa slipcovered in a dark cabbage-rose design. A worn green chair and a black rocker flanked the scuffed Danish-style coffee table before the sofa. The coffee table at least showed signs of Ernie's presence: a filled ashtray, a couple of *Field & Streams*, and ample collection of empty Bud cans. Nearest to her, a low wide bookcase sectioned off a three-foot entry area by the front door. On the bookcase sat a big television that faced the sofa, back to her, its tangled wiring drooping unkempt over the bookcase as it headed for connections in the wall beside her. The voices she'd heard were coming from it, excited but on low volume: "Joy makes my dishes shine every time!"

Ernie led Olivia around the end of the bookcase and across to the sofa, pausing only to say, "Sarge, sit," to the dog. To her he said, "Please sit down," but she obeyed promptly too. She wasn't turning into a doormat, a shame to Steinem and Friedan, she told herself firmly. She was being rational. A man would do the same thing. Don't upset a guy with a gun. And a dog. Not unless you've got a gun and a dog too. Besides, Ernie seemed calm enough, just determined that she would wait here a while. He'd even said please.

But then he looked back at the dog. "Sarge, watch 'em!"

The dog responded with an alert unblinking stare at her. Ernie wandered out through the arch and in a moment she heard him dialing a phone. She sat very still and walled off her fears. Think about other things. She looked around. On the TV, contestants in a quiz show burbled, their preselected all-American faces not too fat, not too old, not too pimply, all wearing eager expressions of all-American lust for the proferred refrigerators, vacations, cars. Well, Olivia could understand lusting for cars. Wouldn't mind one right now herself. She turned her head to look out of the front window, across the porch and down the driveway toward the road. The disabled van sat tipsily in the ditch about two-thirds of the way down, a silvery shape half-hidden by the rain. Nearer the porch was the blue pickup, water sliding over it, giving it the look of a toy under its formfitting transparent plastic packaging.

Ernie came back to the archway, receiver held to his ear, and stood looking at her absently, maybe listening to it ring. The rifle was still slung over his shoulder. In a moment he muttered "Shit" to himself and disappeared. She heard the cradle click. Olivia noticed that the phone was just around the corner in the next room, beside the arch, on the driveway side of the house. Ernie did not reappear. She heard his footsteps retreating toward the back of the house.

Did that mean she could get up? Dash for the door, down behind the hedge, wait at the road for a passing car—well, no, there weren't many of those, he'd find her easily, she'd have to make her way all the way to the construction site before she'd be safe. Hi, guys, sorry to bother you, she'd scream into the wall of noise from the roaring machines.

If he didn't catch her first.

Wasn't really a great plan, was it. If she couldn't escape in the van, she certainly couldn't on foot. Have to get hold of the rifle somehow. But she realized she could test the dog now. At least find out if he'd do anything without Ernie egging him on.

She tensed her legs and leaned forward an inch preparing to stand up.

Sarge did not approve.

She hadn't actually moved yet, but his ears went back, his head lowered, his lips pulled back from his formidable teeth and a rumbling thickened the air. Oh boy. She leaned back again in the sofa and the rumbling stopped.

So. If she did get hold of the rifle she'd have to use it on the dog. How the hell did a rifle work? Only thing she'd ever done with a rifle was stick flowers in the barrel at a demonstration.

Ernie appeared in the archway with a sixpack and a bag of cookies. Pecan Crisps. He placed them on the coffee table, shoving aside the previous collection of cans to make space for the new additions.

"Want a beer, Olivia Kerr?" he asked.

"Uh—thanks, no."

"Cookie?"

"Not just now."

"All right." He tabbed open a can himself, pulled the worn easy chair around to a position near the TV, and sat down, shrugging the rifle from his shoulder and laying it casually across his lap. He was directly between Olivia and the door. He leaned back in the chair, one leg stretched out comfortably before him. "Sarge, c'mere," he said.

The big dog relaxed and trotted the few steps to his master, tail wagging. But Olivia remembered the rumble and didn't move. Ernie scratched the animal's ears, then softly told him to go lie down. Ernie lifted the can for a swig of beer. Finally he looked at Olivia.

"The situation we've got here," he said pleasantly, "is that I've got to make a phone call to check you out."

"Okay. Um, didn't you just call someone?"

"Wasn't there. But I'll try again in a few minutes."

"Oh. Okay." She noticed that Sergeant Rock was not only lying down as commanded, he was dozing already. But dogs were not very sound sleepers. "And after you check, I can go?" she asked timidly.

"Probably. I'll help change the tire," he assured her.

"Is there anyone else you can check with? I can tell you numbers for my editor or—"

He took a long swig of beer without answering.

"I mean, maybe I could suggest someone to call."

"I'm checking what I should do," he explained as though to a child.

"Oh." Olivia licked her dry lips. "I see. Your boss."

"Might say that." Ernie smiled mirthlessly and put the beer can down on the carpet next to the chair. "Here," he said, "toss me another Bud."

Olivia reached for a can. Could she fling it hard enough, and accurately enough, to hit him in the forehead, knock him out? Then grab the rifle, then—

No. She couldn't.

Besides, she saw Sergeant Rock lift his head lazily from the floor, ears pricking at the mere tiny sound of the can being pulled from the six-pack.

She tossed the can obediently at Ernie's chest. He caught it one-handed, pulled the tab, and drank.

"What was this guy Colby after?" he asked suddenly. "The one in the picture?"

"He was just a reporter," Olivia said. "Writing about the plane crash."

"Writing about that Congressman what's-his-name?"

"Yeah. And the people on the plane, you know, and their families."

"Cap'n Corky didn't have a family any more. Divorced."

"Oh. But didn't he have a sister?"

"Oh. Yeah." A frown crackled fleetingly across his face. "Yeah, a sister."

"Do, uh, do you have a sister?" Olivia asked, hoping it wouldn't be a touchy question.

"Nah. There's just me. Dad died and Mother went off to Florida. Sold me her half of the farm."

"I see. It's a nice farm," Olivia said.

He drank some beer and grinned. A heartening grin, really, his face brightening around his beard like sunshine breaking through clouds. "You ever worked on a farm, Olivia Kerr?"

"Um, no, not worked. Used to visit my uncle."

"Thought so. See, it's tough. Chickens, hogs, plowing, rvesting—the whole ball of wax."

"Yeah. I suppose you're right. Maybe some people like working outdoors."

"This weather? They're crazy."

Olivia looked out the window and nodded. This conversation was unreal. She was discussing the weather with a guy who might be Dale Colby's murderer. How had he done it? Rifle, somehow, no doubt, he was a terrific shot. Her van bore witness to that. But there were no bullet holes anywhere in Dale's den. Nor in Dale, Jerry said. Well, this wasn't the time to figure how he'd committed that crime. It was time to prevent this one. And preventing it required discussing the weather. So be it. "Yes," she agreed, "that rain is fierce."

"Regular monsoon," he agreed. "Can't earn a living with this weather going on. Don't know whether to plant cactus or rice." He grinned again.

Cactus or rice. He'd made a joke. Olivia tried grinning back. She wasn't sure if she succeeded or not. "Must be tough. How are the animals doing?"

"They're like me. They survive." He finished the second beer, placed the can neatly by the other, laid his hand on the stock of the rifle, and looked at his watch. "I'll try to phone again."

"Okay."

He slung the rifle over his shoulder and started for the phone. "Sarge, watch 'em."

Instantly, the dog was on the alert again. Not a good idea to try to slip by him in his sleep, Olivia decided. He didn't wake up like her, slow and muzzy-headed until she'd had her coffee. He was ready in a flash, ready to—to—never mind. The point was, it was definitely not a good idea to try anything unless he was somehow locked up. Maybe, if she could get a solid door between him and her— But she couldn't reach the front door before Sarge. The arch to the dining room had no doors, and Ernie was in there dialing now. The only other door to this room was straight across from her. Through it she could glimpse a carpeted hall. Bedrooms, maybe, or stairs. But since the dog sat in a direct line between her and that door, it was of no immediate use anyway.

The windows had screens. But even supposing she somehow slashed an opening and escaped, Sarge could then get through too.

So could a bullet.

Maybe whoever Ernie was calling would tell him to let her go. After all, she didn't really know anything. And Ernie, now lounging against the side of the archway, phone at his ear, thought she knew even less. He'd learned only that she knew he'd known Corky Lewis years ago, and that she was a colleague of Dale Colby's, who'd been killed. But he didn't know she'd found the Donovan's Bar napkin that linked him to Colby's home. And he didn't know that Nick and Maggie knew about him.

Not that they could help. She hadn't told them she was coming here.

Hadn't told Edgy or Nate yet either.

Hadn't told the cops about any of it. Damn, that Detective Schreiner would look pretty good right now.

And getting to that phone to call anyone was even less likely than escaping.

She longed to be back doing rewrites on Joanne Little and Patty Hearst.

"It's Ernie." He spoke suddenly into the receiver. "I—" There was a brief pause. He kicked at the baseboard. "Look, Rosie, it's urgent! Just tell me—" He broke off again, glared at the receiver. "Shit." He ducked into the corner beyond the archway, slammed the phone down, stalked back to the chair, slid the rifle from shoulder to lap again. For a minute he sat with his eyes closed, muscles tense, then slowly relaxed as though willing himself to unwind. He opened his eyes and looked at his dog first. "Good boy, Sarge. Lie down." When the animal had flopped onto the carpet again, Ernie looked back at Olivia. "Sorry," he said politely. "We'll have to wait for a return call. Everybody's always so busy. Hurry up and wait, you know?"

"Yeah." She rubbed her palms together nervously. They were damp. "I spend hours waiting for people to call back too."

He studied her a moment with those opaque dark eyes. "A reporter," he said. "Suppose you were reporting about me? What would you want to know?"

Hoo boy. A lot of stuff, Ern. Like how'd you manage the locked room? Why'd you do it? Why won't you let me go? And so on. Olivia stamped down her journalist instincts and said carefully, "Let's see. You didn't know Dale Colby, so it wouldn't be a news article. A feature, maybe. Human-interest story. So I'd probably ask you what it's like to be a farmer these days."

"Being a farmer. That's human interest?"

"Sure. City people want to know because it's all new to them. Other farmers want to see if you've got the same problems they've got."

"Yeah. Money," said Ernie. "But I got that fixed."

"Oh?" she said cautiously.

"You see those houses they're building down at the corner of Vale?"

"Yes."

"Sold that lot to them about a year ago. Put the money in the bank, get a nice check every quarter. Enough to buy beer, anyway."

A sizeable check if he kept up his present rate of consumption, she decided. She said brightly, "That's good. With real estate going up so fast around Mosby, this farm must be more valuable every day."

"You got it. Just sitting here, it's valuable. Don't have to work it at all."

"So you're thinking of selling it all?"

"Nah." He waved an arm toward the window behind Olivia. "See the woods back there?"

She twisted around to peer out. Was the rain easing? Beyond the driveway and rough lawn, the Virginia woods started up abruptly: tall trees, creepers, bushes. Look long enough and one of Colonel Mosby's men might materialize. She said, "Yeah."

"I won't sell the woods. Half this place is woods. Good hunting patch, backs up to the river. Lots of deer. So I'll sell off lots by the road. Let 'em build their tacky little houses down there. Sarge and I can hang out here, go hunting. No hassles."

"Sounds great. Have you always liked hunting?"

"Yeah. Eight years old, I remember going out with my old man." Ernie was looking in her direction but his eyes were focused far away, somewhere back in those woods. "He died when I was in Nam."

"I'm sorry," said Olivia.

"They sent me home. I was a short-timer already, only twenty-three days to go. Right out of the jungle into the cold here. Thanksgiving time, you know? Christ." He glanced at her, at the dining-room arch, at the dog, finally settled on the carpet at his feet. "Thanksgiving. What a farce. Giving thanks—" His face crinkled suddenly in a grimace and Olivia realized he was fighting tears. She tensed. Soothe him somehow. He was unpredictable enough already. Try the weather.

"I'm sorry," she said again. "Must have been a jolt, summer to winter like that."

He recovered himself, his dark eyes dull again. "Fucking Army," he said. "Buddy dies, they send you back into action next day. No real funeral, no investigation, nothing. Just some damn-fool chaplain bullshitting about how he didn't die in vain. Crap. And they pin medals on the assholes that ordered them into the wrong place."

That frown on his face again. Olivia said hastily, "Yeah, the Army must be pretty unfeeling."

He seemed amused. "Not at all. Civilian stateside dies, it's oh dearie me, young fella, why don't you go home early, have some turkey. Crazy business."

"Yeah. Crazy business," she agreed cautiously. The stateside civilian had been his dad, after all. But in the tight comradeship of war, a buddy's death would be more immediate, more threatening. If her own dad died she knew she would grieve for years. But Dale's death had left her not so much with sorrow as with an urgent sense of unfinished business, of validating his life and her own by carrying on his projects, by avenging his death.

And boy had she ever muffed it.

Ernie was looking glumly out the window down the driveway. The rain was definitely letting up, she saw, the darkest of the clouds scudding away. The people on the TV were shrieking in their small low-volume voices, clapping their hands. Someone must have won one of the all-American prizes.

Okay. Be logical. The best chance for escape was for Ernie's boss to tell him to let her go. But she needed a backup plan. The truck, she decided. Try to get the truck keys. And padding. People who trained attack dogs wore padding against the fangs. Maybe she could snatch up the slipcover as she left. Bundle herself thickly. But all these plans required getting the rifle as well as the truck keys.

And he might have another rifle. Hunters usually did.

Ernie stirred restlessly. To keep him occupied until the mysterious boss rang back, she sought desperately for a safe topic of conversation. "Does your mother like Florida?"

"Oh, yeah." He looked back out the window. "She's got a sister there. And we weren't getting along too well, her and me. She thought I was drinking too much." He snorted. "But if I didn't drink she thought I yelled too much."

"Well," said Olivia. Couldn't respond to that. She returned to the earlier topic. "I'm glad she likes Florida. I was there once, just on vacation. The ocean is great. The beach."

"Yeah. The beach is all right. Even in Nam the beach was great."

"Yeah. I like beaches. I was just over at Bethany Beach, uh, yesterday." Could that be right? Was it really only twenty-four hours ago that they'd been playing volleyball, splashing in the sea?

"Haven't been there. Rehoboth, once." He wasn't paying much attention to this dumb conversation either, glancing back and forth from the window to the archway where the phone lurked.

Sergeant Rock bounced to his feet, quivering, as the phone shrilled at last. Ernie hoisted the rifle to his shoulder and strode toward the arch. He didn't forget to tell Sergeant Rock, "Watch 'em."

"Hello?" Olivia heard him say. "Yeah. Oh, hi, Mitch . . . Okay. I'm doing okay." There was a pause. Was this Mitch the one he was waiting for? Why wasn't Ernie saying anything about her? He said, "Okay, I get the idea. Why all the buildup? . . . Yeah, okay, I know you won't . . . Oh, Christ!" A thump of Ernie's boots. Sarge's ears twitched. "You didn't . . . yeah, yeah, okay, I know you won't. They don't have my name? Well, don't tell the fuckers anything! I'll get back to you, okay?"

The receiver slammed down and Ernie bounded into the room, fury twisting his bearded face. "You little shit!" he screamed. It was the most terrible voice Olivia had ever heard. "You called the cops on me!"

"No, no, I didn't!" she exclaimed, cringing.

"Shut up!" He smacked her across the jaw. A fantail of pain flared from her cheek through her skull.

"No! I didn't! Someone else did!" she sobbed. She'd crumpled sideways, burying her face in the sofa, arms over her head, waiting for the fists, the fangs, the bullets.

"Someone else? Down, Sarge. Like who else?"

There was something salty in her mouth but she forced herself to think through the haze of pain. This Mitch had told him something about cops. Who could have told the cops? Nick or Maggie or Jerry? The bartender? But the cops didn't know Ernie Grant's name, it appeared. Nick or Maggie or Jerry or the bartender would have told the name. So who else was there? "The sister?" she gasped into the sofa cushion. "Maybe Corky Lewis's sister?"

"Jesus. Jesus, that's it." Ernie stepped back a pace. "Mitch said they were asking about him. Asking about his friends. Must have been the sister."

A web of pain still pulsed around Olivia's skull, a net around her brain. The saltiness in her mouth was blood. She could see it on the slipcover. She was aware of her every breath, air pulled across the dusty cabbage-rose slipcover into her nostrils and lungs, forcing her rib cage to move as her chest expanded and then deflated. She hoped the movement of her breathing wouldn't set him off again. She could see his jeans from the corner of her eye, a glimpse past her own arm that was still arched to protect her head. He seemed to be staring out at the driveway. A few feet beyond him the dog sat watching him alertly for clues about what he wanted.

She was watching him the same way.

It was sinking in at last that she would never get away. Take away the dog and the rifle and he still could hurt her. He could keep her here forever.

She could die here.

If only she knew what he wanted!

He turned toward her. "Hey. You okay?" He sounded surprised.

What did he want her to say? She swallowed the blood in her mouth and mumbled "I guess so" into the cushion. She quailed again, waiting for the blow.

"Okay, here, I'll help you sit up." He took her hand, tugged her gently to a sitting position. A fleck of hope sparked alive, deep in her mind. He was being nice!

She said, "Thank you."

"Here. Have a cookie." He thrust the bag of Pecan Crisps toward her.

She ran the tip of her tongue along the inside of her throbbing cheek. The blood was coming from there, where he'd smashed her flesh against her teeth. But if that's what he wanted— "Thank you," Olivia said again, and bit into the cookie.

Chapter 16

"Josie disappeared? When?" Holly demanded.

Nick, a weight of pity in his lumpy face, said, "Hour and a half ago, about. We drove them all over here. Donna broke down when she saw the house and we shooed the three girls into the bedroom so we could talk to Donna in the living room. She was worried about the future, about all that had to be done, and we helped her make a list of insurance people and so forth. After a while we saw the girls all troop across the dining room to the kitchen for a glass of water. The younger two went back and we didn't think anything of it, we were busy with Donna. But then when we finally got her settled down and went back to check on the girls, Josie was gone."

"An hour and a half."

"Yes. Tina said she looked around the kitchen and muttered 'Nazgûl' and then ran out through the garage."

"You called her friends?"

"Yes. She's not there. We also called the grandparents."

"The ones in Roanoke?" The image of that angry old man lingered. But he was talking about disowning them, not snatching them.

Nick nodded. "Yes. And they're both there, in Roanoke." Nick's sad brown eyes moved to Donna again where she stood red-eyed and disheveled by the garage door, nodding without conviction at Maggie. "The trouble is, Donna's convinced herself that they've hired someone. That it's a kidnapping."

Kidnapping. Holly strode over to Donna and Maggie. "Nobody's got Josie," Maggie was saying. "She'll be back."

"But Dale's parents! And the man—the one who hit Dale with the lamp—"

"No, no, it's not that. Josie's just sad and—" Maggie broke off as Holly joined them.

Holly said, "Hello, Mrs. Colby. I understand Josie is gone?"

Donna began to sob again. Maggie glared at Holly and said, "She'll be back soon."

Holly ignored her. "Mrs. Colby, why do you think someone has her?"

Donna, choking on her sobs, gasped, "Dale's parents want them! And there's the man—he got in, he hit Dale—and now Josie—"

"Did you see him?" Holly asked patiently.

"No. But he gets through locked doors—"

Whoopee. She'd seen this state before, FNG's whimpering for their mamas the first time they heard incoming. Still, you gotta try to get through, Schreiner. "He doesn't get through locked doors, Mrs. Colby. We'll find out how he did it," she said soothingly.

Donna stared at her, unseeing. "Someone hit Dale. Why? All that blood—And now Josie—"

"We'll find out." Give up, Schreiner, no hope for answers here. Stress and terror had cut the lines of Donna's logic. Maybe Josie really had run off like a little fool and would be back soon. That would be nice. But it was all too possible that Donna's hunch was right. Maybe the child's grandfather wanted to take control. Or worse yet, maybe the girl had noticed something about the murder, and the murderer knew.

Maggie was watching them, teeth against her lower lip, the occasional gusts of damp wind rippling across her blue dress. Holly asked her, "Was there a message? A note, maybe, or a phone call?"

"No. Nothing."

Donna was shaking again. "They'll take them away!" she sobbed, stumbling toward the street.

"Mrs. Colby!" Holly called harshly. "Listen. If you want Josie back, you have to help!"

"Help?" Donna quieted a little and turned back.

"The best thing would be if you stayed right here in case there's a message. You should be here in case Josie or anyone else calls, to find out what they want."

"That's right. Josie will need you, Donna," Maggie agreed.

"I'll call in to alert the patrol cars," Holly said reassuringly. "We'll check Roanoke too and have her back soon. Your job is to wait for a message."

"Wait for a message." Donna drew a shuddering breath. "Yes. I'm sorry, I'm so—"

"Of course you are," Maggie soothed. "Here's Nick. He'll wait with you, okay?"

"Yes—thanks—" She accepted his burly arm, and together they moved toward the front door.

Holly was halfway back to the car, preparing to radio for a search for Josie, when Maggie laid a hand on her arm. "Look," she said, "Josie will be back soon. Don't bug the kid."

Holly halted. "You know where she is?"

"I know she's a little girl with a lot of grief." Maggie was taller than Holly, her eyes intense as blue flame.

Holly didn't budge. "She could still be kidnapped."

"If so she's long gone. There's no sense looking around here unless there's a message. You've probably got a lot of other things to do."

"Hey, look, get off my back!" Holly spun away toward the car. What an asshole Maggie could be. "*I'll* decide what's relevant in this investigation."

The hand was on her arm again, soft but insistent. "Of course you will. I'm sorry. But Josie will be back. So you might as well work on other stuff."

Holly shook off Maggie's hand but stopped again. Why was Maggie so insistent? Suddenly sure, Holly said, "You know where Josie is."

"No comment."

Lugano in New York had said this woman knew something about a kidnapping there. Holly asked, "Why the hell don't you just tell me so we can get on with this?"

The blue eyes were sad. "You want to know why not?"

"Yeah!" Holly braced herself for a con.

But Maggie's voice was gentle and true. "Because Josie is very young and she's trying to cope with death. She doesn't need to talk to someone who hasn't coped yet herself."

"What do you mean?" White rage licked at the roots of Holly's mind. "I've coped! Anyway, that's all over! I'm the best damn cop around here!"

"Yeah, you probably are," Maggie agreed readily. "But it's not really over for you, is it? You're running from it every minute."

Angry denial flamed and died to ashes before she could speak.

Admit it, Schreiner, Mitch is right. It's phony forgetting, isn't it, when the thing comes snuffling back with every passing chopper, with every glimpse of red dust? But that didn't change things now, on this case. She said, "So what? I'm still a cop. A good cop. And you damn well better cooperate."

"I am cooperating. But right now Josie needs a friend, not a cop."

"We're trained to find missing people," said Holly stiffly.

Maggie shook her black curls in exasperation. "Aren't you listening? I know you're trained! I'm not knocking your brains or your ability. But we're talking about a child. And so far I've seen two Schreiners. I've seen a cold, competent detective who goes quietly and efficiently for the facts. And I've seen a bitter woman full of rage."

"I'm a vet, so you think I'm wacko!"

"No! I just—" Maggie paused, searching Holly's face. "Look, what's all this about wacko? Or last night, that stuff about spitting on you? You think I hate vets? Because of the peace movement. Is that what bugs you about me?"

"It's not bugging me. It's a fact of life. Like rain or termites."

"Yeah. Well, look, number one, I'm married to a vet."

"Not a filthy Nam vet," Holly snapped.

"Number two, it was the war I was against. Not you."

"Don't give me that shit! I got back from Nam, went into a coffeehouse stupidly wearing my uniform. Hey, says this girl, this total stranger, how many kids did you help kill?"

Pain sparked in the depths of the blue eyes. "That wasn't fair."

Damn civilian. If she wanted to dredge up monsters, let her look at them too. Holly said in a cool voice, "Wasn't it? First few months I was there I knew something was wrong with the damn war. But I saw the Montagnard families shot up by the Cong and told myself we were there for the kids. To make a better life for innocent kids. Then one day some ten-year-old shoeshine boy lobbed a grenade into my friend's Jeep. And I'm supposed to stand smiling by? There was no innocence in that phony war. Everyone who touched it became filthy."

"Yeah."

"I cheered when I heard someone shot that kid." She glared at Maggie. "I cheered! Florence Nightingale here cheered!"

Maggie's gaze dropped. In a moment she said in a low voice, "Yes. I might cheer too."

"Yeah! Everyone did. John Wayne himself would cheer."

"John Wayne," said Maggie thoughtfully. "Florence Nightingale. Innocent children. All those dear old ideals—Vietnam killed them for you too."

"Vietnam and you idiot protestors!"

"Come off it! We were saying the same thing you're saying! We were saying this war had nothing to do with American ideals! We were saying, okay, the Commies are bad but the other side is no better so what are we fighting for?"

"You were saying you didn't care that people were dying there!"

"For God's sake, that's exactly what we cared about! You think I would've wasted a minute protesting a war if they used squirt guns?"

Holly shook her head stubbornly. "You don't know what it was like. It was, hey, you went through hell when your country asked? Well, now you're scum!"

"And for us protesters it was, hey, you believe in democracy and free speech and government by the consent of the governed? Well, you're Commie scum!" Maggie pushed long fingers through her curls, black as crows' feathers in the damp breeze, and her glare softened. "God. You're right, you know. The war made us all filthy. The GI's, the protesters, the ten-year-old with a grenade. Made us all scum."

Holly met her grieving eyes and for an instant trembled with the sorrow of it all. She turned away, pressed a hand to her temple. What the hell did all this have to do with Dale Colby, with Josie? She said, "Let's get on with things, okay? I want the truth about Josie."

Maggie sounded weary too. "First I want to know if there's some other problem. Liv and Nick protested too. But you don't blow up around them. Is there something else about me?"

Holly gave a little bark of a laugh. It sounded harsh to her. "You don't want to know."

"I want the truth, even if I don't like it."

No, babe, you don't want the truth. No one in Disney World wants the truth. Holly said, "This is all beside the point. We're trying to find a little girl, who may be kidnapped."

"We're trying to find out if we two can work on the same team or not. Look, you're asking for truth from me. How about some from you?"

"You want truth? It's not like *M*A*S*H*."

"So be it. I just want to know what else is between us."

All right, civilian, you asked for it. Holly gestured at Maggie's swollen middle. "They brought this Montagnard woman in one day. Pregnant. She'd run into the Cong. Hurt bad. We did a Caesarean. Little boy, almost full-term. Healthy except for one thing. He had a frag wound in his chest. We tried—tried so hard—" Holly stared dry-eyed at her shoes. The tiny beat repeating in her mind. *Ten, eleven, twelve.* And then no more. "He wasn't scum. He was innocent," she said thickly. "That baby."

"Yes." Maggie's voice was husky too. Her hands had spread protectively across her own belly. "I see why I upset you. That little baby, and the peace sign."

"Oh, there's more." Holly wasn't about to let her off that easy. "In Nam on leave one weekend I met Helen. A nurse in USAID, you know, pacification stuff. She worked in a Vietnamese civilian hospital. I made the mistake of complaining to her about our facilities. The 18th was just a tent hospital then, undersupplied. And she said, well honey, come have a look at the natives." Holly's eyes returned to her own shoes. "It was horrible. Four patients to a cot, one filthy suction machine, rats in every corner. And I saw this guy with what looked like a mass of gray Jell-O squirming all over his wound."

Maggie winced. "Maggots?"

"Part of the treatment, Helen said. The doctors left them there until they'd cleaned off the necrotic tissue. When the dead stuff was gone they'd remove the maggots and fix the guy up."

"Christ." Maggie was shaken. "You had a year of—of that. And then here comes old Ryan, a bundle of reminders." She crossed her arms as though erecting a barricade to protect Holly. "Is there someone you can, you know, talk to about this?"

"Are you kidding? Who wants to hear about this? I learned as soon as I got back that telling the truth about Nam is like farting in public."

"Yeah. I remember, trying to tell the little bit of truth that I knew— I guess everyone prefers romantic John Wayne wars. God, to go through all that and then be told to shut up and pretend it's all okay—"

"Look, can it, okay? I'm not looking for pity."

"I know." Maggie studied the ground for a moment, face drawn, before she said, "Suppose we took a walk, you and I, and happened to bump into Josie. Would you give me fifteen minutes alone with her before moving in?"

"Fifteen minutes? You're crazy!"

Maggie smiled blandly. "Well, yes, guess I am. No reason really to think we'd bump into her, is there?"

Infuriating creature. This was probably supposed to be a concession. But Holly still had cards to play. She said, "Look, I know you were involved in a kidnapping case in New York."

Respect flickered in Maggie's eyes. "You're not just a good cop, you're a quick one. But as it happens I was one of the good guys in that case."

"Innocent as the driven snow, no doubt."

"I didn't say that." Holly was surprised to see pain cross her face. "There was too much shooting. Too much death. If I'd been quicker—" Maggie looked up at the clouds, steel-wool gray, that were scouring the sky. She spoke almost to herself. "Anyway, the kids come first. There's no such thing as justice if it hurts a kid. I was right about that at least."

Which meant there was no budging her about this kid. What the hell, Schreiner, you always did your damnedest to help kids. Besides, going along might save dozens of man-hours. Holly said gruffly, "You can have five minutes."

The blue eyes returned to Holly's. "Ten and it's a deal."

"Ten. Let's go."

She followed Maggie's long strides to the top of the street, then south a block to the deserted school. Honey Creek Elementary, flat-roofed, red brick, no character except for a white colonial pediment and two thin columns framing the glass doors, puny reminders of Virginia's glory days long ago, before another war. Maggie ignored the rambling building and passed across an asphalt parking lot dotted with gleaming puddles, through a playground outfitted with wet swings and jungle gyms and basketball hoops still jeweled with raindrops. The rough lawn at the rear of the school property sloped to one of Mosby's many little streamlets, drainage ditches really, that fed rows of tall white oaks, tangled bushes, and thick grasses.

Maggie seemed less certain now, slowing to reconnoiter the steep banks as she walked along the mowed edge above the rivulet. It gurgled with about a foot of water from the recent rains. Holly asked impatiently, "What are we looking for? Bicycle tracks?"

"No. Hush," said Maggie, still peering into the ditch. They moved on, but after a moment she murmured an explanation. "We're looking for a hobbit-hole."

Chapter 17

Maggie raised her palm. "Okay, here," she whispered. "Ten minutes."

Holly paused beside an old oak at the top lip of the ditch. The worst of the clouds had blown over but the sky was still overcast, filtering the August sunlight to pale blandness. She was standing a few yards from a back entrance to the school yard, where a little footpath crossed the ditch over a culvert. On the other bank of the stream, a segment of cement curbing from an earlier version of the crossing had rolled halfway down the bank and lodged behind some bushes. Holly watched Maggie pick her way quietly down the bank, step over the water, and brush off the cement before sitting down.

"I like it here, Josie," said Maggie after a moment.

A little startled scrabbling sound from inside the culvert pipe, then silence.

"The sounds are nice. The wind in the treetops, the water gurgling. It sounds like the Shire," Maggie went on.

A small choked voice said, "Go away!"

"Don't worry, I won't come in. I was just wishing I'd known about a place like this back when my friend died."

"Go away!"

"See, I felt really confused. I thought if somebody died you were supposed to feel sad. Well, I thought I was some kind of freak because I didn't feel sad. First I felt nothing. Like all my feelings were locked in a vault. Remember Denethor when his son was dying? He was seized by the power of the death crystal, and was numbed. It was like that at first. But then when my feelings got out of the vault they were terrible feelings. The worst was feeling so angry."

She paused. Holly could feel the rough bark of the oak through her shirt, the touch of a damp breeze on her cheek, the humid air rising from the vegetation like primeval breathing. Her hand rested on the thick branch of a bush laden with damp green leaves. She could just pick up Josie, get her back to her mother, get on with the damn investigation. But Maggie had fulfilled her part of the bargain. So unless the kid tried to run— Was the kid still there? She hadn't heard the noise of flight. Holly listened for Josie's voice but the only sounds were leaves, water, faraway cars. Then Maggie went on, quiet, serious. "I was angry at whoever killed my friend, of course. But what seemed awful was that I was angry at my friend."

She paused again, and this time the small voice responded, "Why?"

"Why was I mad at my friend? Because I still wanted to be with her, to talk to her, to explain things. But she'd gone away and I couldn't reach her. It wasn't fair, I knew. But still I felt angry at her."

The breeze fingered the damp leaves. The water gurgled. Maggie said, "It turns out that most people feel angry. Because most people want things to be fair. But death isn't fair. Not at all. And it hurts a lot. And there's no way to fix it."

Amen, sister. Holly could hear snuffly sounds coming from the culvert now. Maggie still sat on the broken curb, her dress airy blue against the jungle-green of the foliage. Still talking in that pleasant, serious voice. "I was angry because I kept thinking what I could have done differently. Maybe if I'd done this or that she wouldn't be dead. Maybe if I'd been nicer to her, maybe if I'd thought nice things instead of being mad at her, maybe I could magically have saved her. Maybe it was my fault. So I was angry at myself."

Red mud on the floor, water, blood. The young soldier's hand already cold in hers. Nurse, tell me why, his murmur in her ear just before he slid into darkness. If only she'd tried harder, there must have been a way, there must have! And then the surgeon, wearily: C'mon, Schreiner, pull yourself together, there's five more guys waiting. Cut 'em up, sew 'em back together, send 'em to Japan.

Tell me why.

Holly hauled her mind back to the present. Somehow she had broken off the branch in her anger and was holding it, green and dying. She realized then that Josie had crept out of the culvert, and was sitting on the cement block with her face against Maggie's arm. "It was my fault," the girl whispered.

"Yes, I thought it was my fault too, when my friend died," Maggie agreed.

"It's like you said. I was mad at him. I was so mad." Holly had to strain to hear the little voice.

"Even before it happened, you were mad?" Maggie asked.

"Yes. Before. I was mad, and I wished— I wished—"

"Sometimes when I'm really mad at someone I wish he was dead."

It was like pulling a trigger. Josie burst into a frantic fusillade of wails. Maggie held her, absorbing the storm, murmuring softly. Faces swam into Holly's memory, the kids, boys was all they were, dressed like soldiers but sobbing out their fear and despair to her. Twenty, she was; but they were only eighteen so she became mother. Taking on the sorrows of the whole 4th Division. Recruiters didn't mention that little duty, did they, Schreiner?

Maggie had succeeded in calming the girl. She was explaining, "Everybody's mad sometimes at people in their family."

"Yes—but—" Josie's mouth trembled. She swiped at her eyes.

"Did he do something to make you especially mad?"

"It was a t-tape," Josie explained, little hiccupy sobs punctuating her phrases. "There was a John Denver thing on the radio and I needed to—to record it. But I forgot to get—get a tape." Holly could see Josie's unfocused gaze roving around the trees of the little dell. "And Daddy was so busy always. And Mother's so dumb, she'd just tell me to ask him. So I took—took one of the tapes from the living room."

"Oh, boy. Was he mad?"

"Yes." Josie gave another little hiccup. "He yelled and yelled, and he spanked me."

"That must have been awful."

"He spanked me so hard! Look!" Josie pulled up her shirt, twisted around.

Maggie looked and hugged the girl again. "Oh, Josie, I see why you felt mad! You're twelve, you should have your own music. And you're too old to be spanked."

"Yes! And it's like you said, I wished—" She hesitated.

Maggie said gently, "For a minute, you wished he would die. And suddenly he did."

Another burst of sobs. "I was so mad at him! It's like—like I killed him."

"No you didn't. We all get mad at people sometimes. It doesn't make them die. I bet you've been mad at lots of people who didn't die."

She thought that over and admitted, "Yeah."

"But when somebody does die, we wish everything before had been perfect. And of course it never is. So we feel guilty and angry and cheated."

"Yeah." Josie was looking up at the branches again. Holly held still behind her tree, her throat tight. The girl said, "Sometimes he was nice."

"Yes. He was busy but he loved you."

"Yeah. Sometimes he'd watch TV with us. The best was when he'd read us the newspaper." Josie straightened on the cement block, reached down toward her feet, and found a handful of pebbles. She tossed one into the water. "He'd read to us. He was smart, he knew how to explain it. Not like Mother, she just said to ask him. And he'd give us lemon drops. It was good, when he read us the newspaper and we all had lemon drops."

"Yes. He loved you."

"It's only that—well, Mother says I'm smart too. He's not the only smart one. But he acted like I was still a little girl." Another pebble hit the streamlet, kicking up a crown of drops.

"Yeah, that's a problem. When you're twelve you're more grown-up."

"Maybe he was too busy to notice," said Josie. "Mother said he was busy."

"Maybe that was it. I think he would have noticed pretty soon that you were growing up, though."

"Maybe—maybe he was noticing a little. And that made him mad too."

Maggie had picked up a few pebbles of her own and was tossing them too. "Yeah, could be. He liked everything to be under control, your mother says. He liked to be in charge. But when a girl grows into a woman she's in charge of herself. Maybe that bothered him a little. It bothers some people."

"Yeah. Maybe." Josie, her pebbles all gone, stuck out her feet and wagged them slowly back and forth, together then apart. It made Holly think of a butterfly fresh from its cocoon, drying damp new wings. The girl asked, "But what do I do now?"

"Well, that's the hard part to figure out," Maggie said. "It takes a while of feeling frightened and sad and angry."

The feet were still. Josie gave another sad little hiccup. "I don't want him to be gone."

"Of course you don't. And one of the things you'll be figuring out is how to sort of keep his dreams for you. Remember the Fellowship of the Ring, after Gandalf the Grey was killed? They had trouble figuring out what to do. But they got the job done at last." Maggie tossed her last pebble and rested an elbow on her knee. "Did you know that Tolkien's parents died when he was a kid?"

"Really?"

"Yeah. And later, when he was in college, one of his very best friends was a guy called G. B. Smith. They had lots of plans about writing wonderful stories, with trolls and so forth. But World War I started and they both had to go fight. And Tolkien's friend was killed."

"Oh."

Holly was picking nervously at the leaves on the broken branch.

"Well," Maggie went on, "G. B. Smith had written a letter to Tolkien, just a little while before he died. He wrote, 'Say the things I've tried to say after I'm not there to say them.'"

Josie's feet waggled once, thoughtfully. "That's why he wrote the *Ring* books?"

"That's one reason, yes. But it was later. Years later. By then he'd figured out a lot about death and about how much it hurts to survive. And it takes time to figure out what's best to do. Like the Fellowship. You have to find something that's worthy of the ideals you shared. And true to yourself."

Mitch's voice in Holly's ears: something worthy of my dead. Something authentic.

And Nick's: when people started marching to protest some other pointless killing, I marched too.

And that question as the boy slid into the darkness: Nurse, tell me why.

Josie and Maggie were climbing the bank behind Holly, saying something about Mother getting worried, their shoes squishing in the damp weeds. Holly turned her face away from them. Be strong, Schreiner. Maggie paused and said uneasily, "Josie and I better go on to her house. Do you want me to come back for you?"

Holly shook her head, not daring to turn around.

"Okay." Maggie hesitated, then handed her a Kleenex. "We'll see you there in a little while."

Holly nodded mutely. Maggie squeezed her shoulder and then was gone.

Holly lifted the green branch and struck the old oak tree. *One*.

She hit it again and again. *Two, three.* The leaves were ripped, crushed, shredded. Defoliated. Stripped. Wasted. *Whoopee.* Panting with angry grief, she lashed harder and harder until the branch was a scarred naked cane and she was gasping for breath. *Why?*

> *And it's one, two, three what are we fighting for?*
> *Don't ask me I don't give a damn,*
> *Next stop is Vietnam.*
> *And it's five, six, seven open up the Pearly Gates,*
> *Well there ain't no time to wonder why,*
> *Whoopee we're all gonna die.*

It took twenty minutes for Holly to pull herself together and get back to the Colbys'. To her surprise Nick and Maggie were bundling Sarah into the Camaro. Maggie asked, "You okay?"

"Yeah."

"You sure?"

"Yeah." Holly turned to Nick. "Where are you off to in such a rush?"

He paused as he climbed into the passenger side. "We can't find Olivia. She was supposed to meet with her editor hours ago."

"She's still not there?" She'd been late even when Holly had been talking to them.

"Her editor just called here looking for her."

"For you," Maggie interrupted, thrusting some papers out the driver's window. "We're worried, so we want to go check. Here's where we're going. And also—" Her fingers lingered on Holly's hand. "I apologize. Really. It's just that I wanted to protect Josie. Children need to grieve too and I was afraid your questions might complicate things."

"You thought the big bad policewoman would brutalize the kiddies?" Listen, I've nursed more broken children than you could ever imagine.

Maggie shrugged. "Your act convinced me." She gestured at the papers Holly held. "That's why I wanted to keep you busy. It's not Mr. Taynton's fault. Anyway, I'd really like to talk to you again. See you soon."

Taynton? The Mosby Museum director? What the hell was she talking about? Holly flipped through the papers as the Camaro backed into the street and swirled away around the corner. A scribbled name and address on the top sheet meant nothing to Holly. Underneath, sales slips. Dated today, from Mosby Hardware and from the Blue and Gray Frame Shop. Maggie had bought a picture frame, canvas, mat knife—oh, Christ. All the stuff they'd found on the steps of the Mosby Museum that morning. That asshole! Furious, Holly sprinted to the street but the Camaro had long since disappeared. Christ, Winks had spent all day looking for something that hadn't even disappeared!

Not that she wasn't just as pleased to have Winks out of the way.

Christ. What an asshole Maggie was. All to distract the authorities from a sad little girl.

She looked back at the sales slips and felt a grin tugging at her lips. An image flashed into her mind. The barracks at the 18th Surgical. She and Billie Ann and the others had found some cans of red and white paint one day. They'd painted pink polka dots all over their quarters. Tweaking official noses.

Maggie would've loved it.

All the same, Schreiner, right now the official nose is yours. Better get back to work. She shoved Maggie's papers into her pocket and went back up the walk to ring the Colby bell.

"Oh, Detective Schreiner!" Donna's arm was around Josie's shoulder. The girl looked sad and spent, but more alive somehow, her hurt nearer the surface. Tina, eyes red too, hovered in the background. Donna said, "Please come in. I'm so sorry I was upset when you were here before."

"It's natural to be upset," Holly said automatically. She followed them in and sat on the familiar sofa again. "I just have a few questions. I wanted to ask if you'd remembered anything about what your husband was working on. Especially this last week?"

"I've been trying," Donna said, "but I don't know if it will help. I remember a Mr. Bates came here to talk to him. Something about Resler. And a man from the environmental group that opposes the highway came by. And a lot of phone calls. Mrs. Resler, Mrs. Carson from the congressman's office. A woman, Priscilla something, I didn't know her at all. Dale seemed happy to hear from her. She gave him a name and he said it was a new lead. But it didn't seem to work out."

Mitch, no doubt, refusing to cooperate with reporters. Turning the new lead into a blind alley, as he'd done with her. But Holly nodded. "Good. This is very helpful, Mrs. Colby. Now, we've been told there were tapes stored in this room. They're missing now?" She gestured at the empty shelf.

"Yes, Maggie was asking about them too. It must have been the man who broke in that took them. I think I would have noticed if they were gone."

Holly believed her. Josie, who had pulled away from her

mother and was sharing a wing chair with Tina, said, "Except for one."

"Yes, I wanted to ask you about that one," Holly said gently. "Do you still have it, Josie?"

"Yes."

"Could you bring it in, please?"

Josie slid from the chair and moved reluctantly from the room. Holly asked Donna, "What was on the tapes?"

"Interviews," Donna said. "The current ones were in his study. The ones he stored out here were older. He'd already transcribed the parts he wanted, but he'd hold them until the story was finished."

"Do you remember what story these were about?"

Donna shook her head. "I didn't pay much attention. The labels were in code, you know, KC for Knox plane crash. The people he worked with could tell you more about them. I really didn't do much except answer the phone for him when I was home too."

"Mail?"

"No. He always checked the mail. In case there was a tip for him or something."

"Did he ever talk about it?"

"Sometimes. He mentioned a letter from Felicia yesterday morning."

"What was your impression of Felicia Colby?"

"I thought—well, it's probably not fair. We only heard from her when she needed money. She needed money pretty often. It was hard for her, raising that child alone." Donna's blonde head bowed suddenly, as though realizing she was now in the same fix.

"Did she ever ask about Dale's will?"

"Not that I know about. Maggie said I should look for a will in his papers. He never talked about a will." Donna's mouth trembled. "He thought he'd live as long as—as other people."

"Yes." Most of us think that. Some of us wish we didn't have to. Holly glanced at her notes. Check with Gabe, see if they'd found anything in Colby's papers.

Josie came back in and tossed a tape into Holly's lap. "Daddy's stuff is erased," she said. "It's John Denver now."

"Yes, I know, but our people will still want to look at it. We'll try to get it back to you right away, but—"

"No. I don't mean that. You can keep it. I don't want to see it again. Ever!" She dove into the farthest wing chair and buried her face in the back cushion.

"Josie, don't cry!" Donna sprang up and ran to her daughter, her knee on the seat beside her. "Please don't cry!" She had started crying herself. "Things will get better, really."

Tina joined her mother and sister and for a moment all three sobbed together. Whoopee. Holly slowly put the evidence bag into her shoulder bag. The kids come first, Maggie had said, and promptly had reduced that stoic little girl to tears. Wonderful. And she'd almost done the same damn thing to Holly. Mitch was full of it too, all that garbage about facing the pain. After eight years, why face it now? Be strong.

Eight years of nightmares.

Phony forgetting.

Donna raised her head from her daughters. "I'm sorry, Detective Schreiner."

Holly said gently, "It's natural to be upset, Mrs. Colby. I'm finished with my questions anyway, unless you can think of something else."

"No." She straightened, brushed a hand across her hair. "I can't think of anything."

"Well, call me if you do. The girls too, okay?"

Tina just snuffled, but Josie's teary eye appeared, peeking over her shoulder. "Okay," she said.

Holly checked in with Gabe before she left. He was frantic. "Yeah, we got statements typed up and signed from most of them. Not Kerr, not Mrs. Colby. And Taynton at the Mosby Museum is going crazy. Can't figure out which painting was stolen."

"Nothing was stolen, Gabe. Call off Winks."

"What do you mean?"

"Somebody bought a frame and burglar tools and left them on the steps. Practical joke."

"You're kidding!"

"I've got the receipts right here."

Gabe let out a whoop of laughter. "Christ! And old Taynton about to have kittens!"

"Break it to him gently, Boy Wonder," Holly warned. "He can still complain to the chief if we don't handle it right."

Gabe was still chuckling. "Right. I'll present it as the results of tireless police work."

"Good. Anything else?"

"Let's see. Felicia Colby's friend in Harrisburg. This Nan Evans. We finally got through, she said yes, she saw Felicia in the ladies' just before five yesterday."

"How about Doc Craine? Any word?"

"Not yet. And I don't dare call him again."

Holly sighed. "You're probably right. Well, I'm going off to—" she glanced at Maggie's scribbled note in her hand—"looks like Emmie Grant. Maybe Ernie. On Appleyard Road."

"Who the hell is that?"

"No idea. But the Kerr woman is supposed to be there. Wait, there's something else here." There was another line written under the address. She squinted at Maggie's scrawl. *Pelt is found?* No, not *found. Friend,* maybe. And was that an *o* in the first word? *Pelot. Pilot!* "My God, Gabe, it's the pilot's friend! Corky Lewis's friend. His sister told me he met some Vietnam buddy last fall but I couldn't get his name. Maybe this is the guy. Why the hell didn't Kerr tell us?"

"She left messages twice," Gabe reminded her.

"Yeah, and then she wasn't there when I called back," grumbled Holly. "Anyway, I'll check this out. Back to you soon."

Chapter 18

Olivia stirred the scrambled eggs. "Do you like them well-done?" she asked timidly.

"Medium." Ernie stood at the kitchen door, rifle balanced lovingly in his hands. Sergeant Rock snored at his feet.

She looked into the cupboard and pulled out a plate. "Is this one okay?"

"Yeah. One for you too."

The inside of her cheek had stopped bleeding at last, though it still felt puffy. And so far she was doing well, keeping him happy. There had been no recurrence of that instant of uncontrolled fury when he'd thought she had called the police. Except for his growing irritation that the phone wouldn't ring, he was being polite. He'd even noticed after a while that her cheek was swelling where he'd hit her, and had escorted her here to the kitchen, encouraging her to make herself an ice pack. Her jaw still throbbed dully but the ice pack stopped the bleeding and the headache had diminished too. While she held the towel-wrapped ice to her cheek he had said that some scrambled eggs would taste pretty good. "Oh, do you want me to fix you some?" she'd asked eagerly.

"Sure." Ernie had grinned. It really was a nice grin. "How about you? Had any lunch?"

"Um—a little."

"Some for you too. My guest," he'd declared magnanimously.

"Yes. Uh—where's a bowl?"

He directed her to bowl, skillet, eggs. When she picked up the heavy iron skillet he'd said in a tense voice, "No funny stuff, now."

"What?" She'd jerked around to look at him in alarm, dropping the skillet onto the stove. It made an enormous clatter. "Oh, I'm sorry, I'm sorry, I didn't mean—"

"Never mind." His voice was peaceable again and the hands on the rifle relaxed. He picked up his beer, sipping slowly now. He watched her melt the butter, break the eggs, stir them into the skillet, start some toast. She worked carefully. The eggs had to be perfect so he would be happy.

Now she spooned them onto the plates, two thirds for him, and added a slice of buttered toast to each plate. He said, "Forks in that drawer."

She found the forks. "Just put mine here on the counter," he instructed. She obeyed, even though it mean sidling near the napping Sergeant Rock before she could leave the plate and retreat to the other end of the kitchen. The dog raised his head. Luckily he seemed interested in something at the front of the house, his ears pricking toward the dining-room door, away from her.

Ernie put down the beer can next to his plate and forked eggs into his mouth. She waited nervously until he mumbled, "Go ahead, eat." Then she ate. She couldn't taste the eggs but he wanted her to eat.

The dog was still looking alertly toward the front of the house. Suddenly he barked and lunged out into the dining room.

Ernie threw down his fork, grasped his rifle with both hands, and motion impatiently to Olivia. "Sofa," he snapped.

She hurried to obey as Ernie added, "Watch 'em, Sarge." The dog dropped to his haunches and glared at Olivia. Ernie flicked off the TV and took up a stance beside the window.

She could hear it now too, what was troubling the dog. Faintly in the distance, voices. Hope and terror twined tight as a braid inside her. The voices were drunken, yowling voices. Coming closer.

They were trying to sing.

They were trying to sing "Blowin' in the Wind."

They were coming up the drive.

Ernie muttered, "Shit. Couple of drunks. What the shit do they want?"

"The ann-sher," yodeled Jerry's voice, "is blowin' inna wind!"

"Wind!" Nick's baritone, just as uncertain of the notes and half a beat behind, came in at last. He added, "Whatsa next versh?"

"Next. Something something roads?"

"No. That's firsh versh."

"Look. Here we are!" Jerry declared grandly.

Someone started banging on the door. Sarge, distracted from Olivia, looked at it and barked.

"Watch 'em!" Ernie corrected him sharply. The dog's attention returned to Olivia.

"A dog. Hey! Nice doggie! Nice pooch!" Nick's head lurched by the window. She thought he saw her. Oh, God, they were upsetting Ernie. They mustn't upset him! But the banging on the door resumed.

"Shit," muttered Ernie. With sudden decision he stepped to the door and swung it wide, rifle at the ready. Jerry grinned at him boozily through the screen door.

"Hi," said Jerry.

"What do you want?"

"What do we want." He tugged vaguely at the door but it was hooked. His brow furrowed with the effort of thought but his eyes had found Olivia. She looked at him with despair.

"A phone!" said Nick's voice.

Jerry beamed. "Thass right, a phone! The car went in a ditch." He waved vaguely toward the road. "Need a tow truck."

Nick stumbled into view, knocking Jerry aside, and grabbed the doorjamb for support. "Tow truck, yes! Need a phone."

"Look." Ernie gestured with the rifle. "You two get back to your car. I'll call the truck."

They grinned at him stupidly.

"The goddamn tow truck is coming!" he enunciated loudly at them. "Now move!"

"Move. Yessir!" Nick let go of the doorjamb to salute. Over-balancing, he fell against the screen. His fist punched through the wire. "Oww!" he howled. "I'm bleeding! Shit! Oh, God! Ow!" His thrashing arm loosened the hook as he jerked his hand out. "Look!" he whimpered at Ernie, pulling open the screen door far enough to thrust his scratched hand inside. "I'm bleeding!"

"You're puking drunk." Ernie was disgusted but wary enough to step back, keeping the rifle barrel from Nick's drunken grasp. "Come on. Move! Get out of here!"

"Blood? Lemme see!" Jerry jerked the screen wide and stumbled toward Nick, peering at the arm. "Jesus! It is blood!"

The rifle cracked.

Olivia flinched at the sound. Sergeant Rock growled at her. Ernie pumped another round into the rifle. Jerry and Nick tumbled into the room, diving drunkenly over the low bookcase to escape the noise. "Hey, somebody's shooting!" Nick yelped to Ernie. "Better come inside, buddy!"

"Jesus." Ernie was exasperated. "Look, you guys see this?"

He jiggled the rifle. Except for the warning shot, it had remained pointed at Jerry, carefully maneuvered out of reach of their stumblings, swinging smoothly to follow their moves. He jiggled it again. "This is a rifle. Understand?"

Nick sat up, peered over the bookcase, blinked at it. He looked like a giant baby trying to focus. He said, "Yesh. Rifle."

"I fired it."

"That made the noise?"

"Yes!"

"Hey," Nick said importantly to Jerry, "that rifle made the noise!"

Jerry was on hands and knees, staring queasily at the carpet. "I don't feel sho good," he murmured, and pitched forward onto his face almost at Olivia's feet. Had he been hit? She couldn't see any blood. But she could smell alcohol fumes.

"All right," said Ernie patiently to Nick. "You know it's a rifle?"

"Yeh," Nick agreed solemnly.

"And what I shoot next is you."

"Hey, no, not me!" Nick's big-baby face crumpled, on the verge of blubbering.

"Then sit on the sofa!"

In an overanxious attempt to please, Nick clambered to his feet, teetered, and fell back into the end of the sofa farthest from Olivia. Satisfied, Ernie swung the rifle to point at Olivia as he spoke to Sergeant Rock. "Good dog, Sarge. Down."

The dog dropped. Olivia, nerves taut, sensed Nick's flicker of tension, acknowledgment that the animal too was a lethal weapon under Ernie's control.

Ernie, still behind the bookcase, rested the rifle on the top of the TV, still aimed at Olivia. With his left hand he ripped the cords from the TV and stereo and tossed them to Olivia. "Tie him up," he instructed. "Tie his hands behind his back. You! Turn so she can tie your hands and I can see it."

Nick obeyed. The thought of faking the knot crossed Olivia's mind but she rejected it instantly. Ernie would catch her, she knew. Become enraged. Shoot them both. Shoot them all three, because Jerry would try to help. And a second reason was that she was terrified that Nick might try something stupid. She knew better than he that Ernie was balanced on a razor-edge, barely in control. They all had to do things his way or he'd explode again.

Better keep Nick quiet, keep Ernie calm. She pulled the knot tight around Nick's wrists.

"Now the other one," commanded Ernie.

She obeyed, crossing Jerry's wrists behind him and tying them as he lay reeking on the floor. He whispered, "Not so tight," but she didn't acknowledge him.

"Now get their ID. Maybe in their wallets. Put the ID here on the TV."

Olivia obeyed. She found Nick's driver's license and pulled it out. With a sense of panic, she noticed the Actors' Equity card behind it. Ernie mustn't learn that Nick was an actor. Mustn't even think they might be faking. She shuffled the dangerous paper behind a library card and, heart hammering, turned to Jerry's ID. Hospital card would be best, she decided, and slid it with Nick's driver's license onto the top of the TV for Ernie to inspect.

"Sit down," Ernie commanded her. She returned to the sofa. "Sarge. Watch 'em." But Ernie didn't wander off this time. He kept the rifle aimed at foggy, worried Nick, his eyes shifting from him to limp Jerry to oh-so-obedient Olivia. He studied the cards on the TV with quick little downward glances. "Doctor. Damn," he said. "And the other one from New York. Not cops, anyway. You would of been in bad trouble if they were cops, Olivia Kerr." His attention shifted back to the disheveled pair beside her. "Maybe old buddies celebrating."

He seemed to be talking to her, so Olivia said, "Maybe." Her throat was tight and dry, her mouth still puffy and unresponsive. It was hard to get the words out.

"Ole buddies," Nick agreed in a worried voice. "Hey, buddy, easy with the rifle, okay?"

"Do what I say and things'll stay cool," Ernie said.

"Okay. Whassa matter?"

"The matter is, you didn't leave when I said leave."

Nick nodded solemnly. "Sorry," he said. "Needed tow truck."

Sarge growled and Olivia tensed. She hadn't done anything! But the dog's ears were swiveled back. Ernie looked at the door and Olivia followed his glance. "Shay!" Nick exclaimed in delight. "It's my wife! Hi, Maggie!"

But it wasn't Maggie. It was Detective Schreiner. An icy knot clenched in Olivia's stomach. A cop. Bad trouble, Ernie said. He would erupt. They'd all die. She prayed that Detective Schreiner would accept Nick's lie, not say she was a cop.

The detective scanned the scene, frowning, and asked calmly, "What's going on here?"

Ernie seemed deeply uneasy now. "Get inside here!" he snapped.

"Hey, Maggie, honey," Nick said, "better do what the man says. Got a gun and a dog."

Detective Schreiner moved casually out of sight beside the front door. Ernie shrieked, "You call the cops, lady, and these guys are dead! Understand? Or do I have to shoot one to prove I mean it?"

Schreiner's cool voice said, "I understand. What do you want?"

"Get inside here!"

"Okay." Cautiously, the sandy-haired detective pulled opened the screen and stepped inside. The dog growled.

"Sarge, down," Ernie snapped. Olivia was amazed again at the personality change that came over the muscular shepherd with the different commands. From the crouching menace threatening to lunge at the slightest move, he switched to docile, eager to please. Ernie added sharply to Detective Schreiner, "Go sit down. Not next to your husband. In that rocking chair."

Slowly, the detective obeyed. Olivia saw her dark eyes moving in the same quick survey Olivia had taken, marking windows, doors, dog, rifle, beer cans. She sat in the rocker, sandaled feet neatly together, and asked Olivia, "What's happening?"

Nick came in quickly, with a guilty-husband air. "Shorry, baby, we're sloshed. You were right. We asked to use the phone just like you said. To get a tow truck. Din't we?" he demanded of Ernie. "Din't we ask for a phone?"

"Yeah." Ernie watched them carefully, eyes shifting from Nick to the newcomer. Olivia could feel his discomfort and bewilderment at what to do with all these invaders, could feel his dangerous edginess growing.

Nick continued, "And we fell down in the door, and he din't like it. So he made ush stay with thish young lady, whoever she is."

"Jesus. You're too smashed to make sense," Schreiner said with disgust, rocking back in the chair. The dog growled and looked around, perhaps sharing Ernie's unease. The detective halted and looked back at Ernie. "Guess he doesn't like me rocking. So what do you want with us?"

Olivia watched Ernie puzzle over the question, hunting for an answer that would leave him some options. Finally he nodded to Olivia and said, "Reporter here had some questions. We were waiting for a call and then these two broke in."

Everyone looked at Olivia, but she looked only at Ernie.
"That's right," she said. "We were just waiting for a call."

"And these two drunks broke in," Ernie prompted.

"Yes. They're very drunk," Olivia managed to say.

"God. You idiots," muttered Schreiner to Nick and Jerry, and
then directed a question to Olivia. "So now we're waiting for a
call? Call from who?"

Olivia could sense Ernie's tension bubbling, overheating. She
said quickly, "I don't know. From his boss."

Ernie's mouth twitched in a tiny grin and he seemed to ease
down a notch. She'd guessed right, then, it would be okay to tell
them what he'd told her.

"Who's his boss?" Schreiner asked.

"I don't know. We were mostly talking about other stuff.
Ernie's a farmer and a hunter, and he was in Vietnam, so we were
just—"

"Nam?" A quiver of pain seemed to run through Detective
Schreiner. Her eyes squeezed closed an instant. Then she looked
at Ernie with enthusiasm. "You were in Nam? I was a nurse
there."

"You're kidding." He stared at her, wariness and fascination in
his look.

"18th Surgical, Pleiku."

"No shit! We flew out of Pleiku sometimes!"

"Helicopter pilot?"

"Roger. First Cavalry."

"God. You guys were great. When were you there?"

"'69, '70."

"I was earlier, '66 to '67. You pilots were fantastic! Guys were
always telling us how you'd snatch them out of impossible
situations. You saved a whole lot of people."

That pained grimace pulsed across his face again. "Not all of
them."

"I know. Me too. Couldn't save all of them." With surprising
vehemence, the detective added, "Nam sucked."

"Still sucks."

"Yeah. Still sucks."

"Sucks so hard we'll never get away."

Schreiner's eyes closed again. Olivia, taut with terror that
Ernie would freak out again, watched the detective fearfully.
Schreiner was tense too, holding the seat edge of her rocking chair
with both hands clenched as though fighting pain. She said softly,
"We don't get away. It's still killing people. Even now."

"Even now," Ernie agreed, and looked at Olivia. "This lady was asking about Cap'n Corky. He thought he'd got away. Dead now."

Olivia, panicky, wondered if she was supposed to say something. But Schreiner, tense or not, was in there quicker. "Because of Nam?"

"You better believe because of Nam. God." Ernie wiped his mouth with the back of his left hand. His right never left the trigger, Olivia saw. The rifle was propped on the TV, still aimed at Nick, who blinked stupidly every few minutes but didn't move. Jerry was faking sleep, snoring gently. Ernie said, "I thought then it would be over. I thought, hey Mike, we got even. But it didn't—" He looked at Schreiner, bewildered. "It's not over. It's worse."

"Yeah. Goes on and on. They were in Nam with you? Corky and Mike?"

"Mike was, yeah. We flew a lot of missions together. Got through some heavy, heavy stuff together." He frowned out the window toward the far woods. "That guy was like a brother to me. Great big guy, liked to clown around. I had this snapshot of him trying to look like Elvis. He signed it 'To Ernie Grant from the King.'" Ernie grinned a little, shaking his head at the memory. "But a serious pilot. Taught me how to get out of LZ's no one else could get out of. How to spot Charlie's traps before landing on them. He knew everything about that war. He was the one I was betting on. He'd survive."

"Yeah, I knew a couple like that," Schreiner said. "They knew every trick in Charlie's book."

"Yeah. Well, it wasn't Charlie that wasted Mike. I mean, maybe Charlie fired the bullets but anyone could of seen it and avoided the problem. Anyone except that asshole Cap'n Corky Lewis."

"I see." Detective Schreiner sounded weary. Her right hand still gripped the chair seat by her knee but her left moved up to push hair from her eyes. "So Lewis blew it."

"He was an idiot! He'd only been in country a little while, and here he comes, fresh out of officer school, and we're all supposed to take orders from him. He'd had some good helicopter training in the U. S. but he didn't know shit about combat. And we'd been flying missions ten months, and we tried to tell him, but this idiot—" Ernie broke off, struggling to control himself. Still lying down, Sarge wriggled and muttered but Ernie ignored him.

Detective Schreiner said, "Yeah. Happened to us too. New

chief comes in, all of a sudden we're supposed to be polishing the tent flaps instead of setting up IV's."

"That way for you too?"

"Yeah."

"Fucking Army."

"Yeah." Schreiner's hand passed over her eyes again. "So what did Lewis do?"

"Should of been routine. Some platoon was under attack and they asked us for five Hueys to get them out. They had a secure landing zone, and they sent up smoke to show us where it was. Okay. Off we went. I was flying second in formation after Bright Boy Corky Lewis. No problem, it was full daylight. I could see the smoke drifting downwind, I could see the goddamn landing zone. I could *see* it! I could *see* that LZ!"

Olivia sat very still, trying to measure Ernie's mood. The others were quiet too: Nick, looking sleepy although Olivia could sense his tension; Jerry, snoring lightly on the carpet; Detective Schreiner, as taut as Ernie, a strange current running between them. Olivia realized that Schreiner had found Ernie's weak point. What he was talking about tugged at him, distracted him from his task of keeping dog and rifle deployed. But Olivia remained fearful. She knew the tiniest wrong move could trigger Ernie's destructive rage.

Ernie was looking out at the woods again, still gripped by the past. His right hand was steady on the rifle but his left clenched and unclenched in anger. "So Cap'n Corky headed for the smoke. Mike got on the radio and told him the target LZ we wanted was in the clearing beyond the ravine. 'Negative,' says Cap'n Corky, 'I see the smoke.' 'Negative,' said Mike, 'the target is upwind of that smoke.' And Cap'n Corky comes back saying, 'I'm in charge here.'"

"That was always the answer," said Schreiner bitterly. "Anytime I asked why we were doing some asshole thing or other, the answer boiled down to 'Shut up, I'm in charge here.' Guess they didn't have any other answers."

"Yeah." Ernie was still looking at the faraway woods.

"So Cap'n Corky landed in the wrong place."

"Yeah. Like I say, Mike and I were right behind him in the second Huey. He touched down, we touched down, and then Charlie opened up. Heavy, heavy fire. Well, he bounced right up again. Guess he'd finally figured out that this wasn't the secure landing the platoon told us about. And I bounced up too, and the guys behind never landed, so we were out of it in just minutes. I knew we'd taken some rounds but the ship was okay. So I looked over at Mike to make some remark. And—and Mike was slumped over, blood all over his flak jacket. Well, I broke formation and tore all the way back to the Evac hospital. The crew chief and I grabbed Mike and ran him inside. But—but it was already too late."

Ernie's voice was thick, his eyes closed. Detective Schreiner edged forward in the rocker. She said, "And I bet that bastard Corky Lewis wasn't hurt."

"Not a scratch," Ernie choked out.

"What did you do?"

He cleared his throat. "Me? I got drunk. They say I was waving an M16 around and they had to tie me down. I stayed drunk two days. Cap'n Corky stayed out of reach. The instant I was fit to fly he saw to it I was off to other parts. And then after a few days word came that my dad had died. So they sent me home."

"And they said, it's over, forget it." Schreiner was watching him closely, watching the weapon too. But her voice was alive with scorn. "Told you to forget your dead buddies, forget Mike. Told you they didn't die in vain, forget them."

A choked whimper from Ernie. "Yeah—but Mike—see, I thought Mike would want—he would of done it for me, you see."

"Yeah, I see," Schreiner said. Her arms trembled with the effort of the grip on the chair seat. "Me, I would have wanted to hunt down Cap'n Corky. Blow the bastard away."

"Yeah. In a plane, just like Mike. And leave him Mike's photo so he'd know why. I thought then it would be over. So I could get on with my life. But—" Ernie's hands went to his face and his shoulders shuddered. Detective Schreiner edged off her chair, still crouched but ready to move. Olivia realized that Nick had imperceptibly moved forward too. Sarge was growling uneasily but Ernie didn't notice.

"Mike's photo," murmured the detective. "So Corky Lewis knew why."

"I thought it would be over," Ernie whimpered. "But Cap'n Corky stuck Mike's photo in his jacket. And that damn reporter found it, and my name was on it—" His hands fell from his face to the rifle again.

"But you wanted Corky Lewis to see the photo." Detective Schreiner's glance flicked to the window, nervously, Olivia thought. "That's why you had to take the chance."

"Yeah, and he said he'd keep it quiet, but—"

The thin whine of a siren crescendoed to a scream. Tires

crackled on the sodden gravel outside. Olivia's world fractured into kaleidoscopic chaos. Everything happened at once.

Ernie screamed, "Cops! You bastards! You called the cops!"

Schreiner grabbed at her own ankle.

Ernie's hands lifted the rifle, found the trigger.

A hunting boot sailed through the air and smashed against Ernie's head.

A shot.

Another shot.

Nick sprang sideways from the sofa, caroming off the window-sill and up onto the bookcase to kick the rifle from Ernie's hand.

Blood spattered on Nick and Ernie as they disappeared together, falling behind the bookcase.

Schreiner was running toward them.

Ernie shrieked, "Sarge! Take 'em!"

Jerry's body hit Olivia's like a bony feather bed, knocking her down into the sofa, sheltering her.

Over Jerry's shoulder she saw Sarge lunge for Nick and the detective. Somehow Schreiner, turning, had a gun in her hand. She fired once, twice, three times. The quick blasts caught the animal in mid-stride, so that his body jerked in the air, spurting blood, until it thudded against the TV and slid to the carpet.

Schreiner knelt behind the bookcase, disappearing from Olivia's view.

Heavy footsteps thumped on the porch. "Police! Don't move!"

"Police are here already, Winky," said Schreiner's calm voice. "But we could sure use an ambulance."

Chapter 19

Olivia took a deep shuddering breath of relief and disintegrated into a fit of coughing.

"Liv. Hey, Livid, are you okay?" Jerry implored. He pulled back from sheltering her to kneel on the sofa, still half-astride her, hands behind him, his face furrowed with worry.

"Jerry, my love," she gasped between coughs, "you stink!"

"I what? Oh." He looked down at his stained and reeking shirt. "Yeah, guess I do. But Nick said sacrificing my new bottle of Jack Daniel's would add a convincing touch. Here." He turned his back. "Untie this Boy Scout knot of yours and I'll do something about it."

Olivia complied, still coughing. He stripped off the shirt and threw it into the far corner. "But are you okay, Liv?"

The air was a little better now. Olivia fought down her coughs and tried to think, am I okay? Not just Jerry's powerful aroma. Not just the scrambled eggs lumped in her stomach. More like seasickness, the sense that a solid dependable world had betrayed her. She said, "I don't know. Where's Ernie?"

"It's okay, the cops have him." Jerry became very professional, studying her face, expert fingers running over her cheek and chin. "Headache?" he asked.

"A little. And nausea. Is Nick okay?"

"Yeah, he's standing up again. Some blood on his shirt next to the Jack Daniel's. I'll check him next." He peered into her eyes in a cold, unromantic way. "Pupils okay."

She risked a peek past him at the room. Four uniformed cops plus a couple of plainclothes detectives she remembered from the Colbys'. The pudgy one, Gabe something. And the older guy. Nick was there too, leaning against the wall, looking alert enough. They all seemed interested in something on the other side of the bookcase room-divider. Probably Ernie, and Schreiner. The dog lay crumpled at the foot of the television. Ernie's three empty beer cans, miraculously untouched, still sat upright by his chair.

Olivia shuddered.

Jerry said, "You got hit hard."

"He socked me in the jaw."

A wave of hatred washed across Jerry's face even as his fingers continued their professional exploration of her jaw. He said calmly enough, "Doesn't seem to be broken. He hit you on the forehead too."

"The forehead?" she asked in surprise, and ran her fingers across her brow. He was right, there was a definitely a bump, definitely tender. "No," she said. "He only hit me once, when he thought I'd called the cops. This must have happened when the van went in the ditch."

In the background, the police stood looking down at whoever was on the other side of the bookcase. A thin little voice asked, "Sarge. Nurse, is Sarge all right?"

"Take it easy, soldier," soothed Schreiner's voice. Olivia had never heard it so warm. "He's comfortable. Just relax, we'll get you fixed up soon."

The thin voice said, "After I blew up Cap'n Corky's plane I was going to shoot myself too. But Mitch said no, Mike would want me to do something worthwhile." It was Ernie, Olivia realized with a shiver. But he sounded like a little kid.

"I bet Mitch will come talk to you," Schreiner said. "You'll have to go to the hospital but I bet he'll see you there."

"Nurse?"

"Yeah?"

"You shot me, didn't you?"

"Yeah. You were about to fire on our own guys. You're okay now."

"I thought they might be ours." He sounded very sleepy. "Hard to tell the friendlies from the others sometimes."

"Yeah, these were friendlies. Listen, the ambulance is coming. You take it easy, and I'll see you in the hospital."

Olivia heard the approaching siren, the bustle as cops ran to get patrol cars out of the way of the ambulance. Nick moved out of their path and came to sit on the far end of the sofa. "You hurt?" Jerry asked him.

"No. Schreiner's shot stopped him in time. His went into the ceiling." He pointed his chin at the corner of the ceiling nearest the archway, and Olivia saw the cracked and shattered plaster.

Jerry peered into Olivia's eyes to check her pupils once again, then sat next to her. He put a lanky bare arm around her shoulders. Slowly, normality was seeping back. She murmured, "I was so scared."

"Me too," said Jerry darkly.

"The dog and the rifle. He was such a good shot! He hit the van from the porch when I tried to drive away."

"Yeah," said Nick. "We inspected that tire. That's when we knew we needed a special gimmick to get in."

"You shouldn't have come in."

"Maybe not," Jerry said. "But I figured, one guy with a rifle, and three of us—besides, you looked so scared. But I hadn't figured on that dog."

"Yeah." Olivia shivered.

Jerry glanced at her and added grimly, "And I hadn't figure it was really two against two."

"Hey, easy, Jerry," warned Nick.

"What do you mean?" demanded Olivia.

"You tied us up for real, kiddo." Anger lurked behind Jerry's even tone.

"But he told me to!" She was astonished at his implication.

"And if he'd told you to shoot us? Handed over his rifle and told you to do that? Would you have done it? Gone over like Patty Hearst?"

"I—" Olivia hid her face in her hands. He didn't understand. "No. I wouldn't have—but—the dog—" Would she have robbed a bank for Ernie? She had a sudden insane sense of fellow feeling for Patty Hearst. How much would she have done to survive? She turned her face into Jerry's bare shoulder, sobbing.

"Liv, Liv!" Half-contrite, half-exasperated, he stroked her hair. "I shouldn't have—look, I just thought you'd be more helpful."

She still sobbed. "But even if I was—I thought of all that, Jerry! I thought at first that if I could just get the rifle, shoot the dog—but then I realized it was impossible. He'd have other guns."

Jerry looked surprised. Nick nodded. "She's right, Jerry. Detective Schreiner took two handguns off him just now, before she gave first aid."

"Wow," said Jerry softly.

"I tied you up so you wouldn't do something to—to get him mad," Olivia explained.

Jerry nodded and Nick's brown eyes smiled at her. "You did fine," he said. "But now, would you mind untying me?"

"Oh, God, I'm sorry!" Olivia leaned around Jerry to unfasten the knotted electric cord. Nick flexed his fingers and rubbed his wrists. She added apologetically, "I'm still sort of dazed. It was—you know, he was completely in control."

"Right," said Nick. "Jerry, we're all mad as hell, but it was Ernie Grant's fault. What Liv did was reasonable."

Olivia managed a small smile. Reasonable. But Jerry's questions were reasonable too. There must have been something she could have done to help. Some way to be Joanne Little instead of Patty Hearst. To strike back instead of cooperating. But Joanne Little's jailer had only had an ice pick. No rifle. No attack dog. She fingered the lump on her forehead absently. How had she got into this ridiculous dilemma? Stupid eagerness to get a story, a dangerous story. Neglecting to take even the tiniest precautions. And then, once here, pushing ahead blindly, asking about Dale Colby, flashing his photo, too dumb to see danger until it had overtaken her— She frowned at the carpet. Damn it, that was a good piece of acting Ernie had done while he looked at that photo—

Her own name caught her ear. Detective Schreiner, watching the paramedics carry Ernie out on a stretcher, was talking to plump Gabe. Her arms were crossed, her stance relaxed yet ready, talking in her emotionless voice. Pure cop. She'd seemed so much more human talking about Vietnam with Ernie. She was saying, "Olivia Kerr came out here for some reason, haven't had a chance to ask. The others followed. I didn't know it was a major scene until I arrived, found the Ryan woman singing a lullaby to her kid down by the road, in her car. She said Kerr's van had been disabled, and the two men had gone in to check and weren't back yet. That's when I radioed for backup."

"We got right on it."

"Figured you would. I went in and tried to talk him down. Almost did, I think. But that asshole Winks came in with siren screaming and spooked him. That's when he picked up the rifle for real."

"And you shot to stop him."

"Yeah." The sandy-haired detective hesitated a moment, squinting toward the bookcase. "Something else stopped him first,

Gabe. I was still fumbling with the goddamn ankle holster when that boot hit him in the face."

Olivia followed her gaze. That hunting boot! It lay in the shadows at the foot of the bookcase. But she remembered it now, sailing in to hit the side of Ernie's head. The shots had come an instant after. One from Ernie, off balance. One from Schreiner.

But where had the hunting boot come from?

"Ahem," said someone from the door to the bedroom hall.

Detective Schreiner looked over, unsurprised. "Should have known," she said in resignation. "I asked you to stay down by the road."

Maggie stood there, big-bellied and listing sideways to balance a sleepy Sarah on her left hip. "Yeah. Well. It was pretty boring down by the road."

"Even so," said Schreiner sternly.

"Hey, look, this time I didn't mess with your precious crime scene," Maggie said defensively. "Except to toss in that boot."

"From the bedroom hall?"

"Yeah."

"How'd you get in there?"

"Torn screen in the bedroom. Stuck in a hand and unlatched it. The dog growled but the rest of you people had him pretty well distracted. Besides, I stood behind the door so I could slam it in his face if he moved."

"Yeah. And the kid?"

"She went to sleep in the car so I locked her in. Naptime. Just fetched her this minute." She shifted the little girl on her hip. "Okay if we sit down?"

Schreiner made a curt gesture toward the sofa. Maggie carefully deposited Sarah there between Jerry and Nick, kissed Nick's bald head and grabbed his hand. Still holding it, she perched on the arm of the sofa next to him to listen.

Gabe peered at his notes and said, "Okay, Holly, I got it about the shooting. You're all by the sofa, he's here on this side of the room divider. You're talking to him, he hears the siren, goes for the rifle, this lady throws the boot, you shoot him, he goes down."

"Right. He yells for the dog. By then O'Connor has jumped on the bookcase and is kicking at the rifle, so I turn to check the dog. He's charging. I fire again." She looked at the furry heap below the TV and said in a tight voice, "He was a real good dog."

The other detective looked at Sarge, then at Detective Schreiner. "So what was it with this guy? Did I hear him say he blew up the congressman's plane?"

"Yeah."

"Nut case? Or did he have a motive?"

Schreiner clasped her hands behind her, looked at her shoes, and muttered something.

"What?"

"I said whoopee." Schreiner took a deep breath, raised her head to inspect the fractured ceiling. Olivia was shocked at how ravaged she looked. Schreiner said, "He's no more a nut case then I am." A dark smile quivered on her lips. "We'll see if that's enough to get him acquitted."

Olivia saw that Maggie was bolt upright on the sofa arm, still holding Nick's hand but tense, her attention riveted on Detective Schreiner. Glancing in their direction, Schreiner was caught for a moment by the intensity of Maggie's gaze. The bitter smile guttered and died. She jerked her eyes away and pulled out her notepad. "Ms. Kerr," she said briskly, "could you fill us in on what happened?"

"Yeah. Okay." Olivia took a deep breath. "I—well, before I start, I just want to say I tried to call you."

Schreiner's expression was flat again. "Yes. I got your messages. Tried to find you at the *S-D* office."

"Yes, uh, I was in and out."

"Why did you come here?"

"Well—what I called you about was, I forgot to tell you something last night." At the twitch of Schreiner's brow she flared defensively, "I really did forget! I picked it up from the floor in front of Dale's den while I was knocking on his door. Just stuck it into my pocket. And then a few minutes later we found Dale dead, and it just went out of my head."

"What was it?"

"A paper napkin. I didn't even look at it, just thought one of the kids had dropped it and it was messing up Donna's clean house. But after I got home I looked at it. It came from Donovan's Bar. And I knew it wasn't there before we left."

"And you went off to the bar."

"Yes. Late last night. Nick came along." Olivia glanced at him. "The bartender didn't recognize Dale Colby's photo. But he did say that a customer named Ernie Grant had been very interested in the reports about the plane crash in January, because he'd known the pilot. So I came out to ask Ernie Grant about it."

"All alone."

"Look, I'm a reporter! And this is one hell of a story!" Olivia paused, surprised. She'd been blank with terror for so long that the story's importance had evaporated. Now, in a rush, she realized she had it. Pages and pages of it. Maybe a ticket to the Washington *Post*.

"Maybe so." Schreiner sounded weary.

"Listen, you walked into it too!" Olivia flared. "We've all got reasons. And I don't care how many goddamn patrol rides you try to send me on, sister, you're going to get good press."

That at least brought a flicker of surprise to Schreiner's flat dark eyes, a twitch of warmth to her mouth. "Long live the First Amendment," she muttered, and turned to a fresh page. "So you drove out here to talk to Ernie Grant. Then what?"

"Well, I thought he was Corky Lewis's friend. But after we'd talked a minute he started insisting that I should wait inside while he made a call, and it finally dawned on me. I knew he'd been at Donovan's. And if he had one of the napkins in his pocket, it might have fallen out while he was killing Dale Colby."

"I see."

"I tried to get away but he disabled the van and pulled me inside here."

"Is that when he roughed you up?" Schreiner was writing fast.

Olivia touched her jaw. "No. He was very polite, in a funny way. Forced me into the house but kept explaining politely that it was just till he'd made the phone call, after that he'd help me change the tire if I checked out okay. He just seemed puzzled that I was here. No, um, sexual threat either. He didn't even seem angry at me. Except once."

"Yeah?"

"We were waiting for his boss to call back and the phone rang. I'm pretty sure it wasn't the right call, it was just some friend. I think he called him Mitch. And the talk was friendly for a minute, then Ernie asked what he was leading up to. And whatever Mitch said got him agitated. He told Mitch not to tell them anything, and then he ran back in here screaming that I'd told the cops about him. That's when he hit me."

Gabe asked, "Didn't you try to get away while he was on the phone?"

Jerry burst out angrily, "Are you crazy? The van was disabled, an attack dog was watching her, and that guy had a rifle and two handguns! You expect her to just walk out?"

Olivia looked at him in pleased surprise.

Schreiner went on as though the other two hadn't spoken. "What happened then, Ms. Kerr?"

"I convinced him that someone else told the cops. He got

polite again, offered me some ice for my jaw. Let me fix him some scrambled eggs. And then Jerry and Nick came weaving up the drive. Ernie believed they were drunk."

"I can see why," observed the detective drily. She glanced at Nick. "Thanks for clueing me in that cops were not welcome."

He nodded gravely. "I still had some hopes for survival."

"Yeah."

"You were great," Nick told her. "Calming him, finding out about the plane crash, stopping him at the end."

"That's the job." She turned to Gabe. "I need to make a call. Keep an eye on Winks so he doesn't contaminate the evidence."

Gabe nodded and rejoined the uniformed cops clustered beyond the bookcase. Schreiner went into the dining room, flipping through her notebook. In a moment Olivia heard her dialing. She had to strain to hear the quiet voice.

"Hello, Mitch, this is Detective Schreiner." She was around the corner, out of sight. "We've picked up a guy you know. Ernie Grant . . . Hey, we didn't have any choice, he was holding people at gunpoint! Anyway, I just wanted to tell you he's under guard in Windover Hospital, but maybe we can arrange a visit . . . Good." Olivia struggled to hear as Schreiner went on. "Look, help him however you can, that's why I'm calling you, but he'll have to stay in custody. We've got him three ways. Not just holding the hostages, but also blowing up the plane Corky Lewis was flying, and we've got him at the scene of the Colby murder yesterday afternoon . . . What did you say?" Her voice had become sharper. "One-thirty to six? Are you sure?" A hint of sarcasm crept into her voice. "And I suppose you've got an alibi for him for the plane crash too? . . . Oh. Okay, look, I know you're not bullshitting me. But we have evidence linking Ernie to a bar and the bar to the scene of the crime . . . What guy in the bar?" She reappeared in the archway, her hand cupped over the receiver, and asked Olivia, "Did Ernie Grant say anything about a drinking buddy?"

"No." Olivia shook her head.

"But the bartender did," Nick reminded her. "He mentioned someone that Ernie occasionally met there."

Schreiner spoke into the receiver again. "Yeah, we got a lead on him. Why? . . . Yeah, I understand you can't say any more. We'll check with Ernie. Thanks for your cooperation, Mitch . . . Yeah, me too, I want to help the guy too. But I've got to make sense of this Colby thing."

Schreiner hung up and came slowly back into the front room, frowning at her notes.

Maggie asked, "Mitch is a friend of Ernie's?"

"Veterans' counselor."

"So Ernie has an alibi for yesterday?"

Schreiner shot her a dark look and crossed the room to murmur something to Gabe.

Maggie looked down the length of the sofa at Olivia. "I heard her say one-thirty to six, right? So if Ernie did it, and he was at the counselor's all afternoon, he couldn't have killed Dale until six-thirty at the earliest."

"Seems too late to me," said Jerry. "Rigor and lividity were several hours advanced when I saw him at nine. But that's for the medical examiner to decide."

"Yeah, but the ME won't be pinned down yet," Maggie informed him. "So there must be some kind of evidence for a later time of death. And we have the bar napkin there, from a bar we know Ernie visited. So maybe Ernie was there at six-thirty—"

Jerry shrugged.

"But why?" Olivia asked. "Dale hadn't printed anything."

"But apparently he'd found Mike's photo. A signed photo, to Ernie Grant."

"So if Dale knew, and didn't print it—" Nick said slowly, looking at Maggie. "You're thinking blackmail?"

"Maybe."

Olivia examined that possibility. "It's true, Ernie was surprised to hear I was from the *Sun-Dispatch*."

"We know Dale was under pressure from Felicia to get money," Maggie said. "Maybe he figured he would keep quiet a while and collect from Ernie."

"Blackmailing someone like Ernie? Someone who'd blow up a plane? Not very wise," said Jerry.

"Dale did need money," Olivia said. "But it doesn't seem like a risk he'd take."

"No." Maggie combed her fingers through her curls. "And there are other problems. First, Ernie was at that counselor's at the most likely time of death. And a brass lamp seems a strange choice of weapon for a guy who's a walking arsenal."

"Wonder who he went drinking with?" mused Nick.

"Dale?" suggested Jerry. "If Dale was blackmailing him—"

"Dale got out occasionally," said Olivia dubiously. "But it was hard for him. He'd make the arrangements by phone, I think. Besides, the bartender didn't recognize Dale's photo."

"Right," Nick agreed.

"For that matter," added Olivia, "I could have sworn Ernie didn't recognize it either. But we know Dale found Mike's photo, don't we? Oh, God!" She halted in sudden disbelief.

"You've thought of something?" Maggie jumped up and ran to Olivia's end of the sofa.

"But it can't be! But he has a blue Ford—and he was first on the crash scene, he could have picked up the photo—see, Ernie didn't say Dale found it, he said the reporter found it—oh, God!" Things were beginning to make horrible sense.

Maggie, perched eagerly on the sofa arm by Olivia, asked, "Who, Liv? Who?"

"It wasn't Dale who found the photo. It wasn't Dale blackmailing Ernie. See, when Ernie phoned to check on me, he called the person Rosie." Olivia raised her astonished gaze to Maggie's. "It was Nate," she said with certainty. "Nate Rosen!"

Chapter 20

Holly had deployed her forces. Winks had been sent to get a
search warrant for Nate Rosen's home, car and office at the
Sun-Dispatch. Gabe was on his way to Bo Morgan's to show the
boy a set of photos, including Rosen's, in the hopes that he'd
recognize yesterday's visitor. Afterwards, Gabe would visit the
bartender at Donovan's Bar with the same photos.

A couple of uniformed cops had accompanied Ernie Grant to
surgery. They'd wait for him to wake up and let Holly know so she
could get a statement. The next thing on her own agenda was to
take Olivia, Maggie, Nick and Jerry to the station house for official
statements. Right now the four were changing the tire of the van
while Sarah napped in the car, so Holly decided to take a last look
around Ernie's house. She'd leave the place under the care of a
couple of patrol officers and come back for a more thorough search
tomorrow.

She started around for one last quick tour. This house was not
really Ernie's, it was his parents' home still. Their bedroom sat
untouched in the front corner of the house, their flowery curtains
and bedspread still in place. Ernie's own room was the only area
that gave any sense of the man, and even there the message was
split, a boy's collection of model airplanes on one wall vying with
a handsome display case of real firearms on the other. Nothing,
unfortunately, that could fire through a keyhole, knock a lamp
onto a guy's head, and then disappear without leaving a trace. She
stood looking at the well-oiled weapons for a moment. A lot of
them. She could understand his obsession. Nam peeled off your

youthful sense of invulnerability pretty damn quick. Left you always watching your back, building psychological bunkers, setting up defensive perimeters even in the so-called safety of home. All those rifles, shotguns, automatics. Attack dogs. She felt bad about the dog. The only creature in the world that Ernie trusted. She closed her eyes. She felt so bad about the dog.

Cut it out, Schreiner. Don't get sentimental, this ain't Benji we're talking about.

"You okay?"

Maggie. Always hovering around like a goddamn guardian angel, equally ready to produce a lost child or a skillfully thrown boot. Holly swiped hastily at her nose with the back of her hand. "Yeah. Just sorry about the dog."

Maggie mulled that over for a moment. "Yeah. Poor Sarge. Another brave and loyal soldier lost in the wrong cause."

Was that it? Was that what choked her up about the dog?

"He should have been a hero," said Maggie gently, and added, "So should Ernie. And so should you. You should all have been heroes."

Holly was trembling. When Maggie put her arms around her, she shoved back at her angrily. Be strong, Schreiner. But Maggie was stronger, would not be pushed away this time. She held Holly tight. "Let it out," she murmured. "Please don't let it kill you too. We need you."

Holly was shaking uncontrollably. She fought it another moment but then the tears started and she had to give in. Locked in the safety of those arms, she rested her head on Maggie's shoulder and let the shuddering sobs escape, let someone else be the strong one. Maggie held her a long time, stroking her hair, rocking her gently in her arms, until at last the weeping was spent and Holly stood exhausted. Maggie pulled a packet of tissues from her bedraggled blue dress and handed it to her.

"Thanks." Holly swabbed at her ravaged face. "Uh—"

"If you say you're sorry I'll kick you in the shin!" said Maggie fiercely.

"Yeah, okay." Holly pulled herself together, managed a trembly grin. "God, with peaceniks like you, who needs wars?"

"Yeah," said Maggie. Her grin was shaky too.

Holly looked down at Ernie's braided rug, then up again into the blue eyes. "Maggie, can you tell me why?"

Maggie shook her head slowly. "We have to work out the meaning for ourselves."

"And if there's no meaning?"

"Then we have to bear witness to the waste." Maggie shrugged. "All I know is it can't be ignored. Can't be forgotten." She looked at the weapons display. "And there aren't any short-cuts. Quitting before we've worked it out is dangerous. Revenge won't cure grief."

Holly nodded. Ernie had quit too soon. Mitch might have helped, all that talk about confronting pain, renewing life. Helping a guy do it for himself.

Maggie's mind was running along the same track. She leaned back against the wall and said, "This counselor you called, Mitch. Ernie's friend. He works with vets?"

"Vietnam vets. Yeah, a rap group."

"Have you joined it?"

"It's for men only."

"Why? You're a vet."

"Hey, look, are you kidding? Nurses weren't their buddies. If they got wounded, okay, we were their moms. Like Ernie just now. But if we went to a party we found out that off-duty we were nothing but round-eyed pussy." Holly waved away Maggie's indignation. "Guys we worked with were mostly okay, the doctors and corpsmen. They knew we were on the team. But guys like Mitch never saw us that way. Can't expect miracles now."

"Maybe not." Maggie looked glum. "Especially since I bet half the rap group involves telling each other they were scared shitless. Can't do that in front of some broad."

"Yeah. John Wayne dies hard."

"Maybe because there's some truth in John Wayne amongst the lies." Maggie studied Holly a moment, a tiny frown between her brows. "You're a good detective. You like homicide work."

"It's okay."

"No, really. It satisfies something."

"Yeah, okay, I like to figure out why the poor suckers bought it. So what?"

"So maybe—well, it's just that in Vietnam guys died and no one could tell you why. You don't want that to happen to Dale Colby and the others."

Nurse, tell me why. Holly said, "Maybe. Yeah, maybe so." She did feel good when she managed to cut through the crap to a fact. To something real. Something authentic. "Sometimes," she told Maggie, "when I've solved a case, they let me sleep for a few nights."

"They?"

"The dreams. It's as though for a little while—I don't know."

She remembered Mitch's words. "As though my survival means something."

"Yeah. That's good. You're onto something," Maggie said eagerly. "Look, Holly, we've got to find someone to work through this stuff with you."

Holly felt suddenly betrayed. "You think I'm crazy too!"

"The hell I do!" Maggie shook her black curls fiercely. "You're a normal, smart human being who had to go through something inhumanly horrible! Seems to me that hurting and grieving about it proves you're *not* crazy. If it didn't bother you—now, that *would* be sick."

She was right, damn it. It wasn't crazy to hurt. To hell with Alec. With Mitch. Though Mitch almost understood even if he wouldn't help. He knew that the dead refused to go unremembered. Knew that trying to be numb wouldn't work no matter how hard you wished it would. Holly pushed back her hair and looked at the woman who kept prodding her toward this necessary unwelcome knowledge. "You know," she said acidly, "your brother is right. You are a maggot. Always gnawing away."

Maggie grinned sadly. "Guilty as charged. Just trying to uncover what's healthy and alive."

Healthy and alive? That needed some thinking about. Holly said slowly, "There was this other nurse. Billie Ann. She wrote me a couple of times but I didn't answer."

"Call her," Maggie urged. "You need each other."

"Maybe so." Holly looked around the room and returned to the immediate problem. "I just wish I could do something for Dale Colby."

"You've got Nate Rosen, right?"

"No. I mean, even if everything works out, and we get proof that he was at Colby's yesterday afternoon, and that he was worried that Dale would find out he was blackmailing Ernie, and so forth—even then, we don't know how he got in and out of the room. And his attorney will hammer that home for the jury."

"Yeah."

"Except for that, it'd be a pretty case. No sweat."

"Yeah. Oh, God!"

"What's wrong?" Holly stepped toward Maggie, concerned. She was standing with one hand jabbed into the black curls over her forehead, her eyes closed. After a moment her hand dropped and she looked bleakly at Holly.

"Sorry. Just remembered a phone call I have to make. God, did you ever notice how life can be a shitheap?"

"That fact has come to my attention." Holly put her arm around Maggie's dropping shoulders. "Hey, buck up now, Maggot. Let's go get this damn paperwork out of the way."

Near midnight Holly sat across from Nate Rosen in the interrogation room, Gabe quiet with a notebook in the corner. Nate looked even more mournful than usual, worry written in his wrinkled forehead and the nervous motions of his long fingers.

"We're not ready to charge you with anything yet," Holly explained. "But we'd like some information."

"Do I need a lawyer? I didn't do anything." He stuck his hands in his pockets, where his fingers twitched nervously.

"You're not under arrest. But you could clear up some questions for us."

"Arrest?" There was panic in his voice. His hands jerked out of his pockets and a note fluttered to the floor. Gabe picked it up and handed it back politely.

Holly repeated, "You're not under arrest. We just have some questions."

"Do I have to answer?"

"Why wouldn't you want to?" She watched him alertly. "You want to help us find the guy who killed Dale, right?"

He licked his lips. "Yeah." The implications of not answering were sinking in. "Yeah, let's talk, then."

"Okay, let's start at the beginning, with Representative Knox's plane. You went to the scene of the crash as a reporter, right?"

"Yeah, I was in my car. Heard someone talking about the crash on my CB. Drove right over."

"You were first on the scene?"

"One of the first. The wreckage was spread out over the hillside."

"Ernie Grant said you found a photograph in the wreckage."

The name shocked him. He passed a hand over his face and apparently decided to brazen it out. "Yeah. The tail section was burning and a few people were there shouting. I noticed what looked like a hunk of the cockpit. The pilot's, uh, body was nearby. I, uh, looked at his ID and stuff, and put it back. Then the emergency people started arriving so I ran back to the car and got to a phone."

"A phone?"

"To call in the story."

"Yes. Now, Ernie Grant mentioned a photograph he'd left with the pilot."

"Yeah. I found it. Picture of Ernie's Vietnam buddy pretending to be Elvis Presley. But I didn't know that at first." His brown eyes brimmed with worry.

"Nothing was printed in the *Sun-Dispatch* about the photograph."

"No. I, uh, just took it to investigate. But I didn't find out anything right away because there was so much else to do. The first thing I did was check the pilot's name and the air charter company. They said it was a congressman's plane so I knew it was a big story. Started working on the political side. Had to interview all those investigators, too."

"Did you show the photo to the investigators?"

"Uh, no." Nate studied his fingers and decided to add something. "I was so busy with the rest of the story."

Just like Olivia Kerr. Holly sighed. Reporters were such very busy people. Weaselly people, valuable to cops but only when it suited them. Holly said, "Now, Mr. Edgerton said he'd assigned Dale Colby to the story too."

"Yeah, like I say, it was a big one."

"Did you show the photo to Dale Colby?"

"No."

She waited for him to elaborate, but this time he was quiet. She asked, "What did you do about the photograph?"

"Well—I took it because I was curious. See, the signature said 'To Ernie Grant' but his ID had said Lewis. And the photo on his ID didn't match either, so it wasn't a picture of him. I figured he must be holding the photo for a friend, and if I could find this friend I'd get myself a nice human-interest piece out of it, that's all. So I called a few Grants in the directory, asked if they knew any pilots. When this one said yes I told him about the crash, and said I'd found a photo for him. He agreed to meet me. When we did—well, I guess he just assumed I knew everything. Started telling me about the guy dressed up like Elvis in the picture, how Lewis's mistake killed him. Didn't take long to realize this was the guy who'd put the explosive on the plane."

"So you had a nice story," said Holly, her voice tight. "But it never got printed."

"Uh, no."

"Would you like to explain why not?"

Nate was silent a moment. Then he said, "The direction these questions are going, I don't think I want to answer."

"That's your decision, Mr. Rosen. You're not under arrest. Let me just point out that Ernie Grant told me you said you'd keep quiet about the photo. We know that Mr. Grant had just sold some valuable land to a developer so he had the money to pay blackmail. We plan to subpoena bank records and—"

"All right, all right!" Nate flopped his hand nervously. "Yeah, I needed the money. He didn't. Not really, said he just wanted to hang around with his dog, go hunting—hell, I felt for the guy."

Wonderful. Blackmail as a humanitarian act. But there's no time for a lecture, Schreiner, find out about that locked room. She said, "Let's move on to yesterday afternoon, Mr. Rosen. You were in the office until two o'clock?"

"Yes. Approximately. Then I went out to get some man-on-the-street quotes for the heat-wave story. The weather people were talking about cooler air coming in—well, you know what the weather was."

"Yes. And you stopped by Colby's."

He stared at his fingers.

She said, "You were seen by two neighbors."

"Yes," he said at last.

"You rang the bell?"

"Yes."

Holly waited but he didn't add anything. She asked, "Did Mr. Colby answer?"

"No. But I didn't expect him to. I thought he was at the beach. I just rang the bell, well, just in case."

"You went in anyway?"

"I wanted to find out—see, the trouble is, this story of his got a lot of people nervous. Including me, because it told about the pilot meeting a vet before the crash. I wanted to hear Dale's taped interviews, to hear what he really had."

Holly thought a moment. What could Dale have had on those tapes? Priscilla's account of her brother's encounter with an unknown vet who upset him. And Mitch's no-names-given discussion of the rap group. But he wouldn't have had Ernie's name. Or would he? She asked, "You wanted to know, because if he published Ernie's name your payments would dry up?"

The sad brown eyes met Holly's. "You've seen Ernie. If he saw his name in the paper—in *my* paper—before you cops got there to arrest him, you think I'd be alive long?"

"So you were afraid of Ernie."

Nate shrugged uncomfortably and jammed his hands into his pockets. "Yeah! Not the world's most stable guy. It was important for me to know what Dale had. Maybe there was no reason to panic. The front door was unlocked so I went in."

"What time was this?"

"Three-thirty, maybe a few minutes later."

"And what did you do?"

"I went to his den. Knocked and waited." Holly could visualize him, his hands twisting nervously in his pockets as they were now, the bar napkin dropping unseen to the floor. Nate went on, "Nothing happened. So I tried the door, but it was locked. I struggled with it for several minutes. Worked up a real sweat, it was so damn hot yesterday, but I couldn't push the damn thing open. So I went back to the living room to get those tapes and—"

"You didn't go into the den at all?" asked Holly sharply.

"No, I just told you, I couldn't. Locked from the inside."

"Did you hear Mr. Colby in there?"

"No. I realize now—he must have been in there—already—" His thin mouth clamped thinner.

"You saw or heard nothing from that room?"

"Nothing. But it didn't worry me then, I thought he was at the beach, you see."

Holly exchanged a glance with Gabe. This was a clever story, damn it. Admitting only what they could already prove. A good lawyer could make Nate look like the soul of cooperation, waiving counsel, freely answering questions, the innocent little blackmailer and burglar caught up in an unfortunate coincidence. She needed more or he'd slither out from under a murder charge. Presumed innocent. Suddenly angry, Holly slapped the tabletop with both hands and pressed herself to a standing position.

"Thank you, Mr. Rosen," she said. "That's all for now. But we'll be wanting to question you again."

"Well. All right." Surprised by the abrupt dismissal, he looked at her uncertainly.

"You're free to go, Mr. Rosen."

Nate got up, gave Gabe a thin smile, and ambled out.

"Tail him?" asked Gabe.

"Yeah. Set it up, okay? Let's hope he makes a dumb move. We need everything we can get against that weasel."

He was watching her check hastily through her handbag. "Where are you going?"

"Colby's. I was hoping we'd get a hint from Rosen about how he managed the locked-room trick. But he's sharp. So I'm going to go look at that goddamn room again."

Chapter 21

Holly was glad to see a light still burning in the Colby living-room window. It was midnight and she'd worried that Donna would be in a drugged sleep. She stood on the cement platform and knocked instead of ringing, just in case. Donna answered almost immediately.

"Sorry to bother you again, Mrs. Colby," Holly said. She saw that Donna was not dressed for bed, she was still in the sleeveless blouse and denim skirt Holly had seen earlier that day. Holly went on, "We're making some progress toward finding your husband's killer, and I'd like to see the room again."

"Yes, please, come in." Donna stepped back. The hall light glared on her bedraggled blonde hair and on eyes puffy from weeping. She glanced into the living room and said, "Please sit down. Can I get you something to drink?"

"Thanks, no." Holly went into the living room. Maggie was slouched in one of the wing chairs, one leg dangling over the armrest. She'd changed from the rumpled blue sundress into a red cotton maternity shirt and white shorts. She said, "Hi. I take it your suspect didn't explain how it was done?"

"We're getting there. Shouldn't be long before we have what we need."

"And now you want to look at the crime scene again," said Maggie. "Well, tonight's as good as tomorrow. Maybe better."

Holly looked at her sharply. Strange mood here. "What's going on?" she asked. "Why are you here?"

"I was just checking on Donna. To see how things were going. To tell her about a phone call I just made."

Holly plunked herself down on the sofa and pulled out her notebook. Exasperating woman. Just when she thought things were under control she was playing catch-up again. "What have you found out this time?" she asked.

Maggie watched Donna cross the room and sink into the other wing chair before she said, "I've found out that Josie and Tina are smart kids. If they keep making good grades they'll get to college someday." She flipped a hand toward Holly's notebook. "You can put that away for a while."

"It's top secret that the girls are smart?" Holly asked in a vinegary voice.

Maggie pulled her leg from the armrest of her chair and stretched both feet out before her. "I thought you might want to know how Dale Colby died. Donna and I were getting ready to discuss it. But I can't seem to remember with that notebook out."

"You know how it was done?"

"Can't remember."

Holly slapped the notebook closed and shoved it into her pocket. So the take-charge hotshot was back in the picture again. Couldn't trust anyone. She looked coldly at Maggie and said, "Yes, I'd like to know."

"Oh, hey, come on." Maggie breezed across the room to perch on the sofa arm. "We're all on the same team."

Donna was looking at Maggie with eagerness and fearfulness. "You know how it was done?"

Maggie met her eyes. "Yes, Donna."

"The lamp? The blood? The stolen tapes? Everything?"

"Yes. Well, almost everything."

Donna looked down at her hands, squeezed together in her lap. "I want to hear. And I don't want to."

"Yeah. Same here," said Maggie sadly. "But we've all got to."

Donna studied Holly's face for a moment, then the pocket where the notebook had disappeared, then her gaze dropped to her own knotted hands. "Yeah."

"Okay," Maggie said. "We'll start with the phone call. That's what Donna and I were just talking about, that and the girls. I called Harrisburg. Talked to Felicia Colby's friend, Nan Evans."

"About Felicia's alibi? We did that too," said Holly. "Felicia was in Harrisburg at four forty-five."

"Right. But you see, Felicia mentioned that Nan was an old friend. So I asked her another question. I asked why Felicia insisted on a divorce when Dale was so opposed and it made life so rough for her. Nan said it was a secret because of the boy. But she told me Felicia divorced him because he beat her up once too often."

"Beat her up?"

"The baby had been sick and so dinner was late. He beat her up. The next day she packed her bag and walked out."

Holly frowned. That was long ago. And Felicia couldn't have arrived from Harrisburg in time yesterday even if she'd waited all these years for revenge. Holly looked across at Donna, who was still pressing her hands together. "He beat you too?"

"Yes," murmured Donna almost soundlessly.

"Recently?"

Donna looked mournfully at the window, at the door. Maggie said, "I'm sorry, Donna. But we have to go over it again. So she'll understand."

Donna's gaze returned to Holly. "Yes. Recently. And for a long time before. Starting a few months after we were married."

"But you didn't walk out like Felicia."

"Oh, God, I wish I had! But I thought it was better for the kids. He loved the kids. Back then I thought it was better for them."

Was this some kind of a con these two were pulling? Holly glanced grimly up at Maggie on the sofa arm. Maggie said, "It's true. Look." She ran across to the wing chair, pulled Donna upright, and said, "Show her. Okay?"

Donna hesitated, then lifted her blouse. Holly's brow contracted despite herself at the sight of the yellowing bruises and red scabs on her ribs. *Did heaven look on, and would not take their part?*

"He used his belt," Donna explained. "The buckle end."

"And you didn't leave him?"

"He always had a reason, he said." Drooping, Donna sat at the other end of the sofa. "Dinner was late, or the house wasn't neat— For a long time I believed him. I loved him. I wanted to believe him. If I could just do better it wouldn't happen any more. I tried so hard! But after a while I started thinking it wasn't really what I did. I couldn't control it. It was something in him."

"You still put up with it?"

"Because of the girls. And because he could be so sweet sometimes. He'd bring flowers—"

Maggie asked, "Didn't you wonder if it would be better for the children if they weren't in a violent home?"

"Of course I wondered," said Donna with some dignity. "But

you see, he loved them. He was a perfectionist but he loved them. Told them stories, taught them games. And there was Felicia."

"Felicia?"

"She kept asking for money. One day on the phone I got so exasperated with her. I asked her why she kept badgering him when she knew we were in debt over our heads for this little house ourselves. And she asked me if I'd ever thought of how far in debt I'd be with kids and only my income. Well, I knew she was right. The house is in Dale's name. The bank accounts. So I stayed. To be fair to the girls."

"I see," said Holly.

"Later—after he lost the job as managing editor—it got worse. He was so frustrated. He bought the guns then. Every month or two he'd go at me with the belt and wave the gun around. And the Parkinson's frustrated him even more. Ate away at him. He was so afraid it would interfere with his work. And he took it out on me. It got worse and worse." She was squeezing her hands together again. "For a little while I thought maybe the disease would progress fast enough that he couldn't beat me any more. But the doctor got it under control, and then the L-dopa came along." She looked at the window again. "The doctor said he was optimistic about how long Dale would be able to continue as usual."

Happy news on the medical front. Holly could imagine Donna's feelings at the excited announcement of this great breakthrough in medicine. She said, "So Dale did continue as usual."

"It got worse. Last year I was getting some school things and got tied up in traffic. I was an hour late. And he was absolutely furious. Said if I was thinking about running off like Felicia he'd hunt me down and kill me." Her lips trembled. "He would have."

"He didn't kill Felicia," Holly pointed out.

"No. But he hated her. It was partly that—anyway, he would have killed me."

Maggie asked, "Did you ever call the cops?"

Donna shook her head. In the lamplight her disheveled hair glowed gold, giving her the look of a lost waif. The Little Match Girl, maybe, from one of Holly's childhood books. Donna explained, "Before we bought this house we were in an apartment. Neighbors called the cops once when I was screaming. Dale told them we were just arguing. They believed him, told me to keep down the noise, went away."

"And you with bruises?"

"They didn't see them. He always hit me where they wouldn't

show. Anyway, he would just have said I fell down the stairs or something. They would have believed him."

Holly nodded. She could imagine Winks' response. Poor Colby, he'd say, married to a whiny bitch like that. But she hated domestic-violence cases herself. The victims feared the cops because the guy was even angrier afterwards. Cops risked their lives going into those situations and then the women would refuse to press charges, even joining with the abuser to get the cops to leave. Holly remembered, just hours ago, Olivia Kerr's glare of hatred and fear. Instead of welcoming Holly as glorious rescuer, Olivia was terrified that she might rock the boat, might damage the fragile relationship with her captor that had kept her alive so far. Donna Colby had lived with that kind of fear, year after year. And with cops like Winks around she was probably right to avoid their so-called help. "I understand why you didn't call us," Holly said. "But I don't understand why you're telling me now."

Maggie had left Donna's side and was pacing restlessly around the room. "Because it's important for you to know why."

Holly pushed her hair back from her forehead. "Look, for once I've got too many why's. Plenty of people with motives. And I've got people with opportunity. Not you, Mrs. Colby, because you were away when he died. And the worst problem is I don't know how it was done. The ME won't be pinned down about anything except it involved heart failure. Toxicology reports are all negative. So if you're working up to some kind of confession, I need more."

"Not a confession," said Maggie sharply. "At least not yet."

"What, then?" Holly had to turn her head to keep track of Maggie, now prowling into the dining room.

"Number one, Donna and her kids need help. Serious help."

"Yes, okay."

"My brother can help find a therapist." Maggie leaned against the kitchen door frame and looked levelly at Holly. "The second thing is, you know the difference between protecting society and bullshit. And I want you to understand what happened. To know why. I've told Donna to trust you."

Holly met the intense blue eyes. This was personal, then. Maggie wasn't telling Schreiner the cop. She was telling Holly the person. Holly said slowly, "I want to know why."

"Okay. Check me on this. You were a nurse. Why did Dale like lemon drops?"

"Lemon drops?" Holly thought a moment. "He'd been taking anticholinergic drugs for years," she said. "They dry up natural secretions. Lemon drops stimulate saliva—make your mouth less dry and uncomfortable."

Maggie nodded, pleased. "My brother says Dale was on a very high dose of anticholinergics. Is that right, Donna?"

"Yes." Her voice was hesitant. "The doctor said he couldn't safely go any higher. That's why he was eager to get Dale adapted to L-dopa. So he could reduce the dosage of the other drug."

"And if he reduced it, Dale's secretions would improve, probably," said Maggie.

Donna nodded briefly and bowed her head to prop her forehead on the heel of her hand.

"So," said Maggie, "Dale sent us off to the beach. And he stayed here to work on the story, make some phone calls, take his nap. He hated hot weather, Olivia says. He wouldn't have gone out in the heat."

"Yeah, okay," Holly agreed impatiently. "Where are we going with all this?"

"I just want you to have the picture. Dale working quietly inside, taking his nap, in that workroom with all the windows on the south and west."

Windows? Lemon drops? And something Nate Rosen had said, tugging at Holly's memory.

"I'm not telling this to the police," Maggie reminded her quietly. "But just suppose I'd looked back as we left for the beach. Suppose I saw someone standing right here in the dining room by the kitchen door. Suppose her hand was on the wall like this." Maggie demonstrated, then pulled her hand away.

"The thermostat!" said Holly. "You turned up the thermostat!"

She could picture it now: Dale in that southwest room, napping, ninety-five degrees outside, the sun beating through the southwest windows. If she'd turned the air conditioner off that room could have hit 110° in a very short time.

And Dale, on anticholinergics, could not sweat. Could not regulate his own temperature. She remembered the crisp unrumpled shirt he wore. Not just the shirt of a finicky man, as she had thought. It was the shirt of a man who couldn't sweat.

"Nate Rosen said he got very hot trying to open the door to the den," she said.

"Did he? And he wasn't in the hottest room," said Maggie. "The rest of the house was shaded from the sun. It wouldn't heat up so fast."

"But wouldn't you have noticed how warm it was when you got back?" demanded Holly.

"Well, two things had happened by then," Maggie pointed out. "The storm had gone by, and the outside was much cooler by about six o'clock. So some of the heat had dissipated already. And Donna flipped the air conditioner on again as soon as she arrived, then came out to help us unload. The house had been cooling thirty minutes or so by the time the rest of us went inside." Maggie left the dining room and went back to flop in the wing chair again, looking at the two on the sofa. "Actually—it did seem stuffy, even then. But I didn't realize the significance yet. I thought it was just that the rain had made the outdoors seem so much fresher."

"So it was heatstroke," said Holly slowly. She'd seen a couple of cases in Nam: The body's cooling system failed, a high fever cooked the brain centers, leading to convulsions, coma, cardiac failure, death. She remembered something else. "High temperatures speed up rigor mortis a little."

"I didn't know that," said Maggie.

"Yeah. So rigor would have been a little ahead of schedule, but body temperature—that's what happened! His body temperature started out so high that by the time we saw him he'd barely cooled to normal. No wonder Doc Craine won't guess about time of death."

Donna was looking at her fearfully. "But the blood!" she said. "Someone hit him! Someone got in and hit him—and got out—"

"No, Donna." Holly shook her head. "The door was bolted from the inside. He probably went into convulsions before he died. Often happens in heatstroke. Slammed into that lamp on the edge of the desk thrashing around."

"Convul— Oh, God!" Donna doubled over. "Oh, my God! I thought—I thought it would be a coma—very quiet, just going to sleep for his nap and—"

Whoopee. So smirking Death had played another nasty one. A mild woman, seeking a mild escape from violence, and failing.

Donna whispered, "I should have phoned sooner."

Maggie had hurried across the room and was bending toward Donna now. "You had second thoughts? That's why you tried to call him from the beach?"

"Yes. To wake him up. But he didn't answer."

Holly asked, "Why yesterday? After all these years, why then?"

Donna was still sobbing. Maggie, kneeling beside her, arm across her heaving shoulders, raised her face toward Holly's. "We're still just supposing."

"Okay."

"We're supposing he'd started to beat Josie."

"Josie? You mean he never hurt the girls before?"

Donna lifted her head, indignation mingling with her tears. "Never! I would have left!" she said in a choked voice. "But he never hurt the girls. If he was mad at them he'd hurt me. He'd say I should be able to control the kids. That I was a—a bad mother."

"I see. Then Josie took the tape with his interview on it," said Holly slowly. Damn tape. The officer who'd listened to it had reported that it was all John Denver music. None of Dale's stuff left.

Donna said, "The tape set him off. But I realized it could be anything. Josie wasn't safe anymore. He had those guns—" She straightened up at the other end of the sofa and wiped a hand across her forehead. Maggie found a Kleenex in her pocket and offered it to Donna, then sat back on the floor at her feet.

Well, Schreiner, what do you do now? Open homicide investigation. She owed it to Dale, right? She could squeeze a proper confession from Donna, probably. Get a big press play, commendations, promotions. Schreiner the supercop. And Donna? She could go up for quite a few years. Even for manslaughter, she'd be in for six, maybe. Tina and Josie would be, what, fifteen and eighteen then. Father dead, mother in jail for murder, the girls living with—who? Dale Colby's icy parents, most likely. People who had raised a violent son already.

Or suppose a jury let Donna off. Self-defense didn't strictly fit but juries were mulish sometimes. But even if they decided in Donna's favor, there would be months of legal maneuvers. And publicity. There was no acquittal in the press. Olivia Kerr and her colleagues would play it big. Schoolteacher Kills Sick Husband! Murderous Mom Roasts Dad! As for Donna's job—forget it. School boards were politically vulnerable and wouldn't risk hiring a teacher tainted by a murder charge, regardless of her legal guilt or innocence. And even if this fragile battered family got sympathetic treatment from the press, like Joanne Little, the glare of publicity was brutal. To say nothing of the trial itself. She could picture little Josie on the stand, the DA's insinuations gentle so as not to antagonize the jury: "Josie, honey, don't you think most daddies spank their children when they're bad?" The girl's cuts and bruises would be healed on the surface by then, the brutality nothing but cold abstract words to the jury. What was it Maggie had said? It's not justice if it hurts a child.

Was it justice if it betrayed the dead?

How much did she owe Dale Colby?

And how did you measure violence? To save her children, a meek and terrified woman had turned a thermostat dial. A far cry from Ernie Grant's arsenal of explosives and firearms. Much as Holly ached for him, she knew Ernie was an ongoing source of violence.

Like Dale Colby.

Was Donna an ongoing source of violence?

Donna, for years, had responded to violence with peace. Exactly what a nice girl was supposed to do. She'd absorbed the violence until it had touched her child. And when she'd fought back at last, it was with a twist of a thermostat dial. Expecting a peaceful death in his sleep for a violent man.

Holly glanced at Maggie. She still sat, uncharacteristically still, legs stretched out on the rug before her, arms propping her from behind. She was looking at Holly expectantly. Holly said, "In Nam once I was talking to a guy who was door gunner in a helicopter gunship. Wounded bad enough he could have been reassigned to something easier when he went back. But he wanted to be a door gunner. Said he liked shooting people if he wasn't too close. Those little pesky things running around on the ground, it was just a game to shoot at them. Just touch the trigger."

Maggie nodded. "But they were just as dead as if he'd choked them with his bare hands. Face to screaming face. Killing is killing."

Holly said, "Donna?"

Donna twisted the Kleenex in her hand. "I know. His brain—God, convulsions too." She struggled for a moment before she continued. "I didn't know there would be convulsions. But I knew it would be real. I faced it myself, over and over. Those guns—it's like you said, just touch the trigger. I was so scared each time that he would go too far. And when the doctor said he must never get overheated—at first it was a fantasy, but I saw Dale's fear of the heat, and I knew." She raised her head, gazing around the orderly room. "My marriage was a game. Make-believe. All this time I've tried to pretend it was okay, pretend he wouldn't do it to me again. But with Josie—I saw that was real. He was out of control. He'd destroy her too. I had to do something." She looked down at her Kleenex, then, unexpectedly, square at Holly. "But I didn't know I would feel so—filthy. I just thought about the girls, but now—"

"Some situations force us to be filthy," said Maggie soberly, dark memories stirring in her blue eyes. "Because every choice violates someone."

"But if I— Will they send me to jail?"

"Maybe," said Holly. "You'd certainly have a trial. Months of it. The newspapers would hound you. Hound your girls."

Donna nodded.

What the hell, Schreiner, you went to Nam because you wanted to be a healer. Maybe, just maybe, a cop could be a healer too. She took out her notebook. "Tell you what. We have Nate Rosen's evidence that the house was too warm at three-thirty. So I'm writing down that the air conditioner malfunctioned. Doc Craine will be delighted to get a reasonable cause of death. For the rest, well, we were just supposing, weren't we?" She closed her notebook and stood up. "If I get hard evidence I'll have to move on it, of course. It's up to you, Donna. Think about your girls and decide." She started for the door.

"Please," begged Donna, "tell me what to do!"

"She's told you," Maggie said. "She said, think about the girls. You've got to make the decisions now, Donna. And live with the results."

Donna was bent over again, face in her hands.

Holly paused by the entry arch and said gently, "I can tell you one thing. You're on the other side of the great divide now. You've met killing face to face. So whatever else you decide, better put a soft rug next to your bed. You're going to fall out of it with nightmares, lady."

Donna's head, still bowed, gave a tiny nod. Holly's gaze lingered a moment, then her eyes met Maggie's in sorrow. Tentatively, Maggie raised her fingers in a V.

Holly hesitated, then returned the salute. "Peace," she said, and went back out into the night.

About the Author

P. M. Carlson is the author of seven Maggie Ryan mysteries: AUDITION FOR MURDER, MURDER IS ACADEMIC, MURDER IS PATHOLOGICAL, MURDER UNRENOVATED, REHEARSAL FOR MURDER, MURDER IN THE DOG DAYS and MURDER MISREAD. MURDER UNRENOVATED was nominated for both the Anthony and Macavity Awards for Best Mystery of 1988.

If you enjoyed Maggie Ryan in *Murder in the Dog Days,* you'll enjoy P. M. Carlson's next Maggie Ryan mystery, *Murder Misread,* coming from Bantam Books in December, 1991.

Turn the page for an exciting preview of
Murder Misread

MURDER MISREAD

Anatomically, the thing to do was to hit the brainstem. The medulla oblongata, familiar from Intro. to Psych., skipped over quickly by bored professors because it was concerned with plodding functions like reflexes, heartbeat, breathing. The same services it had performed for eons in fish, in reptiles, in shrews, in apes. Professors preferred the neocortex, that Johnny-come-lately that surged out from the humble stem to fill the skull like an atomic mushroom cloud. The cortex had all the exciting functions—intelligence, problem-solving, language, personality, literature. And yet if you damaged the glamorous cortex, the ages-old medulla—aided by some bright young doctor with a set of machines—might still keep the frail, well-plumbed bag of bones and guts ticking along, might even resuscitate a few twitches of consciousness from the cortical remnants. But damage the medulla, and the cortex, too, would wither helplessly on its ancient, bleeding stalk.

The gun was tiny, snub-nosed, but heavy enough to drag down the clothes a little. Or maybe it wasn't physical weight, maybe it was, as they said, psychological. The months of fear, of not knowing enough, of frustration at every attempt to resolve the problems, all now coalesced into a compact steel mechanism in the pocket. A solution of sorts to the insoluble. Something that could clip out poison mushrooms at the stem.

And afterward? Who could tell? Tracks had been covered, loved ones protected. Values conflicted, and choices had to be made.

Muggy with the humid breath of vigorous new maple leaves and young vines, the June morning sent sweat trickling down Associate Professor Charlie Fielding's heaving chest. He was bounding up the railroad-tie steps from the parking lot to Van Brunt Hall, aviator glasses bouncing on his slippery nose, making the solid world appear to hiccup with each step. Charlie was late, and heartbroken. Both Deanna's fault. He'd waited half an hour longer than he should have, hoping, but she hadn't appeared. Probably with her new friends. Damn her anyway. Deanna of the glinting hair, whose special magic could transform a winter afternoon into a tropical haze of laughing mint-scented delirium. No, it wasn't over. It couldn't be over. Just a misunderstanding. He was sure.

But he'd fix it later. Right now, he was late for his appointment. And sweating like Stallone in *Rocky* under his summer tweed jacket. And, he noted with an inward groan, his socks didn't match. One blue, one black. Today was going to be a stinker.

His office was on the first floor of Van Brunt, an unimaginative fifties building that had largish rooms but little else to recommend it. He wrenched open the door and threw himself into the fluorescent-lit white hall.

Charlie raced past the hall clock across from the main office. God, nine-twelve already. He rounded the corner of his own hall and braked frantically. Three people—two quite small, all upside down—blocked his door. He caught himself on the edge of the doorjamb and lurched to a halt. The little girl that he'd almost knocked over returned her sneakered feet calmly to the floor and straightened out of her handstand. Luminous brown eyes, black curls, a mischievous grin. "'Scuse me," she said.

"Ditto." The tallest of the three, a lanky young woman in her twenties, had bounced upright from her handstand too. Black curls again, and an infectious smile, but this time the eyes were jay-blue. He generally didn't like tall women, but this one had an endearing gawkiness that made him think of Big Bird. She pushed her hair back from her face with both hands. "We were just practising our gymnastics. Didn't expect anyone to come around the corner so fast."

"Yes, I'm sorry. I'm running late." Charlie pressed his aviators up on his nose and glanced at the young woman doubtfully. "Are you, um, Dr. Ryan?" Big-boned and slim in her blue jeans and loose sky-blue shirt, she might be student, faculty, or visiting townie.

"Right. Maggie Ryan. And you're Dr. Fielding?"

"Charlie." He nodded as he pulled his office key from his pocket.

The third and smallest member of the trio still had his hands on the floor, kicking one short leg out behind him in vain imitation of the handstands. Now he stood, toddled toward Charlie with a broad grin, and announced, "Da!"

"Will thinks all men are named Daddy," Maggie Ryan explained. She grabbed both children, their dimpled fingers disappearing into her bony hands. "Will and Sarah, this is Dr. Fielding. He's the man I'm going to be working with this summer."

Charlie smiled at the children and was rewarded by twin grins. "Hi," said Sarah.

"Da!" insisted Will gleefully. Sarah rolled up her eyes.

"All right, pick up your stuff," Maggie instructed Sarah, swooping up Will with a practiced arm. "What's next, Charlie?"

"Checking in with our efficient Cindy Phelps in the departmental office. She's supposed to have a sitter ready. Let me just stow my briefcase and we'll take the kids over there." He nodded at an open door with a sign painted on it: Main Office, Educational Psychology. They all trooped in.

The quiet tapping of the Selectric halted. "Hi, Charlie." Cindy Phelps was freckled, muscular, with a Farrah Fawcett-Majors tumble of highlighted hair and a shell-pink dress. She ran the department like a high-fashion spider tending her web.

"Hi." Charlie cleared his throat. "Cindy, this is Dr. Ryan, the project statistician. You've probably got a form for her to sign."

Cindy's prominent blue eyes swept eloquently to the ceiling. "God, yes! I've got forms for every occasion. And to match any color scheme. Today's special is buff and canary." She nodded toward a chair in the corner. "I've also got you a sitter. One of our undergraduate majors. Liz!"

Charlie watched his new statistician size up the tanned, broad-shouldered young woman with unfashionably short, dark hair who came toward them. "Hi, Liz, I'm Maggie," she said. "This is Sarah, and this is Will. I hope you like reading stories and climbing trees."

Liz grinned. "Yep. Also Play-Doh and swimming."

A trace of caution in Maggie's blue eyes. "Swimming?"

"I'm on the team here. And I work as lifeguard at the state park on weekends."

Maggie relaxed. "You're hired! I won't have to tell you about energetic kids, I see. Here, Will, meet Liz." She handed over the little blue-jeaned boy, who looked up somberly into Liz's face. "Don't let them run off too far just yet, okay? I want to talk to Dr. Fielding a little while, then I want to talk to you and set up a schedule. Will needs a nap after lunch or he's whiny and nasty all afternoon."

"Can do. Why don't you come out to the preschool area when you're done? Northeast corner of this building." Liz gestured with her free hand.

"Fine."

"Come on, Sarah, want to go to the playground?" Competently, Liz bustled the children from the office.

Charlie turned back and saw the inner office door open behind Cindy's desk. Bernie Reinalter came out holding a sheaf of papers. Bernie was lean, very fair, no taller than Charlie but with an aloofness that was suitable for the chairman of the department. "Good morning, Charlie," he said.

"Hi, Bernie." Charlie started to smooth his hair but stopped himself. Bernie was always carefully and conservatively dressed. Even now, in shirtsleeves for summer, he was in a pale yellow button-down shirt, and there was a crease in his gray trousers. "Uh, Bernie, this is my statistical consultant for the summer, Dr. Ryan. This is our chairman, Professor Reinalter."

"Glad to meet you," said Maggie.

"Sorry I don't have time to talk to you just now," Bernie told her. "I'm just bringing Cindy some material to type up. I'm meeting a couple of Japanese scientists for lunch, so it helps to have it in written form too."

"Sure, we'll have time to get acquainted later."

Bernie disappeared back into his office. Cindy glanced at the stack of papers he'd left on her desk, then turned back to Maggie. "You'll be using the corner office in Charlie's wing. Professor Schiff's office. He's moved out, but the custodian says he won't be finished cleaning till late this afternoon so I'll give you the key later."

"Okay."

"And now forms. All assembled in one color-coordinated packet. Unlike socks," she added, with just a hint of a glance at Charlie. In his pocket, his fist tightened on his keys. *Bitch*. Cindy continued smoothly, "Why don't you take them along,

Dr. Ryan, and fill them out when you can? I'm here till four-thirty."

"Fine. And please call me Maggie." She scooped up the packet. "The checks come to this office too?"

"Right. I'm the money lady."

"You sure are. Another day, another dollar, eh, Cindy?" said Charlie.

"Now where have I heard that before?" Cindy turned her shell-pink back abruptly and resumed typing.

"Dismissed," said Maggie. Her smile was as mischievous as her daughter's.

"She rules us all," explained Charlie as they walked back toward his yellow hall. "Money, keys, typewriters—she controls the mainstays of life."

"I'll treat her with proper deference," Maggie promised. "Okay, now. Tell me about this project of yours."

"Fine." Charlie pushed his door open and kicked the wedge under it to hold it open. He hung his jacket on the wooden coatrack, then picked up his briefcase and pulled out a stapled manuscript. "You've seen the proposal?"

"Skimmed it." She slid Cindy's varicolored forms into her own briefcase. "But my experience has been that proposals often get altered as the first results come in."

Charlie laughed ruefully. "You've got us pegged, all right. A lot of the details have changed. But we're still hacking away at the same basic question: How does a skilled reader read? When we know what the best adult readers are doing, we can start thinking about how to teach kids to do it too. I mean, just think what happens when you read." He gestured at the papers in his hand. "You pick up a sheet of paper with funny little marks on it, and your eyes look at the marks. Not all the marks—your eyes bounce from one fixation point to another, usually hitting just a few spots per line."

"Right, I remember the basics. You process hundreds of words per minute. More like picking up thoughts instead of letters."

"Something like that. But remember, all you have on the page is letters, grouped, with spaces between groups." He pushed his glasses up on his nose and waved his proposal eagerly. "So an efficient reader must have some sort of plan, or he'd be misreading all the time, having to go back and check. Obviously your peripheral vision will have some blurry information about what's coming up next on the page, so when you know how, you can bounce your eyes to the best possible next fixation point." His fingers stabbed at the pages he held. "The point that will give you the most information about the thought that the writer is developing. We're trying to figure out what kinds of points are chosen for fixation by skilled readers. How the hell do we do it? What blurry peripheral cues do we respond to? It's not easy. As you guessed, we've already given up on half of our bright ideas about how to measure this process."

Maggie cocked her head, her hands thrust into her jeans pockets. "But the other half must be working or you wouldn't have sent for an expensive New York statistician like me to help analyze it."

He couldn't help responding to that smile, a sudden glow like Diane Keaton's. "Well, I have hopes." Boy, did he ever! He'd been promoted on the basis of work that had grown out of his long-ago thesis. This was his first major project since then, his bid to prove that the department hadn't been wrong to choose him to fill the famous Professor Chandler's shoes as reading researcher. If this multitude of interconnected studies didn't work out—well, he'd still have tenure. But he'd seen too many professors scorned and patronized when their early promise had fizzled, human deadwood in their own departments. Last year, two of his pilot studies in a row had fizzled, and for a week he'd had nightmares: rigid shoulders marching out the door, little Charlie screaming, "Wait, wait!" unable to follow.

But he'd succeeded on the next experiment and dared to hope again. "At least we've got a usable method," he told Maggie. "Here, let me show you." He flicked on the television that sat on the side table, and went to the bookcase-covered back wall. The books in fact sat in carefully organized stacks on the floor, crowded out by rows of plastic videotape containers. Charlie selected one and fed it into the machine. Uncooperatively, the screen began lazily to flip up horizontal bars.

"What we're using is basically a double-exposure technique," he explained as he struggled with the controls. "Camera one is recording the reflection of a light on the cornea of the reader's eye. You see the reflection as a white spot on the TV. Camera two is on the page he's reading. So the white spots you'll see superimposed on the page are the places on the text where the eye fixates." The bars were rolling down the screen now.

"Ha! I told you it'd never replace the horse," declared a cheerful new voice.

Trust Tal to be around when anyone new appeared. Charlie turned. "Tal! Hi!"

Tal Chandler was bald, a wiry, twinkling old gnome with knobby nose, knobby chin, knobby red cheeks, as though his face had been constructed of little hard apples. He reminded Charlie of a Walt Disney dwarf. He wore shapeless gray trousers, a heather-gray tweed jacket with leather elbow patches and sagging pockets, and a wide grin. He nodded toward Maggie, who was studying the video controls. "And who is the lovely learned lady?"

"Dr. Ryan. Our statistical consultant, just arrived from New York," said Charlie. "Maggie, this is Tal Chandler. The Meredith Professor of Educational Psychology. Emeritus."

"Talbott Chandler! Of course!" Maggie turned from the video. The screen was behaving itself now, showing a clear page of text with white spots hopscotching across it. She extended her hand enthusiastically, and Tal dropped his bookbag to shake it. "You did that famous stuff on how kids learn French!"

"A linguist as well as a statistician! Delightful!" Tal beamed. "Tell me, are you related to the small children I saw a few minutes ago in the preschool playground? The younger announced that I was 'Da.' The elder told him, I believe, *'Fiche-moi la paix.'*"

"Oh, God." Maggie clapped a hand to her forehead in mock dismay. "I'd hoped that if I did my swearing in French they wouldn't pick up nasty words to shock innocent bystanders. Not a good strategy around a university, I see."

Tal's smile widened, his little round cheeks bunching even tighter. "Fear not, I shan't translate," he assured Maggie.

"Hey, c'mon," protested Charlie.

Tal rolled his eyes at Maggie, beckoned Charlie closer, and whispered in his ear, "It means 'shut the hell up.'"

"Mm. A truly useful phrase," Charlie admitted.

Tal turned back to Maggie. "And where is the lucky father of these phenomenal infants? Will we have the pleasure of his company?"

"He's still in New York, but he'll join us a little later this summer. He'll be acting near here, at the Farm Theatre again."

"Ah, the Farm Theatre. Good outfit, that. Saw a splendid *Cyrano* there a few years back," Tal reminisced.

"That was Nick!" exclaimed Maggie. "He did Cyrano!"

"He did? Send him my congratulations!" Tal snatched up Charlie's borrowed ruler left-handed and waved it on high. "What moments, eh? 'Let death come! I wait, standing proud, with sword in hand!' *Debout, et l'épée à la main!*" He hopped onto a chair, commenting aside, "My wife can do this all in French, you know. She makes a far better Cyrano than I. You must meet her. Let's see . . . something about old enemies . . . ah—"

Maggie's blue eyes were dancing. "'Despite you all, old enemies that round me loom . . .'" she prompted.

"Ah yes!" Right hand cocked behind him in a fencer's pose, he thrust the ruler at the air. "'Despite you all, old enemies that round me loom, I bear aloft unstained, unyielding—my white plume!'"

He swished an imaginary hat and bowed extravagantly. Maggie applauded, laughing. "*Quel geste!*"

Charlie said, "Tal, you're bouncy today!"

"Yes. The delightful company, of course. And I'm celebrating!" He twinkled down at them. It had been months since Charlie had seen him so ebullient.

"Celebrating what?"

Tal shook his head vigorously. "That's a secret! Tell me, Dr. Ryan, will you be free for lunch today?"

"I'll probably have to meet the kids."

"Tomorrow, then! And you must meet my wife. She can't come today either." He jumped down from the chair, stumbling a little but catching himself by grabbing at the jacket on the rack. "But Charlie, you must join today's celebration! Not the cafeteria. Someplace on College Avenue, with proper champagne. Plato's, all right? At noon?"

"It's a deal," agreed Charlie.

Tal's cheeks bunched in another grin. "A celebration! I'll see who else can come. Of course I asked Cindy, but she had another appointment. I told her I'd save her some champagne. But now perhaps you should tend to your tapes." He gestured theatrically at the TV screen, where little white flashes continued to bounce silently across the displayed text. "Do you know how we used to do eye-movement research, Dr. Ryan?"

"No, I'm afraid not."

"One brave fellow, Professor Ahrens, actually stuck a tiny cup on his eyeball with a thin marker attached, so as he read, the pattern of eye movements was traced onto a smoked drum in front of him."

"God! That's hideous!" Maggie shuddered. "How could he read normally?"

"Yes, indeed, that's what the rest of us all said! You see, we didn't want to have to do experiments like that ourselves. We scientists like to think that we can endure anything in the search for truth, but really we hate to sacrifice our little comforts and little vices. But luckily, in this case someone eventually thought of bouncing light off the eye and photographing it, and bright young folks like Charlie here are refining the methods all the time. Though I don't know about Charlie." He shook his head in mock sorrow. "This young sprat thinks we make up hypotheses as we read, whereas anyone sensible knows we look at the words."

"This old geezer says we struggle along word by word without any coherent ideas about what they mean," Charlie returned.

"You see what I mean?" Tal appealed to Maggie. "He twists simple statements of fact. Why, according to him there's no need to look at the page at all, just open the book and start hypothesizing. Daydreaming."

Charlie laughed. "Tal, who's twisting now?"

"Well, wait'll you hear my paper at the MPA convention!" Tal glanced at his watch. "But right now, I'd best return these books to the library. Now that I've finished daydreaming my way through them." He hoisted his bookbag and whisked out as quickly as he'd come.

"Famous scholars never look the way I think they will," said Maggie, amused. "His publications are very sober."

Charlie nodded. "He was a little giddy today, though he's always cheerful. He's been retired four years now, and still bustles around. Publishes a lot even now. We have great discussions about the control of eye movements. And he's curious about everything. You notice the grilling he gave you already!"

"Yeah. A man after my own heart. Now, what do we want to find out from those little flashing lights on the screen?"

They returned to their chore.

Sunlight sifted through the trees. The creek giggled below. A little child galloped down the path, paused to pick up a pebble from the mud, ran back to her smiling mother. They moved on past, until their happy chatter merged into the rustling of the leaves.

A sweet day for a murder.

Anne Chandler's wandering attention was caught by her own stubby fingers pulling yet another Gauloise from the pack. Unwillingly her eyes slid to the ashtray: this would be number seven. No, eight, damn it. She tapped the cigarette back into the pack regretfully and tucked it into her jacket pocket.

"So, uh, do you suppose you could give me the extension?" asked the pimply student sitting stiffly on the other side of her desk. His Adam's apple bobbled in his scrawny young throat. Knot, the French called it; *noeud de la gorge*, knot of the throat. And *noeud de la question*, the crux of the matter. The crux was that this poor kid wasn't suited for college at all. Anne wanted to pat his downy cheek, set him on a tractor, let him earn a living in the healthy open air with no need to decipher any more funny-looking French words.

But no doubt he was pursuing some other, less suitable goal. Ambitious parents, perhaps. It would be kindest to get it over with. Anne squashed her maternal instincts and said briskly, "Three more days. But that's it, Bill. I can see that it's a problem for you to get the paper in by next Wednesday"— somewhere in his maundering account he had made some excuse or other, she remembered vaguely, "but I really have to close the books on this course. It's already a week past the final." She stood up to signal the end of the conversation.

"Yeah, okay, I'll try, Professor Chandler." He stumbled to his feet glumly.

"I'll look forward to getting your paper," she lied with her best inspiring-teacher smile. His gangly height loomed a good twelve inches over her own stocky bantam figure. "See you later, Bill."

"Thanks, Professor Chandler." He shifted his bookbag apologetically and ambled out.

Anne fingered the cigarettes and looked at her phone.

It didn't ring.

What the hell was he up to?

With sudden decision she plopped back into her chair, picked up the receiver, and dialed Ken Little.

"Ken, sorry to call you so late, but I can't meet you for lunch today. Could we reschedule?"

"Sure thing, Annie. I have some kind of bug anyway, woke up feeling woozy, and I wasn't really looking forward to lunch that much. You know, with the food at the Union—"

"We really should get the film schedule set soon, though," she broke in, paging through her calendar. "How about tomorrow, at ten?"

"No good. Eleven?"

"Fine. I'll start my office hours late."

"Okay. Do you know if there are any bugs going around? I mean, this just came out of the blue. When I woke up—"

"You'll feel better tomorrow, Ken. See you then." She pressed down the cradle before he could reply and, without letting herself think, dialed Tal's office. But again, it rang fruitlessly, over and over.

Dr. Lambert, then.

God, why was it so difficult? She had muscled her way brashly into the academic world long before women were welcomed. *La plastronneuse*, some catty old professor had nicknamed her: the pushy one, the show-off. Or, more literally, the starched shirtfront, the breastplate, the chesty one. Tal had been delighted with the pun, burrowing his nose into her ample bosom and murmuring lasciviously, "Mmm, *la plastronneuse!*" and they'd both giggled like kids. Well, pushy she'd been, she'd had to be. She had defended countless papers at conventions, had traveled alone in France and French Africa, had force-fed the glories of French literature to generations of linguistically lazy students. But now, instead of making a simple call, her fingers were again twitching at the Gauloises.

She pulled her erring hand from her pocket, placed it firmly on the receiver, made herself dial the well-known number.

"Can you hold a moment, Mrs. Chandler?" asked the receptionist.

And in a moment, miraculously, John's voice: "Dr. Lambert here."

"John, it's Anne Chandler. I haven't been able to catch Tal, and I wondered . . ." She trailed off. What she wondered could not be put into ordinary English.

And didn't have to be. John exclaimed enthusiastically, "Looked great, Anne! Still shrinking. He keeps on like this another six months and he'll be good as new."

"You're . . . sure?" she faltered.

"The X rays were as clear as they could be. He's winning, Anne!"

"John . . . thanks." She hung up, dazed. Braced to deflect the worst, she found that this good news could not penetrate her defensive walls either. She was adrift, unable to believe or disbelieve.

And Tal? Maybe this was why he hadn't called, this inability to believe. Anne slung her bag over her shoulder, locked her office, and hurried out into the June sunshine.

The air was pleasantly tepid, scented with the first blooms on the rose plants around the Modern Languages building. *To hell with you, roses, with your little pink smell*. She pulled out her Gauloise and lit it defiantly, sucked the delicious stinking smoke deep into her chest, then spewed it contemptuously at the blossoms.

To hell with you, too, cancer.

The Ed Psych office was locked when Anne arrived, the halls nearly deserted in this peculiar between-semesters slack. *Les vacances*, the French said: vacation, vacancy. Tal's office, as it turned out, was vacant too, locked and dark. Puzzling over her next move, she wandered back toward the door. Maybe she shouldn't have cancelled that meeting about next year's French film season. But she couldn't face Ken and his need for mothering today.

At the door she met Cindy Phelps approaching from the library walk. "Oh, Cindy! Just the person I wanted to see!"

"Really?" Cindy's light blue eyes looked kindly at Anne from under shelves of enhanced black lashes. She dragged her rose-colored cardigan from her shoulders and tossed it over her forearm, then reached into her bag for the office key. "What can I do for you?"

"I'm looking for my wayward husband."

Cindy glanced over her shoulder at the hall clock. "Twelve-thirty. He'll still be at lunch."

"Yes. But do you know where he is?" Anne followed Cindy into the departmental office. Eric, the plastic brain model on the shelf, stared at them with blank blue eyes.

Cindy stowed her bag and hung up her cardigan. "For once, yes. He said he'd be at Plato's. Invited me to come with him and celebrate."

"Celebrate?" An avalanche of hurt battered Anne's heart, stirring buried memories of that horrible long-ago winter when she'd discovered Tal's affair with that bosomy premed student.

Cindy laughed, preening. "Oh, God, that sounded wrong! This wasn't like a tryst or anything. A bunch of people went. He asked Bernie too, but Bernie had to have lunch with some computer people from Japan. I couldn't go, so Tal said he'd save me some champagne." The hand patting her exuberant hairdo into place slowed, and she frowned at Anne. "Are you okay? I mean, he said you had an appointment. How come you're here?"

"Oh, it got cancelled." Anne smiled at Cindy, the weight lightening. It was true—Tal had known about her lunch with Ken. Still, why hadn't he called? "So he's at Plato's?"

"Right. Say, what's he celebrating? His birthday? Seventieth, right?"

"Right, you might say that. Cindy, I tried to call him this morning but he didn't answer."

"Well, he got in late." Cindy lifted the cover from her typewriter. "And he was running around the halls, in and out of everyone else's office. Busy busy. So you didn't have much of a chance of getting through."

"Well," decided Anne, "I'm going over to Plato's. If I happen to miss him again, tell him I want to talk to him, okay?"

"Sure thing."

"Cindy, how are you doing?"

For an instant their eyes locked. "Okay," said Cindy. "It'll be okay." Then her gaze slid away and she glared at the smiling man who was pushing a wire cart laden with manila envelopes into the office. "Oh, damn, here comes the mail to sort."

Anne waved good-bye and walked back out into the sun. She was jumpy today, wasn't she, unable to make phone calls, thinking of that curvy premed for the first time in years. Well, months. She crossed the parking lot, surprisingly full for vacation time. Probably people who usually had to park at the peripheral lots, taking advantage of *les vacances*. A high proportion were the old rusting hulks driven by grad students, instead of somewhat newer Toyotas or Vegas favored by the faculty. The undergraduate Porsches were probably off to the beach.

The woods were lovely, washed by yesterday's rain, each leaf defined in the chiaroscuro of June sun and deep shade. The noises of civilization—motors, sirens, voices—faded rapidly as she descended. Birds called, a squirrel ranted in high-pitched hoarse indignation, foliage rustled. Almost nice enough to take that old bastard Rousseau seriously, all his drivel about getting close to nature. Anne tramped stolidly down the path, her bag swinging from her shoulder, her face turned up to catch the occasional dazzle of sky beyond the rippling leaves.

She heard the voices first, from the fork in the path. Men's voices, gruff working-class voices, down by the creek. As she hiked along the upper path, she tried to peer down through the ragged screen of young maples to see what was happening. Nearing the bridge, she could glimpse flashes of light and paused, squinting. A photographer of some sort? She pushed aside a young branch so she could survey the activity.

The photographer was squatting, stretching, clambering onto logs and rocks, even into the stream in a strange ritual ceremony around a quiet heather-gray form on the path. Well outside the circle of his dance, others stood watching: men in uniforms, the gray of the campus safety officers, the navy of the city police, the white of ambulance attendants who stood with a stretcher vertical between them. Beyond them, clumps of university people—tweeds, blue jeans, Aran sweaters. A tall black man in a blue blazer was talking to the largest of the tweedy ones. Looked like Bart, Anne thought. Next to them, a lanky young woman with black curls had a comforting arm around a sobbing female student in a jeans jacket.

Anne stepped back onto the path, letting the branch spring back across the view. With shivering hands she pulled a cigarette from her pocket, lit it, and inhaled deeply. Then she marched back to the fork in the path and down toward the crowd.

She was stopped after a few yards by a big gray-jacketed safety officer, young, taut-faced, a trace of acne on his jaw. Dixon, said his badge. "I'm sorry, ma'am," he croaked hoarsely, and cleared his throat. "Please use the other path. This one is closed."

"Someone's hurt?" asked Anne, drawing in the sustaining smoke. She knew it was a dumb question. The ambulance attendants had been standing idly by, waiting.

"Someone's been shot and killed!" confirmed the youthful officer, his murky blue eyes troubled and lively in his stiffly held face. "So we have to ask you to go the other way until they're finished with the body."

"But you see," explained Anne, enunciating carefully for the benefit of his dazed young ears, "I think I'm married to that body."